ALMA

OTHER BOOKS AND AUDIO BOOKS
BY H.B. MOORE:

Out of Jerusalem: Of Goodly Parents

Out of Jerusalem: A Light in the Wilderness

Out of Jerusalem: Towards the Promised Land

Out of Jerusalem: Land of Inheritance

Abinadi

ALMA

a novel

H.B. MOORE

Covenant Communications, Inc.

Published by Covenant Communications, Inc.
American Fork, Utah

Printed in The United States of America
First Printing: September 2009

16 15 14 13 12 11 10 09   10 9 8 7 6 5 4 3 2 1

ISBN 10: 1-59811-864-1
ISBN 13: 978-1-59811-864-3

Praise for H.B. Moore's Books

"H.B. Moore takes the reader on an incredible journey of a man who makes the ultimate sacrifice. *Abinadi* is a historically rich, well researched, poignant account of one of the most influential prophets in the Book of Mormon. Moore's creativity, mixed with the heart of Mesoamerican culture, brings new insights to the influence that the prophet Abinadi had on generations to come."

—Dian Thomas
#1 *New York Times* Bestselling Author

"Heather Moore once again establishes herself as the best Book of Mormon fiction writer in the business. She has created a flesh-and-blood Abinadi that will forever change my perception of this remarkable man, his influence on Alma, and the importance of his mission in Book of Mormon history."

—Charlene Hirschi
The Herald Journal

"Scripture invites fresh thinking, and H.B. Moore has done just that. Her story of Abinadi, the first martyr, captures a world of human relationships set against the inner struggles of individuals to come to grips with what matters most in their lives. In a word, her story is real, breathing life into the daily routines of people who lived thousands of years ago and highlighting the dramatic moments that must have occurred in the lives of a few—Abinadi, his family, the king and his priests, and the man Alma. Moore's deft and lively style makes this book a delectable, and informative, reading feast."

—S. Kent Brown
*Director of the Laura F. Willes Center for
Book of Mormon Studies, BYU*

"This book is a delightful combination of careful research and getting inside an inspiring character. Although H.B. Moore disclaims being a scholar, her Abinadi not only lives and breathes but is authentic to the time and place in which he lived. While she paints a fuller picture of a fascinating Book of Mormon character, she stays close to the facts, as presented in that book."

—Ann Madsen
Ancient Scripture Department, BYU

"[*Abinadi*] holds drama and excitement, reveals serious research, an understanding of a mature commitment to God, and the ability to speak directly of the sins and excesses of King Noah's court."

—Jennie Hansen
Meridian Magazine

"Moore takes an imaginative approach to the lives of three scriptural men: Abinadi, King Noah, and especially the life of Alma. Who were these men, really? What were their thoughts, their desires, their goals in life? H.B. Moore explores these thoughts and fills in the relatively unknown inner-linings of these individuals."

—C.S. Bezas
BellaOnline

"In *Land of Inheritance* . . . Moore persuasively renders as must-read historical fiction the rich (and growing) body of scholarship about ancient life in Mesoamerica. I highly recommend this exciting, well-written, faith-centered and faith-enhancing novel."

—Richard H. Cracroft
BYU Magazine

To the honorable men of my family—
my brother, Scott, and my brothers-in-law:
the Moore Boys—Corey, Jason, Jeff, and Derris—
Russell Pearson, Jason Clegg, and Joel Jacquart

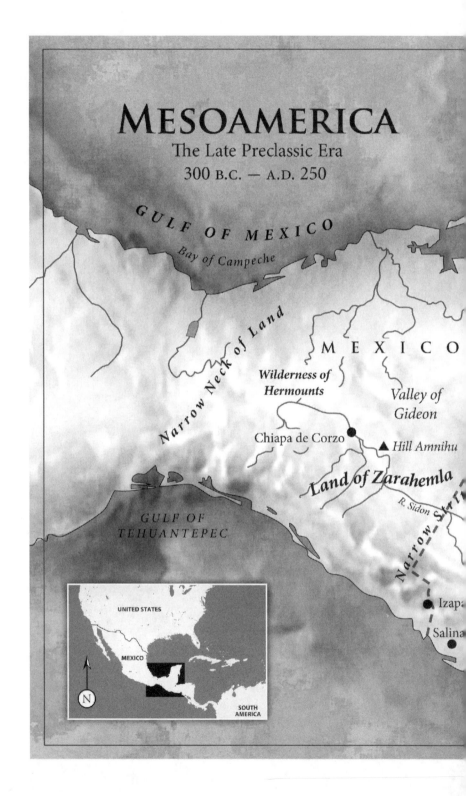

MESOAMERICA
The Late Preclassic Era
300 B.C. — A.D. 250

GULF OF MEXICO

Bay of Campeche

Narrow Neck of Land

M E X I C O

Wilderness of
Hermounts

Valley of
Gideon

Chiapa de Corzo

▲ Hill Amnihu

Land of Zarahemla

R. Sidon

Narrow Str[...]

GULF OF
TEHUANTEPEC

UNITED STATES

MEXICO

Izap[...]

Salina

N

SOUTH
AMERICA

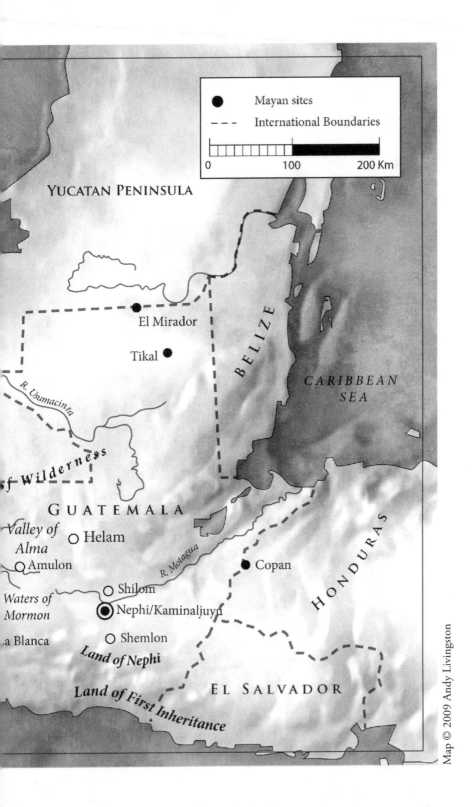

Acknowledgments

Every writer has an extensive support system in order to stay motivated since writing is often a solitary task and frequently mind-numbing. This year has marked a slight change in my audience as my two older children read my books—and actually liked them. Perhaps they now understand more that Mom isn't just "playing on the computer." Special thanks to my children for being the rock that holds me steady, and to my husband, Chris, who has been supportive from day one.

Next, eternal gratitude goes to my parents, Kent and Gayle Brown, who are always the guinea readers. They have to wade through the very beginnings of a plot and sketches of the characters. After the first draft is completed and revised, I hand the book off to several beta readers—not to be confused with beta fish—although sometimes I do feel like they are circling my manuscript, nipping at every sentence. Lu Ann Staheli, Annette Lyon, and Michele Paige Holmes—thanks for your invaluable help. And to J. Scott Savage and Robison Wells—the action scenes would be lost without your input.

Additional thanks to my father-in-law, Lester Moore, for his careful reading and continued support. Many thanks to Phill Babbitt, webmaster; Andy Livingston, map designer; Karen Christoffersen, friend and consultant; and my writing family—the LDStorymakers.

Also, a huge thank you to those who take the manuscript from the computer to the bookshelves—my publisher, Covenant Communications, and the wonderful staff of editors, designers, and marketing personnel. A thousand thanks to my editor, Noelle Perner, and managing editor, Kathy Jenkins—I'm privileged to work with such wonderful ladies!

Preface

Following the death of Abinadi, a priest named Alma went into hiding and recorded the teachings of the deceased prophet. These teachings proved to be a catalyst, prompting Alma to return to the city of Nephi under the cloak of darkness to deliver the Lord's message to friends in secret. Within the chapters of Mosiah 18 through 24, an incredible physical and spiritual journey unfolds, centering around Alma and those who choose to follow him—a journey fraught with fear, death, and ultimately survival.

Book of Mormon scholar Hugh Nibley characterizes Alma as being a direct descendent of Nephi. Alma was a man born with the right to hold the priesthood (*Teachings of the Book of Mormon—Part Two*, 77). Even though Alma served as a priest in King Noah's court, he may not have carried out the priesthood functions as they were intended in the local temple. Once free of King Noah, Alma was able to perform the ordinances that were necessary to establish a church and baptize the believers.

Interestingly enough, Nibley points out that Alma was not baptizing the people for the remission of sins. For in this pre-Christ era, the sacred duty of following the law of Moses was still required. Instead, Alma baptized the people as a "witness," allowing them to enter into "a covenant with [the Lord]" and to have "his Spirit more abundantly upon" them. (See Mosiah 18:10, 13; and *Teachings*, 88–89.)

Alma established a colony at a place called the Waters of Mormon. The majority of scholars have joined in the opinion that Lake Atitlan is the most likely location. Joseph Allen informs us that the lake is located ninety miles west of Guatemala City (where the

city of Nephi is believed to have been generally located). Pottery and
other archeological finds in this region have been dated to the middle
and late pre-classical periods (*Sacred Sites,* 34).

As we learn from the Book of Mormon, when the Lamanites
invaded the city of Nephi after Alma had gone, King Noah took his
priests and some of his men and fled, leaving behind the women and
children. The Nephite men began to regret their action and ended up
turning on King Noah, killing him. The priests fled again, led by
Amulon, who functioned essentially as a chief priest among them.
Incredibly enough, years later, he and his men abducted twenty-four
daughters of the Lamanites and married them. When the Lamanites
discovered their colony (the land of Amulon), they showed compassion on these renegade Nephites. Amulon rose to power and was
appointed king over the land of Helam—ruling over Alma and his
people.

Nibley reminds us that Amulon was one of the most dangerous
men in the Book of Mormon, and he should not be taken lightly.
Throughout history it was common for a king to appoint leaders, or
lesser kings, over communities. When Amulon was appointed king of
the land of Helam, he took it to the extreme—following in the footsteps of his predecessor, King Noah (*Teachings,* 125). We learn in
Doctrine and Covenants 121:39, that "it is the nature and disposition
of almost all men, as soon as they get a little authority . . . they will
immediately begin to exercise unrighteous dominion."

Through researching the Mesoamerican culture, I've come across
many similarities in what we know about the Nephites and Lamanites
versus the histories of the Maya people during the late pre-classical era
(300 BC—AD 250). I've documented some of these details in chapter
notes at the end of this book.

Various scholars hold differing opinions about the chronology of
the Book of Mormon. In the appendix of *Voices from the Dust,* S.
Kent Brown suggests that Abinadi's martyrdom takes place around
128 BC. Thus, this story begins shortly after the prophet's death.

It is a daunting task to write a story about or fictionalize part of
Alma's life in any way. He has certainly been one of the most influential prophets in my life—his teachings have impacted me as few
others have. As I studied the chapters on Alma within the Book of

Mosiah, time and time again I was struck by parallels to our modern-day challenges. Alma was the only priest who was willing to stand up to King Noah. And only when his life was put in danger did he flee. His reliance on the Lord was complete and utter as he was forced to escape Noah's army a second time. Years later, when he was required to live under Amulon's tyrannical rule, Alma must have wondered if he'd ever be free. Yet inside his soul he was truly free. He was true to his convictions, his faith, his Lord. His increasing burdens were made light, and deliverance finally came.

In reading Alma's story, I was reminded of the burdens that each of us carries throughout our lives—some are but short trials, while others may be lifelong hardships. The Lord did not take away the burdens placed upon Alma's back, but through prayer and righteous living, the burdens were made light. And in spite of all the difficulties along the way, Alma was able to continue the work of Abinadi and bring countless people unto Christ.

Character Chart

Alma—Former high priest of King Noah's court

Helam—Brother of Abinadi

Amulon—High priest in King Noah's court
    Married to Itzel
        Daughter: Raquel

Maia—Married to King Noah
    Daughter of Jachin and Lael

Raquel—Widow of Abinadi
    Son: Abe

Gideon—Former high priest of King Zeniff's court

CHAPTER 1

As one whom his mother comforteth, so will I comfort you.
(Isaiah 66:13)

128 BC

Amulon stared at the king's red face, wondering if he'd ever hated a man more.

"What do you mean you can't find him?" King Noah yelled. He gripped his elaborate bird headdress and yanked it off, throwing it at Amulon.

Ducking the sailing headdress wasn't hard, but it was humiliating. The entire court had stopped to watch Amulon deliver the bad news—the same news—week after week. The former high priest Alma had disappeared, and more people left the city each night. Guards had been stationed at every possible road, but somehow the "believers" managed to escape. Women, children, men. *Humiliating.*

Amulon straightened to his full height. Even though he wasn't the king, he still commanded fear and respect. To be berated in front of the court would earn him ridicule. He could already see it in the other priests' eyes. For a strange moment, he wished his old friend Alma were here to give him advice. But that was impossible now. Alma was a traitor.

Amulon looked at the ground, hoping the king would mistake his bowed head for a gesture of subservience. "I pledge not to rest until Alma and his followers are found."

The king was on his feet now, his beady eyes fiery. "The court has heard your promise, and now they will hear mine. If you do not deliver Alma into my hands by the next moon, you'll suffer punishment that will have you begging for death." He tightened his pudgy, jeweled hands into fists.

Amulon raised his gaze and nodded at Noah's fury. "Yes, O King." The two men locked eyes for a moment—two men who had shared every luxury, every conquest, every victory, even a few women. Two men who lived for power at all costs. Amulon stared into the king's eyes and saw his future—a future that didn't include this preposterous king.

A future where *he* was in power.

He kept his smile to himself as he turned and strode toward the back of the court room. A young boy passed him, eyes wild with fear.

Amulon paused and watched the child bow before the king and request permission to speak.

"O King, another family has abandoned their home," the boy said in a trembling voice. "Jachin and Lael of the lower district. All animals and goods were left behind."

Amulon left the scene, not interested in hearing the sure explosion from the king. He walked out of the court and toward the front entrance of the palace, having nowhere else to go, at least not in the palace. The harlots had all but sequestered themselves in their rooms. Not much time for making merry or celebrating when the king was in a rage day and night. So Amulon left the palace and headed for home. At least there he would find some quiet—if only because his house was empty.

It didn't take him long to walk the dark, silent streets. They were deserted because of the new curfews. When he reached his home, he walked through the courtyard and entered the gathering room where one of the servants had left an oil lamp burning. He sank onto the cushions piled along the wall and looked around the room. Rugs, vases, and carved idols decorated it. Had it really been so long ago that his wife and daughter had lived with him under the same roof? He hadn't seen his daughter, Raquel, since that day in the plaza when her husband, the traitor Abinadi, was put to death.

He tried to push thoughts of his disowned daughter from his

mind, but the questions crept back. *Where did I go wrong?* Amulon thought. *How did my daughter go from a young, beautiful child to a defiant woman running from marriage to a king? And what possessed her to marry a poor farmer who called himself a prophet?*

It had torn at his heart to see her at the plaza during Abinadi's final moments. But her pleas for her fanatical husband had closed the door on his sympathy once and for all. His wife, Itzel, had apparently empathized with their daughter—and had disappeared that same day. Rumors circulated that she'd followed Raquel back to the hidden community of the elders.

If the other rumors were also true, and Itzel had left with Alma's believers, then she was as good as dead to him.

Dead!

After struggling to his feet, Amulon went into the cooking room. He spotted a jug of wine and took a long drink. To think of his wife disobeying him—by following the man who'd betrayed him so deeply—infuriated him in the worst way.

Alma. It seems I found a man I hate worse than the king.

Amulon took another drink, trying to determine how he could avenge himself of the wrongs that had been committed against him. It had all started with that preacher—Abinadi. But since he was dead, Amulon had to find another to bring to trial. The next logical person was Alma—the ever-evasive high priest. Amulon thought hard. There had to be a way to discover Alma's whereabouts—the believers that still remained in the city *had* to know his whereabouts. Finding out who the believers were was nearly impossible, but there must be a way.

Something tickled at the back of his mind. What had the boy said earlier? The most recent deserters—Jachin and Lael. They were familiar to him . . . they were the parents of Maia, the king's own wife. And Maia was the one whom Alma had risked his own life to defend.

Amulon took another long drink, this one in celebration. If Maia's parents were believers, then it wasn't unreasonable to assume that she was, too. He knew she had returned to her parents' home for a short time after the death of her son but had since been granted a private residence, though he couldn't recall where. Nothing a little research couldn't take care of.

He wiped the excess wine from his lips and grinned. He'd just found a way to redeem himself in the eyes of the king—and perhaps exact some revenge of his own.

* * *

It had been a good day—a hard day. Alma's back and shoulders ached from constructing shelters for the two dozen families now living in the wild country of the Waters of Mormon. More Nephites arrived daily—travel-weary, but joyous to reunite with their fellow believers. And Alma welcomed them all.

The sun dipped toward the horizon, splashing its rays across the lake. Alma paused to watch the final light illuminating the rippling water for a few more moments—blue, green, orange, and violet. The ibis and jabirus birds had long since retreated but would be back in full force to welcome the morning.

Footsteps approached behind him, and Alma turned.

The face was hard to distinguish in the fading light, but the hooded form was familiar. "Hello, Helam."

The man nodded once. "We have a new family."

Alma smiled. "Take me to them." He cast a glance at the lake again; the sun had disappeared, leaving the water a deep violet. Then he followed Helam silently, walking along the shoreline and turning toward the spring. There beyond the thickets sat rudimentary structures housing the families. Children gathered in groups playing with a rubber ball, using only their elbows and hips, while mothers and fathers watched, enjoyment replacing the exhaustion of hard labor on their faces.

Alma greeted those they passed by name. He knew each person, each child. A young boy ran up and tugged on his arm. "Will you play ball with us?"

He patted the boy's head. "Another time. Tonight I have to welcome some new arrivals."

Disappointment shadowed the boy's face, but it was gone the instant he set off toward his friends.

Helam laughed. "You're everyone's favorite uncle."

He smiled at Helam's laughter, grateful that the quiet man had warmed up to him. Helam was Abinadi's brother.

And I was a part of the court that condemned Abinadi.

Although Alma was an outcast when the judgment was passed down, he had served many years as a part of Noah's corrupt court. The thought still made him shudder.

If Helam noticed Alma's sudden change of mood, he didn't say anything. As the two continued around the makeshift shelters, Alma thought about all Helam must have endured—not only as a youth when he was badly burned in a crop fire, but as a scarred citizen of the city of Nephi. When it came to appearances, King Noah was a perfectionist. His palace, his food, his women, and especially his city were without blemish—on the surface. The crippled or the scarred were simply driven out, and Helam had spent most of his years living in exile with a colony of elders who accepted him—elders such as Gideon, a former priest from King Zeniff's time, when the land had been ruled by a righteous king and the law of Moses was revered.

No longer. The creeping decay of the original temple had been replaced by newer, higher, and more elaborate temples. Carved idols guarded the doors, and altars were used for illegitimate sacrifices of all manner of beasts—even humans.

Tears pricked Alma's eyes, and he shook the gloomy thoughts away. That life was behind him now, yet he couldn't forget. Although he was twenty-three years of age, it still took some doing to accept his leadership position among the believers. He spent every moment trying to make up for his previous wrongs. Trying to undo everything he'd done. Trying to do as much good as he'd done harm, hoping to surpass it one day.

They rounded the final hut, and Helam stopped, letting Alma pass by. There were only two people sitting on top of their bundles, food and drink in hand. Alma felt his breath catch as the man and woman raised their gazes. Jachin and Lael—Maia's parents—had arrived.

The man stood on shaky legs and grinned. "We came to join the Lord's fold."

The lump in Alma's throat tightened as he walked toward the couple and pulled the man into an embrace.

"Welcome, Jachin." He turned to the woman, who rose, and embraced her too. "Welcome, Lael."

She pulled back, wiping joyful tears from her face. "We were afraid we wouldn't make it before nightfall."

Jachin put his arm around his wife's shoulders. "Every night the sounds of the wild beasts seemed closer."

Alma let out a sigh of relief. It had been over a month since he'd last stood in their humble home, sharing the teachings of the Lord. "We've been praying for you. Each day when you didn't come . . ." He couldn't help but look past them, searching.

"It's just the two of us," Jachin said, a knowing look in his eyes.

Alma snapped his focus back to the couple, questions burning on his tongue. But now wasn't the time to ask them, not when they needed food and rest.

Lael touched his arm. "She is well."

Alma nodded, a measure of relief trickling through him. Perhaps Maia had been able to find some semblance of peace as one of King Noah's wives, even after all that had happened. If that was so, then he could sleep with one less burden. "Very good. You can report the latest news to the colony in the morning. I know they'll all be eager to hear what you have to say. You may sleep in my hut until we can build you a shelter."

"We don't want to intrude," Jachin began.

"No intrusion." Alma smiled. "I have a favorite sleeping spot near the lake." He motioned toward Helam, who stood a few paces away. "This is Abinadi's brother. He'll take you to my hut."

At the mention of the prophet's name, Lael and Jachin stared at Helam for a moment before gathering their bundles. He bowed slightly. "Welcome to Mormon." He reached for Lael's bundle and led them toward the huts.

Alma watched them leave, his heart filled with a mixture of relief and heaviness. Maia's parents had arrived safely and she was well. But she was still in the city—still at the mercy of a wicked king. Alma knew firsthand the torture of hiding a converted heart. He feared for her life if her conversion were discovered. The king hadn't hesitated in bringing her to trial for the death of their infant son—a child who had been born too early to survive. The king's abuses of his wife had almost certainly been the cause of the premature birth. What if Maia incurred the king's wrath again?

Like a whisper, her words came to his mind: *I could no longer live with the king when I love another man.* He shook his head at the tangible memory. She'd wanted to request a divorce from the king, but Alma knew it would be a death sentence. He'd pleaded with her, and finally she had agreed not to seek such action.

I'm not asking you to love me, she had said. At the time he'd known it was too late for that. But he had changed. He had overcome his unrighteous feelings toward a married woman. He had repented and been forgiven by the Lord.

Yet still he worried about her. The last words she had spoken to him were, *Somehow, I'm going to make it to Mormon.*

His prayers over the last weeks had been for the safety of all those who desired to join the believers. Including Maia. But if the cost were too great, he could only pray that her life would be spared.

Alma walked around the spring and arrived at the lake once again. The water was almost black now, peaceful, quiet. The three mountains surrounding the lake had blended into the sky, yet he could feel their protective force even without seeing them. He moved to a small grove and unrolled the rug he kept there for such occasions. It was still early for sleep, but he sat on it, resting his weary body. He clasped his hands together—the new calluses a sign of hard labor—and thought about the chores that would have to be done the next day: start on Jachin's small home, finish cultivating the modest fields, and prepare for the Sabbath eve.

His message tomorrow night would be one of redemption and repentance. Most of the new believers struggled with leaving their old lives behind and truly accepting that the Lord had forgiven them. Alma understood perfectly. He'd had the same struggle.

But I know better now, he thought. *The Lord has forgiven me. The Lord has taught me a new way—through Abinadi. And I will spend my life teaching others what I know in my heart to be true. But how can I help the believers understand the true scope of the Lord's forgiveness and the meaning of redemption?*

Alma moved to his knees and bowed his head. He had so much to pray for, so much to ask the Lord for. But first, he must thank Him for the safe arrival of Maia's parents.

As he prayed, a familiar warmth spread through him, seeming to expand his chest. Clenching his hands together, his whispered prayer fell quiet as he listened. Then, as gentle as a lamb, yet stronger than a lion, the Lord's voice came.

Organize my Church and invite my people into my fold. If they are willing to bear one another's burdens and mourn with those that mourn, they may be redeemed. If they are willing to comfort those that stand in need and stand as my witnesses, they shall be baptized, that they be numbered with those of the first resurrection and have eternal life.

The words flowed through Alma as the Lord continued to instruct him in the way to baptize the people into the Church of God. Alma's heart soared. The believers would have their own church—one organized by the Lord Himself. This was the key to their redemption and would start them on the path to eternal life.

Tears spilled onto Alma's face as gratitude blossomed in his heart. Through him, through the Lord, the believers would be counted among the fold of God. They would become as one—united in heart and purpose—as witnesses of the Lord at all times and in all things. As the Lord's voice went silent, Alma found that he was trembling. Humility and joy blended together until he didn't know if he'd be able to catch his breath.

After several moments, his breathing returned to normal, and he lay down on his bedroll, exhausted and exhilarated. He closed his eyes against the quiet night, knowing that his journey as an instrument in the Lord's hand was only beginning.

CHAPTER 2

For this shall the earth mourn, and the heavens above be black . . .
(Jeremiah 4:28)

An insect buzzed close to Raquel's ear, waking her. After swatting at the obnoxious offender, she reluctantly opened her eyes. Morning seemed to come too early now. It was easy for her to sleep well past dawn and even the morning meal—if little Abe let her. But not today. She glanced over at the child sleeping next to her mat. Each of them seemed to derive comfort from the other—comfort that came in the smallest of measures.

On the other side of a room, behind a curtain, slept Raquel's mother. Bringing her this far had been difficult since she wasn't used to such heavy work, but she stayed determined. And now, Raquel had never seen her more at peace. The other women had been patient in teaching her the skills she lacked.

Raquel stood and moved away from Abe. The longer the one-year-old slept, the happier he would be. It seemed that with his father gone—and now his favorite uncle—he'd developed an ornery nature. *When are you coming back, Helam?* she wondered. After her husband's death, Helam had been the steady hand in her life. But he'd traveled to Mormon to help build a colony for the believers. He promised to return to the elders' community for her and Abe, along with his mother, Esther, and hopefully Raquel's mother, too.

Raquel crossed to the small window at the back of the hut. It looked over a stretch of carefully tended fields. She had grown to love this narrow valley, which the elders had established when they were

banished from the city of Nephi. But since her husband's death, it
hadn't felt the same. Everything reminded her of Abinadi. The grove
where they had their wedding, the secluded forest where they camped
the first nights of their marriage, and of course this hut. She looked
around at the rudimentary room. Abinadi had built it with his own
hands, all the while making plans to build a bigger one for their
growing family.

But with him gone, there was no need for a larger hut.

Inevitable tears pushed their way to the surface as her chin trembled. Although she was only twenty, she wondered if she'd spend the
rest of her life feeling this much pain. Mornings were the most difficult, when she woke and remembered all over again in the second or
two that it took to move from sleep to awareness—and the ache
always twisted her heart. It would take her an entire day of hard work
to feel better. By nightfall, she would reconcile herself again,
exhausted with work, so that as soon as she curled up next to her son,
she'd fall asleep.

Raquel wrapped her arms around her body and sank to the floor.
Her chest heaved as she silently cried. It was for this reason she hated
waking before the settlement had come to life. The quiet was discon-
certing, and the loneliness amplified itself into every crevice of her
home. She was almost tempted to wake Abe or her mother, but
instead she allowed herself to feel the sorrow, alone.

She squeezed her eyes shut and prayed for Helam to return soon.
If only for her son, if only to leave this settlement, if only to start
anew.

"Mama?"

Raquel raised her head. Two brown eyes blinked at her. Abe
bounded to his feet and toddled over to her, his arms outstretched.
She pulled him into a fierce embrace, hoping that the hut was still too
dim for her son to see her tears. He was too young to articulate his
observations, but she knew he *felt* when she was sad. After all, they'd
both suffered the same loss, though in time it would fade for her son.
He was already starting to forget. He asked for "Papa" less and less.

Noises came from outside. Raquel stood, Abe still in her arms,
and stepped out of the hut. Esther crouched near the cooking fire,
stoking the embers from the night before.

Raquel watched her mother-in-law for a moment. Here was another person who had suffered. First with the abandonment of her husband so long ago and now with the death of her son.

"Mama," Abe said, stretching his hands toward his grandmother. His vocabulary didn't differentiate between the two women yet.

Esther turned, shielding her eyes from the rising sun, and grinned. "Good morning, sweetheart, come see your grandmother."

Raquel smiled and set Abe on the ground. He swayed a bit, gaining his balance, then walked over to her. Raquel followed him closely, ready to catch him if he stumbled on a rock.

"Mama," he called again.

Esther scooped him up in her arms and planted a hearty kiss on his cheek. Looking over Abe's head, she met Raquel's gaze.

She hoped that all traces of her tears were gone. Her mother-in-law didn't say anything, just bounced Abe for a few minutes, getting him to laugh.

Raquel crossed to the stone and started to grind kernels into flour for the cakes. Soon Esther was at her side, taking up her own stone and making the work go twice as fast. Raquel kept an eye trained on Abe as he picked up a rock and brought it to his mouth.

"No, Abe," she said. He looked directly at her and popped it in. "No, no." She straightened and grabbed her son, then fished the rock out of his mouth. "You could choke."

His lips puckered, and he started to cry.

She sighed and shook her head. "He's getting ready for another ornery day."

A knowing smile on her face, Esther straightened. "Here, let me take him for a little walk, and you can finish with the maize."

Raquel handed her son over to Esther then bent over the grinding stone again. She didn't know what she'd do without her mother-in-law. Just simple things like taking Abe for a few minutes meant so much. A short time later, Raquel had created enough flour to start the first two cakes. She mixed the flour and some water in a bowl and formed a sticky ball. She relaxed with the mundane task.

Suddenly she had the distinct feeling she was being watched. She looked up just as a hooded figure stepped into the circle.

"Helam!" she cried and leapt to her feet. Rushing to him, she threw her arms around his neck. He laughed and returned her embrace, then pulled away. Sticky dough covered his shoulders, but Helam didn't seem to notice.

"You're finally back," Raquel said, feeling a little awkward at the display of affection. He *was* her brother-in-law, but still.

He peered at her through his hood, his smile shaded. "It took longer than expected. New families arrive each day, and the work is never-ending."

She nodded. "Once you take us there, I can help."

"There's still uncertainty, Raquel." He hesitated. "The soldiers haven't given up the search, and the king is coming down hard on his commanders."

Squaring her shoulders, she tried to push back her fears. "We *have* to go to Mormon. I don't know if I can bear living here any longer." She glanced around at the group of huts. She'd loved living here with Abinadi, but now the memories were too painful. Her voice dropped to a whisper. "It's difficult . . . I see Abinadi everywhere. Each morning I wake up in our home, and it's like I can't breathe." Immediately, she was chagrined. She hadn't been this forthright with anyone in the settlement. She dropped her head, knowing that she was selfish in her grief. Everyone had loved Abinadi, and everyone mourned him.

"I know," Helam said, touching her arm. "I miss him too." He looked away for a moment, then said, "You should see how fast the community of Mormon is growing. It is invigorating working with Alma. Teaching people that have so many questions. Building a community of people who want to be righteous and seeing their numbers and faith growing each day."

Raquel looked up again. "That's what I need. A different place. Hard work. A new life."

Just then, Esther called out, "Helam?" She and Abe came into view, back from their walk.

Helam crossed to his mother and embraced her. Then he grabbed Abe and swung him around. Screeching with delight, the child laughed.

Raquel waited, smiling at the two. They'd developed a strong bond on the journey from the city after Abinadi's death. Abe tugged at his uncle's hood, and Raquel said, "How many people are in Mormon, and how long is the journey?"

Helam turned, a smile on his shadowed face. "So many questions."

Raquel put her hands on her hips.

He laughed. "Fifty or so believers and five days' travel."

Just then, several people exited their huts and joined them at the cooking fire. Raquel's mother, Itzel; Gideon and his wife, Tia; and another elder, Ezra. Ben, a boy of eleven, also ran out of his hut. He'd mourned Abinadi fiercely and stayed close to Raquel for weeks. Recently, he'd spent most of his time making swords. It seemed his grief had been replaced with the obsession to make the perfect sword—the perfect sword to defend those he loved against any future threats.

Helam was soon surrounded by all the greetings and questions from the others. Raquel didn't have a chance to ask more questions.

The day passed agonizingly slow as Raquel waited for a chance to speak with Helam alone. She'd brought up the topic of traveling to Mormon once with her mother, but her mother had seemed reluctant to make a decision. *Then I will have to make it for us,* Raquel thought. It didn't help much that Ben continued to ask *her* questions. If it were possible, he was more eager to travel to Mormon than she was.

"I need to try out my swords," Ben told her that afternoon. He carried two swords, each carved with angled designs that looked like mountain ridges.

Raquel had to restrain Abe from reaching out and grabbing the sharp obsidian. "Maybe one of the men can practice with you."

Ben scrunched up his nose. "They're always too busy."

"All right," Raquel said, setting Abe down and handing him a strand of bird feathers to occupy him.

She took one of Ben's swords and held it straight out.

"No," Ben said. "Like this." He brought his sword in front of his face and narrowed his gaze. "It's all in the eyes."

Raquel tried to hide her smile. "Like this?" She angled the sword close to her body, then squinted back. Soon they were hopping around, tapping swords.

"Do you think Abinadi would have liked my designs?"

She halted and turned her sword over. "I'm sure he would have loved them. What are they?"

Ben stopped too and pointed to the horizon. "I outlined the landscape. See?"

She did and was impressed. "We'll always be able to remember this place."

"Yes, and if we ever need to come back, we'll have a map to show us the lay of the land," Ben said, looking at her. "When are we going to leave for Mormon?"

"I have the same question," she said. "Maybe tonight I can speak with Helam about it."

When Abe was down for the night and her mother inside the hut, Raquel sought out Helam. She found him huddled with the elders near the fire. More waiting. Since the other elders didn't seem eager to leave this place, Helam was probably her one chance. He'd been to Mormon, and he'd enjoyed the work there. Only when the moon sat high in the sky did the council break. Raquel waited for the other men to leave, grateful that Helam stayed behind, then she crossed to him.

He turned from the fire. "What are you doing out this late?"

She hid her annoyance. He used to shadow her when Abinadi spent time in the city preaching. It seemed his old protectiveness had returned.

She neared the fire, feeling the heat of the dying blaze on her legs. "I want to go back with you."

Helam shook his head. "The country is untamed, with wild beasts at every border. Even fifty people aren't enough to keep the colony secure. Mothers have to keep their children close by at all times."

She was prepared for the argument. "This valley was untamed when the elders first came. I didn't shy away from the hard work then, and I won't now. I know there are risks." She stared into the moving flames. "I think it will be good for all of us—your mother and my mother."

He fell silent for a moment, and Raquel hoped that she'd finally broken through to him. "We discussed it tonight in the elders' council. A couple of men expressed interest, but Gideon pointed out something that quieted anyone's desire to leave."

Raquel looked at Helam, curious. Gideon was one of the bravest men she knew—he wouldn't be concerned about a wild territory.

"Noah's soldiers are still scouring the countryside. Rumors say they've started to break into homes unannounced, trying to find evidence of any of the citizens planning a departure. Then those citizens are brought to trial."

She lifted a shoulder. "I'd expect no less of the king, but we'll stay clear of the city when we travel."

"Don't you see, Raquel?" Helam said, keeping his voice low. "On the right, we have King Noah's soldiers; on the left, we have the Lamanites. Before us, the unknown. But if we stay here, we'll be safe." His gaze bore into hers. "And that's all I care about—that you and Abe are safe."

"But Helam, surely—"

"You are the most stubborn woman I know," he interrupted. "I wouldn't be surprised if I discovered you packing a bundle before dawn."

Raquel shrugged, an apologetic expression on her face. When she'd tried to sneak out of the village and go after Abinadi, Helam had caught her, then accompanied her—his stubbornness matched hers. But the wild country of Mormon? Even that was a journey she didn't dare make on her own.

"What if we just went? Then if, after some time, it proved to be too difficult, we could return here?" Raquel said.

"Just you, Abe, and me?" he asked.

"No, I'm sure Esther and my mother—" she started.

"So I'm to escort and somehow protect three women and a baby, lead you through dangerous, warlike territory, watch you labor in a temporary settlement, then help you flee anytime the king's soldiers come near."

Raquel stared at him for several seconds. "Exactly."

* * *

The morning dawned in a haze, at least in Amulon's mind. He groaned as he sat up, blinking at his surroundings. He'd fallen asleep on the cushions in the gathering room, an empty wine jug nearby. Then he remembered—he'd been celebrating.

A smile crept to his lips as he reminded himself of his plan. Find Maia. Force her to admit that she was a believer. Bring her to trial. The king would make an example of her to the people and reward him later. It would be *almost* like bringing in Alma. Almost.

Amulon pulled on one of his best feathered capes and ate a meal of maize cakes and pitted cherries prepared by his servant. By mid-morning he set out for the lower quarter. Even though Maia's parents had received a generous bride price from the king, he heard that they hadn't upgraded their residence. Perhaps neighbors could direct him to Maia. As Amulon passed through the streets, most of the people bowed their heads when they saw him. A couple even ran up and handed him a painted ceramic vessel. He smiled generously and moved on his way. He loved being revered. The road narrowed until it became a series of paths, leading in several directions. He stopped when he came to a cluster of three huts—all of them simple, only two or three rooms each, but the courtyards were well tended.

Amulon hesitated, wondering which one belonged to Maia's parents. He heard someone singing. He walked to the edge of the courtyard of the middle hut, realizing with surprise that the voice belonged to Maia. He'd heard her sing many times at court, and her voice was unmistakable. She must have returned here after it became known that her parents had fled. He smiled gleefully. This was going to be even easier than he had thought. He listened to the words of her song carefully. It was a traditional tune he'd heard before, nothing to do with a new belief.

He scanned the two surrounding huts. He'd need a reason to bring her to trial—so he'd have to find something that she was guilty of.

A plan formulating in his mind, he left Maia's home. He hurried through the streets, barely acknowledging those who paid homage to him. Reaching his estate, he gathered supplies—food, wine, and servants' clothing. He'd learned one thing from his daughter—how to wear a disguise.

Before he put his plans into action, he spent part of the day strategizing with the captain of the border guards. All manpower was to be doubled, and nighttime patrols would be increased.

When the sun crossed the sky and began its descent, Amulon headed for home. Once there, he put on the servant's robe and wrapped his feathered cape in a bundle of clothing. As twilight began to fall, he strapped a parcel of food and wine, including a pouch of silver onties, to his back. Then he set off.

It was only a short time until curfew, so if he hurried, he wouldn't be stopped or questioned. Not that he couldn't reveal his identity and continue on his errand, but he didn't want to raise any interest.

In a short time, he arrived at the collection of three huts. The glow of oil lamps came from all three, and now it was just a matter of guessing which hut on either side of Maia's to approach. He went to the left and peered in the window. A woman and baby sat inside, with a young boy playing on the floor. Amulon crept away, skirting Maia's hut, and peered into the window of the hut on the right. A man and woman sat inside, eating supper. No children in sight.

Amulon smiled and rounded the hut. He pulled the feathered cape out of his bundle, swept it around his shoulders, and knocked on the door.

When the man opened it, Amulon held out the pouch of silver. "On authority of His Highness, King Noah, you must vacate this home immediately."

The man's eyes widened, and he looked from Amulon to the pouch.

Amulon thrust it toward him. "Count it, if you must." He waved his hand. "It will more than pay for this place."

The woman moved to her husband's side, bowing her head.

"Any one else live here?" Amulon asked.

Both the husband and wife shook their heads.

"Very well," Amulon said, "I'll wait outside until you have gathered what you can carry." He looked at them pointedly. "Tell no one about these orders."

The woman clutched her husband's arm, fear in her eyes. But they turned away silently and started to gather their things.

Satisfied, Amulon moved out of the doorway. He scanned the other two huts. There didn't seem to be any sign of outside activity. Sooner than he expected, the couple emerged, and Amulon handed them the bag of silver.

They hurried off into the darkness. Amulon watched them disappear then entered the hut and shut the door with satisfaction. The first part of his plan had gone perfectly. He took off his cape and wrapped it into a bundle. He would save it again for the right time. Next, he blew out the oil lamp and left the hut. He climbed over the low wall that separated his new hut from Maia's, then picked one of the trees where he'd have a good angle and pulled himself up on the first branch. From his position, he could see directly through her window.

He settled back, enjoying the night air and the vision before him. He'd forgotten how beautiful she was. Her dark hair shone in the lamplight. Her features were still flawless, even though she was no longer a young bride of sixteen. How exquisite. If it were possible for a woman to become more beautiful as she aged, Maia was the example at the age of nineteen.

She sat near the flickering oil lamp, bent over some handiwork. Her dark copper hair had come loose from its plaits, and every so often, she brushed it back from her face. Then she started singing softly. Amulon found himself leaning forward, trying to hear each melodic phrase. How the king had allowed this wife to live apart from him he couldn't understand. He could well understand Alma's interest in her—even though she was forbidden as a king's wife.

A smile touched Amulon's lips. Perhaps being forbidden made her all the more enticing. Their twenty-five-year age difference didn't hurt either. He continued to watch her for several minutes before reminding himself that he should be looking for any incriminating items in her home. From his angle, he could see most of the gathering room, except for a couple of corners. He looked for any idols that might prove she still worshipped the sun god or the moon goddess. He couldn't see any. That might be proof alone.

Then suddenly Maia stood, yawning. Amulon gripped the branch below him, ready to run for cover. But she didn't come near the window—she turned and moved into the next room. Amulon slipped from his perch and walked along the side of the hut, keeping to the edge of the trees, following the glow.

She was in her bedchamber. Amulon climbed the next tree and balanced a little more precariously than before. Maia yawned again, then unbound her hair. Maybe he would catch her praying. His heart started to hammer. She pulled the robe from her shoulders, and Amulon held his breath. Before removing anything else, she blew out the oil lamp.

Amulon let out his breath, blinking in the sudden darkness. When his eyes adjusted to the new dark, he silently climbed down from his perch and crept toward the window. He peered inside, trying to make out her form, huddled beneath a cover on the bed. She was quiet. No words, no praying, no singing. He watched for several moments, disappointment throbbing in his chest, before he finally pulled back.

Tomorrow would be another day. Another chance.

CHAPTER 3

For, behold, the day cometh, that shall burn as an oven . . .
(Malachi 4:1)

About a week after Helam's return, Raquel knew she had to approach
him again. The more time that passed, the harder it would be to
convince him to take her to Mormon. Everyone had settled into a
comfortable routine, as if Helam had never been absent, as if Abinadi . . .

Raquel met Helam's gaze across the evening fire, but he quickly
looked away. Gideon, the head elder—the Teacher—continued to
expound on the teachings of the Lord and His Ten Commandments,
something Raquel was quite familiar with now. She remembered
when she'd asked Abinadi several questions about the laws of God—
especially the ones King Noah had chosen to ignore.

Raquel folded her arms, feeling sleepy as Gideon's soft voice rose
and fell in the night. Her son was already asleep in the hut, her mother
with him—likely asleep as well. Raquel stifled a yawn, then noticed
Helam looking at her again. Maybe he'd changed his mind. She pulled
her worn mantle tighter about her shoulders, looking around the darkened settlement—the huts neatly lined up, the fields beyond. There
was nothing here she would take except the memories.

Gideon finished, then offered a prayer. The meeting had ended.
Next to her, Esther stood and stretched. "Good night."

Raquel watched her mother-in-law bid good-night to several
others then walk to her hut. By the time Raquel rose to her feet,
almost everyone had left. Helam, Gideon, and Ezra remained. She
walked up to the three men and folded her arms.

Gideon arched a brow, his expression turning serious before she could speak. "I'm sorry Raquel, but our decision remains the same."

Next to him, Ezra nodded, but Raquel turned her gaze on Helam. "All right," she said. "You have your way . . . for now."

He nodded, his face hidden in the shadow of his hood. Sometimes Raquel wished she could just pull the hood off. What was he hiding from? Who was he protecting? Everyone knew him and knew of his childhood burns. No one here would shrink away or treat him differently.

"For now," she repeated, then looked at Gideon and Ezra.

Gideon put a hand on her shoulder, his face full of fatherly concern. "We know it's been difficult for you to stay in this place with all of Abinadi's memories. And if we had another option, one of us would take you to Mormon."

Raquel's eyes stung. *Not now.* She had warded off her emotions all day. It was easier to feel angry at the elders than to think about *why* she was in this situation of being dependent on other men for her well-being instead of on a husband.

She took a step back, and Gideon's hand fell away. She didn't want anyone's pity; she just didn't want to live here anymore. Turning before tears could appear, she called good-night over her shoulder, then walked toward her hut. She didn't know if the men discussed her after she left, but suddenly she felt ashamed. She'd been ungrateful and selfish. Hot tears burned against her eyelids. She had her own mother to think about, plus her mother-in-law, and her son. How could she even consider putting any one of them in danger, just because she missed her husband with every breath?

She would always miss him—some days more intensely than others—but his presence would always be in her heart. Then she stopped cold, a shiver of realization trailing down her body. She wasn't the only husbandless woman here. Esther had been abandoned by her husband years ago, and her own mother had left her husband and home. She was not the only one in this situation. A half-sob rose in her throat. With one more backward glance at the faltering fire, she escaped into her hut.

Once inside, Raquel pressed the backs of her hands against her eyes, taking several deep breaths, trying to calm herself against a deluge of grief. "Not tonight," she whispered as she felt her way through the dark until she reached Abe. Lying next to him, she wriggled close, smelling the slight dampness of his neck. His breathing was steady, quiet. She kissed his hair, then closed her eyes against the moonlight mixed with the glow of the fire coming through the lone window.

She must have fallen asleep, because the next thing she knew, the room had brightened. Something was wrong. She opened her eyes, tasting something acrid in her mouth. The taste traveled to her throat, making her feel like gagging. Smoke. The hairs on her neck bristled as she sat up.

The door of her hut burst open, and smoke billowed in. Helam ran in to the room, shouting, "We have to leave, now!"

Raquel scrambled to her feet, fear piercing her heart. "What is it?"

"The Lamanites," he hissed. "Gideon's hut is already burning."

"Oh, no!" Raquel's mother cried out from the corner. She started grabbing things to pack.

"There's no time," Helam said.

Panic welled inside Raquel as she scooped up her son. "Where's your mother and Ben?" she asked Helam.

"Here!" Ben spoke from the doorway, smoke coming in behind him. Esther and Ben stood together, looking frighteningly small and vulnerable. Esther put a hand to her mouth and coughed violently.

"Let's go!" Helam said, leading the small group out of the hut.

The women filed out after him, staying huddled together.

Raquel looked around at the burning village in horror. Several huts had caught fire. She gasped when Lamanites rushed into a hut just three away, and screams erupted from inside. Flashes of Abinadi being beaten with burning sticks leapt to her mind, and she froze, gripped with fear. But someone pulled her arm, and she numbly followed.

"Run! Run! Don't stop no matter what you hear or see." It must have been Helam, because in the next instant he took Abe from her and grabbed her hand.

Raquel stumbled alongside him, her eyes stinging with smoke. The cries from within the village became her own, and soon she couldn't tell the difference between them.

Her legs ached as she plunged into the nearest field, gripping Helam's hand, following the others. Behind her a man shouted, but she didn't understand what he said. Then he shouted again, a terrible piercing sound. A war cry. Dread pulsed through her.

In front of her Ben stumbled. She nearly tripped over him, but Helam caught her just in time. He helped Ben to his feet. "Go! Go! They're coming after us."

One look behind sent a shock of terror through Raquel. At least half a dozen Lamanite warriors were leaping over the waist-high maize, whooping and hollering as they drew closer.

"Drop to the ground!" Helam whispered in a fierce voice. "Turn to the left and crawl as fast as you can."

Abe whimpered in Helam's arms, and Raquel longed to comfort her child. In front of her, Esther, Itzel, and Ben dropped to all fours and started to scurry away.

Raquel threw a fearful look at Helam.

"If they get too close," he said, "take Abe and run as fast as you can. I'll only be able to hold them off for so long."

She nodded, trying to hold back the tears. She started crawling, ignoring the sharp jabs of the small rocks beneath her hands and knees. Half the time she held her breath, listening as the war cries drew closer. Then suddenly, they curbed. When they seemed to move farther away she turned to look at Helam behind her. "Have we lost them?"

"I hope so. We'll keep going until we reach the other side of the field."

They still crawled, but a little slower, as if they didn't dare disturb the stalks they moved between.

Finally they reached the far side of the field and moved to a group of trees at the base of a hill. Raquel stood and helped Itzel and Esther to their feet. Both women stood unsteadily, panting. Raquel's entire body trembled. She looked over at Helam, who was still holding her son. Abe's eyes were wide open—staring at the blazing settlement.

She took her son in her arms, cradling him against her. *Thank heaven we are all safe.* She turned to see at least half of the huts burning and the dark shadows of Lamanites moving against the orange backdrop.

"Look over there," Ben whispered.

On the adjacent side of the field, a group of people emerged and seemed to melt into the trees.

"Must be Gideon's group, heading for the city," Esther said.

"Where's everyone else?" Ben asked, sounding frightened.

"Some escaped before we did," Helam said. "They're probably well on their way." He looked over at Raquel. "Do you still want to go to Mormon?"

She stared at him.

"It looks like you finally get what you wanted."

She shook her head, feeling a tear slip down her cheek. "This is not what I wanted."

"I know." Helam moved closer to her and put a hand on her shoulder. "I think it will be a better choice than the city. Even with Gideon and the others going, there will be no guarantee of safety." He hesitated. "Especially yours. If I thought that we could find refuge in your father's home or elsewhere . . . but I'm afraid it would be too tempting for some citizens to turn you in."

She nodded. The city wasn't exactly friendly to her—not only had King Noah threatened to put her to death, but her father would follow the king's orders, no matter what.

Helam faced her as he spoke to the small huddled group. "Our best option is going to Mormon."

Raquel let out a breath and tightened her hold on her son, knowing she had everything she wanted in her arms. Her mother was with her, and if Ben, Esther, and Helam were safe, what more could she ask for? She shivered. She had wanted to leave the settlement and start a new life, but not like this. Not in this horrible way.

"Look. They're burning another one!" Ben whispered loudly.

Raquel and Helam simultaneously hushed him, but their eyes were drawn to the village. Orange flames rose in the sky.

"They're going into your hut!" Ben said.

Raquel couldn't speak, clearly seeing the light from the torches spill out of the window and doorway. Her stomach felt sick as she thought about her enemies going through her belongings. Then the Lamanites left her hut. Raquel held her breath.

"It's on fire," she whispered in the deathly silence.

No one spoke as they watched flames reach out the window and doorway, slowly consuming the home.

Raquel stroked Abe's hair as he buried his head against her chest. Somewhere in the back of her mind she realized that Helam had put an arm around her shoulders. Then she felt tears streaming down her cheeks.

As if he could hear her agony, Helam answered, "They don't want to give us a reason to come back." His grip tightened around her shoulders.

Raquel stared at the rising flames, and even though they were far away, it was as if she could feel the heat singeing her face. Soon the rest of the huts went up in flames. She didn't know how much time passed as she stood there, watching. It was sickening and mesmerizing. Fire had taken almost everything she had.

Helam's soft voice finally broke through. "Let's go." He reached for Abe and took him from her.

Raquel followed the others numbly, looking back time and again. Ben sidled up next to her and took her hand, and she held on tight.

"I brought my swords," he whispered.

She nodded, knowing exactly what he meant. At least they had one part of the valley the Lamanites couldn't burn.

* * *

Amulon watched Maia day and night, growing more impatient each day. She seemed to be a model citizen. She'd even come over to check on her neighbors and knocked on the door. Fortunately, she didn't try to enter.

He had her day memorized—rise, then fix an early breakfast. Feed the turkeys, fetch the water, weed the garden, travel to the market and barter with some of her embroidered wraps, then return home again in the evening. Sit by the oil lamp and embroider.

It wasn't a schedule that befit the wife of a king, but it was unvarying. Predictable.

He was wasting his time. He'd send a soldier to watch the house instead. Tonight would be his last night.

The light glowed from her home as Amulon watched. He could see her bent over her embroidery. He was half-asleep when she raised her head, her expression startled.

Amulon straightened, listening. What had she heard? Then he heard it too—a soft knock on her door.

Maia rose and walked slowly to the door, and Amulon had to move to get a view of the visitor.

In the doorway stood a man Amulon thought he'd never see again.

Gideon. The man who'd been banished from the city years ago— the man who was responsible for the strength of the elders—the man who must have sent Abinadi to the city to preach.

Amulon strained to hear the conversation. It seemed Maia didn't know him, that Gideon was introducing himself.

Why is he here? Amulon wanted to know. His chest burned as all the possibilities spun in his mind. Regardless of the reason, Maia's associating with this man was against the law. Now she could be tried for treason against her own husband.

He held his breath as Gideon spoke to Maia in quiet tones. She seemed to agree with whatever he said, as she kept nodding. Then Gideon moved out of the doorway. Half a dozen people entered the hut.

Amulon stared. They were dressed like . . . believers. They wore simple tunics made of linen, with little adornment. Their capes were of woven material, not a feather in sight.

Maia's home is full of believers! Amulon almost shouted with triumph. He needed more men. Gideon would put up a fight.

Without wasting any more time, Amulon grabbed his cape and fled the area, keeping to the side streets and out of sight of any curfew-breakers. As he reached the central marketplace, he donned his feathered cape. Now no one would mistake his identity. Two soldiers lazed near a corner. When they saw him approach, they straightened to attention.

Amulon spoke only two words. "Follow me."

He traveled the city until he had gathered a dozen more men, all of them curious but obedient. No one asked questions.

When they finally reached the road to Maia's hut, Amulon stopped and pointed. "Inside is a host of traitors to the king. Some might be hostile, so we must be prepared to use our weapons. One of the traitors is the king's own wife. Make sure she is not harmed; she must be brought before the king."

The soldiers nodded their understanding, their eyes wide.

"Move," Amulon said. He led them to the front door, then directed one of the soldiers to kick it open.

The soldiers rushed inside, shouting. Then they stopped and quieted.

Amulon entered the hut. It was empty.

CHAPTER 4

. . . judgment and justice take hold on thee.
(Job 36:17)

Amulon turned in a slow circle, disbelieving his eyes. The hut was empty except for a stack of cups on the low table. Just a short time ago it had been full of people. Where could they have gone so quickly? "They can't be far," Amulon said to the soldiers who crowded the room. "How many of you would know Maia or Gideon by sight?" When most of the soldiers raised their hands, Amulon nodded his approval. "Excellent. Now divide up and search the surrounding roads and homes for Maia or Gideon or any of their followers."

Amulon pointed to a couple of the soldiers. "You'll remain with me. We'll wait a while and see if they return." He ordered the others out of the hut, then he scanned the place one last time, fury welling up inside of him. He'd been so close.

"Let's go," he said, moving out, followed by the soldiers. He led them to the hut he'd been staying in.

The hours stretched on, one after the other, as Amulon watched Maia's hut. Finally sleep got the better of him, and he commanded the soldiers to wake him if there was any movement.

As dawn streaked across the sky, Amulon woke with a start. The first thing he noticed was that the soldiers were asleep. The second thing was that someone was singing. Amulon rose and peered out the window, kicking the nearest soldier in the process.

Maia knelt in the soft earth behind her home, digging or planting something. How long had she been back? He roused the other soldiers, motioning for them to be quiet. Pulling his cape over his shoulders, he took a deep breath then exited the hut. He skirted the low wall, then entered through the back gate.

Maia instantly detected his presence and raised her eyes to study him. Then she stood and brushed off her hands. She surely recognized him, yet she didn't say anything.

Amulon crossed his arms over his chest. "The king has had you watched."

Maia didn't move, just narrowed her eyes slightly as if trying to decide whether to believe him. She glanced at the soldiers, then back at Amulon.

"Last night, you hosted a group of rebels in your home," he said.

Now her expression changed. Her eyes widened, and she pursed her lips.

"Do I need to outline the charges?"

She shook her head.

For an instant, Amulon felt a twinge of regret, but just as quickly he pushed it away. "Come with us. I think your husband will be interested to hear what you've been doing."

Maia's expression was defiant. "I've done nothing to be ashamed of." She paused, eyeing him carefully. "At least *I* can say that."

Amulon practically growled, "Take her!"

He glowered as they walked through the streets. It was still early enough that few people saw them, but word of the arrest would spread soon enough. In fact, Amulon wouldn't be surprised if the king knew about it before he arrived at the palace.

The palace guards straightened, their eyes bright with curiosity, when they saw the small entourage coming toward them. Everyone loved a trial.

"Summon the king," Amulon told one of the guards. The stout man hurried away as fast as his short legs would allow. Amulon nodded at the soldiers who held Maia and led them into the throne room. It was empty of people, with last night's leftovers scattered across the low tables. A couple of servants scurried in, knowing looks on their faces, and began to remove the food and rearrange the cushions.

A short, thin man entered, carrying a sheaf of skins and writing instruments. It was Eli, the scribe who had almost offered marriage to

Amulon's daughter. Eli bowed, his gaze lighting on Maia for an instant. Although he raised an eyebrow, the scribe took his place without asking questions.

Perhaps the king would call for a formal trial at court, requiring everyone to convene later in the court room. But Amulon hoped that the matter could be resolved right away, here in the throne room.

Amulon paced the floor as he waited for the king to arrive. From time to time, he glanced over at Maia. She offered no resistance to the surrounding soldiers but stood looking at the ground. Her clothing was simple—still finely woven linen, but nothing like the other women at the palace. Had the king cut her income? Maybe it wasn't just boredom that caused her to barter her needlework at market. Perhaps she was so out of favor that this new transgression would hardly raise Noah's interest.

Amulon's palms started to feel moist. He didn't want this matter to be an annoyance to the king. For an instant, he second-guessed his great plan of redeeming himself. What if the king were displeased?

A guard announced the king, and everyone stood to pay their respects.

Amulon whirled around and bowed just as the king entered the room. He had two women with him—neither of whom Amulon recognized. They must be new harlots. The women glanced at Maia, apathy in their eyes, then turned their full attention back to Noah.

When the king was settled comfortably with the women sitting on cushions at his feet, he finally looked directly at his wife.

Maia kept her head lowered. The king stared, but still she wouldn't meet his eyes. His face reddened, and he finally turned to Amulon.

"What's the meaning of this?"

"O Highness," Amulon said, his voice dripping with allegiance. "A few days ago, her parents disappeared with the believers . . . You remember the young boy who brought you the news of Jachin and Lael?"

The king nodded, impatience in his eyes. "Go on."

"I decided to have her watched—in case she has become a believer like her parents."

Understanding dawned in the king's eyes, and he pushed away a female hand stroking his arm.

"Last night," Amulon said slowly, deliberately, "she received an interesting visitor at her parents' house."

The few people in the throne room murmured. Maia finally lifted her eyes and looked at her husband. But there was no pleading, no begging in her expression.

Amulon braced himself for the impact of his next words. "It was Gideon."

The king's brows shot up as he straightened and moved his leg away from the woman who was stroking it. "I banned him years ago."

Amulon didn't even have to nod, since the king was staring straight at Maia, their eyes locked.

"Speak, woman!" Noah roared.

She flinched, her expression pained. "Amulon speaks the truth."

Noah stood, his face red. But instead of shouting, he spoke in an even tone. "Why?"

"He came to seek shelter in the city. The Lamanites have burned their settlement."

The king's eyebrows shot up. "The Lamanites?"

Amulon watched the king closely. *No!* he wanted to shout. *Your wife is a traitor. That's what this is all about.*

Noah walked toward Maia, all of his attention on her, Amulon forgotten. "Tell me exactly what Gideon said."

The women at the throne pouted as they watched the king leave. Eli scribbled furiously in his corner.

Amulon's mouth went dry. *This can't be happening to me.*

"He said that everyone had to flee the settlement," Maia said. "He had only a portion of them with him—just families. More should be arriving in the city. He estimates about forty in all."

"Why did Gideon seek *you* out?"

"He thought my parents' home was empty. Someone told him that they were believers and had left to follow . . ." She looked directly at Amulon. "I had only been staying in the home recently. He didn't expect to find me living there."

The king looked at Amulon as well. "Is this true?"

Amulon spread his hands. "I didn't question the woman. I just brought her directly here so that you could make the judgment of her actions for yourself. She certainly welcomed him inside—despite knowing he was a traitor."

Noah weighed Amulon's answer for a moment. "It may have been an honest mistake." He turned back to Maia. "Or maybe not."

She held his gaze, not shrinking as Amulon might have expected. He couldn't let this turn sour, so he spoke up. "But what about her parents? They have been breaking your laws. Surely their daughter has been a part of their activities."

Noah glared at Amulon. "Surely?" He looked at Maia and took a step closer. "Are you a believer?"

She stared at him as if rooted in place.

Noah folded his arms. "Is my own *wife* a believer? Will she betray her own husband, her own king? The man who has given her everything?"

Amulon held his breath, looking back and forth between Maia and Noah. Even the scribe had stopped writing.

Maia's face paled as she clenched her hands into fists. "Yes," she whispered.

Noah leaned toward her, speaking through clenched teeth. "What—did—you—say?"

"Yes." Her voice was little more than a whisper. "I am a believer. I believe that Abinadi was a true prophet of the Lord. That he was wrongly convicted and wrongly put to death. That his prophecies will come about. That we must stop idol-worshipping and unclean sacrifices. And I believe that a man must have but one wife."

Noah's face worked itself into a rage. But instead of screaming, he squeezed his eyes shut and took several deep breaths.

Amulon drew back, fear pounding in his chest. The king's silence was worse than his yelling.

After a moment, Noah opened his eyes, his face remarkably calm—no, cold.

"Take her to the prison!"

The soldiers led Maia toward the door. She didn't even offer so much as a glance toward Amulon.

The king's eyes were on him. Cold, calculating. "You will personally gather a group of men to find Alma, if it's the last living act you perform. I don't want you sending out scouts. I want *you* to find him." He turned his back. "Now!"

* * *

It was Alma's turn at the night watch. Even though he spent his days in physical labor, then his evenings teaching from the recorded words of Abinadi, Alma insisted on taking his part in all things. Two days before, a band of Lamanites had been spotted, but they had turned another direction before reaching the Waters of Mormon. The whole community had been relieved, but Lamanites weren't their worst fear.

At least death by the Lamanites would be swift, whereas death by the Nephites would be slow and painful—perhaps in the manner of Abinadi's. Alma tried to ignore his hungry stomach as he watched the moonlight playing across the terrain. It seemed he was always hungry, but didn't notice it much until nighttime, when he wasn't so occupied. A group of men regularly brought in beasts for food, but they had little else to supplement their diets yet.

He sat on the top of a hill that gave him a good view of anyone that might try to waylay his people. Another watchman was stationed several dozen paces below him. It would take one signal from Alma for the watchman to issue the warning.

A snapping sound reached him—from somewhere down the hill. Alma's fist clenched around his sword, the obsidian spikes gleaming in the moonlight. "Who goes there?" he hissed.

"Jachin," called a loud whisper.

Alma immediately relaxed. The man was almost as tireless as he.

"Any movement?" Jachin huffed when he reached Alma.

"Nothing." Alma let out a sigh and turned back toward the landscape. He worried each night—and each day, for that matter. The three-day journey from the city to the Waters of Mormon was perilous. The king's guards were still searching for him, and the Lamanites seemed to be ever-present, just beyond the borders.

"Look there," Jachin whispered, pointing.

Alma looked just beyond a thick section of trees, where he could make out several figures.

"Do you think they're Lamanites?" Jachin asked.

Alma watched for another moment. "No."

"Guards?"

Alma peered through the darkness, studying the forms. One of them was short, the size of a child. "I think we have new believers. We should go down and help them."

Together the men scaled the other side of the hill, still alert to any other intruders. As they drew within hearing distance, Alma called out, "Hello there!"

Immediately the group slowed and one person stepped forward—tall and hooded.

Before the man could speak, Alma knew it was Helam.

"Alma?"

"Yes. Follow us; we'll guide you the rest of the way in." Alma waited for the small group to reach him. He was surprised to see so many women. They were all women except for the two children and Helam. Then his eyes widened as he recognized Itzel, Amulon's wife. And . . . He bowed his head when he saw Raquel—Abinadi's widow.

She carried Abe in her arms, the young son of the prophet.

"Welcome," he said, looking at her. He'd forgotten how young she was.

She smiled, no guile in her eyes. Her son blinked at Alma but didn't seem too curious.

"You know my mother, Itzel," Raquel said. "And this is my mother-in-law, Esther."

Alma nodded toward the two women. "Welcome to Mormon. This is Jachin."

"And I'm Ben," the boy standing by Helam said. Alma turned to him with a smile and was about to welcome him too, when his breath caught. It was the boy who'd been whipped in the king's palace. The boy who'd refused to turn in Raquel when the king demanded it.

Alma took a deep breath. "It's an honor to have you here." His gaze went to the women, then stopped at Helam. He felt humbled to have all of them here.

Helam stepped forward and clapped him on the shoulder. "Let's show them around."

Alma and Jachin grabbed the bundles from the women as they

moved up the hill. Alma wondered why Helam would bring such a vulnerable group, with him as the only man. "How was the journey?"

Helam was quiet for a moment as they hiked. He now held Abe in his arms, and it appeared the child was asleep. "The Lamanites burned our village."

Alma turned and stared at him. "Did everyone make it out all right?"

Helam nodded. "I think so. Gideon took a group back to the city, where they'll try to find shelter."

His worry lessened only slightly. Alma knew it wasn't the best option, but perhaps better than being at the mercy of the Lamanites.

They reached the top of the hill then started down toward the cluster of shelters. "I'm happy that you made it here safely," Alma said. "This week I've been teaching the principle of baptism to the believers. The Lord has made it known to me that He desires His people to be cleansed and for them to enter into a covenant with Him."

"How many want to be baptized?" Helam asked.

Alma grinned. "All of them."

"That's amazing. A true congregation gathered according to God."

* * *

With Abe fast asleep and the other women nearly so, Raquel crept out of the tent. The male voices had stopped, and Alma and Jachin had left. Only Helam remained, sitting on a rock. He'd insisted on sleeping outside.

Raquel gripped her pouch and pulled her cape tighter about her shoulders. Being near the large lake made the air cooler than she was used to. Helam looked up as she approached.

He shook his head when he saw the pouch she carried. "Again?"

"Again." The past several nights on their journey, she'd been adamant about applying curaiao salve to his face and arms. Of course, he'd only let her do so at night when the others couldn't see.

Obediently he removed his hood, and Raquel opened up her pouch and removed the shell case containing the salve. In the moonlight, his scars seemed to be nothing at all—just a few lumps and crevices. And Raquel knew it didn't hurt when she touched his skin, but he seemed to squirm anyway.

"Hold still," Raquel hissed. "You're acting like a child."

Helam let out a heavy sigh, closing his eyes. "This really isn't necessary."

"Yes, it is. I can already see a difference."

"Really?" He brought his hand up.

"Don't touch," Raquel said. "It has to soak in."

Helam lowered his hand.

"No hood tomorrow," she said.

He stared at her, then started pulling his hood back up.

"I mean it, Helam." She stopped him mid-motion with her hand. "We're starting over here. This is a new life for you. From the beginning, you need to be your true self." She let her hand fall.

"I *am* my true self." With irritation in his voice, he stood, moving away.

Raquel shook her head. "Do you want to remain hidden the rest of your life? The only reason people treat you differently is because you *act* differently."

"You don't understand. I've seen the horror in people's eyes when they see my face."

"I've also seen the love in their eyes when they get to know you." She paused, watching his reaction. "Besides, there will be a lot of young women here—young, faithful women. If you ever wish to marry, the women must get to know you."

She waited. He did nothing, and she wondered if he'd even heard her.

Finally he lowered his head and removed the hood.

"Good. And don't you dare put it back on." She smiled and thought she could see amusement in his eyes. "Or one of these mornings you might find it missing."

She turned from him before he could respond and entered the tent full of sleeping people.

Once inside, she laughed to herself. She knew her mother-in-law, Esther, would approve if she could get Helam to stop wearing that hood. He was more threatening with it on than off.

Raquel settled next to her sleeping boy. Ben was on the other side, snoring lightly. She closed her eyes and thanked the Lord for delivering them safely to this new land. She also prayed for the safety of Gideon, the other elders, and their families. After such an exhausting three-day journey, sleep came quickly, but it didn't stop her from hoping that when she awoke, the bad dreams would finally be gone.

CHAPTER 5

One Lord, one faith, one baptism.
(Ephesians 4:5)

Alma looked over the gathered crowd filling the entire hillside. Behind him, the Waters of Mormon reflected the morning light. If he had to estimate, there were around two hundred believers gathered. Alma's breath caught at the sight. It was incredible that in such a short time so many had left the city and come here to worship as a community. So many had embraced the Lord's teachings, so many had converted as if they were prepared all along and only had to be taught—only had to hear the truth.

He remembered the citizens protesting when Abinadi had preached in the marketplace. Just a few angry people could dissuade potential believers from hearing the truth. And now here was a different crowd—a crowd of believers, or people who embraced the truth. His heart constricted as he wondered what Abinadi would think if he could see these people now—believers who were a direct result of his sacrifice.

To Alma's right, Helam sat on a boulder, shoulders hunched, but his head exposed. The day after his arrival with Raquel and the others, he'd removed his hood. Alma sensed it had something to do with Raquel. Already in the short time he'd known her, he was impressed with her courage. It seemed she was afraid of very little and would reasonably expect a man like Helam to be likewise.

Helam's scarring was significant, but after a few days of staring, no one seemed to pay much attention. His face had become a common sight in the community—his teachings revered and his humor appreciated. Alma felt deeply grateful for the friendship that grew between them. With all his heart, he wished Abinadi's life had been spared, but the good that his testimony had brought would never be forgotten.

Extending his arms toward the gathering, Alma said, "Here we are, overlooking the beautiful Waters of Mormon." He caught Raquel's gaze in the crowd. She sat near the front with her son and mothers. Her expression was open, teachable, and she smiled when his eyes met hers. Beneath the smile, Alma sensed that she still grieved for her dear husband, but her heart was strong, and she was determined to honor Abinadi's name.

"You have come to this place desiring to join the fold of God and to be called His people," he continued, remembering the recent tender words of the Lord. Heads nodded in agreement. "You have been willing to bear one another's burdens so that they have become light.

"We have left behind family, friends, and homes that we love," Alma said. "You have mourned with those that mourn. You also have comforted those that stand in need of comfort." He looked at a small child who clung to his mother. "And through it all, you stand as witnesses of God at all times and in all things, and in all places." He smiled as his heart thudded. The warmth was back, and it was as if the Lord were looking on, adding His approval.

Alma took a deep breath and continued. "The Lord had promised that if we do these things, we will be redeemed of Him and be numbered with those of the first resurrection."

The men and women returned his smile and drew their children closer.

"If eternal life is the desire of your hearts, then what have you against being baptized in the name of the Lord?"

Several people murmured their desire to be baptized, but most just stared at Alma, tears in their eyes.

"Being baptized in His name means that we enter into a covenant and become His witnesses. And we promise to serve Him and keep His commandments. Through baptism, we will be privileged to have His Spirit poured out upon us."

The people started to clap. One woman wiped the tears from her face and called out, "This is the desire of my heart."

A man stood and echoed her sentiment. Soon the entire crowd was on their feet, repeating that they, too, desired baptism.

Alma smiled, his eyes burning with emotion. After several moments, the people quieted and most of them sat down again. "Very well," Alma said, his heart pounding. He met Raquel's gaze briefly, then he turned to Helam, who still stood, his arms crossed, wearing a lopsided smile. Alma stepped toward him and clasped a hand on his shoulder.

"Helam, would you like to be the first baptized?"

Helam looked at him in surprise, then his expression turned serious as he glanced at the crowd of people. "I'm not—"

"I would be honored if you would be first," Alma said.

Helam's eyes grew moist, and he nodded. They walked down the hill together, through the parting crowd.

The crowd reassembled at the freshwater spring that ran into the lake. They quieted as Alma directed Helam into the water, scattering the herons on the shoreline.

Alma gazed at those standing along the bank and felt his heart swell. Today the desire of their hearts would truly be realized. Today he would be baptized, along with the believers. He turned to Helam and, taking his arm, directed, "Hold onto my arm with your other hand."

When Helam was positioned, Alma looked to the heavens, feeling peace flood through him. The words the Lord had given him seemed to come with little effort. "O Lord," he cried loudly, "I pray that thou will pour out thy Spirit upon thy servant, that he may do this work with holiness of heart."

He took a deep breath. The atmosphere was absolutely silent except for the gentle lapping of the water. "Helam, I baptize thee, having authority from the Almighty God, as a testimony that ye have entered into a covenant to serve Him until you are dead as to the mortal body."

Helam's grasp tightened on his arm.

"And may the Spirit of the Lord be poured out upon you," Alma said, then took a deep, stuttering breath. His voice faltered with emotion as he continued. "And may He grant unto you eternal life, through the redemption of Christ, whom He has prepared from the foundation of the world."

Helam's grip remained firm as Alma plunged both of them into the cool water. The water enveloped them, and, after pulling Helam back up, Alma embraced him. Although soaked, Alma felt as if he were covered with unbelievable and gentle warmth. The two men clung to each other for a moment, Alma thinking about the incredible turn of events, from Abinadi's first appearance in King Noah's court to this joint baptism. Then they broke the embrace, wiping their eyes.

"Thank you," Helam said, his voice thick with emotion.

Alma reply was a whisper. "Thank *you*, my friend."

They walked together to the shore, where a line had formed. Alma wasn't surprised to see Ben at the front, a grin splitting his face. He ran to Helam and wrapped his arms around his waist. Then he turned expectantly to Alma.

Tears pricked Alma's eyes. "Come on, son. You can be next."

* * *

Amulon walked along the line of soldiers. He'd requested eight of the finest men—hardened in battle and skilled at picking up on the minutest details. No leaf or stick would go unexamined by these men.

"We need a four-day food supply and all the water we can carry on our backs." Amulon used his best commanding voice. "Prepare to travel both night and day. Sleep will be rare."

The soldiers nodded in unison. They knew that if their mission was successful, they would be well rewarded.

The king had requested that his oldest son, Limhi, accompany them on the search. Amulon had resisted; the young man was hardly the seasoned hunter. In fact, Amulon had his suspicions about the way Limhi spent his time—mostly in studying the ancient records in the royal library.

By the time the sun had reached its zenith, all of the preparations had been made. Bundles of the most necessary supplies were strapped to each soldier's back, and, with weapons in hand, they set out.

A few people lined the streets and waved as they exited on the north side of the city. Several women stepped forward, calling out blessings of the gods and goddesses. Once out of the city, Amulon led the group at a fast pace. He smiled to himself as he thought of Maia in prison, an example for all those who dared defy the king. And now he had only to bring Alma to justice. He turned to the soldiers. "We're heading north, and just before reaching the borders of Shilom, we'll turn west."

The soldiers looked surprised, probably thinking that the country west of the mountains was too wild for women and children. But Alma would most likely go to a place with which he was familiar. Back when Alma served in King Noah's court, they'd gone on several hunting trips on the west side of the mountain.

They reached the pass by nightfall, and Amulon instructed the soldiers to set up camp. After a meal of dried meat and a guava, he stretched out on his mat, thinking of his wife, Itzel. When he had heard the news that the elders' settlement had been burned, he was sure that his wife had been among those who fled to the city. Had she traveled back with Gideon? Would she attempt to come to his home?

It was better that he wasn't in the city if she appeared. He'd have to publicly denounce her and request a divorce to keep her out of his home. The only way to maintain his status as a favored high priest was to push away anything or anyone resembling treason. He closed his eyes as the night deepened. A couple of soldiers stood watch and all was quiet. The conversations between the soldiers had stopped, and most of them had fallen asleep.

The king had never questioned Amulon about his wife, although he was sure Noah had heard the same rumors as everyone else, which proved the king didn't hold Amulon's wife's desertion or his daughter Raquel's betrayal against him. King Noah's loyalty was another reason Amulon simply couldn't fail at this mission.

He tossed until sleep finally claimed him. By the time dawn touched the mountain, he was ready to go. The soldiers closed up camp, and their second day of travel began. An hour into the journey, one of the soldiers stopped.

He crouched and examined something on the ground. "Animal droppings."

Amulon reached the soldier's side and crouched too. "Goat dung." He picked up a piece and rolled it between his fingers. It was still quite soft. "The believers must have traveled through this pass recently."

The soldiers walked slowly, finding a well-traveled trail. Amulon's heart soared. This evidence was indisputable—he didn't know how much farther they'd have to go, but at least they were on the right path for now.

They kept to the forest as much as possible, staying concealed from sight should they cross any pockets of Lamanites. Every so often, a soldier ventured to the trail again, finding more evidence of travelers. By late afternoon, they came through the mountain pass and stopped, looking across a valley. It was surrounded by towering mountains, and a large lake spanned a good part of the wide escarpment. *The Waters of Mormon, a place I've visited before.*

Amulon directed his men to take shelter. They would sit and watch. This area was still wild country, but it had plenty of water for a community to build itself and grow. It was also a fertile hunting ground. It made sense that Alma might consider stopping here. It was only a day and a half travel for soldiers, maybe two or three for a family carrying grains, tents, and leading any flocks—yet still relatively close to the city of Nephi.

Surely Alma would realize he'd be discovered sooner or later. Amulon smiled to himself, thinking of how Alma may not have made the wisest decision. Yes, the man was skilled in the art of woodworking, but perhaps not in the matters of warfare or strategic positioning. *As I am.*

He'd been standing still for so long that one of the soldiers approached. "Are we to continue this way?"

Amulon turned. "Not yet. We'll wait for nightfall and let their fires guide us in."

The soldier nodded.

Amulon looked at the others. "Let's set up camp and make ourselves comfortable. The night will reveal exactly what we are looking for."

Darkness came slowly, but it turned out that Amulon didn't have to wait long. Just before the sun set, a plume of smoke rose from the north side of the lake. Then another followed, and another. *How many people are down there?* Amulon wondered. The king had estimated at least one hundred. But by the number of cooking fires, the amount could easily be double that.

The soldiers stood ready for their next instructions. It was with great pleasure that Amulon said, "Let's go visit Alma."

They traveled with only the moonlight as their guide. The terrain was rocky in places as they moved across the valley toward the lake, but no conversation was necessary. Amulon planned to find a good hiding place before the morning, when they'd be able to watch the people and strategize their plan of attack during the day without being detected. His pulse quickened as he thought about catching Alma unaware and hauling him back to King Noah. Amulon couldn't think of a prisoner he'd rather have in custody more.

"The fires are going out," a soldier whispered next to him.

Amulon halted, watching as the orange glows started to disappear. Maybe Alma was smarter than he thought. Or maybe they'd been spotted.

A chill crept along Amulon's neck as he strained his eyes in the darkness to see if they were being spied upon. He silently directed the soldiers into the nearest line of trees. They crouched there, listening for any sound, waiting for any movement. Then he heard footsteps moving through the undergrowth.

He sent a warning look to the soldiers and brought his finger to his lips.

Someone was walking along the trail they'd just abandoned. Amulon crouched closer to the ground and gripped his sword. One figure appeared in the moonlight, then another. He held his breath, counting. Eight people. Several adults and a few children.

A child's voice said, "I can't see the fires anymore."

"Hush," a man's voice came. "We're still going in the right direction."

Amulon's mouth fell open. More believers. More deserters. He watched them pass, wondering if these people knew how close they were to death. They had no animals with them, only the bundles on their backs. They must have left almost everything behind. *Just like Jachin and Lael.* Amulon gave his soldiers the signal to let them pass.

The longer he watched the silhouettes moving, the angrier he became. These people were openly defying their king. How could they think that life would be better outside the kingdom? Why would they choose to come to this place to start completely over and spend their days in hard labor?

When they were out of earshot, one of the soldiers said, "Why are we letting them get away?"

"We don't have the manpower to take a lot of prisoners back," Amulon said. "Let's save it for the one who really matters."

"The high priest Alma?" the soldier asked.

"*Former* high priest," Amulon said. He spat on the ground. "He'll never know what's coming. Let's make camp."

The soldiers bedded down for the night, trading watch hours. When dawn was near, Amulon turned to the waiting soldiers. He wanted to see Alma's face in the light of day before he captured him. "Let's go. We have a traitor to find."

They broke camp, then silently moved just above the faint path taken by the believers the night before. They wound their way through the trees and brush as the darkness began to lift, startling a few birds as they went. When they pushed through the thick foliage, Amulon felt his heart pound. They were getting close—he could sense it. He licked his dry lips and gripped his sword. The moment would be sweet when he finally came face-to-face with Alma. The fear in his eyes and the inevitable pleading would be well worth the journey.

The group slowed as the trees thinned and the morning light hit the valley beneath. Spread below them like an oblivious herd of animals was the colony that had so successfully evaded the king. Rows of lean-tos and crude huts had been built. A large area on the west side of the colony had been cleared. It looked like it was almost ready for seeding. Amulon spotted a group of men working to build another shelter in the early light. However, it was the size of the colony that surprised him most. He'd judged the fires correctly. There were enough shelters to house close to two hundred people here, maybe more.

He let out a breath of air through his nose. The soldiers next to him seemed astounded as well.

"Where did they all come from?" one asked.

Amulon shook his head, too caught up in the scene to answer. The more he focused, the more he noticed. People emerged from their huts—moving about their chores. Amulon watched for several moments as quick meals were shared, and the men set off to haul wood, tend flocks, or fish, leaving the women behind to weave and grind grain. He studied the men—surely Alma was among them. But the men looked basically the same—hurrying about, heads bent, wearing similar clothing.

"Someone's coming," a soldier hissed.

Amulon immediately crouched to the ground. They were off the path, but the foliage was light. The soldiers waited in silence as another group of believers climbed the hill and passed by several paces from them.

Amulon counted. Another eighteen who had escaped the city of Nephi. It was unbelievable. Men, women, and children alike, and this group with about a dozen goats. He clenched his fists together, the wrath building inside of him.

He watched as the group reached the colony. People rushed to greet them, relieve them of their bundles, and bring them food and water. Then something astonishing happened. Everyone stopped their work and gathered to the shoreline. Two men stood in front of the gathered group. The two hundred people he'd estimated was incorrect. The crowd had swelled to more than three hundred.

For a moment, he wondered if his wife, Itzel, was one of the throng. Had she escaped with the community of elders? Had she dismissed their years of marriage so easily? The people at the lake represented many who had betrayed him.

One of the two men raised his arms, and Amulon sensed that the crowd had quieted. Then he stared hard. The man with the raised arms was Alma. Amulon was sure of it. After several minutes, a few people in the crowd stepped forward and walked into the water with Alma. With one hand he grasped the arm of the person nearest him, then raised the other hand and tilted his head upward for a moment. Then he lowered his free hand behind the person and dunked him in the water.

"What are they doing?" the soldier next to him whispered incredulously.

Amulon's face heated as he said, "He's performing the rite of immersion." He shook his head, his stomach twisting in anger. "He's mocking the priesthood." *As if he had permission from the king.* "The king will be furious when he hears."

He straightened, sick of looking at the sight. His mind was made up. His army of eight would do little good against a colony of three hundred, so he'd have to return and gather more forces. It might take several days—or up to a week—but the wait would prove worth it.

He turned to the soldiers. "We'll return to the city and gather an army. Then we'll wipe them all out."

CHAPTER 6

I will heal thee of thy wounds, saith the Lord.
(Jeremiah 30:17)

As the community bustled with building and expanding to accommodate new arrivals, Raquel could find time to hunt for herb cuttings only when Abe was napping. This afternoon, her mother agreed to watch over Abe, so Raquel was grateful for the respite as she walked through the trees surrounding the cleared field.

"Good afternoon, Raquel."

She looked over to see Alma crossing the clearing.

"How's your health?" he asked.

"Very well," she said.

He tilted his head, the sun slanting on his face. "And your mother and son?"

"Also very well, thank you."

"If you need anything, let me know," he said with a smile.

Looking after him when he departed, Raquel marveled at his genuine kindness. She could only imagine the hardships he'd been through. She'd seen his heart truly changed and observed his humility at her husband's burial place. She'd heard him pray for his people, seen him blessing, baptizing, and leading them. No, she didn't hold him responsible for her husband's death.

When she saw his occasional trepidation around her and Abe, she wished she could tell him that she admired and respected him. Maybe he still thought of Abinadi—as she did. She also saw Alma's complete joy and love when he spoke of the Lord.

Just like Abinadi.

Her throat constricted, and she bent over and plucked several hibiscus flowers. Hibiscus tea helped alleviate Abe's running nose. She wished it could heal a heart. Coming to the Waters of Mormon hadn't healed her grieving heart as she'd hoped. She was still surrounded by the people who'd known Abinadi best, and she still felt the hole he'd left. But each day was a little easier—and each day her son grew and learned. She found happiness in Abe's delight of discovering new things. She also marveled at Ben's easy adjustment. He had immediately found a blacksmith who took a look at his swords and gave him advice.

As Alma baptized the believers, including herself, her heart had swelled. The Spirit of the Lord had comforted her. She was in the right place, doing the right thing. Abinadi's death hadn't been in vain.

A few days after the baptisms, Alma had organized the Church of God, or the Church of Christ. With the authority of God, Alma ordained priests, Helam included. Each priest was responsible for teaching and administering to the people. The admonitions delivered by Alma rang true in Raquel's heart: "Teach nothing except that which has been spoken by the mouth of the holy prophets." Alma had also commanded the priests to preach about repentance and faith on the Lord.

"There should be no contention one with another," Alma had taught, "but look forward with one eye, having your hearts knit together in unity and in love." He commanded the priests that they should labor with their own hands. And on one day every week, the Sabbath, the people gathered together to teach and to worship.

Raquel marveled that the true teachings of the Lord were so opposite of King Noah's and the way he ran his court. His priests never labored with their own hands. They lived a lazy and idolatrous life supported by heavy taxes on the citizenry.

Yet Alma only asked the people of the Church to impart of their substance so that everyone in need would be cared for.

It made perfect sense. Even when everyone worked hard and did the best they could, there were still some in need of additional support. New families arrived at the settlement each day, bringing only what they could on their backs. Many had tales of their narrow escapes, but all had faith in their hearts and hope for the future in their eyes.

One of the best things about coming to Mormon was seeing Helam finally shed his hood. After a couple of days, Raquel no longer noticed his scarred face, and she was sure the others hardly paid attention to it. She'd even seen a few of the unmarried women notice him. Perhaps marriage would be possible for him after all. She knew it would make his mother happy.

She arrived at a small grove of apple trees and picked several of the custard apple leaves—they would make an excellent poultice for sprains or broken bones.

"There you are."

Raquel turned to see her mother-in-law coming toward her.

"Did you watch the baptisms this morning?" Esther asked.

"Yes. It was a family that I knew from the city." Raquel set the leaves on top of the basket she carried.

"I can't believe how much we've grown in the past few weeks," Esther said. "I overheard Alma and Helam discussing the numbers. Close to four hundred altogether."

Raquel raised an eyebrow. *Four hundred believers.* If only Abinadi could have known.

Esther must have noticed the shadow pass over her face. She placed a hand on Raquel's arm. "How are *you* doing, my dear?"

Raquel smiled. Her mother-in-law never delayed the real questions. "I'm happy to be here. Abe is thriving, and my mother has made many friends—it's like she's a different woman. I don't think I've ever seen her so content. And Helam. It's amazing that no one even pays attention to his scars. To think of all the years he hid himself—"

"Raquel . . ."

"I know." She ducked her head. "That wasn't the question." She glanced at Esther. With a deep breath, Raquel said, "I'm better."

Esther nodded, apparently satisfied. She patted Raquel's hand. "The light is returning to your eyes," she said. "I've been watching more than you think."

Raquel laughed as she turned and pulled off a few more apple leaves.

"See? A month ago you wouldn't have laughed at anything I said."

"Have I been that bad?" Raquel asked, turning back.

Esther put an arm around her. "You are an amazing woman and are raising a fine son. One that Abinadi would have been proud of."

Raquel felt tears burn, but this time she wasn't afraid to let them fall.

"I'm not the only one who's noticed," Esther continued.

"What do you mean?"

"There are a few eligible men in the community who have been watching you."

Raquel laughed again. "Who would pay attention to a woman who's a widow with a child and goes around sniffling all of the time?"

"Anything is possible," Esther said in a gentle voice. "Even with Helam. In fact, I've had a man approach me about his daughter and Helam."

"That's wonderful," Raquel said, lifting her head and smiling. Finally, someone for her brother-in-law. She had been right in making him remove that hood. It was already working. He'd be married with his own family in no time.

"It's wonderful, of course. But he already sent a refusal," Esther said, sounding dejected.

Raquel looked at her with surprise. "What? Why? What's wrong with the woman?"

"Nothing that I can tell—at least not with *her*," Esther said. "I don't think Helam is quite used to the idea of marriage. With his scarring, he never considered it a possibility."

"Well, it's time he changed. He can be so stubborn." She shook her head. "He really turned that woman down?"

Esther nodded. "I hope he'll realize his duty soon and find a good woman. Having a family would bring him much happiness." She paused, then said in a gentle voice, "As Abinadi's mother, I'm probably the person who needs to tell you . . ."

"Tell me what?"

"It's not good for you to be alone either."

Raquel stiffened. "I'm far from alone."

"Abe needs a father."

Raquel's heart pounded, disbelief pulsing through her chest. "My son *has* a father, one who loved him more than life itself. I'll never replace him!" She took a step closer to the tree.

Esther placed a hand on her arm. "Raquel . . . you're not being disloyal. As his mother, I'm telling you it's all right. I know it's difficult to hear. But you need to search inside yourself. Abinadi is gone. You have a son who is wonderful, beautiful, but he has already forgotten his father."

"Of all people," Raquel said, her voice trembling, "I'd think *you'd* understand. It's only been a few months since he died." She wiped tears with the back of her hand. "*You* have survived by yourself. You raised two of the greatest sons ever—alone."

Esther looked down. "It wasn't by choice. Their father is likely still alive, out there somewhere." She raised her gaze, her eyes now filled with tears. "I do not doubt your abilities. And I do not mean to rush you. I just don't want you to live the rest of your life alone. You're still very young. You have a lifetime ahead of you—one in which you can love and be loved. I don't want you to miss out on any of that."

Raquel gripped the basket. "I haven't missed out on anything," she said in a measured tone. "My husband's love will sustain me for the rest of my life. I don't need anything or any *one* else." She turned away, her eyes smarting again. She loved Esther with all of her heart, but no one understood her pain. She could barely catch her breath some days, let alone look at another man in that way.

"I'm sorry," Esther began. "I didn't mean to—"

Raquel shook her head.

"You wouldn't be betraying Abinadi. I know he'd want you to be happy."

"I *am* happy," Raquel said, tears flowing down her cheeks.

Esther took her into her arms, patting her back. "I know, dear. I know." She drew away. "In time, you'll understand what I mean. Maybe not tomorrow, or next month, or even next year. But maybe in time."

* * *

Amulon watched the slight figure huddled in the corner. Even in this filthy prison cell, surrounded by damp walls and dirt, Maia was still beautiful.

"Maia," he said again.

Finally she lifted her head. Her face was streaked with dried dirt and stained with tears. Her eyes were red and swollen, her hair matted. But still something about her glowed, as if this prison couldn't really touch her.

"I know you can hear me." He spoke quietly so the other prisoners wouldn't overhear. He didn't want to listen to their pleading requests.

Just a few months ago, he'd stood in this exact place to unlock the door and escort Abinadi to trial.

Maia met his eyes, her gaze surprisingly steady. Still she didn't speak.

"The king has been merciful," Amulon said. "He has declared that if you will recant your statement about being a believer, he will forgive you. You will resume your life at court among his other wives." He hesitated, waiting for relief to flood her face. But she only blinked her eyes.

"This is a great favor, one not easily given," he continued. "If you value your life, you will ask your husband and king for forgiveness."

At this Maia rose to her feet. "I have done nothing wrong."

Amulon laughed aloud, forgetting his resolve to keep things quiet. "You are a foolish woman to speak so. You have done *everything* wrong." He gripped the latch of the door. "You have abandoned your husband, your king; you have welcomed traitors into your home; you have believed the man who blasphemed against the king."

Maia's gaze remained steady. "I have followed my heart."

A smile twisted on Amulon's face. "You certainly have. I know who you've given your heart to." Finally, the reaction he was looking for. Maia's face reddened, and she reached out and touched the wall behind her.

"Yes," Amulon hissed. "Remember, nothing is a secret at court. The object of your affection is skilled at deceiving others and leading them away. Until two days ago, he remained concealed."

Maia shrank back, fear in her eyes.

"But I have found him and his followers—several hundred of them. And on the morrow I will march a large army to Mormon, where we'll wipe all of them out." He crossed his arms over his chest.

"Then we will see where your heart truly belongs—with a living king or with a dead traitor."

Maia brought her hands to her stomach and took a deep breath. "You are lying."

Amulon grinned. "I have no reason to lie to an audience consisting of a harlot."

Maia lowered her hands, her fists clenched. "I am no harlot. I have never betrayed my husband. I have remained faithful, despite what some might say . . ." Her voice faltered, and she looked down.

"I was right," Amulon said in a low voice. "Some believer you are. A woman with an adulterous heart." He paused, taking pleasure in his next words. "When I return from killing Alma and your parents, I'll look forward to presenting you as a traitor to the king—"

"Amulon!" a voice shouted from the corridor.

He grimaced and turned to see a guard appear. The man stated, "There's a rebellion in the streets. The king requests your counsel immediately."

"I'm on my way." Amulon adjusted his cape and cast one more glance at Maia. He couldn't read her expression, but he relished the thought of her begging for his mercy in a few days.

He hurried after the guard as he passed the other prison cells. Hands reached out, grabbing at his cape. "Release me! I will fight for the king!" He yanked his cape free and increased his pace. He followed the guard up the steps and out into the fresh air. His bleary eyes blinked against the brightness of the morning.

Soldiers had already gathered in front of the palace. One of the other high priests shouted orders above the commotion.

At the top of the stairs, King Noah stood in all his finery. Amulon broke into a run, passing the guards at the gate of the palace and through the courtyard.

"There you are!" Noah roared.

Amulon didn't have time for formalities. "How many rioters?"

"At least one hundred," the king said. "North of the market."

Amulon thought fast. Several alleyways spread from the market into neighboring clusters of huts. With enough soldiers, he could surround the rebels before they knew what had happened. "I need fifty soldiers. The rest will stay here to guard the palace."

He turned from the king, not waiting for a reply. He made quick assignments, and within minutes he was fully armed, leading the fifty men at a jog through the streets. This delay frustrated him—it would postpone tomorrow's departure to Mormon. As they neared the market, Amulon divided the men, and they separated into four groups. "No prisoners," he said, giving his final instructions. "We'll let them know how serious their offenses are."

Amulon led his twelve soldiers through several courtyards and over low fences that surrounded the homes. Shouting soon arose; they were close. The next bend confirmed it. A handful of soldiers and two high priests were in the middle of a crowd of rebels. "We are not slaves," one citizen shouted. "If we choose to leave the city, we may do so."

One of the high priests held up his hands. "You have sworn allegiance to King Noah. By leaving the city, you are declaring yourself an enemy—no better than the Lamanites."

"Then the king must change the laws of the city," another man said.

Amulon stiffened. He recognized the voice. Sure enough, the tall man turned slightly. *Gideon.* Amulon felt anger heat his face. How dare the man come out in the open and show defiance? Amulon stepped to the edge of the crowd, signaling for the others coming out of the alleyways to do the same. Within seconds the crowd was surrounded by armed soldiers.

"Silence!" Amulon yelled. The crowd turned and quieted. "The king has sent his soldiers to put out this rebellion. All traitors will be immediately put to death—no trials or appearances at court."

The crowd hushed and seemed to shrink together. But Gideon strode forward, his eyes blazing. "The people are tired of the king's repression."

Amulon pushed out his chest and brought his sword in front of him. "Are you willing to defy the king and risk the lives of all these people?"

Gideon's gaze remained steady. "The king has put to death one man too many. The prophecies of Abinadi will come true, and the king will—"

"Silence!" Amulon shouted. "Seize him!"

Confusion ensued as those in the crowd started to run, throwing dust into the air and pushing past Amulon's soldiers, swallowing up Gideon in the process. Amulon looked frantically about, searching for the rebellious leader. He shouted orders at the soldiers, and they scattered through the crowd. When most of the people had dispersed, and Gideon was nowhere to be found, Amulon shouted to his soldiers, "Find him!"

He stormed his way back to the palace. The rebels had been broken up, but they'd band together soon enough. Someone needed to be made an example. Gideon . . . Alma . . . Maia . . . he didn't care which. But he was tired of waiting.

He entered the throne room and bowed to the expectant king. "The rebels have fled—among them their leader, Gideon."

Noah moved off of his throne and took several steps forward. "Gideon? The one I banned with the rest of the elders?"

"The very same," Amulon said, watching anger work itself across the king's face. He rushed on. "A group of soldiers will bring him in soon. Meanwhile, we need to start our march on Mormon."

Noah let out a sigh of frustration, sinking back onto his throne. "Go. Bring him back."

Him. Alma.

Amulon bowed once more and backed out of the room. Finally he was on his way.

CHAPTER 7

To whom shall I speak, and give warning, that they may hear?
(Jeremiah 6:10)

Alma stared at Jachin as he delivered the dreaded news.

"Maia is in prison—thrown there by the king, her own husband," Jachin said. Next to him, his wife, Lael, cried out and buried her face against her husband's shoulder.

"You're sure?" Alma asked, clenching his hands together. It was nearly dark, and most in the colony had been ready to settle in for the night when a group of believers had arrived and shattered the peace with their news.

Jachin nodded. "The newest arrivals didn't have many details, but what they told me was enough. There are also uprisings all over the city of Nephi, led by Gideon."

Lael raised her tear-streaked face. "We have to go back. We have to rescue my baby."

Jachin turned and put his arms about his wife, trying to comfort her.

Eyes burning, Alma turned away, staring at the peaceful lake as the moon began its ascent. Everything about coming to the Waters of Mormon had been a blessing—except for knowing he wasn't able to protect Maia.

"It would only take a few days to reach the city of Nephi—I could be back in less than a week," Alma murmured.

"Then you'll go?" Lael's voice cut across the distance between them.

Alma turned, his eyes boring into Jachin. "I don't trust the king for even a moment. There's no telling what it will take to make him stop. But I have to try."

Releasing his wife, Jachin crossed to Alma. "No," he whispered in a defeated voice. "More than anything I want my daughter by my side. But for any of us to return to the city of Nephi and try to rescue her will be an immediate death sentence. I can't have that on my head."

Behind him, Lael covered her face with her hands, sobbing.

Jachin looked over at her, then back to Alma, his eyes rimmed in red. "All of our hearts are broken, but you must understand." He put a hand on Alma's shoulder. "*We* need you here more than *she* needs you." He hung his head. "The sacrifice will be great for her mother and me, but we knew that when we left everything behind in the city to come here."

"I can take several men with me—" Alma began.

"No," Jachin said again. "If anything should happen to you, we would all be lost. We look to your as our leader, as the reason we have taken the risk of coming all this way."

Alma blew out a breath, knowing that Jachin was right. But how could he do *nothing?*

"Prayer is our weapon," Jachin said in a quiet voice. Then he returned to his grieving wife and led her away.

Alma paced along the muddy shoreline as the dark waves lapped serenely, in contrast to his taut nerves. He stopped, turned, and then started walking again. Maia was in prison—a filthy, dark, damp place filled with rats and criminals.

I ran while she stayed, Alma thought. *And now look what's become of her.* He shuddered to think of all that she'd gone through under King Noah's reign of terror, since her own husband would stop at nothing. *But I'm no longer there to protect her.*

Yet he knew Mormon was where the Lord wanted him to be, welcoming the believers, teaching them further truth, and performing baptisms. He had made the right choice, yet it didn't lessen the pain he felt about Maia's situation.

He breathed a heavy sigh, wishing he could reach across the distance and somehow pull all the believers to Mormon, to safety. But that would take away their choice. It was hard for them to leave their homeland, and if Abinadi's prophesies about the king's demise came sooner rather than later, perhaps it wouldn't be necessary. But the more time passed, the more dangerous the situation grew within the city.

Though Alma knew he would sleep little tonight, he found the mat he kept near the shore and unrolled it, settling down then folding his hands behind his head. The night was clear and the air comfortably cool. Insects buzzed by the lakeshore, but they didn't stray close enough to bother him. His mind was tortured with thoughts of Maia in prison. He also worried about Gideon and the uprisings—all those innocent people who just wanted to learn the truth. Finally, the sound of the lapping water caused his body to relax and his eyes grow heavy.

He must have dozed, because suddenly he awoke. *Something is wrong.* His heart hammered, and dread shot through him. He sat up and looked around, listening. Nothing. But the uneasy sensation didn't fade. In fact, it grew stronger. He knew the Lord was warning him about something.

Rising to his feet, Alma walked toward the nearest cluster of lean-tos, every sense in his body on alert. *What is wrong?*

Alma wound his way through the various tents and shelters, finding the community quiet. Then a flood of urgency overwhelmed him, and he started running for the south hill. The watchmen would be there, vigilant, but Alma still ran, charging up the hill.

As soon as he saw Helam and Jachin, he whispered loudly, "Helam! Jachin!" When Alma reached the men's side, he caught his breath for a few seconds as he scanned the terrain. "Do you see anything?"

"No. What's the matter?" Jachin asked.

Alma brought a hand to his chest. "Something's wrong. I can feel it." After taking another deep breath, he said, "Have you checked on the flocks recently?"

Jachin nodded and pointed west. "Ben is with them just beyond that rise."

Alma followed his direction, seeing the bumpy shapes in the moonlight. He tried to ease his breathing even more. "What about—"

"Shh!" Helam hissed. He put a hand on Alma's arm. "Look over there."

A chill crept up Alma's neck as he turned. The faint glow of fire rose from the next hill over. Then it suddenly went dark. It was as if someone had lit a fire, then quickly smothered it. Then another flash of fire came.

"More people coming to join us?" Jachin asked.

Both Alma and Helam shook their heads and exchanged glances. The three men watched the far hill in silence. Sure enough, a moment later, another flash of fire.

"A signal," Jachin said.

"For whom?" Alma's chest grew tight. They watched in silence as every few minutes a flash of fire burned against the darkness.

"Do you think it's a scouting party?" Helam asked, his voice a whisper.

Alma nodded, a shiver trailing along his arm. At the lakeshore, he'd been warned, and now, seeing the flash of fire, the warning in his head multiplied. "I think the scouting party is signaling to someone or something bigger."

"Should we alert the people?" Helam asked.

Alma hesitated, not because he didn't want to evacuate as soon as possible, but because if they fled Mormon, the believers still en route would be left behind.

Helam seemed to read his mind. "A small group can remain and wait for any others who might come from the city."

Warning pulsed through Alma's body. "It's too dangerous. Besides, I don't know where we'll end up."

Jachin said, "Surely the people in the city know of the king's army coming to find us. If the army overtook any believers coming to Mormon, it is already too late for them."

With a heavy heart, Alma realized that Jachin was right. "Wake the men and have them gather their families, tents, and belongings. We leave before dawn. I'll be back before then."

Helam's eyes bored into him. "Where are you going?"

"To see how many there are."

"Let me come with you."

"No," Alma said, knowing that he needed Helam's leadership to unite the community in their preparations. "I'll travel quicker alone, and I need you *here*."

Helam opened his mouth then closed it, understanding in his eyes. "Take this." He handed Alma the sword he carried for his watch patrol.

Alma gripped the weapon and turned to Jachin. "Alert Ben to gather the flocks. I don't know how much time we have left."

As Helam and Jachin went their separate ways, Alma looked at the moon, hoping the night sky would stay clear, lighting his way. Then he started to run in the direction of the flashing fire. Working day and night building up a settlement had strengthened his muscles more than working as a high priest ever had. He reveled in stretching his legs and moving along the terrain. After several minutes, he settled into a fast pace. The intermittent fire signals continued to be his guide. When he grew closer, he slowed, not wanting to make any noise.

Dawn was still hours away, but the sky had released its inky black and now stood a deep purple. He stopped for a few minutes, trying to calm his breathing. Then he crouched and moved forward.

At the top of the hill sat three rather small tents. Soldiers usually slept out in the open, so he was surprised to see tents at all.

Short bursts of flames arose, and in the brief light Alma noticed that the tents looked royal in nature, the entrances lined with jaguar fur.

Four men sat huddled together, tending to the flame signal. Alma's hands grew clammy. The feathered cape one of the men wore was unmistakable—that of a high priest.

Amulon.

It had to be. Alma waited until the man turned. Even when the fire went out again, beneath the clear moonlight, Alma recognized his former friend.

His mouth went dry. Everything he'd been dreading was all confirmed in this instant. The king was after his people. He'd sent his commander and soldiers—or worse, his army—to capture the believers.

When Amulon turned back to his men, Alma crept away, ever so slowly and quietly. Who was Amulon signaling to?

Alma continued east, up one ridge, then another. The second offered a better view of the trail his people had forged.

He scanned the surroundings beneath the moonlight then stared at the part where the trail disappeared around a hill. That's when he saw shadows moving on the hillside. To his horror he realized the dark shadows were men—soldiers. He estimated at least a hundred.

As the stars began to fade with the coming dawn, Alma was drawn to another hillside. Another group of soldiers. Another hundred. How many more were coming? How long would they wait before attacking?

Alma half-slid, half-ran down one hillside and up the next. He dodged the trees, staying concealed as he sprinted toward the lake. When he topped the final ridge, the sky had changed from purple to gray—night was fading fast. The flocks had been rounded up, the tents taken down, and most of the people seemed to be ready and waiting. Helam and Jachin had made good on their tasks.

The people quieted as Alma approached them. Young babies fussed, but for the most part, everyone was quiet and attentive. Catching his breath, he put his hand on his pounding heart. He could see fear reflected in the eyes of the people. *His people.* He swallowed against the lump in his throat, meeting the gaze of several—Raquel, Itzel, Esther, and Ben. "King Noah has sent an army."

A gasp rippled through the crowd.

"Two hundred at least, but I suspect more are coming. Amulon is the commander." In the front of the crowd, Itzel, who stood next to Raquel, buried her head on her daughter's shoulder. He glanced at the ever-changing sky. "Dawn comes in less than two hours. I want to be well on our way before the first light touches their camp."

Heads nodded and mothers drew their children closer. Alma looked at Helam, whose face was hardened.

Alma raised his hand, pointing northwest. "We will go through that mountain pass as quickly and as quietly as possible. Once we are out of sight from the lake, we can slow our pace." His gaze met Raquel's as she tried to comfort Itzel. "Men, be mindful of the women who travel alone." He looked across the faces of the people who had come to mean so much to him. "We will travel in the small groups that we previously organized. Please stay together and keep your children quiet. I want the last person to be inside the pass before the sun reaches the horizon."

Alma focused on several men on the front row, Helam and Jachin included. "Scouts?"

A dozen men stepped forward. "Three of you will lead the way. Four of you will remain here, watching the actions of the army until we are safely through the pass. The remainder will station themselves in the rocks above the pass."

Helam nodded to Jachin. "Let's go." He stepped up to Alma and handed him a bundle. "We'll meet you on the other side."

"Thank you," Alma said, grateful that Helam had gathered his belongings.

As the scouts went to their assigned positions, the crowd started to shift, men, women, and children shouldering packs and turning northwest.

Alma joined the moving crowd, staying to the side, urging people forward. Ben walked alongside him, carrying his ever-present sword. "I'll protect you," he said, his face gravely serious.

"Thank you," Alma said, keeping his tone equally somber. "But I need you to protect the women and children."

Ben beamed when Alma said "children"—making it clear he no longer considered Ben a child. He nodded and melted into the crowd. For such a large group, the people kept a rigorous pace. The morning dew was still heavy as they plunged into the foliage. Soon the lower part of Alma's tunic was wet, but eventually the sun would warm the land, and his clothing would dry out.

Just as the sun crested the eastern hills, Alma reached the pass, where everyone was concealed by the high cliffs. But Alma knew it wouldn't take long for the king's soldiers to discover the route.

Amulon would be enraged. All the more reason to keep a fast pace. The lack of sleep would catch up with them all soon enough, but now wasn't the time to rest.

It wasn't long before Helam and Jachin finally joined him.

"Are they coming?" Alma asked.

"Not yet, but I expect they'll start heading toward the lake soon," Helam said, his mouth a grim line. "Maybe they're enjoying a morning meal first."

"Whatever gives us more time," Alma said. The two men disappeared into the pass, and Alma gazed down at the lake a final time. The surface moved serenely with the slight breeze that had picked up. The beauty of the valley was still breathtaking but no longer a safe haven. With any fortune, the army would be delayed, and the four hundred and fifty believers would be far beyond the army's reach.

He whispered a prayer of gratitude for safe delivery so far, then turned toward his people and took the head of the group again. With a heavy heart, he left behind the beautiful lake and any connection he'd ever had to the city of Nephi.

He said a silent good-bye to his parents in their graves, Maia in prison, and Gideon forging a rebellion.

* * *

Amulon stood near the lakeshore and stared in disbelief at the abandoned settlement. They'd been through every hut, every lean-to, every scrap of cloth that remained. He was disgusted with himself.

He berated the soldier closest to him then ordered two sets of men to scout the lakeshore, going in different directions. Scanning the surrounding mountains, Amulon marveled at their size. Alma's journey wouldn't be easy. And it wouldn't be easy to find him either. *But I'm not giving up,* he decided.

His gaze landed on the nearest mountain pass—certain it was the way they had gone. "To the pass," Amulon said. He and the remaining soldiers moved through the abandoned community, then scurried up the side of mountain that led to the opening.

"Slow down," he commanded his men as the opening loomed before them. The warning came too late. An arrow zoomed through the air and struck the man next to him.

Then another soldier fell to Amulon's left. Diving to the ground, Amulon peered upward, scanning for the assailants. His men quickly spread out, taking cover.

Three more were struck before Amulon could get a count on the believers. He could see only four, propped in various crevices along the face of the cliff—one man was at least a dozen feet off the ground. After several more moments of watching, Amulon decided his soldiers could easily get the upper hand—one or two might be lost, but they needed to breach the first line of attack to make it inside the corridor.

"On my signal," Amulon hissed. "Ready to rush . . . Now!"

The men burst into action, screaming as they sprinted toward the pass, shooting arrow after arrow as they went. Amulon was seconds behind.

Five soldiers fell immediately, then two more. Amulon looked about wildly—there must be more believers than he'd first counted. An arrow whizzed past his head, finding its mark in another soldier. Three more men collapsed in front of him.

Raising his bow, Amulon spiraled his arrow at the man on the ledge. It veered just to the right. *Missed.* He slowed his pace and aimed again. Suddenly his shoulder seared with heat. Looking down, he saw that an arrow had grazed him. Ignoring the seeping blood, he fired another arrow.

A sharp cry sounded to his right—another soldier down.

Amulon's thigh exploded with pain. Another arrow. He yanked out the arrow, then stumbled forward. But he kept going, losing count of the soldiers who dropped around him. "To the pass!" he screamed. He was only a dozen paces away.

Then abruptly the volley of arrows stopped. Amulon ran the last bit of distance to the passageway and halted. It was empty.

"Through here!" he shouted. "They can't have gone far."

Soldiers rushed around and ahead of him. Then the arrows started again, coming from above. Man after man fell to the ground. Then another burst of pain—this time in his side. He watched as a soldier turned and saw the arrow between his ribs. "Hold still," the soldier said. He took hold of the arrow with both hands and yanked it out.

Amulon screamed as the pain shot through him. His knees buckled, and he grappled for balance. He stared at the red-soaked arrow in the soldier's hands.

Someone grabbed Amulon's arm and tugged him backward.

"No!" he yelled, struggling to free himself. "We must reach them." He was shouting, but his voice sounded strangely muffled. His head throbbed as he blinked to keep his eyes focused. The soldiers, the rocks, the arrows all seemed to blend together.

"You're injured," a man said, dragging him backward.

Amulon tried to yank free, but dizziness engulfed him, and he slumped in the man's arms.

"Come on! Let's get out of here!"

Amulon looked to see who had given the order, but everyone seemed to blur together. Before he knew it, soldiers were rushing past him in the opposite way.

"No!" Amulon tried to scream, but the sound was barely heard. "I command you to stay and fight!"

No one was listening to him. Then the dizziness gave way to black.

CHAPTER 8

If ye . . . keep my commandments . . . I will give you rain
in due season, and the land shall yield her increase.
(Leviticus 26:3–4)

One Month Later

Alma walked through the settlement in the early Sabbath morning, surveying the newly fashioned huts. They'd narrowly escaped the king's army in the wilderness, pushing as fast as they could, in case Amulon picked up their trail. Eight days after leaving the Waters of Mormon, they'd arrived here. It didn't have the pristine lake that Mormon had, but it was beautiful nonetheless. Several streams of pure, delicious water ran through the valley. And with the Lord's prompting, Alma had declared that this was where they would live.

They'd spent the past few weeks clearing land for maize and beans, planting, repairing tents, and constructing shelters. Several groups of hunting parties rotated, bringing in meat for the whole community.

As Alma continued along the road, he saw that tools and timber had been laid aside in preparation for the holy day. Gardens would go unattended and all weaving, blacksmithing, and potting had ceased for the day. Alma had looked forward to the Sabbath all week—not just for a rest from the hard labor, but to consecrate the newly appointed priests. He was also excited to make a special announcement and couldn't wait to see the reaction of the people.

He reached the court building first—it was still under construction and served as their civil and worship center until the temple could be laid out. But for now, the court building provided ample shade for the gathered congregations.

Alma set down the writing implements—ink, brush, bark paper—that he'd brought to record the ordinations today. He glanced at the position of the sun—dawn had just arrived, so he knew he had a couple of quiet hours before the congregation would gather. A couple of hours to review his writings of Abinadi's words. Perfect.

He set his things on a low table and carefully unwrapped the leather satchel that held the sheets of bark paper he'd first written on after being cast out of the city of Nephi. Had it only been a few months since he'd fled the city and gone to Mormon?

He closed his eyes for a brief moment, remembering his hiding place on the hill above and how, overlooking the city, he'd written all that he remembered of Abinadi's teachings. Alma brushed the bark paper with his hand, as if it could bring back the memories. Just touching the records brought tears to his eyes.

He scanned the words, then found himself caught up in reading about the Ten Commandments.

That will be the focus of my teaching this morning, he decided. And like Abinadi, he'd teach the people that living the commandments alone would not save them. *All of the law of Moses points to Christ,* Alma thought. If the people understood the higher purpose of following the commandments, they'd be more willing to follow the lesser laws as well.

He knew the people would continue to grow in number, and the Lord wanted everyone be to taught correct principles. *But I am only one man,* Alma thought. *I need faithful priests and teachers to strengthen the people.*

Approaching footsteps caused Alma to look up. Helam came into view from around the corner of the building.

"Thank you for coming early," Alma said as he stood. He started to pack away the records.

"What do you have there?" Helam asked.

Alma glanced down. He hadn't showed anyone his actual writings, although he referred to them often. "This is what I recorded after I fled the city. I wrote down all that I remembered from Abinadi's teachings."

Helam crossed to the table and met Alma's gaze. "Can I take a look?"

Alma pushed the paper toward Helam, who gingerly picked up the records. Moments later, he was sitting at the table, poring over each page.

Alma studied Helam as he read, and he watched the various emotions flit across his face—from happiness to sorrow. After several moments, Helam looked up, his eyes watery.

"He was only speaking the truth—and they couldn't see it."

"No," Alma said in a quiet voice. "But now it's up to us."

Helam nodded, falling into silence and reading.

"Today I will officially ordain priests and teachers to help me teach the word of the Lord," Alma said. "The reason I called you here early this morning is because I want you to be one of those teachers."

Helam snapped his head up, eyes widening in surprise.

"The more our community grows, the harder it is to get instruction to everyone at the same time," Alma said. "And you are just the man to help me."

Helam shook his head. "I haven't spoken in a public setting, ever."

"I've heard your contributions to the council, and I know that you have an incredible foundation of the teachings of the Lord," Alma said. "Besides, it's the Lord's will. He will provide a way."

Folding his arms, Helam looked down. "But would the people accept me in your place?"

"This morning I'll organize the congregations, and they will see that it's the Lord's will."

Helam lifted his head, trust in his eyes. "Then I'll do it."

Alma smiled and reached across the table to grasp Helam's hand. "I have a feeling Abinadi would be pleased."

A couple of voices filtered in from outside the building. "Ah. It must be the other men that will join you as teachers," Alma said, leaving Helam's side.

Less than an hour later, a large congregation had formed. Alma studied the faces that were now so familiar to him—each one he'd come to know, each one he'd come to love as if they were part of his own family. This was his new family, he realized.

The soon-to-be ordained teachers stood at the front of the crowd, and Alma raised his hands for quiet.

"Before I start into the sermon," Alma said, "I want to present to you a select number of faithful and just men. These men will carry my word, the Lord's word, to each and every one of you as we divide into smaller, more manageable congregations."

He took a breath and smiled. "We have been blessed to find this beautiful piece of land. We grow and continue to prosper each day. But we need to continually learn and study the word of God in order to become a righteous nation."

Murmurs of approval went through the crowd.

"So it is that today I present ten men who will fill the callings of priests and teachers over our congregations of fifty." Alma looked at the front row. "Please come forward."

Helam, Jachin, and eight other men stepped forward. One by one, Alma offered a blessing over their heads, consecrating them to their new responsibilities.

When he finished with the ten, they took their places at Alma's side.

"And now, one more announcement before we immerse ourselves in the Lord's teachings." Alma scanned the crowd, waiting for their full attention. "We need a name for our choice piece of land here. And I propose that we call it the land of Helam."

* * *

"The land of *Helam*. Hmmph!"

"Don't be so sour, Helam," Raquel said, trying to stifle a laugh. "It's an honor." Abe played nearby while she sat weaving a swath of ceiba cloth on a back-strap loom. The young boy climbed over a large rock, then back again.

Helam studied her, his expression baffled. "Alma didn't even ask my permission, just announced the name yesterday in front of everyone, so I couldn't talk him out of it."

"That's because he knew how you'd react." Raquel smiled at his grouchiness, then looked around at the area where they'd camped.

Nearby, Abe laughed as he discovered a beetle scuttling across the rock. She watched her son for a moment then turned to look at Helam. His mouth was drawn into a familiar frown.

"It's an *honor*," she said again. "Please don't let Alma hear you complain."

Helam's expression became contrite. "It's not that I don't think it's an honor; I just don't deserve it. It should be named after Alma."

Raquel lifted a shoulder. "Maybe the next place will be." Although she hoped there wouldn't be a next place—that would mean they'd have to pack up and run—again.

The land of Helam is fitting, she thought, though Helam didn't seem to agree.

He rose to his feet. "It's getting late. Mother is probably looking for me."

"She's likely had another offer for your hand," Raquel said in a teasing tone. But when Helam's serious expression didn't change, she tried again. "Have you *ever* heard of a man getting so many proposals?"

"My father is not here to take care of that duty. It wouldn't do very well for my mother to approach another man about his daughter."

"Certainly not," Raquel said, wondering if Helam wished his mother would approach a particular family. "But it's not as if you're the only eligible man around here. It must have been the hood that kept them all away at the beginning." She put a hand on her hip, teasing. "Really, Helam, we all wish you'd make up your mind and let the women fight over someone else."

When his gaze met hers, Raquel drew in a breath. She hadn't expected to see *pain* in his eyes. Confused, she released her loom and rose to her feet. "I'm sorry, I didn't mean to suggest you need to marry right away . . ."

But he took a step back, and suddenly his eyes seemed normal again. Maybe she'd imagined it. "What's the hurry?" he said, forcing a smile.

She opened her mouth but didn't have a response. *What is the hurry?* Helam was twenty-nine, older than Abinadi had been when she'd married him, but men usually married older anyway. Helam waved to Abe as he walked away. She settled back to her weaving, tugging too hard on the loom. Now she had to reset the weft thread.

She was almost relieved when Abe ran over to her and grabbed her leg. "Papa?"

"No," she said, patting Abe's head. "Uncle Helam isn't your papa. He's your uncle. Can you say un-cle?"

"Uh-kuh," Abe said, his eyes watching for her approval.

Raquel grinned and scooped him into her arms. "You grow smarter each day." *Just like your father,* she thought. She buried her face in his curls and kissed the top of his head. "Come, Grandmother is probably wondering why we aren't helping with the meal." She gathered up her loom and spindles of thread then hurried to her mother's tent. Tonight, not only would they be eating with Esther and Helam, but Alma would be coming.

Abe had taken a recent liking to Alma, who had been delighted when the young boy learned his name: *Am-ma.*

Raquel reached the tent and found her mother stoking the fire. Raquel gave Abe a pouch of shiny stones to play with while she and her mother cut up wild avocado to go with maize cakes. It was a simple meal, especially for a guest, but no other person in the settlement had anything different.

The two women worked mostly in silence, until Itzel finally said, "Esther is worried about you."

Raquel let out a deep sigh and fought to keep her eyes from rolling. "She's dropped hints many times. I think she's trying to arrange a double wedding. Helam is also growing impatient with his mother's insistence."

Itzel nodded, remaining quiet for a moment. "Raquel, no one expects you to raise your son without a father. Abe is growing before our eyes, and soon he'll need to learn things only a father can teach him."

Raquel's cheeks flamed. "First Esther tells me to remarry, now you. How can you forget about Abinadi so quickly?"

Itzel's hand touched her arm. "No one's forgotten about him, dear. But no one's forgotten about *you,* either."

Raquel's eyes started to burn, and she tried to push the anger away. It seemed everyone was too eager to move on and forget. But she'd never forget. And she didn't want to. "What about you? You've been perfectly happy without Father." As soon as the words left her mouth, she regretted them. Had her mother been a more passionate woman, Raquel would have expected to be slapped.

But all Itzel did was turn her sad expression toward her daughter. "You have choices I never had."

Raquel lowered her gaze, feeling as stung as if she had been struck.

"Tonight," Itzel said, "try to be nicer to Alma. Esther says he seems interested in you."

"*Alma?* I *am* nice to him. But . . . it's not like that . . ." She stared at her mother, shocked. "Esther needs to stop meddling. She's practically driven Helam insane, and now this. Alma has no interest—"

"Esther seems to think so," her mother broke in.

Abe started screeching and throwing his rocks. Raquel walked over to him and picked him up, her face still heated. She whispered in her son's ear, "You like having your mother all to yourself, don't you?"

He squirmed to get down. Raquel let him and watched him pick up the shiny rocks and move them through the dirt. A new game, apparently.

She folded her arms and thought about Alma, even though she really didn't want to. He was a good man, of course. A leader. Very kind and handsome. He also had a terrible past, like her own father's, but *unlike* her father, he'd overcome it and completely changed. Not that she'd ever hold the past against him, but . . . she and *Alma?* No. There was something wrong she couldn't quite identify. She'd seen the appreciative look in many men's eyes when she talked to them. She'd never seen more than genuine concern and friendship in Alma's. Either he was focused on his new leadership role or his heart belonged elsewhere.

That was it. She must pay better attention to find out who Alma really cared for. Then she'd get Esther to keep quiet.

Raquel didn't say anything else to her mother as they finished arranging the food on the plates. Just as the sun set, Esther and Helam arrived. Ben joined them, still perspiring from working all day with the blacksmith.

Raquel greeted Ben, then plastered a smile on her face to welcome Esther, even though she was tempted to give the woman a good scolding. *I'll just have to prove her wrong,* she decided. She tried to catch Helam's eye to gauge whether she was forgiven for her comment on his marriage proposals, but Alma arrived before she could make a guess. He graciously greeted everyone.

Not lingering or spending any more time on me than the others, Raquel noticed. But that alone wouldn't prove much.

As the men ate, Raquel listened to them talk, half-interested.

Then Alma said something that caught her attention. "Helam, I hear that you don't care for the name of our settlement."

Helam stopped mid-motion and lowered his plate of food. "I, uh—" He threw a furious look at Raquel, but she shook her head slightly, hoping that Alma wouldn't notice.

Alma chuckled. "Don't worry, no one *here* told me."

She let out a sigh as Helam relaxed. He was already upset with her about the marriage comment; she didn't want to add to his displeasure.

Helam's eyes were intent on Alma. "If anything, this place should be named after *you.*"

Alma leaned back and nodded with an amused smile. "A few recommended that."

Looking surprised, Helam said, "Then why *didn't* you call this the land of Alma?"

Alma lifted a shoulder. "It didn't feel right. Not that I wasn't honored by the suggestion, but I knew it should be named after you." He looked at Raquel for support.

She nodded, then caught Esther watching Alma look at her. *Oh, no,* she thought. *Esther is speculating again.*

"You should have listened to the people," Helam continued. "Everyone admires and respects you—they want to show their gratitude in some way."

With a casual shrug, Alma took a bite of avocado.

"The people are talking about you being made their king as well," Helam said.

Alma's head snapped up, his eyes round. "I know." He shook his head vigorously. "Never."

Raquel watched him with interest. Most men, especially a man like her father, would jump at the offer.

Helam folded his arms. "The people look to you as their ruler— it's only a natural request—especially after you divided the congregation into groups. They want to know that you are still in charge."

Alma put down his plate and spread his hands. "I will *never* be king to this people or any other. Tomorrow, I will assemble all the priests and send out word to each congregation. This rumor must be stopped immediately."

Raquel smiled at him, pleased with his fervent stand; it was impressive to say the least. The people would love him even more for it, if that were possible. She looked at the others and again caught Esther watching her. Raquel stifled a groan. Instead of dissuading Esther, she'd more than encouraged her. Raquel immediately rose and started the cleanup.

The other women followed suit.

"I'll settle Abe down for the night," Esther said, capturing the little boy and throwing Raquel a significant glance.

"Thank you," Raquel said politely, although she felt like laughing right out loud. If she couldn't beat her mother-in-law, she might as well find some humor in Esther's hints. When her mother said good night to the men, Raquel determined not to hover and give Esther more reason to speculate, so she left the clearing to wash the plates.

She walked along the dark path that led to the nearby river. She set the plates beside the bank downstream from where the women gathered water. In the light of the moon she worked, relishing the cool water splashing her arms. After taking a long drink with cupped hands, she stacked the plates and began carrying them back.

When she approached the campsite, she slowed her step. Helam and Alma were both still there, talking.

She decided to go around, through a grove of trees, so she wouldn't disturb them, when she heard Alma say, "Can't you just settle on one of the women already following you around?"

Raquel froze. Alma was brave to approach the topic with Helam, she thought, remembering the backlash she'd received. But maybe it was different between men.

"I've tried," Helam said.

This surprised Raquel even more. It sounded like he *wanted* to marry.

"Over the past two months, I haven't been able to shake this feeling," Helam continued. "At first I thought it was only protectiveness, but now I realize it's much more."

Who is he talking about?

"And you don't think she returns your affection?" Alma asked.

"I *know* she doesn't," Helam said in a quiet, pained voice.

Raquel frowned. She hadn't guessed Helam was in love with someone . . . How sad that the woman didn't feel the same. Her mind sorted through the unmarried women in the community. Had she noticed Helam's attention toward one of them?

"Maybe she needs more time," Alma suggested.

"That's what my mother would say," came Helam's reply.

Raquel gave a wry smile.

There was a moment of silence. Then Alma said, "Would it be so terrible to just ask her?"

She heard a snort.

"I could imagine nothing more frightening," Helam said.

She stifled a laugh. Helam finding something frightening was amusing indeed. Usually people found *him* frightening. Then she sobered immediately. Of course he was worried about his scarring, so that probably accounted for his reservations. But with the other women in the community seeking his attention, shouldn't that bolster his confidence regarding this one woman he was interested in?

"Maybe *I* could speak to her about it," Alma said.

Helam's laugh was bitter. "I can just see the horror in her eyes now. Then I'd have to live with the knowledge that she despised me. Seeing her every day would be too much."

Raquel's mind spun. *Who* in particular did he see every day? A woman working the fields?

"Perhaps I could approach her mother," Alma said.

"No," Helam said. "I don't think her mother would know her feelings anyway. I've decided that I don't have a chance. She's still in love with her husband."

Raquel's fingers tightened on the plates she held. *Helam was in love with a married woman?*

"Besides, I don't want her to think it's just to take care of her son," Helam said.

Raquel's stomach tightened. She felt light-headed as a new possibility entered her mind.

"She'll always love her husband," Alma said. "The question is if there's room in her heart for more than one man."

Raquel gasped and dropped the plates. Her face flamed as she realized that the men had undoubtedly heard her. She turned and ran.

Helam was speaking about her, she was sure of it. "No," she whispered as she arrived at the riverbank and stopped short of plunging into the water. *Helam is like a brother.*

"Please be wrong," Raquel whispered. She sank to the ground and drew her knees to her chest. Disbelief coursed through her. She put her fist to her mouth, trying not to cry out. She didn't know whether she was angry or grief-stricken. It was just too unbelievable to consider.

She closed her eyes and wished she'd never overheard their conversation. Wished she'd just gone through her days and weeks thinking of Helam as nothing more than a dependable brother-in-law. A man who had protected her and watched over her son. A man who had buried his own brother. A man who was honorable and faithful and righteous and kind and giving . . .

Her stomach twisted. It didn't make sense. How could this have happened? Had she done something to encourage it? She'd never been anything but courteous, yet—

"Raquel?"

She turned, startled at the sound of her name. She hadn't even heard anyone approach. *Helam.* She stared at him in the moonlight. He had heard her drop the plates, and now she was going to hear his torrid confession.

"Go away," she said, her throat thick. "I've heard enough."

But Helam took a step forward. "Just let me explain, and then I'll leave you alone."

She rose to her feet, her entire body trembling. "I'm your sister-in-law. You promised Abinadi you would take care of me—but that didn't mean . . ." She tried to steady her breathing. "He *trusted* you. *I* trusted you. How can you insult his memory in this way?"

Helam looked shaken. "I'm sorry," his voice was barely above a whisper. "I thought you might react this way. That's why I didn't want to tell you."

"Tell *me?* What about your mother? What would *she* think?"

"I don't know," Helam said, holding her gaze. "I'm sorry you heard me talking to Alma. I should have been talking to you. Please accept my apology."

Raquel's breath stopped. She shrank back, her thoughts tumbling together. Impossible, all of it. Yet Helam's eyes confirmed the truth. He was watching her carefully, waiting for her response. But she couldn't come up with a single reply.

His gaze turned pleading. "I never thought this would happen . . . didn't expect it."

Raquel gripped her hands together, tensing all her muscles. She didn't think she wanted to hear his explanation.

"It came on gradually." He looked away. "If Abinadi hadn't died, this wouldn't have happened. I never would have let my heart open to this possibility."

Raquel shook her head, unable to believe this was happening.

"I've always cared for you, or cared *about* you, of course," he said with a weak smile, looking at her again. "It was when I stopped wearing my hood that I realized that the only person I had really wanted to accept me was *you*. My mother introduced me to one woman after another, but instead of their faces, I saw only your eyes, your smile . . ."

Raquel blinked against her stinging tears. She and Helam made a hopeless pair. She couldn't imagine replacing Abinadi, ever. And Helam was in love with her—a woman who couldn't give her heart in return.

Tears broke free, so she turned away and stared, unseeing, at the flowing river. Her mind still reeled at all she'd believed of Helam . . . And now it was all so different. Completely opposite, in fact.

"I don't blame you if you hate me," he said. "You have every right to."

She didn't respond. Several minutes later she heard him walk away.

"I don't hate you, Helam," she whispered after him.

CHAPTER 9

. . . the Lord is the avenger of all such . . .
(1 Thessalonians 4:6)

Amulon slumped against a pile of cushions in the throne room, examining his injured knee. The shaman had just finished a prayer over Amulon and was stitching the large gash from a recent skirmish in the streets. His knee throbbed, so he took another swallow of agave wine straight from the jug—though he'd probably have to drink the whole thing before feeling any relief. His arrow wounds from the month before had finally healed—and now this.

At least his injury would grant him the chance to continue his plot to capture Gideon instead of rushing to every skirmish that took place in the city. Plotting against Gideon was about the only thing that took Amulon's mind off of Alma. It still stung when he thought of losing the conquest. His stomach felt sick as he thought about the embarrassment of returning and reporting to the king—the covering up he had to do to explain how he let the man slip through his fingers—again.

With a groan of frustration, Amulon gingerly propped his leg on another cushion as he glanced around the room. A few women congregated around Noah as he told them some outlandish tale while two scribes sat in one corner, dedicating more energy to drinking than to recording the king's words. At the door, a thin man was trying to offer a guard a turkey to gain audience with the king but was quickly rejected. Another typical day in the palace.

Since Amulon's failed mission to Mormon, he refocused his anger of losing Alma to tracking Gideon by bribing or threatening citizens to turn over information on his whereabouts. A few had even been given death sentences for their failure to do so. As soon as his knee stopped throbbing, he'd call his top soldiers together and give them their assignments for the night.

A group of dancers entered the throne room. Their anklets and bracelets jingled as they walked. Amulon studied them, noticing two he'd never seen before—rather young and beautiful—wearing fine multicolored linen tunics, their long, dark hair combed smooth and unbound. He sighed with a new realization—he wouldn't be able to do any dancing this evening because of his injury. Besides, finding Gideon was top priority. The women chattered and giggled as if there were no troubles beyond the palace wall. One of them reminded him of Maia—and how she used to dress beautifully. With a self-satisfied smile, he thought of her wasting away in the prison.

He watched the dancers to see if one sparked his interest more than the others. One of the women crossed over to him, clucking her tongue. "What happened, my sweet?"

Amulon flushed with pleasure at the attention as more women gathered around, exclaiming at his wound. Somewhere in the background, music started up and more food was brought in. The king would feast, regardless of the tense atmosphere surrounding his empire.

It was still early in the evening for dancing. But one of the women brought Amulon a staff and insisted he dance with her. He stood and put some weight on his knee, but the pain was still too fierce. He begged off, and the woman stayed with him, bringing him a dish of spicy tamalitos, a platter of honey-soaked pears, and more agave wine.

Just as the wine was helping him forget his knee, shouting erupted outside the doors, and the forlorn sound of a conch shell rose above the merry music. A red-faced guard burst into the throne room, the front of his tunic stained with blood. "The prison's been breached!"

Amulon grabbed the staff and struggled to his feet at the same time Noah bellowed, "Stop any escapees!"

The guard bowed, his breath coming in gasps. "The prisoners are already gone."

Noah's face darkened with rage. "How?"

"Gideon freed them—he's drawn his sword and sworn to slay the king."

"Bring him to me," the king roared. "I don't care if he's dead or alive."

Amulon stepped forward. *Maia.* She must have escaped with the others. The rage inside him matched that of the king.

Without being asked to leave, Amulon stumbled through the dancers and left the throne room. Before he was out of earshot, he heard the king shouting again—the monarch had just realized that one of his wives was among the released prisoners.

Amulon hobbled as fast as he could to the underground prison. A guard lay on the ground at the entrance, sword wounds on both his legs. He peered upward and shook his head with a grimace.

"How could you let this happen?" Amulon growled. "And lose the king's wife, no less."

The guard raised himself on an elbow. "There were at least a dozen men, led by that . . . Gideon."

Amulon nodded and passed through the entrance. A quick tour told him that the cells were indeed empty. He wondered how far such undernourished and beaten prisoners could get, even with Gideon's help. Amulon turned, leaning heavily on his staff, and made his way along the damp, dark corridors until he reached the steps. Toward the top, he heard Noah's voice. As soon as Amulon came out of the entrance, he froze.

Gideon stood there. "Greetings."

Amulon stared. Gideon's hair and beard were tangled together in a dark, curly mass. His tunic was torn and stained—probably with blood—and his face and arms glistened with perspiration. Amulon shuddered at the scar that ran the length of the man's right arm. This warrior had commanded many soldiers during King Zeniff's time—his successful campaigns were legendary.

Noah stood on the other side of the entrance, his chest and abdomen heaving as he panted. Amulon moved toward him. *Where are the other soldiers?* How had the king dared to come out here without any guards?

Noah kept his focus on Gideon. "Where's my wife?"

Gideon shifted his weapon from one hand to the other, then back again. "Maia was wrongly imprisoned. As were the others."

Noah bristled, his chin jutting out. "They blaspheme against their king. My wife would have been put to death a month ago but for *my* mercy."

Spitting on the ground, Gideon narrowed his eyes. "Mercy?"

The king flinched, and Amulon noticed a long knife in the king's hands—he didn't even carry a sword. *Fool.*

Amulon waited for the king's order to attack Gideon—although he knew that with his injury it would be a less-than-favorable match.

Gideon lifted his sword and took a step forward. "You are the one who deserves a death sentence."

"Let me take him." Amulon moved closer to Noah as he raised his knife in defense.

"No," the king said through gritted teeth. "This—man—is—all—mine."

Lunging, Gideon swung his weapon toward Amulon, nicking his right wrist.

Amulon cried out in surprised pain. He switched his sword to his left hand to attack, but Gideon charged the king. The two men battled—Gideon with the clear upper hand.

The king fought off Gideon's sword remarkably well, but he couldn't last long against the seasoned warrior.

Amulon charged Gideon, shouting, "It's *you* who must die today!"

Gideon turned and deflected the sword. He fell back and lifted his sword with both hands, then charged again.

Jumping out of the way, Amulon narrowly avoided full contact with Gideon's weapon but received a glancing blow on his arm. He cried out as the obsidian blade sliced his flesh again. His vision was blurred with the searing pain, but he managed to remain standing. Turning slowly, he gripped his sword with both hands. "You're finished, traitor!"

From the corner of his eye, Amulon saw the king lower his knife, then turn and run.

For an instant, both Gideon and Amulon watched the king in disbelief. Amulon kept his weapon raised, blood running down his arm, ready to deflect the rebel's sword.

Gideon glanced at Amulon and shook his head with disgust, then turned and ran after the king.

"Stop!" Amulon cried out. He tore a strip from his cape and wrapped his throbbing arm. The strip of cloth was soaked before he could even start a loping run after Gideon and the king.

Amulon followed as the king led the way around the prison grounds and north of the palace. He skirted the palace courtyards, cutting across several stretches of gardens. Amulon was losing ground, but he could see Gideon closing in on the king. The sound of a conch shell burst through the air, louder, more urgent this time. Amulon wondered if some of the prisoners had been found. Otherwise the warning was unnecessary. All of the palace guards knew there were prisoners on the loose.

As Noah neared the main temple, he veered left and started up the stairs to the tower.

"No," Amulon gasped. The king would be cornered. "Turn and fight him until I can get there!" he yelled.

But Noah continued to climb, with Gideon closing in on the tower.

Gideon reached the base of the steps at the same time the king reached the top of the tower. Amulon increased his pace although his knee felt as if it were on fire. One glance confirmed his fear; the stitches had pulled loose.

Just as another burst of a conch shell cut through the air, Noah yelled from above, "Spare me! The Lamanites are coming. They'll destroy us."

Gideon paused on the first step of the tower and looked south.

Amulon slowed and followed Gideon's gaze toward the land of Shemlon. It was true. Even from the base of the tower, the setting sun illuminated the hordes of Lamanites marching toward the city, their dark bodies glistening like fiendish silhouettes against the orange-streaked sky. The warriors were naked except for loincloths. Their weapons were held high, and their fierce pace seemed to increase by the moment.

The only way they could have breached the borders is by slaying all the outlying patrols, Amulon realized with horror. The first line of Nephite defense had crumbled.

The conch shell had been the warning of the coming Lamanites, not the escaping prisoners.

"They'll destroy my people," the king cried in anguish, his voice snapping Amulon and Gideon to attention.

Amulon came to a full stop—Gideon still blocked the steps. Their eyes met for a brief moment, and Amulon thought he saw a flicker of pity there.

Keeping one eye trained on Amulon, Gideon shouted so Noah could hear. "Throw your knife off the tower, and I will spare your life!"

Seconds later, Noah's dagger plunked on the ground. Gideon's gaze never wavered from Amulon's.

"I need this to defend the king against the Lamanites," Amulon said, tightening his grip on his sword. He took a few steps backward to show he wasn't threatening Gideon any longer.

After a long moment, Gideon finally broke his gaze and gave a slight nod.

Both men glanced again toward the land of Shemlon and the advancing Lamanites. Tangible fear pulsed through Amulon. Gideon was the least of his concerns now. The entire city was about to be attacked.

"Throw your sword toward me!" Gideon said. "When I am gone, you can pick it up again."

Amulon tossed his weapon. All was quiet from the top of the tower.

Gideon gave a self-satisfied nod. "Today I'll spare your life, if only to let you command your army and defend this city against an enemy who is not much better than you, or your king."

He stepped back, and Amulon gave an audible sigh of relief.

Then Gideon was off the stairs and around the tower before Amulon could try to dive and wrestle away Gideon's sword.

"Let him go," Noah said in a hoarse voice from above. He appeared at the top of the steps, breathing deeply, wild fear in his eyes as he turned to look at the approaching warriors. "There are too many of them . . . not enough time to prepare defenses." He shook his head, his hands clenched in fists. "We must flee."

* * *

Raquel sat on the riverbank until her neck and back became sore from being in one position for so long. She'd cried, she'd ranted, she'd fallen into a stupor, but still Helam's words continued to echo in her mind. And she continued to reject them. Everything had been fine when she believed Helam was interested in someone else. But now . . . She didn't know what to think.

What would her mother think? Her mother-in-law? Her son—when he was old enough to understand? It wasn't unheard of for a widow to marry a brother-in-law. In fact, according to the history of her ancestors, it was quite common, and almost expected in some cases. It was merely an arrangement to care for the widow and her children. It was a duty of sorts. A loveless marriage.

But Helam had said he was in *love* with her. Quite different than duty.

"Completely different," she whispered. She took a deep breath, admitting he'd been more than a relative to her, more than brother-in-law. Over the past couple of months, he'd been a true friend. Perhaps her only real friend. Someone who seemed to understand her feelings completely. Someone who seemed to love Abe as much as Abinadi had.

And now Helam had just destroyed their friendship. It would never be the same again. And she already missed it. How could she look him in the eyes now that she knew his true feelings?

Her head and heart felt heavy. In her stupor, she hadn't noticed dawn approaching. She finally stood and made her way back to her tent, where she found her mother and son sleeping peacefully. She lay down next to her son and closed her eyes.

The heat of the late afternoon woke her, and it took Raquel a moment to remember why she was sleeping in the middle of the day. Then she remembered. Sitting up, she took a deep breath. Somewhere outside the tent, Abe chattered. She wondered why her mother hadn't awakened her. Maybe she knew about Helam already. Raquel took a couple more deep breaths, trying to compose herself, and stepped out into the sunshine.

Itzel sat near Abe, working on an embroidery piece.

"Good morning, Raquel," she said, not even looking up.

"Hello, Mother," Raquel replied, then turned to Abe. He squealed and ran toward her. Raquel picked him up and held on tight, relishing the scent of his sun-warmed curls.

Itzel busied herself again with her embroidery, throwing Raquel a questioning gaze, but not asking anything.

Raquel set Abe down when he started to squirm. He grabbed her finger and started to tug her toward a tree. "Where are we going?" she asked.

Abe led her for a few paces then stopped and squatted in front of a rock, pointing at a trail of ants.

"Oooh. You found some ants?" Raquel asked.

Abe grinned and touched his finger to the rock until an ant crawled on it. He laughed with delight.

Raquel smiled, feeling the tightness in her chest start to relax. She could do this. Just focus on Abe and all that entranced him. Forget about Helam's confession. Maybe it had never really happened—maybe she'd just had a disturbing dream. But the tiredness in her body told her otherwise. She felt emotionally exhausted. She spent the next hour with Abe, then as he grew sleepy, her mother offered to put him down for a nap.

"Why don't you work on your weaving?" Itzel suggested, a knowing look on her face.

Raquel thanked her and started the short walk to the weaving place. Every few weeks, duties and chores were rotated in the community. She'd spent the first two weeks preparing the fields for planting. Now other groups of people were given the job of tending the fields while she rotated between spinning, weaving, and collecting herbal plants. She'd even assisted in two births by preparing pain remedies and soothing poultices.

On the way, she passed Esther. Dozens of thoughts passed through Raquel's mind as her mother-in-law approached. Surely the woman knew about Helam and was now about to confront her. Would she be angry that Raquel had rejected her son, or would she understand?

"Raquel," Esther said, hurrying toward her. The woman's face looked flushed.

Raquel's stomach tightened as she prepared herself for an onslaught.

"Have you seen Helam?" Genuine worry crossed Esther's face.

"Not since . . ." Raquel peered closely at her. Maybe Helam hadn't said anything.

"We've been invited to another family's camp for the evening meal." Esther smiled in a harried way. "They have an unmarried daughter who is quite pleasant . . ."

Raquel couldn't help but gape at her mother-in-law as she spoke. Esther didn't know.

"I haven't seen him," Raquel interrupted, more than ready to be on her way.

But Esther continued. "I don't know what's wrong with him. He barely spoke to me this morning, and he told me he refused to go to any more 'arranged' meals. But I'm going to insist that he come tonight since I accepted the invitation days ago. It wouldn't be polite to—"

"I'm sorry," Raquel said, pulling away. She swallowed against the anguish in her throat. "I hope you find him, but I'm in a bit of a hurry. I've fallen behind on my weaving, and Abe will only be asleep for so long."

Esther regarded her for a moment. "Sorry, dear. If you see Helam, tell him that he's not to miss tonight."

Raquel nodded, not knowing whether to laugh or to sit down and weep.

She practically ran from Esther to avoid either outcome. She slowed as she reached the weaving place. Through the trees she saw that someone was already there. Her heart sank since she didn't feel like company today. As she drew closer, she noticed it was a man.

Helam.

Raquel froze, wondering if it was too late to turn back. He probably hadn't heard her or else he would have turned around, wouldn't he? But what if he was waiting for her? Before she could speculate any further, Helam stood and turned.

"Raquel?"

She was caught. She had to face him, if only to restate what she had said the night before.

She walked slowly through the trees and stopped half a dozen paces from him.

He held her gaze for a moment, but his eyes were tired, dull. "I've been waiting for you."

She nodded, unable to think of what to say.

"I wanted to apologize and tell you not to worry about what I said." A slight smile touched his lips, although it stayed far away from his eyes. "My mother does enough worrying for all of us."

Raquel clasped her hands together and looked down.

"The only person that I've confided in is Alma." He hesitated. "I don't want this to come between our mothers . . . nor should it ruin the friendship between you and me, between Abe and me."

Raquel looked up, noticing that his eyes were reddened.

"I want us to be friends," he said in a pleading tone. "Only friends. I know it won't be exactly like it was before, but . . ." He looked away, seeming to struggle with his words. "You're too important to lose. I'll find a way, somehow, to forget last night, and hopefully you will as well."

For a long moment, Raquel held his gaze. She knew every scar on his face, every expression in his eyes, every laugh, every frown. She *did* love him, but as a brother. She took a deep breath and answered, "All right. It's forgotten."

CHAPTER 10

And the land shall mourn, every family apart . . .
(Zechariah 12:12)

"You want us to *run?* Our army should have the chance to defend our city," Amulon said, staring at the king in disbelief.

Noah shook his head. "There's no time." He swept his hand toward the approaching Lamanites. "They've covered half the distance to the city since we've been up in this tower."

Amulon turned toward the Shemlon border again, dread running through his body. The colossal body of Lamanites was indeed closer—so close that Amulon imagined seeing the whites of their eyes. "Then we run."

The two men hurried down the steps, Amulon gritting his teeth against the pain coursing through his leg and arm. He fetched his dropped sword and found the king's knife.

The men ran for the palace. Once they reached the entrance, they split up, shouting through the corridors. "The Lamanites are coming!" Amulon yelled. "Flee to the west!" The high priests ran out of the throne room and other parts of the palace. Several joined him in evacuating the palace. He ordered soldiers to run through the streets and warn the citizens.

The women and children streamed out of the palace, some carrying bundles of clothing.

"Flee to the west!" Noah shouted to the crowd in the courtyard.

The king's oldest son, Limhi, ran to his father. "The men should stay and fight—defend what's ours."

The king shook his head. "There are too many of them."

Limhi's shoulders sank. "So we just let them have the city?" He waved his hand toward the palace entrance. "Take over everything?"

"If you want your life to be spared, yes," Noah said, his eyes burning. "There's no more time to waste in argument." He started to flail his arms wildly. "Everyone run!"

Limhi stared after his father as Noah crossed the courtyard and started running. The women and high priests followed. Amulon was one of the last to vacate the courtyard. The few who remained grabbed whatever they could carry. Amulon knew that most of the possessions would be dropped along the way.

Cursing his injuries, he moved into the streets, passing the temple. People came from all directions, everyone headed west. Amulon hobbled alongside women, children, and men who ran with only the clothing they wore.

Once they exited the inner city walls, they ran through the maize fields. A cry went up among the people—the Lamanites had reached the south end of the city. *They're coming too fast,* Amulon thought. *Our warriors are no match against them.* Among the people were soldiers, but they were ill-prepared, scattered. Most carried nothing more than a knife.

Amulon ran past discarded items—clothing, food bundles, water-skins—things that didn't matter now that the people were faced with imminent destruction. The moving mass finally cleared the last field on the borders of the land and plunged into the thick trees. Many fell behind, exhausted, giving up—women cried, children wailed, men yelled. Amulon passed Limhi, who carried one of his siblings on his back.

Looking behind him, Amulon saw that the Lamanites were only a hundred paces behind the last stragglers. He scurried up a hill, weaving in and out of trees, trying to find a place to hide—a cave, a crevice, anything—hoping the Lamanites wouldn't take the time to track one man. The king was farther ahead with two good legs to run on, and several guards kept pace with him, ready to defend their king.

The first screams reached Amulon's ears as he neared the crest of the second hill. He turned for a breathless moment and watched in horror as the Lamanites descended upon the stragglers. The warriors cut down any man who stood against them, passing over the women and children.

"Look at that," a voice said.

Amulon looked above him to see King Noah, who had stopped and waited at the top of the ridge to watch the carnage. "They're ignoring the women and children, who don't fight back. How noble." Noah's voice dripped with sarcasm.

Then Noah roared, "Men! You will leave your women and children behind. We must flee now or perish!"

Limhi had just reached the base of the hill when Noah issued his command. "Father, we can't leave the women and children," he called up to him.

Noah's face went red, his hands clenching and unclenching. "They have slowed us down too much already. It's your choice." He turned and scurried down the other side of the hill, shouting as he went, "The men must flee or die at the hands of the Lamanites!"

Amulon watched the confusion on Limhi's face for an instant. Men crowded around the prince, vowing to stay with him to protect the women and children.

For a moment, Amulon wavered, then decided his first and foremost duty was to protect the king. He watched the approaching Lamanites briefly. He could see the fury on their faces and their murderous focus. As lame as he was, he would be no match for even the smallest warrior.

Every moment counted.

Amulon turned away from the battle and descended the other side of the hill, following his king.

* * *

Maia crouched against the damp cave wall. From somewhere outside, screams pierced the air, but no one stumbled into the cave. She shuddered to think of what would happen if the Lamanites discovered her—alone and unarmed.

She was beyond exhausted. It had taken every bit of strength she had to reach this place Gideon had told her about. The other prisoners who fled with her had dropped off one by one as the Lamanites invaded the city. They'd panicked and scattered in all directions.

The screams faded, but Maia still didn't move from her uncomfortable position. Truth was, she was more comfortable than she'd been in weeks. The dampness in this cave was nothing compared to the rot of Noah's prison. King Noah—her own husband—had condemned her to die a slow death, and all because of his wrongful pride. Why should he care if she wanted to worship the one true God? He was so dependent on his idols and pleasing his nature gods that he could no longer see anything beyond himself.

Not that he'd been any different when she'd first married him. She'd had no choice in marrying the king, but she always knew what he was. When she'd overheard Alma teaching her parents about the Lord, she knew she had to change. The value of her own life mattered little since the loss of her baby son. But if she could teach others what she knew in her heart, then it was worth making the effort to live.

A loud war cry interrupted her thoughts and sent a deep shiver through her bruised body. She held her breath, listening for the slightest sound. When several moments passed, she relaxed—but just a little. Her body trembled and begged for food and water. Then she remembered: Gideon had told her that the cave was well stocked.

Gaining courage, she rose and crept through the cave. Her eyes were well adjusted to the dark interior, but the patches of light coming through narrow crevices from above made negotiating the rocky cave floor easier.

She came to a cavern that housed a small spring. She stared at it for a moment, wondering if it were a mirage, then tentatively walked toward it and knelt at the side. Dipping her hands in the water, she cupped them then took a drink. She closed her eyes as the pure water slid down her parched throat. She drank long and hard until she had to force herself to stop.

She left the pool in search of food. Supplies were stacked along the walls, and Maia found bedding, a jar of honey, wrapped lengths of dried meat, an herbal collection, and a sword. As she chewed the dried meat, she stared at the sword, wondering if she could carry the heavy weapon very far, let alone wield it. She'd seen plenty of sporting fights while living at the palace, but hadn't ever tried to use a weapon herself.

Feeling better than she had in weeks, Maia curled up on a rug and tried to fall asleep. But the panic had pervaded her nerves too deeply, and every speck of sound rattled her to the core. When she gave up on sleep, she realized it must be dark outside—evidenced by the increased darkness of the cavern. Her energy somewhat renewed, she took another drink, then a few more bites of dried meat.

How much time has passed? She wouldn't know until she saw the position of the moon. So she exited the cave, peering cautiously and listening for any human sounds. It seemed all was quiet. Looking up, she estimated that it was an hour after midnight. In less than a day, her whole world had changed. Who knew how far the Lamanites had pursued her people or what destruction had been done?

She stepped away from the cave, vowing not to stray too far, but hoping to find someone she could at least help.

Walking through a patch of trees, she reached a small clearing illuminated by the moonlight. The first thing that drew her eye was a dark shape on the ground. No matter what she'd expected to find, she wasn't prepared for this.

A man lay on the ground, his limbs twisted at odd angles. Maia stared at the inert figure as dismay pierced her heart. She took a tremulous step forward, realizing the man was a Nephite by his clothing, probably around twenty years old. Not much older than she.

With a deep breath she took a step closer and watched for any sign of life, but his chest was still. She wanted to flee back to the cave and hide from anything else she might see, but something propelled her to keep moving. She looked across the clearing and saw another body—another Nephite. Tears touched her cheeks as she mourned the senseless death of these strangers. What had been their final thoughts? What loved ones had they left behind?

These men had died defending their homes, their families. Maia's head snapped up. Where *were* their families? She weaved in and out of the huddle of trees, coming back to the clearing time and time again. She found two more Nephites and one Lamanite dead, but no women, no children. Where were the families? All of those women who were herding their children? Had they somehow escaped as their husbands and brothers fought off the enemy?

Again Maia stood in the clearing where the two Nephites slept the sleep of death beneath the moonlight. It was too late to help these men—yet there was a sense of peace surrounding them.

The least I can do is pay respect to these fallen men, she thought. Maia took a couple of steps into the clearing and stopped between the two bodies. Then, quietly, she sang in a whisper a farewell song.

When she finished, Maia returned to the cave and waited until dawn, finding a little sleep. As the first light hit the cave entrance, she rose and stretched. She packed the bundle of herbs, hoping that it might help someone along the way, then chose a few strips of meat to take with her. She wanted to survey the city—see if the Lamanites had already set up headquarters. Then she'd leave for the Waters of Mormon. She would see Alma again, and her parents would be there—welcoming her with open arms.

The smallest of hopes lightened her step. She avoided walking through the clearing and headed for the first field, staying on the edges and concealing herself in the surrounding trees. A few goats wandered around aimlessly, as if looking for their herdsman. Maia was surprised not to see any more bodies in the field. Then she stopped. At the far end, a group of men emerged from the trees— four Nephites and several Lamanite soldiers. Two of the Nephites carried a body.

They're cleaning up the dead. Maia stared as the men moved to the next field. The other two Nephites stopped, then stooped to pick up something heavy. Another body.

So the Lamanites have taken over the city, she decided. *We're under their rule now.* She let out the breath she'd been holding. *It seems they're letting us live, but at what cost?*

She drew back into the trees, bumping into something. Just as she turned, a hand clamped over her mouth. She tried to scream, but the hand tightened, and she struggled just to breathe. She looked up to see a face belonging to one of the darkest men she'd ever seen. And one of the largest.

He grinned, and Maia was taken aback by the whiteness of his teeth. She hardly had time to notice his shorn head and nearly naked body.

"Another stray," he said in a sharp voice, but his eyes were amused.

Maia wriggled against his grip.

"No, you don't," the Lamanite said, then looked at another soldier next to him. "Take her."

As the Lamanite handed her off, Maia was able to get a good kick in, but the large man just laughed.

"Don't think you're the first," he said with a chuckle. "I've found the Nephite women to be very spirited." He motioned for another soldier to come forward. "We'll have to tie up this one."

Before Maia could move, the soldier fixed a piece of cloth about her mouth then bound her hands and feet. Suddenly she was lifted in the air, dangling like an animal on a spit.

She struggled against the two soldiers who held her, but pain shot through her shoulders.

"In no time we'll have you as docile as a Lamanite," the first man said, then laughed. The others joined in.

Maia tried to shout, but it came out muffled. She shook her head, trying not to choke on her own fear.

"Take her back to the city."

"Yes, O Highness," said one of the soldiers.

Maia threw a look at the man who'd captured her. He was the *king?* Her mind reeled. The Lamanite king had come into the battle? He was dressed no different than a common soldier.

The Lamanites started moving at a swift pace. Maia's body bounced painfully as she was jolted along. She closed her eyes so she didn't have to look at the two Lamanites carrying her. What would happen to her and the other captured Nephites? Would there be mass killings or burnings? Would the king make a spectacle of her—like her husband had? She wouldn't expect anything less of the Lamanite king.

CHAPTER 11

Yea, the light of the wicked shall be put out . . .
(Job 18:5)

The believers sprawled across the land—fields, homes, and gardens had all multiplied quickly since the people's arrival in the land of Helam. The early mornings were Alma's favorite time to climb the hill behind his homestead and observe all of the changes. It seemed that each day more improvements were made.

This morning was no different. As the dew evaporated from the tender maize and bean plants, he climbed the hill and turned to watch the sun rise. He had been blessed—*they* had been blessed. Finding refuge in Mormon, baptizing all of the believers, narrowly escaping from King Noah's army, then finding this fertile land unoccupied . . . Alma breathed in deeply as he gazed at the young fields, the outline of several roads, and the patches of homesteads surrounded by new gardens. A common area had been set up near the largest river. An open building was under construction where marriages could be officiated and other community events would take place.

Soon, the hill that Alma sat upon would be under construction too—for a new temple, a place to worship and make the appropriate sacrifices according to the law of Moses. Alma had spent time each evening training the newly ordained priests, Helam included.

Alma thought about Helam and his confession about Raquel. In the days that followed, a change had come over Helam, and he'd become more withdrawn than ever.

Alma understood some of the angst Helam was experiencing—falling in love with the wrong woman. And as Alma watched the community below him come to life in the early morning, he couldn't help but wonder about Maia and what had become of her. Was she taking care of her parents' home and garden? Did she see King Noah often? Was he kind to her?

Alma took a deep breath, closing his heart once again. It was too painful to think about—the part of his life that he'd left behind and forsaken. All he could do now was pray for the believers who hadn't made it to Mormon—pray that their lives would be spared if they were discovered and pray that they would enjoy the fullness of the gospel as the others who had fled to Mormon.

He took out the writing utensils he'd brought along and thought about the men who served as priests in the community. When living in Mormon, Alma had taught them the way of the Lord, but to make the instruction easier for future ordained priests, he wanted to record the previous instruction he'd given to the first priests.

One priest to every fifty in number will preach to their congregation.

The priest will teach nothing except what is taught by Alma, or what is spoken by the holy prophets.

The priest will preach repentance and faith on the Lord.

The priest will teach that there will be no contention with each other.

The people will be taught that they should look forward with unity of purpose, having one faith and having one baptism.

The people will be taught to love one another and knit their hearts together in unity.

The people will be commanded to keep the Sabbath day holy, and give thanks every day to the Lord their God.

Each priest will labor with his own hands for his support.

After reading over his list of instruction, Alma added a few more lines.

The people of the Church will impart of their substance according to what they have, of their own free will, to every needy, naked soul.

The people will be taught to walk uprightly before God, and share with each other their temporal and spiritual blessings.

Satisfied, Alma straightened and stretched. He'd grown strong over the past months compared to his idle life as a high priest in Noah's court. It was time to get to work. He hurried down the hill, looking forward to another long day of work, sure to accomplish much. When he reached the common area, he greeted the men who were already working on the newly delivered timbers. Alma set about stripping the bark with an obsidian-edged scraper.

"Need help?" a deep voice said.

Alma looked up to see Helam wearing his hood again. "Not in the fields today?" Alma asked.

"Too many inquisitive stares."

The two men worked side by side in silence for the better part of the morning, although Alma sensed Helam wanted to talk.

Finally, as the heat of the day crept upon them, Helam removed his hood and cloak. He turned to Alma and said, "Thanks for listening the other night."

"I'm afraid I wasn't much help—if we hadn't been discussing it, Raquel wouldn't have heard."

"And I'd still be in agony trying to decide if I should confess to her. Now I don't have to worry about that anymore." He laughed in a bitter way. "Now I don't have to worry about her at all."

Alma put down his scraper and studied his friend. "Have *your* feelings changed?"

"No," Helam whispered. He took up his own scraper again and put all of his strength into it for a few minutes.

Alma watched, trying to find a way to comfort his friend. "Perhaps time will change her heart."

Helam grimaced. "Perhaps." But he didn't look convinced. "Perhaps it will change in time for her to become interested in another man." He stopped scraping and met Alma's gaze. "Meanwhile, I have to endure every family dinner and every remark from my mother about why I'm not finding a wife."

Alma hid a smile. "Not much different than it was before, eh?"

"It *is* different. Raquel can't even look at me without thinking about it. I'm an annoying beetle under her feet—always there to remind her of what is so disgusting to her."

"Hold on," Alma said raising a hand. "She never said that."

"She didn't have to," Helam said, his eyes downcast. "I've put her in a position she should never have been in. I'm her brother-in-law, for heaven's sake. I should be protecting her, not antagonizing her. I—"

He took a deep breath. "I promised Abinadi that I would take care of her, but now I've brought her grief."

Alma leaned forward and placed a hand on Helam's arm. "Maybe time will help you out as well. There may be another woman who gains your attention in the future."

Helam pulled away as if he had been burned. "You don't understand. It's not my choice. I'm going to have to try and forget, try and move on, but it's not that easy."

"I understand more than you think," Alma said in a quiet voice. He turned away and resumed scraping the bark.

"What do you mean?"

Alma slowed his pace and glanced at his friend. He had pushed his own dilemma so far into the past, but maybe telling someone would ease the pain that kept creeping back into his own heart. "I was in love with someone at King Noah's court before I changed my ways and repented."

"Did she turn you down?" Helam asked.

"Not exactly. There was no hope from the beginning. She was married."

If Helam was surprised, he didn't show it. "Is that why you haven't chosen another?"

Alma lifted a shoulder. "I suppose. That, and I've been so busy with the work."

Helam merely nodded, and the two of them carried the log to where the men were planing the wood. Then they started stripping off the bark from a fresh log.

Alma was sure Helam would ask more questions, but in a way he was relieved when he didn't.

After a while, Helam finally said, "I guess we are both hopeless. At least you don't have to face your woman every day."

Alma chuckled. "That's one way to look at it." The two men looked at each other, assessing. "I don't know if it makes it any better though, *not* knowing how she is or what happened to her."

Helam arched a brow. "Why is there any concern?"

"Because she's a believer, and her husband is not."

Helam fell silent as the two men worked together. Just before midday, a man approached Alma.

"You're needed to settle a blacksmith's dispute."

Wiping the perspiration from his brow, Alma nodded. "Take me to them." As he followed the man, he looked forward to the day when the court building would be completed and he and the other priests could rotate civil duties. For now, Alma usually traveled to where the conflict occurred.

They walked along a series of paths until they reached a small blacksmith hut. Standing outside was Ben, his arms folded, his face hardened in anger.

"Ben?" Alma said, surprised to see the young man.

Behind Ben, a blacksmith named Gad emerged from the hut, his face red. "The boy is stealing from me," he growled.

Alma knew the man had a quick temper. "Gad, what is the problem?"

Gad crossed his soot-streaked arms over his ample girth. "I told the boy he could use scraps to work on his own swords—but I found him making this—" He produced a long narrow sword, made entirely of metal.

Alma waited for the blacksmith to continue. "And what is wrong with it?"

"The metals are precious—and he used everything that I had for just one sword." Gad sent a searing look in Ben's direction. "It's a fool's waste."

Ben narrowed his eyes but was smart enough to stay quiet.

Alma crossed to Gad and took the sword. It was an impressive-looking weapon. "Like our father's of old," he said in a quiet voice.

"What did you say?" Gad asked.

"The sword—it's like the swords that our forefather, Nephi, used to make."

Confusion crossed Gad's face. "Well, I don't know about Nephi, but here in Helam we have little metal—can't be wasting it all on just one sword."

Alma handed the sword back to Gad and turned to Ben. "I think this is just a misunderstanding, don't you agree?"

Ben nodded curtly, but his eyes still remained hard. "I used only scrap. It was just an experiment to see if I could do it."

"It's a fine experiment," Alma said, turning to Gad. "I think the boy meant no real harm. I'm certain he'd let you take back the sword if you wanted to reuse the metal."

Gad let out a breath then scratched his head. "I suppose he can keep it, but no more metal—by scraps I meant the wood or the smaller bits of obsidian."

"That sounds fair," Alma said, looking at Ben, who nodded his agreement. "Come, let's walk a little."

Ben followed Alma as Gad returned to his shop. Placing a hand on Ben's shoulder, Alma said, "How did you know how to fashion a metal sword?"

Ben cast a sly glance at Alma then took a deep breath. "Because I saw one once."

"Once? Where?"

"Well hidden. Gideon showed me—said it was the sword of Laban."

Alma stared at the young man. "It really does still exist?"

Ben grinned. "Of course."

* * *

Maia was shoved into the palace throne room, then handed off from one Lamanite soldier to the next until she was pushed against the crowd of women in the corner. She looked around at the frightened faces of the women huddled together. Some were crying, while others stared blankly around the room. There were no children. This made Maia worry even more.

She sidled up to a woman about her age who looked familiar. "What's going on?" she whispered.

The woman looked at her. "Maia?"

She nodded. "I thought I knew you."

"I'm Gideon's daughter, Neriah."

"That's right," Maia said, trying to smile. But even the comfort of knowing someone wasn't much comfort after all.

"Where did they capture you?" Neriah asked.

Maia explained about the cave Gideon had told her to flee to, then how she had been starting her journey to Mormon.

Neriah shook her head. "No one is at Mormon now. The king's army drove them out."

Maia stared at her. Had anyone been killed? Where had Alma's group gone to? She looked around at the frightened women. "Where are your mother and sister?" Maia asked.

Neriah leaned close. "I haven't seen them since Limhi sent me to plead with the Lamanites."

"What do you mean?"

"The king fled with his priests and men. He ordered the men to leave their wives and children behind. Limhi stayed with the men who refused to abandon us, so when the Lamanites overtook us, he sent us out to plead for our lives."

Conflicting emotions battled within Maia. Her husband's cowardly actions disgusted her. And Limhi—the next in line to be king—had remained against his own father's wishes. Maia's eyes stung as she thought of the young prince who was more of a king than his father.

"And the Lamanites' hearts were softened?" Maia asked.

"Look around you," Neriah whispered. "Limhi sent the fairest women to plead with the Lamanites. The soldiers seemed charmed by our beauty, but perhaps they are now planning something much worse than death."

Two more women were practically dragged into the room and shoved into the corner with the rest.

"What are they waiting for?" Maia whispered, gripping Neriah's arm.

"For their king to return." Neriah's eyes reflected fear.

The king. The man who looked as rough as any soldier. He did seem humored by the fighting women, but when faced with a roomful would he have them all put to death? Or would he and his soldiers enjoy some sport first?

"We have to get out of here," Maia said. "If we all work together, we might have a chance. There are more women than soldiers. We can overpower them."

Neriah looked at her sharply. "They have swords. It would be a death sentence."

"I'd rather die than—"

"Shh," Neriah said then put a hand on Maia's arm. Outside the throne room, people were shouting.

Maia couldn't make out the words, but suddenly Limhi came into the room, followed by several Lamanite soldiers. Maia's breath caught as she stared at the young prince. He looked so vulnerable, so young and desperate. She wished she could protect him.

Then Maia recognized one of the soldiers—the Lamanite king.

He surveyed the women for a moment then turned to Limhi. "We have taken compassion on your people, but you are still our enemies. The wrongs of your people against ours go back genera-tions—unforgiveable generations. But your father is the man we really want. He must pay for the attacks on the border."

Limhi squared his shoulders. "My father has fled with his priests."

The king scoffed. "And this is the man your people call king?"

Limhi looked abashed but held the king's gaze.

Maia could sense the prince's inner struggle. She guessed he didn't know where Noah was, but if he did, would he reveal the Nephite king's location to the enemy?

The Lamanite king started to pace, hands behind his back. "If we do not receive your father into our hands by the week's end, you will take his place and be put to death for his crimes against my people."

"No!" Maia called out. Before she considered what the conse-quences might be, she rushed forward. "This boy has done nothing. He is not his father—not in word, deed, or action."

Two soldiers rushed her and grabbed her arms.

Maia twisted and tugged against them. "Take our homes, our possessions, but do not harm the innocent!"

"Silence!" the king shouted. "Or we'll have to tie you up again." He turned to Limhi. "Who is this woman?"

Limhi's face paled as if he were struggling with the answer. "One of my father's wives."

The king turned back to Maia. "Well, well. A Nephite queen." He walked toward her and stopped right in front of her. "We have not been formally introduced. I am Laman, king of the Lamanites."

Maia could almost smell the blood of Nephites on him. She wanted to spit in the man's face, but the look on Limhi's face held her back.

King Laman touched her face, and Maia flinched. He laughed then said, "Yes, Nephite women *are* beautiful, but it's a pity that one man is allowed to take so many for himself." He paused, studying her in the deathly silent room. "Being born a beautiful woman in this land must seem a curse."

Maia's breath caught. How could this fierce enemy see straight into her heart?

King Laman looked at the rest of the cowering women. "You fear my people and my soldiers, but if you could observe the way our women live and the respect with which we treat our wives and daughters, your judgments would be less harsh."

He turned to Limhi. "You will deliver up one half of your property to house my men, one half of your gold, silver, and precious things to pay for your protection. You will be subject to my rule, or punished dearly." He cast another glance at Maia. "And I want the king of the Nephites at my feet in seven days."

* * *

Amulon limped along, trying his best to keep up with Noah and the others. Several dozen men had followed the king, and now the group had slowed significantly. But the pace didn't help the pain in Amulon's leg and arm, even though one of the men had restitched the gash in his knee. They had traveled all night, and now that morning was upon them, sheer exhaustion was setting in.

Finally Noah stopped, his face and clothing covered in perspiration and dirt. "We will rest here," he said, then pointed. "You five men need to keep watch."

Everyone nodded, but there was little conversation as the men settled onto the ground. Some were asleep instantly.

Amulon closed his eyes, grateful for the reprieve. He couldn't go on much longer in this condition.

What seemed just seconds later, he was awakened by shouting combined with the smell of smoke. He struggled to sit up, his arm throbbing no matter how he moved. Some of the men had built a fire and were cooking a small animal over it.

A large man by the name of Zacharias was arguing with one of the high priests. "I swear by my own heart that I will take these men and return to Nephi. We shouldn't have left our women and children to perish."

The high priest tried to shush him. Not too far away, the king still slept. "We'll stay with the king to protect him. When enough time has passed, we'll return and reclaim the city."

Zacharias shook his head. "If our wives and children have been slain, we'll seek revenge and perish as well."

Others had awakened and started to gather around Zacharias. They well outnumbered the high priests. Amulon picked up his sword and limped over to face Zacharias. "If we return, we'll lose our lives. Then where will our women be?"

"Where are they now? Being ravished by those savages?" Zacharias spat out. "Being subjected to slavery and all manner of vile things? Dead?"

"No one is going back to the city!" King Noah's voice sailed over the crowd.

Zacharias turned and stared at the king in disbelief. "Not even the king can tell us to abandon our children and wives."

Amulon raised his sword and brought it close to Zacharias. "Disobey the king, and you'll perish here and now."

Zacharias remained still, but the men behind him pushed forward. Suddenly, mayhem erupted. The men who supported Zacharias swarmed the king.

"To the fire!" someone shouted.

Amulon swung his sword wildly. Two men pounced on him, knocking it out of his hand. He fell back, crying out, "Help the king!"

As Noah fought against the attackers with his fists, the high priests tried to reach him through the crowd. Dragging his leg, Amulon pushed through the fury. "You commit treason. Stop!"

Someone kicked Amulon in the face, and he went down, holding his nose. Blood streaming, he staggered to his feet, and, grabbing the nearest man, Amulon punched him. Suddenly, a hand grabbed the back of his hair and shoved him to the ground.

The shouting was deafening.

"Release the king!" Amulon screamed, struggling to get up. There were men all around him, jostling and fighting. On his feet again,

Amulon shoved men aside as he made his way toward the king, who wasn't fighting back anymore. Where were all the high priests who should have been defending Noah?

Amulon's stomach twisted—the king's beaten face lolled to the side as the surrounding men continued to strike him.

"Tie him up!" someone shouted.

"No," Amulon tried to scream, but his voice couldn't be heard above the din.

Another shove, and Amulon was pitched to the ground. When he staggered to his feet, he saw that the king's hands and feet were bound with rope, and the men were dragging him away.

With horror, Amulon watched as they threw Noah into the flames.

"Stop!" Amulon yelled, his own cries mixing with the screams of the suddenly alert king. Amulon clawed through the circle of men surrounding the fire. The king's cries pierced the commotion. Maybe it wasn't too late—maybe—

"The priests are next!" Zacharias called. "Deliver them to the fire."

Amulon backed away as the men turned on him. He looked around wildly, searching for his sword. Seeing nothing, he turned to face the charging crowd.

"There they are," someone shouted, pointing toward the forest. The other high priests were making a break for it. Amulon took a deep breath, turned, and ran after them.

CHAPTER 12

Blessed is the man that trusteth in the Lord, and whose hope the Lord is.
(Jeremiah 17:7)

This palace bedchamber is stifling, Maia thought, *especially housing a dozen women.* At least they were being fed and taken care of—in the most basic way. King Laman still hadn't decided their fate; it seemed the decision rested upon whether Limhi brought in King Noah. Six days had passed, and tomorrow was the final day. Tomorrow, Limhi would suffer for his father's crimes.

Maia moved to the window and watched the sky change into hot colors with the setting sun. She thought about her parents and how they had made such a timely escape from the city. Whatever her fate might be, she hoped they were safe from all of this.

"Maia," a voice behind her said. She turned to see Neriah. Her sister and mother were still at large, and Neriah's father, Gideon, had accompanied the Lamanites in search of the king.

"Do you think they'll harm my father if he fails?" Neriah asked.

"I don't know," Maia said, wishing she could somehow comfort the frightened girl. "Limhi was the one whom King Laman singled out." She shuddered at the thought of the young prince, or anyone for that matter, being put to death. She put an arm around Neriah, feeling helpless. "We must pray," she said, then turned to the other women who were in the room. "Let's gather together and pray to the true God."

Several of the women looked confused.

Neriah nodded. "Yes, we will let God know what is in our hearts, then submit to His will."

Maia grasped Neriah's hand, who then took the hand of the woman next to her. Finally, after some reluctance, all of the women held hands. "Together, our voices will surely reach the heavens," Maia said.

She bowed her head and prayed for her people. She prayed for Limhi's life and for the protection of all those who were still living. She prayed for the women in the circle, that their lives and virtue would be spared, and that they could be reunited with their families.

When Maia concluded her prayer, she opened her eyes and saw that most of the women were staring at her—some with disbelief, others with reverence. Maia was certain that there were several new believers in her midst. She smiled at the women, and a few of them returned it.

A Lamanite guard appeared at the door, and the women broke apart. "The king demands an audience with the woman called Maia."

She turned, taking a deep breath. She'd been questioned several times on the possible hiding places her husband might seek out, but she had no new information to give the king.

Maia followed the guard out of the room, the pitying gazes of the women trailing her. But she walked with her head held high—she was a queen after all. She was equal in rank to the enemy king she was about to face again.

The throne room was nearly empty of people. This surprised Maia. Usually King Laman had dozens of soldiers occupying all of the corners, waiting for any command from their leader. The low tables were piled with half-eaten food, but it appeared that everyone had left. Only two guards stood by the king, and Limhi sat several paces away. A couple of Nephites were with him, and one very bored-looking Lamanite seemed to be guarding them.

Limhi looked up when she entered. He held a stack of folded books. *What is he doing with the records of the Nephites?*

She dared a glance at the king, who was watching her. She stopped several paces from him, refusing to bow or show any subservience. After all, he wasn't *her* king.

She could feel Limhi's sorrowful gaze on her and wondered why.

King Laman studied her for a moment before finally speaking. "I see you've been well taken care of."

Taken care of? She had bathed, yes, though in full clothing under the watchful eyes of the Lamanites. She'd been fed, yes, but being cloistered in a small, stifling room was hardly what she'd call well taken care of. Of course, it was better than the prison her husband had condemned her to.

She folded her arms, her glare saying everything.

The king laughed, his eyes glinting as if he enjoyed her internal debate. "Have you always been this hard to please?"

Maia opened her mouth with a retort, but in the corner, Limhi stood and cleared his throat.

"Ah, yes," the king said, looking at the prince. "We have much to discuss." He motioned for Limhi to come forward, and that's when Maia recognized one of the other Nephites who sat with him. It was Eli, a scribe.

"We have found something new," Limhi said in a hushed voice.

"Speak up, boy. Your moments are numbered," the king said.

Maia stiffened at his words.

"There's a vault that was used during King Zeniff's time." Limhi held up the record in his hand. "This says that sacred records and royal artifacts were kept there. Only the priests of Zeniff knew the exact location."

Maia's skin grew clammy with nervousness. Was it the cave that Gideon had led her to? She hadn't noticed everything inside.

The king grinned and steepled his fingers together. "A perfect hiding place for a king." He looked at Maia. "Wouldn't you say so, dear queen?"

She lifted a shoulder. Would telling them of the cave send them on a chase and give Gideon more time to look for Noah?

King Laman's gaze was still on her. "But that's not why you're here tonight."

Maia couldn't help but stare at him. His dark skin seemed so fierce, yet he'd been reasonably fair for an enemy, more so than her own husband had been to his own people when they broke a rule.

The king leaned forward on the Nephite throne. "Tell me about the place called Mormon and the Nephites who fled there."

Maia looked at Limhi. His expression was placid. Did that mean Limhi had said he didn't know anything? Or that he'd told the Lamanites about the hundreds who had fled the city?

She swallowed, her stomach twisting at the thought of saying the wrong thing. What if the Lamanites went to Mormon and found Alma and the others—maybe they'd returned after Noah's army gave up searching.

"I've never been to the place," she finally said.

The king chuckled. He stood and crossed over to her, looking skeptical.

She didn't flinch and waited for the next question.

"Your husband had many enemies within his own city, it seems." He walked around her, regarding her thoughtfully. "It seems that not all the Nephites would be sad if he were caught and punished."

Maia didn't move or speak.

The king stopped in front of her, standing so close she could see the sweat upon his chest. "Tell me, dear queen, about the high priest Alma—the man who led this insurrection out of the city. The man your husband loathed."

Maia took a deep breath, feeling her eyes burn. "He was—he was a man with conviction in his heart. A conviction he would have been punished for." She hesitated, throwing a glance at Limhi, but he remained silent.

"My husband was baffled that so many could escape his guards without detection. Every day, new reports of missing families poured into the palace." She chanced a look at the Lamanite towering over her.

"Missing families . . . such as your parents?"

She drew her breath in sharply. What was this man driving at?

The king wore a pleased expression. "Limhi estimates that over four hundred people fled to the land of Mormon, following this Alma. He says that the king imprisoned *you*—his own wife—for becoming a believer."

Maia swallowed the burning tears back again. She'd do anything, say anything, to protect Alma and his people. She raised her chin. "The people fled Mormon when our king pursued them."

Laman nodded as if considering her answer to be truth. "But the fact remains that there are perhaps four or five hundred Nephites out there who might try to return and claim their inheritance."

"Alma is a peaceable man, opposite King Noah in every way," Maia said, praying in her heart that this king wouldn't try to pursue Alma's clan.

The king looked at Limhi. "Is this true?"

"Yes," Limhi said. "The man spoke to me just a couple of days before he left for Mormon. His only intention was to teach people what he believed about God."

Maia glanced at Limhi. She hadn't realized he'd had contact with Alma after Noah had banned him. She looked at Limhi with new eyes, appraising him. There had always been something different about the prince. Was it possible that he was a believer too?

Several guards entered the room, and one of them rushed to the king, bowing. "The Nephite called Gideon returns. He bears news of the Nephite king."

"Send him in," King Laman commanded.

Maia drew back as more guards entered. She edged toward Limhi until she was only a few paces from him. She leaned against the wall. Her heart hammered with fear as Gideon entered. Had her husband finally been captured by the Lamanites? Would she witness his execution here and now?

But Gideon was alone, looking ragged, as if he'd been traveling for some time. The surrounding guards gave him respectful space. Gideon strode to the king and put a hand over his heart, signifying that he was about to speak the truth. He took several deep breaths before beginning. "We met a group of Nephites who had fled with the king. They were returning to the city to see if their wives and children had been slain."

King Laman set his mouth into a tight line.

"They rejoiced to know that their women and children had *not* been slain," Gideon said. "They agreed to pay one half of all they possess to the Lamanites for their protection. Your guards rounded them up and brought them within the city boundaries. When I questioned the apparent leader, Zacharias, he said that they had slain the king."

Maia covered her mouth with her hand as disbelief pulsed through her. King Noah's own people had killed him? She steadied herself against the wall behind her.

"They tried to capture the king's priests as well, but they fled farther into the wilderness," Gideon said.

The king remained quiet for a moment. "This man Zacharias speaks the truth? King Noah is truly dead?"

Maia looked over at Limhi, whose fists were clenched at his sides. By custom, Limhi was king of the Nephites now. His eyes were red around the edges, and Maia could almost see the pain working its way across his face. His father had been a tyrannical man, but a father nonetheless.

"Bring in Zacharias. I want to hear the truth of it from him."

Gideon stepped to the side, and it was then that his eyes locked with Maia's. He shook his head apologetically.

As many times as she regretted marrying King Noah, Maia could hardly believe that he was truly gone. Although he'd mistreated and abused her, shock still rippled through her body—shock, relief, and sorrow for a life so ill spent. She bowed her head, realizing her prayer for Limhi's life had been answered. Limhi had been preserved, though at an awful cost to another.

"Zacharias!" a guard announced.

A large man bumbled into the room, his face pale with fear. He bowed before King Laman, then raised his gaze.

"King Noah is dead?" the king asked.

"Yes," Zacharias said. He looked the king over with curiosity.

"How can you be sure? Did you slay him and wait for his breathing to stop?"

Zacharias's round face was grave. "We burned him alive."

Maia gasped. When the prophet Abinadi preached against the king, whispers had circulated in the court about how he'd prophesied that King Noah's life would one day be valued as a garment in a hot furnace. She looked over at Limhi, feeling sick to her stomach as Zacharias described the final moments of Noah's life.

Limhi stood rigidly straight as Zacharias's words filled the room.

"We tried to do away with his priests too, but they fled. So we returned and buried King Noah's charred body," Zacharias continued.

It was true. All of it. Maia's knees gave out, and she sank to the floor. Her husband was dead—just as Abinadi had prophesied.

* * *

"I'll help you in any way I can," Gideon whispered, standing near Maia.

King Laman was in the process of issuing orders. He had promised to spare all Nephites who agreed to pay tribute to the Lamanites. At the insistence of the Lamanite monarch, who needed a Nephite head of state with whom to conclude a taxation treaty, Limhi had the kingdom conferred upon him and swore his own oath to King Laman.

"All he wants is one half of our possessions," Maia said to Gideon. Her only possessions were her parents' home and whatever remained inside. "He can have *all* of mine." Her greatest desire was to flee the city and find her parents. As a widow, there was nothing holding her here now.

She turned her attention back to Limhi and King Laman. The king held the court's rapt attention as he declared the terms of surrender. "I'll set guards about the land, so that none of your people will be able to depart into the wilderness."

Limhi nodded, his shoulders already looking as if they were weighed down with his new responsibilities.

"My soldiers will be supported by the Nephite people. In a day's time I'll return to my land, leaving most of them here," the king continued. His gaze strayed in Maia's direction, and she deliberately looked away.

He had been more than fair—at least to the women. Maia couldn't help but admire the king's seeming loyalty to the Lamanite women back home. He could have easily included many Nephite women in his cache of spoils.

She looked up again when she realized the court was silent. The king was walking directly toward her. She slid closer to Gideon—not that he'd be able to protect her in a room full of Lamanites, but she didn't doubt his desire to fight.

The king stood in front of her for a moment, his gaze penetrating. Maia didn't dare look away.

After a tense moment, he said, "I'll need a guarantee that the Nephites won't kill my soldiers."

Maia stiffened as he continued to stare at her. She felt the appre-hension radiating from Gideon as well.

Finally, the king broke his gaze and turned to the court. "The queen comes with us."

Maia felt the breath go out of her, and she grabbed onto Gideon's arm to steady herself.

"Keeping a Nephite queen with us will ensure that Limhi keeps his word."

Maia opened her mouth to argue, but Gideon whispered, "I will find a way to rescue you."

She stared at him, disbelieving. No matter how strong and skilled Gideon was, the Nephites were still outnumbered. One wrong move from her and war would erupt inside these walls, spilling out into the city. There was no telling how many lives might be lost if she didn't make this one sacrifice.

The king turned to look at her, as if expecting her to disagree. She lowered her head in acceptance.

When the king turned away, Gideon started whispering promises again, but Maia stopped him. "Stay in the city of Nephi where you can protect our new king," she whispered. "He will need your experi-ence and wise guidance. I am but one woman—no lives should be lost over mine. In the name of peace for my people, I accept this assignment."

Gideon shook his head. "It's wrong. They've received a solemn oath from our king. That should be enough."

Maia put a hand on his arm. "I know, but few rules are followed in the course of warring nations. The safety and freedom of my people is more important than where I spend my time." She took a deep breath. "Don't you see? I am a widow now. I have no family here, no one to . . ."

Gideon held her gaze for a long moment. "You make a noble sacrifice."

"No more than those men who refused to follow my husband into the wilderness," she said. The king glanced in her direction, so she drew away from Gideon. She didn't want the king to focus his attention on the good Nephite. When she glanced over at Limhi, she saw sorrow and frustration in his eyes. She wanted to tell him not to worry. She'd find a way to take care of herself. After all, what was her lowly life compared to a nation? A nation that finally had a chance with a new king.

The Lamanite king motioned for her to join him. As she walked toward him, she passed Limhi and paused. "Teach the people the truth," she said.

He blinked in surprise, then nodded. "Of course. The words of Abinadi and Alma will be taught in every home."

She smiled, her eyes burning with tears as she wondered if she'd ever see Limhi or Gideon again. Ducking her head, she moved toward Laman and stood by his side. He smiled and raised his hands. "Your people will have nothing to fear so long as they abide by our rules." He turned to Maia. "And I promise that you'll be treated much better in my city than you were by your own husband."

CHAPTER 13

. . . believe his prophets, so shall ye prosper.
(2 Chronicles 20:20)

TWO YEARS LATER

"Every man should love his neighbor as himself." Alma cast his gaze over the Sabbath-day congregation gathered in front of the newly finished temple. The message he shared today would be taken to the outlying hamlets and farms surrounding the city of Helam by his appointed priests and teachers.

The Nephites had prospered, and the city of Helam grew as they multiplied. Yet, as the people flourished, more contention arose.

"If you love your neighbor as yourself, there will be no contention among you," Alma continued. He glanced at the priests next to him. A couple of them were transcribing the words as he spoke. Helam sat in their midst. He remained reserved most of the time, unless he was teaching—using his natural gift for sharing messages of the Spirit.

Helam met his gaze and nodded encouragingly. Helam was still unmarried, much to his mother's chagrin. There had been no progress in a relationship with Raquel that Alma knew of, but Helam remained close to Abe. In fact, the child sat on Helam's lap now, his solemn three-year-old face taking in every word.

Alma turned back to the crowd at the base of the temple stairs. "The Lord has blessed us with many things. He's heard our cries and answered our prayers. He has granted us a beautiful land in which to raise our families and has given us liberty, which we should always cherish. But we must remain true to our baptismal covenants and remember Him in all things." He took a breath, hoping that his message would be received. "Loving our neighbors as ourselves will ensure that we maintain the liberty God has given us."

He bowed his head and offered a blessing over the congregation. When the crowd started to disperse, Alma turned to Helam. Abe scrambled off his uncle's lap and ran to his mother, who was approaching.

Alma greeted Raquel with a smile. Right behind her was her mother, Itzel. The two women waited for the crowd to thin. Then Itzel drew near and said, "Would you like to join us for supper this evening?"

"I'd love to come," Alma said.

"Wonderful," she said, then hesitated.

Raquel grabbed Abe's hand and walked away, speaking to another woman. Alma looked back to Itzel. "Would you like me to bring something to the meal?"

Itzel shook her head and leaned close. "I'd like to speak to you privately."

Alma hoped nothing was the matter. "Of course. We can talk inside the court room."

He led Itzel to the building housing the court room at the base of the temple hill. It wasn't used on the Sabbath, so they found the room empty. Once inside the cool interior, he turned to Itzel.

She didn't waste any time saying what was on her mind. "My daughter needs a husband." She wrung her hands together and rushed on. "She thinks her son is fine without a father, but he's growing older. In fact, he'd prefer to spend more time with his uncle than with his mother or myself."

Alma nodded. Helam took the boy fishing and let him tag along whenever possible. Alma also knew that Itzel didn't know about Helam's fizzled proposal to Raquel.

Itzel lowered her voice. "It's been over two years since Abinadi's death. If she received counsel on the matter from you, I think she might listen."

"I don't think I can force anyone to choose a marriage partner," he said.

Itzel folded her arms. "I guess it doesn't help that you aren't married yourself."

"No," he said, not sure how to react to the comment. "I believe that when Raquel finds a man she can truly love, like she did her husband, she'll remarry."

Itzel took a step closer. "You are unmarried, she is unmarried . . ."

Alma moved back slightly. "I—I have been so weighed down with organizing the Church and building up the community that I haven't given serious thought to finding a wife. Believe me, your daughter is a fine woman, and any man would be blessed to marry her. Yet I know we are not meant to marry."

Itzel covered her trembling mouth, and it hurt Alma to know he was rejecting such a personal request from such a dear and faithful woman.

"Please do not misunderstand me. I am humbled by your offer, and if this is Raquel's offer too, I am deeply touched. But I cannot give her the love and devotion she deserves."

Itzel turned away abruptly, her shoulders heaving. After a silent moment, she said to the far wall, "Raquel knows nothing of this—it's all my idea. I can no longer bear to see her alone."

"She has you and Abe," Alma said. "And she has the friendship, love, and admiration of so many in the community. We don't know what the future will bring, but perhaps she is doing the right thing for now."

Itzel turned back around, her eyes reddened. "Perhaps you're right." She looked away for a moment. "I have been praying every single day for this to come about. Why does the Lord not hear my cries?"

Alma put a hand on her arm. "The Lord hears your cries, but it takes time for a heart to heal." He took a deep breath, feeling his own heart pound at the realization. "When she is ready, she'll find the right man."

Her face brightened. "You're right. I need to be more patient." Her smile was thin as she wiped her eyes. "Although I had hoped . . ."

Alma dropped his hand. "There's nothing wrong with hope."

She nodded. "I'd still like you to come for supper tonight. But don't worry—I won't try to throw my daughter at you."

Alma chuckled and said, "I don't think you'll ever have to worry about throwing Raquel at anyone." As he watched Itzel leave, he remained in the empty court room for several moments. He'd told himself that he'd been far too busy to consider marrying. It wasn't that he didn't want to be a husband and father—he'd seen the sweet devotion of his parents' marriage—but the unsavory memories of King Noah's court still remained with him.

And it didn't help much that he spent almost every day with Maia's father, Jachin. Every day, Maia's memory surfaced, and he wondered whether he'd ever feel the same affection for another woman as he had felt for her.

Alma left the building only to run into Jachin.

"Good Sabbath," Jachin said, his expression serious.

"Is something wrong?" Alma asked, wondering what dispute he might have to settle now.

"It's Lael."

Concern immediately flooded through Alma. "What is it?"

"She discovered a stash of carved wooden idols in the shed at the back of our home. She thinks they're from the boy who helps us with the garden once a week." Jachin shook his head. "We don't want to get him into trouble with his family, so we wondered if you might be able to talk to him."

Alma was already nodding. "What's the boy's name?"

"Sam."

"All right. I'll let you know what happens."

"Thank you," Jachin called after him.

Alma hurried from the court building and turned in to a row of houses. Sam's mother was a widow and had recently lost her youngest child to an illness. He'd grieved with her and prayed over her, and this, he knew, would be tough on her. Inside his own heart, he ached. He knew that Sam had likely carved the idols out of curiosity—just as Alma had done as a boy—but the fact that idols had made it into the city of Helam, no matter how innocently, was alarming. He could understand how upset Lael must feel and how Jachin would be reluctant to confront the widowed mother.

Alma stopped when he arrived at the modest hut. The street was quiet due to the Sabbath day, but he heard humming coming from somewhere behind the house. Alma made his way through the court-yard and around the hut. There sat Sam—carving wood.

He looked up when he heard Alma. His face brightened, then quickly seemed to close up.

"How are you?" Alma asked, noticing Sam move one hand behind his back. In the other, he held a small dagger.

"I'm fine, sir," Sam said, his gaze anywhere but looking at Alma.

Alma crossed to him, then sat. "I used to be good at carving."

Sam raised his dagger. "With this?"

"Let me see what you're working on," Alma said in a gentle voice.

After a moment's hesitation, Sam brought his other hand around, then handed over the piece of wood.

"Ah," Alma said, turning the object in his hand. It was a fair like-ness of a bird. "Quite good, I must say." He held it up to the light, then reached for Sam's dagger. "Let me show you a trick I discovered myself." He bent over the wood piece and made several quick strokes, then held it for Sam to see.

"Those look like real feathers," Sam said, his eyes wide with appreciation.

"Do you want me to teach you?"

"Yes," Sam said, then his brows furrowed. "I'm not in trouble?"

A smile crossed Alma's face. "You guessed why I came." He took a deep breath, considering the best way to teach this young boy. "There's nothing wrong with carving animals for trinkets and chil-dren's games. It's when you start to combine the animals—such as a serpent with a bird—that you need to be careful."

Sam nodded, but Alma could tell that he didn't completely understand.

"Many people create idols so that they can worship them." Alma held up the wooden bird. "It becomes a symbol of something they desire, yet they turn to it instead of the true God. The Lord asked us to put no other gods before Him."

Sam crossed his arms, listening intently.

"You are still quite young, but you must trust me when I say that crossing the line just a little will eventually lead to a wider chasm." Alma pointed to the wooden bird. "It's a harmless bit of wood, but it represents something not so harmless."

Pushing out his chin, Sam asked, "What can I carve?"

"Carve your birds—I can teach you a few more tricks—but choose carefully. If you have any questions, you can ask me." Alma ruffled the boy's hair.

He dipped his head and smiled. "Are Lael and Jachin really angry with me?"

"Not so much angry," Alma said, "but fearful. They well remember the idol-worshipping that went on in the city of Nephi and how it blinded people to the true God."

Sam let out a breath, relief crossing his face. "All right. No more serpents mixed with other animals."

Alma patted the boy's shoulder then stood to leave. Sam bent over the bird to try his own hand at creating realistic feathers. As Alma left the courtyard, he thought back to another boy who'd loved carving every spare minute. He smiled to himself as he hurried down the path.

* * *

"I want to swim," Abe said, his lower lip pushed out.

"No, son," Raquel said, "I have to teach weaving to the girls this afternoon. I need you to stay with Grandmother, and she won't be able to chase after you if you float away."

"I won't float away." Abe folded his little arms across his chest in defiance, and Raquel had to hide a smile.

"Tomorrow you can swim," Raquel said with a sigh, patting her son's head. Ever since she'd let Helam take her son swimming, he wanted to do nothing else. He and Helam spent most evenings swimming and fishing. But Abe demanding that she take him every moment was getting out of hand. "Maybe Helam will take you fishing tonight."

"He said he can't."

So that was why Abe was being so pushy, Raquel thought as she wondered idly what other obligation Helam had tonight. He was probably courting. Several weeks ago, Esther had proudly announced that Helam was finally courting a woman. Raquel had wondered if he would term it "courting" as well. But that was a taboo subject between them.

Of course, curiosity had driven Raquel to find out everything about the woman. She had been strangely pleased to find the other woman quite ordinary and actually plain-looking. It wasn't that she didn't think Helam could attract someone beautiful, but it was comforting to know he might just marry a regular woman.

For the first few months following Helam's confession, they'd hardly spoken to each other. Then one day, Helam had asked to take Abe fishing. The boy was not even two, but Raquel knew Helam probably just wanted to spend some time with him. Since then, they'd fallen into a simple friendship, where nothing below the surface was ever discussed.

Raquel left Abe in the care of her mother and trudged through the streets on the way to teach a weaving class. Much had changed in the city of Helam, she thought as she smiled to herself. Helam hadn't been too happy when the *land* was named after him, and now he had a land *and* a city. Much more to impress women with.

She arrived early in the quiet courtyard belonging to one of Alma's priests. The young women of the city gathered here to learn the art of weaving, and Raquel enjoyed teaching the girls and hearing the latest news from around the settlement.

The first girl to arrive was Kesare. She was a tiny thing, but outgoing and talkative. She greeted Raquel with an embrace. "How is your boy?"

Raquel smiled at Kesare's thoughtfulness and the way she truly seemed to care about others.

"He's upset that I'm here, since he wants to go swimming."

Kesare grinned and smoothed the curls from her face. "You should bring him to class so he can see how popular his mother is."

"He's quite a handful just doing things that he loves. I had to promise him swimming and fishing tomorrow."

"Oh, do you fish?" Kesare asked, her expression curious.

Raquel's face warmed. "Uh, no. He goes with his uncle, Helam, most of the time. I usually just sit and watch."

"You *watch* them fish?" Kesare asked.

"I mostly watch out for Abe. It's not that I don't think his uncle can handle him, but a three-year-old around water is always a concern."

Kesare tugged a lock of hair with a thoughtful look on her face. "I must tell you that since we've become friends, a lot of people ask me questions about you."

Raquel stared at the girl. "What kind of questions?"

Kesare turned and walked over to her loom, looking a little sheepish. "Oh, things that are nobody's business."

"Now that you brought it up, you must tell me." Raquel followed the girl.

Kesare ducked her head, twisting her hands in her lap. "I shouldn't have said anything, but your comment about sitting and watching Abe and Helam reminded me."

Raquel folded her arms and waited. When Kesare didn't say anything, she cleared her throat. "I thought we were friends."

The girl looked up and sighed. "All right. People wonder why you and Helam spend almost every evening together, yet you are neither married nor betrothed."

Raquel took a step back, her cheeks feeling like they were on fire. How dare people gossip about her and Helam that way?

Kesare stood, putting a hand on Raquel's arm. "Don't be angry with them," she said softly. "Helam obviously loves you. You just need more time—"

Raquel gasped and flinched away from Kesare just as three other girls entered the courtyard, carrying bundles of spun cotton. "Sorry we're late," one of the girls said. The other two echoed the apology.

Raquel took a deep breath, trying to compose herself. She hoped the girls didn't notice her red cheeks. As a precaution she welcomed the girls quickly, then turned away, busying herself with one of the looms to give her face a moment to cool—and her heart to calm down. In truth, she wanted to run from the courtyard, from Kesare's words. What did this girl know about love? Raquel had been in love. Deeply. With her *husband*. Nothing could ever replace that.

But the afternoon seemed destined to turn into a bad dream—worse than she could have imagined. After Raquel's initial instruction, the girls worked quietly for a few minutes, and then one started talking about Helam.

Raquel's breathing grew short. Kesare threw several sympathetic glances her way as the girls chattered on, oblivious.

"The whole city is named after him; no wonder he's choosy."

"That's not what my mother said. He's pining after some woman who rejected him."

Raquel felt as if someone had just kicked her in the stomach.

"Who would reject Helam? His sons will probably be great leaders and have rivers or mountains named after them. I mean, he does have scars all over his face, and some say over his whole body, but he's so . . ." A giggle.

"*Perfect*—otherwise." Another giggle.

Kesare finally broke in. "Helam is Raquel's brother-in-law."

All three girls turned and stared at Raquel.

"Maybe you can tell us why he's so stubborn," one girl said.

Despite herself, Raquel laughed. "That's exactly what he is, *stubborn*." She thought of the last real conversation they'd had about . . . She almost blushed to think of it. He told her he'd never bother her with his feelings again, and he hadn't. It seemed that he never bothered *any* woman with his feelings, which certainly made him a man of his word. *Stubborn* seemed to be the least of it.

"My mother says he spends excessive amounts of time with his widowed sister-in-law . . ." one girl began. Then her voice faded and her eyes widened as she realized what she'd said.

Raquel stood slowly, trying to keep a smile on her face, but it faltered, and tears burned at the back of her eyes. The girl apologized. Raquel shrugged it off and stayed busy with her loom until the end of class. Finally, when the last girl had left, she hurried from the courtyard.

Avoiding the main road, she walked along the neighboring line of trees. She took a deep breath, thinking hard about what she could have done better to stem the budding rumors. But the more she thought about it, the more she wanted to berate those who talked about her. They knew nothing. They hadn't lost the love of their lives. They didn't have to look into their son's eyes every day and know he'd never know his father.

Her steps slowed, and she dried her tears. She veered onto the road again and hurried home. Once there, she went directly to her mother.

She found Itzel putting the finishing touches on the hem of a new tunic and Abe playing nearby with another little boy.

"Mother," Raquel said as soon as she reached her. "What have they been saying about me?"

Itzel looked up, confusion in her eyes. "What do you mean?"

"About me, about Helam; please tell me everything."

Her mother's eyes clouded for an instant, but she tucked the bone needle into her sewing project and held out her hand. "Come sit with me, dear."

Obediently, Raquel sat but kept her distance.

Itzel looked down at her lap. "People have been speculating about you and Helam. They say that he is in love with you." She raised her pleading gaze. "I knew none of it was true, so I took a drastic step."

Raquel's stomach flipped. *Has she confronted Helam?*

"I spoke with Alma."

Raquel dreaded what her mother might say next.

"I asked Alma why *he* wasn't married and suggested he might find interest in *you*—"

"No!" Raquel gasped. She stared at her mother in horror. *What had he thought?* "What was his response?"

"He . . ." Itzel brought her hands to her face. "He told me that he thought you were a wonderful woman, but—"

"I can only imagine," Raquel cut in, feeling literally sick. She didn't want to hear about the polite rejection. She wondered how many proposals Alma received on a monthly basis. Now he could add hers to his growing list.

"He also said something very wise," her mother said in a quiet voice.

"Oh?"

"That I needed to be more patient. He said that when your heart was ready again, you would find the right man."

Raquel couldn't imagine a time when her heart would ever be ready, but she respected Alma's viewpoint. She shook her head. "I can't believe you asked Alma to consider me."

Itzel let out a deep breath. "It was wrong. I only want you to be happy. I wanted my grandson to have a father again. But most of all I wanted to somehow put a stop to all of the speculating about you and Helam." She paused, studying her daughter. "The rumors are false, aren't they?"

She looked at her hands, feeling them start to tremble. "Oh, Mother."

"Raquel?" Itzel whispered.

Raquel squeezed her eyes shut, trying not to let the tears start. "I didn't tell you before . . . And now . . . Now I don't know what to think. Sometimes I feel so confused."

"Oh, dear," Itzel said. She wrapped her arms around her daughter and pulled her close. "Oh, my dear."

Raquel let her mother hold her as the tears came.

CHAPTER 14

. . . love the good, and establish judgment in the gate.
(Amos 5:15)

"Tell me if you like it," Maia said, dropping her hands from Inda's hair. She'd just plaited both sides of the young Lamanite's long thick hair, then wrapped it with ribbons.

Inda picked up the polished copper plate and peered into it. Her mouth twisted into a half-smile. "It looks a little too . . . *Nephitish*."

Maia laughed out loud. "Perhaps, but it's very pretty on you."

The girl continued to study her image then finally nodded with satisfaction. "At least it's different." She smiled. "Anything different will make all of the girls envious at the moon goddess festival. Even the goddess Ix Chel should be pleased."

Maia tilted her head, admiring her handiwork. Inda did look pretty with plaited hair—not that she needed much help to look beautiful. As the daughter of King Laman, she was well pampered, but as the middle daughter, she was perhaps overlooked more than the others.

Two years before, Maia had been brought to Shemlon under the protection of the king. She was held in a private room for several days until King Laman decided where to put her to use. First, she went to the cooking rooms, then she worked her way up to gardening, which she enjoyed because she could be outside. That's where she met Inda. The girl took an instant liking to her and promptly begged her father to let Maia be her personal servant. He would have none of it.

The weeks passed, and Inda remained determined. The king had finally changed his mind when, while Inda and Maia were walking in

the garden one morning, Inda had startled a poisonous viper.
Without hesitation, Maia had come to Inda's aid, putting herself in
harm's way by grasping the serpent by its tail and flinging it a safe
distance. When the king heard what had happened, he had become
convinced of Maia's loyalty and trustworthiness.

Maia and Inda had been inseparable ever since. Maia felt sisterly
toward the young woman, even motherly, and enjoyed attending to
her. And though Maia was only five years older, she felt much older
and many times wiser. Inda was very passionate about every little
thing, often leaving reason behind. At times, Maia had to explain that
the smallest disappointment was not going to bring immediate death
or destruction. Perhaps some of Inda's fears came from being the
daughter of a king who seemed to constantly be involved in a battle
on one border or the other.

Inda rose to her feet, pulling Maia from her thoughts. "Now I
must choose what to wear," she said, clapping her hands in excitement. Inda rushed over to a line of beautiful robes. Maia felt a twinge
of envy as Inda brooded over which one would be just the right color
and fit. She chose a dark red garment.

"You'll look beautiful in that color," Maia said.

Inda held up the scarlet robe and spun around. "Do you really
think so?"

Maia smiled. "Let me help you with it so you don't mess your
hair."

Once Inda was dressed in her fine clothing, Maia applied crushed
powder to Inda's eyelids for a darkening effect and painted her finger-
nails with henna.

"There," Maia said as she finished. "You'll be the envy of all the
women at the moon festival, and every man will have to take a second
look as you travel through the city."

A shadow of melancholy fell over Inda's features.

"What's the matter?" Maia asked.

"I want you to come with me."

Maia smiled tenderly. "My place is here. You are nearly seventeen years
old—much too old to have your maidservant following you around."

"But I don't fit in with the other girls. They roll their eyes every
time I speak."

Maia touched the girl's shoulder. "Most of them are just older than you. Besides, once the dancing begins, you'll be enjoying yourself too much to care."

Inda pushed her lips into a pout. "Please come with me?"

"Even if I wanted to, I doubt the king would allow it."

"My father knows you're my best friend—better than a sister to me. He won't mind. In fact, I don't think we even need to request permission. As long as my mother—"

"Inda," Maia said in a quiet voice. "I'm happy to help you in any way, but this wouldn't be appropriate."

"Oh," Inda said, narrowing her eyes. "Is it because you used to be a queen and dancing with us would be beneath you?"

Maia let out a breath. "No . . ." She looked away from Inda's inquisitive eyes. She couldn't explain that although she'd grown to love Inda, she was still a Nephite at heart. Celebrating and enjoying herself at a Lamanite celebration wasn't something she could bring herself to do. She also couldn't bring herself to participate in the pageantry of worshipping the moon goddess Ix Chel.

"You wouldn't have to dance," Inda pressed. "You could just watch and eat the food."

Maia laughed. "I've known few people as persuasive as you."

"Does that mean you'll come?"

Maia shook her head. "I'd love to see you make all the other girls envious, but I'm afraid that I just wouldn't belong." She gave a half-hearted smile. "You shouldn't worry. I'll have plenty to keep me occupied while you're away."

Instead of Inda's usual childish protest, she nodded and turned away.

Maia was surprised but pleased. The girl was finally starting to act her age. Yet, a twinge of sadness passed over her as Inda left the room in a flourish to join her sisters. Maia would spend another evening alone.

* * *

Raquel sat by her favorite spot on the river, watching the water move around the rocks and push against the bank in the fading light. She'd told her mother everything. It had felt good to share her burden, her questioning thoughts, her confusion about the man she had flatly rejected two years before.

Why *hadn't* Helam married? She couldn't assume it was because of her. He had been nothing but cordial toward her and Abe—kind like any uncle or close relative, nothing more. Maybe he was afraid of losing his relationship with her son. If he had his own wife and children, there wouldn't be much time for Abe. Could he be waiting for her to marry first, ensuring that she and her son were taken care of before he made his decision?

Only Helam would be so courteous.

"Mama!" a voice screeched. "Helam's here!"

Raquel stood, surprised to see Helam. She pasted a smile on her face, grateful that at least her son called him Helam now. For a while he'd called him Papa, and she had to keep correcting him.

Abe came through the trees, tugging Helam, who wore his usual crooked smile. When Helam saw Raquel's questioning gaze, he said, "My plans changed, and I thought I'd catch up on some fishing."

The two set right to work tying line on their wooden rods. Raquel fell back, watching as their heads bent together in concentration. Abe said something, and Helam laughed out loud.

Raquel smiled, an ache growing in her chest as she watched the two of them together. She thought about what her mother had told her—about opening her heart—about seeing if there was room for Helam in it. But even if somehow this was the case, surely he had long since changed his mind about her.

She followed the two of them as they walked along the river, Abe's small hand in Helam's large one. She supposed the three of them created the image of a family to anyone who might observe them.

Helam stopped and lifted Abe onto his shoulders. Abe squealed with delight. "Now I'm bigger than ever-body!" he shouted.

Helam laughed in response. He turned and winked at Raquel. She smiled. When he turned back around, she concentrated. *Open your heart,* she told herself. *How do you feel right now? Content. Happy.*

But what does it matter? she argued with herself. *He probably changed his mind long ago. Yet I feel safe. Secure.*

They'd reached the fishing hole, and Helam lifted Abe from his shoulders. The two were soon immersed in positioning their rods directly over the calmer waters.

Raquel settled several paces from them and perched on a rock, watching. But instead of soaking in the peaceful evening, her thoughts tumbled against each other. *Has Helam heard the rumors? What about his mother? What does she know?* He hadn't mentioned anything and probably wouldn't. Yes, he'd been quiet around her, but his relationship with Abe was stronger than ever.

Open your heart, she thought again. She stared at Helam's profile and tried to consider for the first time what it would be like to be married to him. To have him greet her as a husband would a wife. To kiss him.

A warm shiver traveled along her arms, and she let it wash over her for a moment. She noticed the strength in his arms and shoulders as he cast the fishing line across the water, the tenderness of his touch as he ruffled Abe's hair, and the surety in his voice as he explained why the fish liked deeper, calmer waters.

Raquel drew her knees to her chest, her heart racing. *Open your heart.*

She squeezed her eyes shut. It was too much. She couldn't possibly love Helam like a husband. It just didn't seem . . . She opened her eyes and stared at the man on the bank of the river—the man who had loved Abinadi as much as she, the man who loved her son.

But did he still love her?

Too afraid to think about the matter any further, she closed her heart. It was safer that way.

Helam turned just then and looked at her. What she saw in his eyes made her breath catch for just an instant, but she chided herself. Perhaps she'd mistaken his gentleness for something more. His gaze shifted past her, and she turned to follow it.

Coming along the bank of the river was Esther. And she looked furious.

She practically stomped as she bustled up to Helam. Raquel had the feeling she was about to witness a grown man being berated by his elderly mother.

"Where have you been?" Esther asked once she reached Helam. She didn't acknowledge Raquel or Abe.

"Right here fishing, Mother," Helam said, his voice filled with tired patience.

"You know we have a supper engagement. If we leave now, we'll only be a little late." She looked him up and down. "I'd hoped that you'd dress a little nicer."

Helam ignored her fussiness. "I'm sorry, Mother, but I told you I had another commitment tonight."

Raquel's curiosity increased. Maybe Helam was seeing a woman on his own, without his mother's interference. Esther couldn't help but be pleased by that.

"Hmmph." Esther put her hands on her hips. "*Fishing* is your other commitment?"

Helam nodded with a smile. "I know you've worked hard to find me a wife, but it's not really necessary."

Raquel felt uncomfortable. She hadn't heard Helam speak so directly about marriage or other women for a long time. Suddenly she wanted to be anywhere but here.

"Abe, come here," she called, deciding to get him out before he was in the middle of the argument.

"He's fine where he is, Raquel," Helam said, still looking at his mother.

Raquel froze. She looked from Helam to Esther. The woman's face had reddened considerably. "If I leave finding a bride to you, you'll be in the grave before I ever see grandchildren."

Helam tilted his head with that crooked smile on his face again. "You *have* a grandchild."

"Yes, yes," Esther said, looking flustered. "You know what I mean. I can't keep answering everyone's questions, and you should hear the women talk. Some of the things I can't even repeat."

Helam threw his head back and laughed. Raquel smiled but quickly became sober when Esther threw a disdainful glance in her direction.

"Perhaps the women should busy themselves with something of greater consequence than rumors," Helam said, laughter still in his voice.

"Look at you," Esther said, her tone sharp. "You spend all of your time with Abe and Raquel. No wonder everyone is talking." She looked at Raquel as if something had just occurred to her. "And both of you single, at that."

Raquel stood, intent on taking Abe no matter what Helam said.

"Perhaps the two of you should marry," Esther blurted out.

The smile on Helam's face froze, and Raquel's heart sank. She hoped Abe hadn't understood.

"Perhaps," Helam echoed quietly. His gaze met Raquel's, and she was sure her face had gone redder than hot coals.

Esther's eyes widened as she looked from Raquel to Helam.

Raquel wished she could hide her flaming cheeks, but she knew it was too late. Esther had already seen.

Esther brought a hand to her heart. "You—you mean . . . ?"

"Yes, Helam asked me to marry him," Raquel choked out in a whisper. "And I turned him down."

Esther looked at Raquel, her expression shocked. "I didn't know. I never thought . . ." She turned to Helam. "But she was your brother's wife." When he only nodded, she continued, "When was this?"

Helam's shoulders seemed to slump, his voice barely audible. "Two years ago."

"Two years?" Her expression was incredulous. "Even after all that time, you still cannot choose a wife?"

He looked away, and for a moment, Raquel wished she could reach out and smooth away the embarrassment flaming on his face.

"Two years is plenty of time to recover from a rejection, Helam." Her eyes narrowed, then her eyebrows arched. "Son?"

He looked at his mother, then his gaze strayed to Raquel. "I don't think twice the years would be enough."

The silence was palpable. Raquel's heart seemed to slow so that each beat pulsed against her ears.

"So this is why you do not marry," Esther practically whispered. "I understand." She pursed her lips for a moment.

"I tried," Helam said in a strained voice. "I tried to convince myself that I could be happy with another woman. Yet, I failed. Miserably. I couldn't let go of what I felt." He looked at Raquel, and her heart almost stopped at the pain she saw there. "Of what I *still* feel."

The fire in his eyes pierced her to the core, and Raquel had to look away. Her mind numbed at the realization that he still loved her. He still wanted to marry her.

"Two *years?*" Esther whispered again with a shake of her head.

Helam nodded with a sad smile. "Life isn't always what we think it will be." He put a hand on his mother's shoulder. "We are all managing in our own way."

But Esther was staring at Raquel again. "You have known about this for so long?"

Raquel swallowed against the thickness of her throat and nodded.

Suddenly Esther chuckled. Helam, Abe, and Raquel stared at her in confusion.

"Son, if Raquel is as stubborn as you are, it might take a lifetime to convince her." Esther reached for Abe and gave him a squeeze. "Come on, dear, show Grandmother where the best place is to catch those transparent butterflies."

Abe grinned. "Can I go, Mama?"

Raquel nodded and watched her son lope off with Esther. When they disappeared from view, she turned to see Helam watching her. The sun had nearly set, and the orange splashes of color topped the river behind him. For a moment, she thought of how Helam was just like the river—constant, patient, enduring. The course of his heart had never changed.

Open your heart. Raquel stared at him, and he stared back. Finally, she took a deep breath and said, "I don't think I'm nearly as stubborn as your mother might think."

A flicker of hope touched Helam's eyes.

Then, slowly she smiled, warming the distance between them. He smiled back. He took a step forward, holding her gaze, assessing her reaction. When she remained still, he took another step, then another.

He walked toward her, his gaze full of wary optimism. When he reached her side he stood there for a moment, just looking at her. Then, slowly, she raised her hand; he took it and brought it to his lips.

Warmth spread through her hand at his touch. "You're going to miss your supper appointment," she said, trying to keep her voice steady.

He kept her hand in his. "I've been avoiding them for two years. Missing one more won't make a difference." His tone was light, but his eyes said so much more.

"I'm afraid," she whispered.

He tugged her hand, pulling her closer, until she was a breath away from him. "So am I."

CHAPTER 15

*(For the Lord thy God is a merciful God;) he will not
forsake thee, neither destroy thee.*
(Deuteronomy 4:31)

Amulon wiped the oily meat from his mouth and turned to the other priests. The full moon would rise in just a couple of hours, and they were already late starting. "Tonight," he said. "We'll bring them home with us."

The men laughed through their yellowed teeth with him, their eyes eager with anticipation. Once a month during the night of the full moon, Lamanite girls gathered by the lake and danced in celebration of their moon goddess. Their servants brought food and wine, then left the girls to themselves.

Foolish Lamanites, Amulon thought, but it was to his advantage. Living in the wilderness for over two years had taken its toll on his small group of men. They'd practically killed each other several times, and with no women to temper any outbursts or to care for them in any way, they'd become desperate.

Amulon had long given up on returning to the city of Nephi. With the king dead and the Lamanites ruling the land, he and the other priests were wanted men. So they'd spent the past two months building huts in a remote valley. At least it gave them something to do and a sense of purpose. Early on Amulon had taken over the leadership and had named the small valley the city of Amulon. And why not?

He rose to his feet and held his arms up for silence. "Tonight we'll have women to warm our beds. In the morning we'll have women to cook our meals. In the afternoon, we'll have women to weave our clothing."

The men stood and cheered.

"Let's go." Amulon strapped a bundle to his back, similar to the other men's. They doused the fire and loaded up plenty of rope and extra skins of water. The women wouldn't be accustomed to journeying such distances, though it was only several hours' travel to the location. But by the time the priests returned with them to the city of Amulon, they'd be well tamed—that he was sure of.

The group of eighteen men reached the forest just as the sun set. Beyond was the secluded lake where the women gathered. Amulon stopped his party to rest before moving on. He scanned the faces of the men—they looked tired, but the excitement in their eyes had only grown.

Sitting on the ground, Amulon leaned his back against a tree.

"How many do you think there will be?" one of the priests, Paan, said.

"At least a dozen. Last month there were more," Amulon said.

All of their heads nodded in anticipation.

"How will we decide who gets which girl?" Paan asked. He was one of the younger priests who had come to Noah's court after Alma's time.

Amulon shrugged. "Casting stones?"

A couple of the men groaned. One offered, "A dancing contest?"

"I like that." Amulon laughed, but then he grew serious. "These women will become our wives and bear our children, so perhaps we should let them choose."

The men speculated as they considered more possibilities.

Finally, Paan said, "Can I have two?"

The men burst out laughing, nudging elbows and slapping each other on the shoulders. But Amulon hushed them. "There'll be plenty of time to decide later." He looked toward the rising moon. "First, we have a job to do."

It was nearly dark now, and Amulon motioned for the men to follow him. They moved through the trees until they could see the edge of the lake. He breathed in sharply at seeing the Lamanite servants moving along the perimeter, unloading supplies. Several torches had already been lit, and the woven rugs were piled with food. His mouth watered at the extravagant display. The women wouldn't even eat close to half of the delicacies—agave wine, cacao drink, guavas, pears, avocados, a variety of meats, and squash.

Amulon had to order the men not to rush the food. The women would certainly be coming along very soon. They didn't have long to wait. Moments after the food was arranged, the women appeared on the path that came out of the trees on the far side of the lake, walking in a long line. Even at this distance, Amulon could see their beauty. Some Nephites may have found their darker features unattractive, but Amulon found them exotic . . . enticing.

Whispers surrounded him as the men exclaimed about the women.

Amulon recognized a few from the previous month when they'd been spying. Tonight it seemed there were more than usual—apparently the dancing festival had grown in popularity.

"How many?" Paan whispered next to him.

As the women turned along the bank and headed for the display of food, Amulon counted. "Twenty-three . . . twenty-four." The last woman was veiled, and her arms were lighter in color. Perhaps one of her parents was a transient Nephite, he thought. No matter. Women were women.

Amulon smiled, anticipation blossoming in his chest. In a matter of hours, the women would belong to them. He imagined reaching out and touching a woman's soft, dewy skin.

"Look!" Paan said.

Amulon turned—four women had broken away from the main group and started dancing with no music. He stared at the women's strangely seductive movements, which they did with no music to keep rhythm. It was as if the women had a rhythm all their own.

Then he heard someone singing. Over the chatter of those who were eating, Amulon listened to the words of the unfamiliar Lamanite song. He narrowed his eyes in concentration—there was something familiar about the singer's voice. He scanned the dancers and those eating to try to find out who it was. Finally, he saw a shadowed figure several paces from the dancers. It was the veiled woman with light skin.

Paan nudged him. "I want that one."

"Which one?" Amulon said, pretending not to notice who Paan pointed to.

"The veiled one. Only a beautiful woman could sing like that."

Amulon nodded, exhaling slowly as his mind raced. "Indeed."

Paan put a hand on Amulon's shoulder, squeezing. "How long are we going to wait?"

"Until the servants leave and the women start to grow tired."

"I don't know if I can wait that long," Paan said.

"I promise you," Amulon said, turning to his friend with a broad smile. "The wait will be worth it."

* * *

Maia smiled at Inda through her veil as she sang the second verse of the Lamanite song an octave higher than the first. She still couldn't believe she'd let Inda talk her into coming tonight, but when Inda discovered that her other sisters wouldn't be coming, her pleas turned to begging. Then the queen mother suggested that Maia's presence would be best since Inda was younger than most of the girls and Maia could look after her. So, after being promised a veil and that she wouldn't be coerced to dance, Maia finally agreed.

Inda looked radiant in her scarlet robe and plaited hair. The other girls had exclaimed when they saw her, and Maia promptly received requests to do more hairstyles for the next month's dance. She watched as two more women joined in the dancing, and the group that had gathered around the food quieted so that Maia's voice seemed to soar over the lake.

Maia didn't sing as much as she had when she lived in the city of Nephi, but Inda always ordered her to sing a song before she retired for the night. So this was the first time that Maia had sung in front of the others. She sang traditional Lamanite songs, which Inda had been eager to teach her.

A few of the women started to softly play a shell trumpet, keeping rhythm with Maia's song.

Inda approached Maia with a grin on her face. "It's beautiful! I'm so glad you came—all of the women love your songs. Next time we'll have to invite the men."

Maia smiled indulgently, but her heart raced at the thought of sharing her talent in front of men. That's what had caught King Noah's attention in the first place. No matter the feelings of tenderness she had toward her Lamanite charge, Maia was first and foremost a Nephite. She dreaded the possibility of the king ordering her to marry a Lamanite man, though so far he'd made no arrangements. It was in her best interest to keep from drawing unnecessary attention to herself.

Another girl approached, asking for another song. Soon, Maia was singing again and surprisingly enjoying herself quite a bit. As the night wore on, the servants left the lakeside to return in a few hours to clean up.

"Gather into the circle of the moon," one of the women cried out.

Inda tugged Maia along with her. "Now the real celebrating starts."

Maia allowed herself to be pulled and then seated next to Inda in the circle. Several torches had been set on the ground together, creating a blazing fire. Maia could see the women across the circle now, their faces illuminated by the fire.

"I'm to represent Ix Chel tonight," Inda whispered. She stood, her eyes bright and face flushed. She pretended to weave cloth in the air—a divine talent of the moon goddess. The women started chanting a tale of how Ix Chel tried to attract her true love—the sun god. When she completed her phantom cloth of beauty, Inda acted as if she were presenting the cloth to the sun god. Then she spun around in delight. The chanting told how the sun god fell in love with the moon goddess.

The chants softened and the cup of wine passed from person to person, celebrating the union. When it reached Maia, she took it under her veil but did not drink. She passed it on, hoping that no one noticed she hadn't participated. In her heart, she knew there was only one true God, and His Son, the Savior. She wondered if she might someday share her true beliefs with Inda or any of the other women.

One by one the women rose to their feet and clasped hands, swaying together, praising Ix Chel's skill of securing her love. Maia swayed but didn't chant. She looked up at the moon and thought about her homeland and how different it was from here. She thought about her parents and wondered where they were on such a bright night. Were they safe with Alma? Had they already been baptized? Here she was, feeling alone, although she was surrounded by women. It seemed the Lord had preserved her, protected her for a reason, though she didn't yet know why.

The fire dimmed as the chanted story continued. The tendrils of smoke seemed to follow the women's voices as they rose to the sky. Suddenly a cloud passed over the moon. The women's voices fell, and someone screamed.

Maia whirled around to see what was happening when a hand grabbed her arm. A man's hand.

She screamed and reached for Inda, but she, too, was struggling against another man. The men were everywhere. Maia resisted as another hand gripped her other arm. Her wrists were tugged together and a rope tied around them. Then she was shoved to the ground, and a wad of cloth was stuck into her mouth.

A male voice shouted over the screaming. "Be quiet or you will die!"

The screams died to whimpering. Maia turned her head, trying to see what was happening. Men leaped over women who had already been tied and grabbed anyone who tried to flee. One man held a woman at knifepoint, threatening to kill her.

A Nephite!

With horror, Maia watched the Nephites tie the women up one by one. Why would her people do this? She'd heard the rumors when her husband was in power of Nephite soldiers attacking Lamanite families. But weren't those attacks for defense?

Maia's throat constricted as the cloud moved away from the moon, once again illuminating the night. The Nephite holding Inda looked familiar. Maia turned slowly on her side to get a better view of the men's faces. She recognized several—they were high priests from Noah's court.

Maia started to breathe rapidly, bordering on hysterics. One by one she recognized them . . . Paan . . . Amulon. They looked different—wild, lean, beards grown long—but it was undoubtedly those men. How long would it be before they recognized her? Maybe she could plead for the Lamanite women. Or maybe doing so would make things worse.

She was grateful for her veil, but her disguise wouldn't last. The men prodded the women to their feet and started tying them one to another until they formed a long line. *What are they going to do?*

Amulon's recognizable voice rose above the commotion. "Listen to me, women, *if* you want to live." He paused and walked along the line, gazing greedily into the frightened pairs of eyes. "If even one of you tries to escape, we will hunt you down. Then you'll watch one of your friends killed before your eyes."

The woman he stood in front of shrank away. Amulon chuckled. "Yes, you should fear for your lives, since there is no one here to protect you now." He glanced at the moon as if to judge the time.

"Anyone who speaks or makes a sound will immediately be put to death." Amulon brandished a knife in front of the next woman, who drew back. He grinned, seeming to enjoy his power.

One of the younger girls started crying, loud heartbreaking sobs. Amulon was at her side in an instant, his knife pressing against her throat.

The girl cut off her sob and stared at him, trembling.

"I said, silence!" Amulon hissed. "That was your final warning." He looked at the surrounding priests. "Blindfold them."

Maia watched the men blindfold the women down the line, drawing closer to her. Would they lift her veil and recognize her? Paan was the nearest Nephite, and soon he was at her side. He stepped behind her and in one swift motion tied a strip of cloth around her head. He had changed from the young man she'd known—he seemed hardened, thinner, his beard long and scraggly. "Greetings, fair one," he whispered.

A chill ran along Maia's neck. Did he recognize her?

"Don't worry," Paan continued. "You'll soon be under my care."

She tried to draw away from his rancid breath. If the words were meant to comfort her, they had the opposite effect.

He didn't pull away like she hoped, but instead ran a hand along her arm, then slid it to her waist. For an instant he pressed against her, then suddenly he released her and moved to the next woman.

Maia breathed a sigh of relief, but her heart still pounded. How long would it take for the Lamanite servants to return and discover the women missing?

They walked for what seemed like hours. Many times Maia stumbled, catching herself just before tumbling against Inda, who walked in front of her. She strained to see through the coarse cloth over her eyes, but the darkness made it impossible.

I wish I had the answers, Maia thought. For the moment she, too, hated the Nephites. At least these ones.

Finally the procession came to a stop. The priests removed the blindfolds. Maia blinked and looked around. They stood at the top of a rocky hill bathed in moonlight. Below were crude shelters and a row of huts near a river.

"Welcome to the city of Amulon!" Amulon said, triumph in his voice.

Maia looked at the self-proclaimed leader and shuddered. His eyes briefly scanned the tied women, his gaze staying on Maia a moment longer than the others. It seemed that he, too, had noticed her fair skin.

Amulon started the procession again and led the women to one of the first huts. He divided them into two groups and allowed them to be untied. Fortunately, Maia was able to stay with Inda. Once inside the dark hut, Inda latched onto Maia. They sank to the ground together in exhaustion. "What's to become of us?" Inda whispered.

Maia put her arms around the girl and held her tight. She was afraid for herself. Should she confess to Inda that she knew these men? What would Inda think of her then?

Some of the women started to panic and cry.

"Shh!" several said.

Maia strained to hear what the men were saying outside the hut.

"Let them sleep. Tomorrow we'll perform the marriages," a man's voice said.

"Why go through the pretense of marriage? We shouldn't limit ourselves. It should be like King Noah's court—"

"Silence!" Amulon yelled. "We're not welcome in the city of Nephi, and we're certainly not welcome with the Lamanites. We need to build our own colony, our own people, so my original decree will stand. These women will become our wives and bear our children."

No! Maia wanted to scream.

A man who sounded like Paan said, "I agree. Amulon is our chosen leader, and we must obey his orders. Now the question becomes, how do we choose our wives?"

"And why do we have to wait until tomorrow?" someone shouted.

"Men, I told you the wait would be worth it. We want our women well rested. All I ask is for you to be patient, and we'll cast lots in the morning to choose our women."

"And how many women we each get!"

Maia pulled Inda closer to her. How could these men even think of abducting Lamanite women and marrying them? Had they no fear of the repercussions? The Lamanite army could wipe them out in a matter of moments.

"Do you think my father will be able to track us?" Inda whispered.

"Yes," Maia said, hoping it was true. "If they start soon, maybe by morning they'll find us."

Inda pressed closer, her body trembling. "I don't want to marry a Nephite."

Maia kissed the top of the girl's head. "I know," she whispered.

As the sky brightened outside, most of the women fell into a fitful asleep. Maia gazed over the bodies of the women attired in their best dancing robes. She rose to her feet and walked to the crude window. Peering out, she saw three men guarding the door. Another three guarded the next hut.

Maia's stomach turned. She'd rather die than be married to someone like Amulon. These were men who had abandoned their wives and children and left them in the hands of their enemies. Men who had abused their wives and taken harlots for pleasure. Men who had abducted innocent women and girls . . .

I can't do this, she thought, looking furtively around the hut. The silence was worse than the fearful crying of the women or the shouting of the men. It left her to her own thoughts. *Please spare me, O Lord,* Maia prayed. *Spare us all. Protect us from these evil men.*

She sank to her knees, eyes burning. And finally, for the first time since the Nephites appeared, she let her tears fall. *O Lord, have mercy upon my soul. Preserve our dignity.*

She lifted her silent voice to the heavens, pleading over and over until she couldn't remain upright anymore. She slid to the ground and fell into an uneasy sleep.

CHAPTER 16

Take heed unto yourselves, lest ye forget the
covenant of the Lord your God.
(Deuteronomy 4:23)

Alma surveyed the temple grounds in the fading light. The bright reds, oranges, and yellows were vibrant against the darkening backdrop. Each shrub, flowering plant, and tree had been carefully cultivated by the women of the community. Alma could almost feel the love exuding from the living plants as he passed by them, but tonight his heart was heavy.

Contentions seemed to multiply by the day, and he spent most of his time inside the court building now, passing down judgment after judgment. The land of Helam had prospered exceedingly. The people had multiplied, and the building throughout the land nearly rivaled that of the city of Nephi. The market teemed with activity from dawn to dusk as people sold their handmade goods and precious wares unearthed in the surrounding hills.

The women wore fine jewelry and soft linen. The men carried daggers with jeweled hilts, and feathered capes had become a popular commodity.

And contentions grew. It was no surprise, really, Alma thought. But still he had hoped for better—prayed for better. His ordained teachers put in a full day's work in their professions, then spent their evening hours meeting with families who were troubled, helping to resolve minor disputes.

The greater disputes came to Alma. And he was heartsick over them.

He climbed the temple steps as he thought about those people who had lost the humility that had brought them here. They had become comfortable again and started to want more than just freedom to worship. They compared themselves to each other and disputes became petty—a missing goat, a wayward child, a noisy neighbor—all had become sources of contention.

Reaching the top of the steps, Alma entered the quiet walls of the temple. Its construction was simple, though built with loving and strong hands. He walked to the far side of the room and ran his hands along the fine rug that a group of women had spent two months weaving. A labor of love.

He turned and peered through the dim light at the carved window frames—some of which he'd carved with his own hands. The quiet was peaceful and he could almost imagine that everything outside the temple walls was just as peaceful.

But it was not.

Alma walked to the center of the temple and stood before the altar for a few minutes. The stones had been shaped into a waist-high edifice. On top was a smooth stone slab, meant for offers of sin and thanksgiving. Two more altars were positioned outside—for use by the general public. But the altar inside was used for the priests and the teachers.

Kneeling, Alma rested his folded hands upon the altar and bowed his head. "O Lord, O God of Abraham and Isaac and of Jacob," he prayed. "We have been blessed exceedingly. Lift up Thy people so that they remember Thee in all things."

As Alma prayed, the time passed until it was pitch dark outside. Finally, exhausted both in mind and in soul, he concluded his prayer and stood. He made his way toward the moonlight spilling through the temple doors. At the threshold he paused, looking down on the land of Helam. He could see several cooking fires throughout the area coming from individual courtyards. He hoped this meant that families were coming together to enjoy each other's company.

Then his gaze strayed from his community in the direction of the city of Nephi. It had been two years since they'd left the turmoil and iniquity of that place. What had become of the believers who hadn't made it to the Waters of Mormon? Had they been forced to flee the city?

He sank to the top step and stared across the moonlit expanse. Then he saw movement on the grounds below. Someone was walking toward the temple. He stood as the person started up the steps. *Raquel.*

She lifted her head, and by the expression on her face, he could see she was startled. She continued to climb the steps, stopping two below him.

"Alma," she said.

"Is anything wrong?"

"No," Raquel said. She climbed the final two steps and stopped near him. "I just hoped that coming here would help me think better."

He nodded. "Me too."

They stood in companionable silence for a moment.

"Do you ever wonder what's happening in the city of Nephi?" Raquel finally said.

"All the time." Alma turned to look at her. "But that's not what's troubling you, is it?"

A smile flickered across her face. "You're too wise." She hesitated. "I've come to pray about whether or not to marry Helam."

"Ah, that."

"I'm sure I've exhausted him by stalling for so long," she said, folding her arms, "but I want to be sure."

"You're going about it the right way," he said. "The decision of marriage should always be a matter of prayer." He felt her curious gaze on him and wondered if he'd said too much. There was probably plenty of speculation about why *he* wasn't married yet.

"Now what could *your* troubles be?" she asked.

He let out a breath of relief. She wasn't going to ask him the marriage question. "The court has been very busy lately."

She nodded as if she understood completely. "I can't imagine how hard it must be to make those types of decisions."

"I do everything in my power to run a fair court, but there are always those who disagree."

"As is the case with every leader," Raquel said in a quiet voice. "As we've become more settled and prosperous, some of the old ways have crept back in."

"Yes, and it seems almost impossible to stop," Alma said.

"Don't give up," Raquel said, her voice urgent. She stepped toward him and touched his arm. "You must know that we pray for you every day, so even when you feel underappreciated and over-worked, remember we are praying for you."

Alma was taken aback by the sudden rush of sentiment.

"I know that if Abinadi were here today," she added, "he would be humbled by all that you are doing for the believers."

"Compared to what Abinadi went through, a few minor disagreements seem like nothing," Alma said.

Raquel dropped her arm. "It can be frustrating and difficult all the same. I remember when Abinadi returned from his first time preaching and he thought he'd failed." She met Alma's gaze. "But when you warned him of the coming mob, he was certain that he'd made a difference to someone, somehow . . ."

Alma's throat constricted as he remembered that night of chaos. The king had ordered a death sentence on Abinadi's head, and every able body had been hunting him down. When Alma had run into him on the streets, it seemed that Abinadi gazed directly into his soul. Even then, even when Alma had been denying the Spirit of God for so long, he knew there was something of truth in Abinadi's words.

And it had changed his life forever.

"One man converted after such a sacrifice," Raquel said in a quiet voice. "Only one. But that one man brought hundreds to Christ." She gazed at Alma, her eyes moist. "Thank you. I wish Abinadi were here to thank you too, because I know he'd feel the same measure of gratitude for your faithfulness and perseverance."

Alma took a deep breath. "It means a lot to hear that from you."

Raquel stepped away, wiping her eyes. "It's amazing we've come so far." She looked toward the temple. "Even with the challenges we've had, I always feel peaceful when I come to the temple. It makes me feel like we can rise above any foolishness and that anything is possible."

"I believe that anything is," Alma said.

Suddenly she was back at his side. "Do you think I should marry Helam?" she asked.

Alma smiled. "I don't think you need me to answer that."

Raquel slowly closed her eyes. "I suppose you're right." She opened her eyes and smiled in a sad way. "Some days are harder than others, and sometimes I doubt. Other times I—" She broke off, staring past Alma.

"Like you said, being near the temple makes you feel like anything is possible—that and a lot of praying." Alma watched her reaction and waited for her to look at him. "The peace that you are feeling may just be your answer."

* * *

"I still need some time," Raquel whispered.

Helam released her hand. "Certainly."

She wanted to take his hand again, but it was already late in the evening. They'd been meeting this way for weeks, each evening after the sun had set. It wasn't that Raquel didn't want her new relationship with Helam to be known to others. In fact, she was sure that everyone knew, but she wasn't quite ready to tell Abe. The boy saw Helam as his best friend, his uncle—what would Abe think when she told him Helam would become his father? The questions would get even harder as he grew older and understood who his real father was.

Raquel met Helam's gaze. She hated asking him to wait longer, but—

"Raquel?" Helam said, his voice as quiet as the night. "I'll wait as long as you need me to."

She nodded, her throat tightening. He *would* say that. It made her feel even worse.

"Besides, you know how obsessive my mother gets when there's a wedding to plan," he said. "Putting it off a little longer is just fine with me."

Despite herself, she smiled.

Helam touched her chin and tilted her face upward. "It's enough for me to know you feel the same way about me as I do about you. I could die happy knowing that."

Raquel flinched.

Helam grabbed her hand. "I'm sorry. I didn't mean it like that."

Then suddenly, Raquel was in his arms, burying her head against his chest. "I don't want you to leave me, ever."

"I'm not going anywhere," Helam said, stroking her hair.

"I don't think I could live through that again." Tears burned her eyes.

"You're not going to lose me, Raquel."

She clung to him more tightly, wishing she had more of his solid strength and assurance.

"The Lord has protected us thus far—leading us out of danger time and time again," he said. "We have to trust in Him and move forward according to our hearts."

Raquel nodded, knowing he was right. What was in her heart? She knew she wanted to marry Helam. The fear of losing another husband didn't really measure up to any other insecurity she might have of remarrying.

"All right," she whispered. "You have me convinced."

Helam's hold on her loosened. "I don't want this to be a matter of convincing."

"It's not." She pulled away slightly and looked up at him, *really* looked at him. In the depth of his eyes she saw a man who loved her and loved her son. She knew he would be faithful to her in every way. But it wasn't just the way he felt about her. She loved him too. She'd come to depend on him and felt safe with him. She wanted to make him happy, to take care of him, to live with him as his wife.

Helam leaned down and gently kissed her on the cheek. "Thank you," he whispered.

She smiled at the warmth that spread through her body. "Tomorrow we'll make the announcement."

"So soon?" he said.

She tried to slug him, but he moved out of the way, laughing. Then his face sobered, and he reached for her hand. "Tomorrow, then."

She tugged him toward her, raised up on her toes, and kissed his cheek. His eyes widened, and he placed a hand against his cheek. She turned and hurried to her hut, refusing to give him the advantage of knowing that her face was even redder than his.

Once inside, she took a deep breath. Her thoughts were spinning in every direction, and her heart felt like it would burst with happiness. She knew she'd made the right decision. She wanted to shake her mother awake and tell her, but instead she crept to Abe's side. He was curled up on the mat next to hers. She knelt and touched her son's shoulder, stirring him awake.

When his eyes opened, he automatically put his arms out, and Raquel pulled him into her embrace.

"Time to play?" Abe asked, his voice still sleepy.

"No," Raquel said, smiling. "I just wanted to tell you that you're going to have a new father."

"Helam?"

Her breath caught. "Yes. How did you know?"

Abe nestled closer against her neck. "He told me you're the best mother."

"He said that, did he?"

"So maybe he wants to be the best father."

"Yes," Raquel whispered. "He *will* be a wonderful father. You're very blessed."

"Can he take me fishing tomorrow?"

Raquel chuckled quietly. "I'm sure he can."

* * *

"Well, well, well," Amulon said, gazing at the sleepy women with a smile. Just seeing them crowded in the hut and inhaling their sweet fragrance made his stomach flip with delight. It was late morning— time to get moving. "You'll certainly need to prepare yourselves for the big celebration." His gaze alighted on the fair-skinned woman at the back of the hut. She sat close to one of the Lamanite girls, eyes lowered.

Amulon stared at her, ignoring glares from the surrounding women. "Maia?"

She lifted her face. Her cheeks were stained with tears and dust, but her eyes were steady. It was unbelievable. After all this time . . . why was she with the Lamanites?

Then he noticed her clothing's simplicity—just a plain tunic.

Compared to the other girls, she looked like a mere servant. He nodded his head with the new knowledge. "What a surprise."

Maia held his gaze, but she didn't speak. There would be plenty of time for questions and answers later. But right now, he had seventeen restless men waiting for their prizes.

"All of you, out of the hut," he said in a sharp voice. "You'll be guarded as you make your preparations. If someone tries to escape, one of the other women will die." His gaze bore into Maia's. "Make your choices wisely."

He left the hut and finished his list of orders to the men. The women were to refresh themselves and have something to eat before the voting.

The sun was at its zenith when Amulon called the meeting. Flies buzzed among the men as they gathered under the open tent. Despite the shade, the heat seemed to permeate the animal-skin roof.

"Welcome," Amulon said, remaining standing. He smiled at the eager expressions that gazed back at him. Paan sat cross-legged toward the front of the group, his fingers tapping impatiently.

"The women are preparing themselves and will join us momentarily."

A murmur of approval darted through the men.

"I appreciate your patience," Amulon said, raising his hands. He nodded to Paan, who stood and turned to the men.

"We've captured twenty-four women," Paan said. "Yet there are only eighteen of us. We've determined that some of the women are too young to marry as of yet. They'll be saved for a later time."

"How young?" someone shouted out.

Amulon moved to Paan's side. "Too young."

A couple of men grumbled until Amulon held up his hand for silence.

Paan continued. "Each man will select one wife today. The remaining women will be saved for later. The leaders will have first priority in choosing a second wife."

A ripple of objection moved through the men.

Amulon stepped forward again, holding a knife so all could see. "The only way our community will be successful is if we all agree to the rules. If any one of you plans to go against my orders, you're invited to leave now."

The complaining stopped, but several men still glowered.

"To enjoy the privileges in my city, you'll live under *my* rules," Amulon said, waving his knife.

A couple of men ducked their heads.

Amulon looked each man in the eye. Some avoided his gaze, others stared him down, but no one stood to leave. "Very well, then. We'll cast lots to see who gets the first pick after me."

When the men obligingly nodded, Amulon's serious expression dissolved, and he grinned, motioning for Paan to follow him. "Let's go and fetch the women, ready or not." As they walked toward the women's huts, he said, "Do you know who the fair woman is?"

"So that's who you want," Paan said, looking at Amulon, disappointment on his face.

"You probably won't want her when I tell you her name," Amulon said. "Remember Maia?"

"King Noah's wife? The one who . . . What's she doing with the Lamanites?"

"I haven't had a chance to find out," Amulon said. "But since she's a widow now, I thought she'd make a good choice for myself."

Paan shook his head. "You're right. I don't want her. I'd rather have one of the less broken women."

Amulon threw his head back and laughed. "That you will, my friend."

The guards bowed as the men approached the first hut. "Bring them out," Amulon said.

He and Paan both drew their knives as the women were led out of the two huts. They still looked tired but were less dirty than earlier. Amulon grinned as some of the women scowled at him. When the last one had passed by, he turned to Paan. "It will be an experience taming them."

Paan nodded with a smile. "Are you taking one or two wives today?"

"Two. What about you?"

Paan looked at him in surprise. "Do I have a choice?"

"Of course you do," Amulon said, putting a hand on his shoulder. "You're my most loyal man."

"All right, I'll take one for now then perhaps one of the younger ones at a later time." His laughter joined with Amulon's as they followed the colorful robes to the meeting.

By the time the women were settled beneath the canopy, a couple of them were quietly crying. "I don't want a crier," Paan whispered to Amulon.

He nodded in answer but was looking for Maia. Her hair was the first thing he saw—the dark copper resplendent as ever. She had cleaned up well, and her smooth skin and gray-green eyes were remarkable. He remembered the envy of the men as they watched her sing for her husband in court. Soon, he'd be the same object of envy.

His gaze landed on the slip of a girl next to Maia. They seemed to be very close—almost like sisters.

"I want the little one next to Maia," Paan whispered.

"I'll save her for you," Amulon whispered back. He continued to gaze at the frightened women, seeking one that looked healthy enough to bear him sons. His eyes drew back to Maia—she had born the king a son but had lost it soon after birth. Had she fallen out of the gods' favor? A twinge of misgiving passed through him. Yet, if he didn't choose her, certainly another man would . . .

Amulon cleared his throat and moved in front of the curious men. "The time has come. Men, cast your lots." Each man came forward and cast a handful of maize kernels. The man with the least number of kernels grouped together was a lower number in line.

Paan lined the men up in the order they were selected.

Amulon walked around the group of quivering woman. "Not every woman will be chosen today. Those who are not will live in a guarded hut and serve the community by cooking our meals and weaving our clothing." He pointed to one girl wearing a blue robe. "You. Stand and move to the far side. You'll be a cook."

The girl rose unsteadily to her feet, gratitude written across her face. She hurried to the far side. Amulon singled out four more girls who looked too young to marry, ignoring the groans from the men waiting in line. The girls hurried to the far side and clung to each other.

Amulon turned to the remaining women. "Each of you will stand and tell us your name." He watched as they stood, their robes swirling at their feet, their bracelets and anklets tinkling. He took a deep breath of pleasure. It was wonderful to have women in their presence again.

One by one the women stepped forward and pronounced their names. Most were strange-sounding to Amulon, but he was sure they'd all know each other in no time.

Maia stepped forward, and Amulon noticed all of the men eyeing her. He smiled inwardly, rather pleased with his cunning. The Lamanite girl next to Maia stepped forward. "I am Inda," she said, her eyes flashing. "And I'd rather die than be married to any of you!"

Maia grabbed the girl's arm and pulled her backward.

Amulon laughed. "We're sorry, Inda. You'll not get your wish today."

She turned her fiery gaze upon Amulon, and he smiled indulgently.

When the women had finished, Amulon said, "As you well know, I'm Amulon, leader of this community." He pointed to Paan. "This is Paan, my second in command. It will be a special honor for the women who are chosen as our wives. We expect you to act in the manner befitting your position as the wife of one of the leaders in the city of Amulon."

Paan stepped forward and joined him, adding, "Together we'll build a strong community and families."

A couple of the women buried their hands in their faces and groaned.

"Fear us not," Paan continued. "We'll treat you well according to your behavior."

Amulon lifted a hand to his chest. "I'll be the first to make my choices. Paan will choose one wife, and I'll choose two." The women stared back at him in horror. Amulon dropped his hand to his side. "You'll learn quickly that the Nephite way is different than the Lamanite way."

Maia soberly met his gaze, and Amulon smiled. He could see in her eyes that she knew he was going to pick her. He could also see how much she loathed him.

"Maia, come forward."

It took a moment for her to react, and Amulon was about make his demand again when she took a step. The Lamanite girl Inda clasped her hand and squeezed. Maia tugged away and held her head high as she passed through the women. When she reached Amulon's side, she bowed her head and stood by his side.

Triumph burst through Amulon's heart. She wouldn't be so hard to tame after all. He took another moment to let his gaze slide slowly over the rest of the women. He must choose carefully. One woman sat near the front. She looked to be older than some of the others—slightly plump, but healthy and vibrant.

Amulon pointed to her, not remembering her name. The woman walked toward him, looking a bit tremulous, but she didn't cry. She crossed to Maia, and the two women clasped hands. *Excellent,* Amulon thought. He didn't have any criers.

Amulon let Paan make his choice—Inda, who scowled. Amulon chuckled. With the fire of Inda, Paan would have his hands full.

As the other men chose their wives one by one, Amulon looked at Maia and his other woman. They both kept their gazes lowered. A very good sign indeed.

CHAPTER 17

The Lord . . . heareth the prayer of the righteous.
(Proverb 15:29)

Maia could hear Inda screaming at Paan somewhere behind the hut. She waited for the inevitable and flinched as she heard the slap. Inda stopped screaming, and now it was Paan's turn to yell.

Maia turned to face the wall, avoiding Cochiti's pained gaze. The woman had so far been strong, but the look on her face revealed the horror she felt at overhearing Paan and Inda.

The marriage ceremony had been farcical at best. It seemed the men had been planning to abduct the Lamanite women for quite some time. They had prepared all manner of meats and soaked wild fruit in a honey concoction. Of course, Amulon officiated at all of the marriages, except his own. The men even had gifts of rough-hewn jade jewelry for each woman. Paan had married Amulon to Cochiti, but when it came Maia's turn, she couldn't speak. Literally.

Amulon had grabbed her shoulders and shaken her, but even though Maia tried to make the words come, they didn't. Finally Paan suggested that a nod would suffice, but Amulon had crossed his arms. "She will become my wife when her voice returns."

Maia could see that he worked hard to control his anger. She half-expected to be beaten in public, or at least inside Amulon's hut. But when he brought the women to the hut, he merely shoved them inside and said he'd return soon.

So now they waited. At least Inda and Paan had stopped screaming at each other, and Maia could only imagine what was happening now. A hot tear budded against her eye, and she quickly swiped it away. There was no room for tears in this place, and she refused to pity herself. In fact, she was the lucky one right now—not that it would stop Amulon and his advances tonight. The former high priest had taken many harlots in his days at court. Tonight would be no different.

In the near darkness, Cochiti moved closer to Maia. "Who are these Nephites of yours?" she whispered. "They take more than their share of women. They beat us. We treat you with nothing but goodness, and now—"

Maia touched the woman's arm and tried to explain. But still her voice would not work. She lowered her head, ashamed of herself, ashamed of her people. She wanted to explain that not all Nephites were like beasts. There were good men—

The reed door burst open. Amulon came into the room, holding a small torch. The brilliant orange blinded Maia for a moment, and then her eyes adjusted. Amulon also carried a large swath of cloth.

"Woman," he said, looking at Cochiti. "Hang this across the room."

Cochiti scrambled to her feet and tied a corner to one wall, then pulled the cloth across the hut and tied the other corner. The room was now divided in half.

"Very good," Amulon said. He moved to the back portion where the two women stood. He looked at Cochiti briefly, then focused on Maia. "Has your voice come back?"

Maia shook her head as Cochiti placed a hand on her arm. "She has tried," Cochiti said. "Perhaps in the morning I can make her a tea that will help."

Gratitude flooded through Maia for this Lamanite. She didn't know why her voice would not come, but to have Cochiti speak for her to appease Amulon was a blessing indeed. A blessing—Maia's breath stalled to think of it. Was she being blessed? Was the Lord protecting her for some unknown reason? Her skin warmed at that thought. Why not the other women? Why not send an army of Lamanites to rescue the women from these Nephite men?

Amulon studied Cochiti with new interest, his smile almost kind. "Very well. I can wait one more day." His gaze moved to Maia again.

"You will stay in the front part of the hut. The back area is reserved for me and my wife."

Maia looked at Cochiti, whose face seemed to pale. But she raised her chin, her expression resolute, and nodded.

Leaving the back portion of the room, Maia wished she could stop the inevitable somehow. But she knew it was impossible.

* * *

The next morning, Maia woke early and started to clean the hut. It looked like it had suffered years of neglect, even though she knew it couldn't have been built more than a few months ago. She was careful to make very little noise and not disturb Amulon and Cochiti. The two seemed to be sleeping late. Amulon's snores reached through the curtain clearly enough.

Maia tried to put out the memory from the night before. She'd witnessed plenty of men taking advantage of women in King Noah's court, so she'd braced herself for the worst. But she heard no complaint from Cochiti, which was a relief. Maia shuddered to think of what would happen when it was her turn. She had been down this unsavory path when there was perceived honor in being a king's wife, but there would be no honor in being married to Amulon.

A yawning sound cut through her thoughts, and Maia straightened. Amulon was awake. The hairs on the back of her neck stood as she waited for the confrontation. His slow footfall seemed to thud in her ears, and he parted the curtain. His searching eyes found hers. He grinned.

Maia looked away, heat flaming her cheeks.

"It'll be your turn soon enough, dear queen," Amulon said. He didn't bother to lower his voice as he laughed. Maia was sure that Cochiti heard every word.

"Is the morning meal not ready?" he asked, a glint in his eye.

Maia shook her head and made a movement toward the door.

"Let your *wife* prepare your food," a voice said behind the curtain.

Amulon and Maia turned with surprise. Cochiti came into view, a serene expression on her face. "Good morning, Maia," she said, then looked at Amulon. "Give me a short time, and your meal will be ready."

Amulon arched an eyebrow and stared after Cochiti as she left the hut. Then he looked at Maia, triumph in his eyes. "Well," he said, "Go help her. You may not be my wife yet, but you must work as if you were."

Maia hurried to the door and stepped outside. The day was still early, but several women milled about. Some huddled around cooking fires; others just stood and talked. The men also stood in groups talking, although they kept a watchful eye out as the women worked.

It looks almost . . . normal, Maia thought. She folded her arms as she approached Cochiti, who was building her own cooking fire.

Maia wished she could speak but hoped that Cochiti would understand her concern.

Cochiti looked up. "I thought you'd follow me out here." She stood and drew close to Maia. "Inda said you used to be revered by all of these men in your husband's court—that they were forbidden to touch you and that they paid deference to you. So this must be . . . especially difficult for you to think of becoming a wife to one of these men." She took a deep breath. "Inda made me vow to protect you. Even if your voice does return, pretend it hasn't." Her lips formed a half smile. "I know you pity me, but in the eyes of the gods, I am a married woman now. And I will do my duty."

Maia stared at her, shocked. This woman was accepting her lot so readily. Maia nodded, hoping that Cochiti could see the gratitude in her eyes.

"We need more tinder," Cochiti said matter-of-factly.

Maia moved away to look for scraps of wood on the ground. She also kept an eye out for Inda, wondering how she'd fared during the night.

Then she saw her. Inda met her gaze at the same time. They hurried to each other, and Inda threw her arms around Maia's neck.

"You still can't talk?" Inda asked.

Maia shook her head, squeezing her friend's arm.

"I can tell you worried about me all night," Inda said with a gentle smile. "You should know that Paan left me alone," she whispered.

Maia's eyes widened.

"I don't know why he did. I certainly made him angry enough . . ."

She sent a sly glance in the direction of a couple of men. Maia followed her gaze and saw Paan watching them together. She couldn't read his expression, but at least he didn't look angry.

She put an arm around her friend and kissed her forehead.

"You don't need to protect me any longer," Inda said, her smile returning. "I think I can handle my husband."

Maia shook her head.

"What?' Inda asked. "Look at him. He may have been some great priest in Noah's court, but after I stopped screaming at him, he became quite . . . nice." She paused. "When they abducted us, I'd never been so scared, but I also felt sorry for them. Paan told me that all the men lost their wives and children when the Lamanites invaded the city of Nephi. He said the new king would kill them if they returned, and they're certain their wives have remarried and that their children have forgotten them."

There was much more to the story, Maia thought as she stared at Inda. Paan had left out the fact that they'd *abandoned* their families.

"And what if my father sends an army?" Inda continued. "Will we not still be married to these Nephites?"

Maia wanted to shake sense into Inda. What Paan and Amulon had done was an act of war, of treason. Marriage or not, it didn't make it right.

"I can see you're upset," Inda whispered. "I am too, in a way. But after Paan explained things so gently . . . and when he didn't touch me last night, I suppose my heart softened."

Looking away, Maia had a hard time with Inda's conclusion. She looked around the settlement. The other women couldn't possibly be content like Inda. Just then Amulon exited the hut and crossed over to Cochiti. He touched her arm and said something. Then she smiled at him. *Smiled!*

What was happening to these women? Maia wondered. Why couldn't she talk when she needed to? She looked back at Inda, who shrugged. It was as if the women had taken a powerful herb and forgotten where they'd come from.

Was this what the Lord had in store for them after all? *What about me?* Maia wondered. Her voice wouldn't remain silent forever. And when it returned, she'd become a wife again.

* * *

It took several weeks before Maia regained her voice. She didn't know what had caused it to go away—but it was indeed a blessing. Her voice came back slowly, but she still pretended it was lost, even two months later. The only person who knew her secret was Inda.

Amulon left her alone most of the time as she worked. Once in a while he'd make unsavory comments about her becoming his wife, but so far he hadn't taken her by force. She had to be grateful to Cochiti for that. The woman was more than kind and generous to her new husband. She practically spoiled Amulon, and he enjoyed the attention.

Overall, the community was relatively peaceful. Most of the husband-and-wife combinations were congenial. Many of the women were with child, and there was much anticipation in the air about the coming births.

This morning Maia had risen early as usual and started the cooking fire. Since Cochiti had announced her growing child, Maia had let her sleep in each morning. She didn't mind the cool mornings, in fact, she relished the peace and quiet. She methodically ground maize kernels, the scraping filling the silence.

Most times when she was alone, her thoughts turned to her homeland and her family. Even though her parents were no longer in the city of Nephi, Maia pictured them there and the thought of memories they had shared. They'd been more than willing to take in their ill-contented daughter—even when she was married to the king. She wondered what they'd think of her silence now. They would probably think she had truly gone mad this time.

Maia swept the maize powder into a clay bowl as her mind strayed to Alma. He seemed like a distant figure in her memory. He had been part of her life when she was so miserable—the only shining light even with no hope of them ever being together. She closed her eyes and visualized his face. He had certainly been handsome, but his eyes were what she loved the most—kind and honest. Especially that last time she saw him in her parents' courtyard. He'd looked surprised when he confessed her true feelings, yet so concerned when she said she wanted to seek a divorce from the king.

Adding water to the flour, Maia stirred the sticky dough with her hands, thinking of the irony in her widowhood. Alma was likely married with at least two children. A man like him would certainly waste no time in marrying.

And what am I then? Where has my life gone? Backward, she decided. *At one time I was married. No longer. At one time I had a son. Briefly. At one time I had parents. Now lost. I was even a servant to royal Lamanites; now I'm a servant to outcast Nephites.*

Maia bit her lip, hating the feelings of self-pity washing over her. She finished forming the maize cakes and set them to bake over the fire. Watching the dough sizzle, she realized she was leading herself down the wrong path. The Lord *had* protected her. He *had* answered her prayers. Maybe in a way she never imagined, but at least she still had her faith—even if it was a faith she couldn't share with anyone.

Opening her eyes, Maia blinked back stinging tears just in time to see Inda coming toward her.

Maia put a smile on her face and rose to greet her friend. The relationship between Inda and Paan had mellowed over the past few months. This morning Inda's eyes were bright with excitement, and her cheeks glowed.

Maia looked around to make sure there was still no one else about to see her speak. "What is it?" she whispered.

Inda grasped both of her hands. "It's happened. I'm with child." She smiled. "Oh, Maia. I never thought . . ." She looked down as her hand touched her stomach. "I'm going to have a child with a man I've fallen in love with."

Maia nodded slowly. She'd seen the way Inda looked at her husband and had guessed. But to hear it from Inda herself was truly remarkable. *A blessing,* whispered her mind. To have endured so much, then to find a semblance of happiness at the end of the ordeal.

Maia put on her brightest smile. "Then today is a good day indeed, and there should be no complaining at all."

Inda laughed. "No complaining indeed."

"Have you told Paan?"

"Not yet," Inda said. "For some reason I wanted to tell you first." Her voice faltered. "I know this has all been difficult for you, and that you detest these Nephites. But I want you to know that I have forgiven them, and I am now a part of them."

Amazement coursed through Maia. She didn't know what to say.

Inda touched Maia's arm. "I don't want you to worry about me. We're going to make this a strong community and raise many children and grandchildren. You can keep your silence as long as you must; your secret will always be safe with me. Maybe in time you'll find happiness, too."

Maia embraced her friend, heart pounding. She couldn't believe that Inda had forgiven the Nephite men. As she watched Inda hurry to her hut and pondered the news she was about to deliver to her husband, Maia sank to her knees next to the cooking fire. She remembered Alma's words of redemption, repentance, and forgiveness as he spoke to her parents. She'd received forgiveness from the Lord for her mistakes, but had she sufficiently forgiven those who had wronged *her*? She knew she'd never trust Amulon, but could she forgive him?

There was so much—too much to let go of. The only way she'd been able to hold on the last couple of years as a slave had been to keep that anger close to her heart. It gave her strength. Motivation. Purpose.

But what if it was all wrong? What if Inda was right and Maia still needed to forgive? No matter what? Wouldn't that weaken her and make her become even more of a pawn to be pushed around?

"No."

Maia turned her head, wondering where the word had come from. She clasped her hands together to keep them from trembling. Could she find happiness like the others around her if she decided to forgive the vile Nephite men? She removed the maize cakes from the fire to let them cool, then left the cooking area and walked through the huts to the edge of the first field. It stretched out flat until it reached a hill where the sun peeked over.

All right, I'm going to try, Maia thought. *I'm going to try to forgive my dead husband. One person at a time.* She stared across the field she'd help to cultivate. The harvest season was just weeks away, and soon the people of Amulon would reap what they'd sown.

Maia was just about to return to finishing the morning meal when something caught her gaze. There were several strange shadows near the top of the hill, on the far side. She peered through the sun's glare and realized they were not shadows, but men.

Had a hunting party gone out the night before? She waited to see if the men came closer, but they remained in place. As she watched, more appeared at the top of the hill. A shiver ran through her as she counted. Twenty, with more appearing every second.

The sun moved higher in the sky, reflecting off the bare torsos of the dozens of men, and Maia suddenly knew. Lamanites had found them.

She stared in disbelief as more Lamanites crested the hill. She estimated at least a hundred of them, and more coming. Her heart leapt as she thought of these warriors rescuing their women at last.

Turning, Maia fled to the huts to warn Inda and Paan. Perhaps they could flee before the inevitable carnage began. At least they should be given a chance. Several people had woken, and Maia waved wildly at them, pointing to the far hill.

She reached Inda's hut as Paan stepped outside. "Lamanites are here!" she said, grabbing his arm. "You must take Inda and flee. They'll surely kill you."

Paan looked at her, shock on his face, whether more from the fact that she was talking aloud or that the Lamanites had arrived, Maia didn't know.

But there was no time for explanations.

Inda appeared at the doorway, her eyes wide.

"Please," Maia said. "You must flee now. An army of Lamanites is coming—they'll surely kill your husband."

Inda clutched Paan's arm, her eyes filling with tears.

"Well, well," a deep voice said behind Maia.

She turned to see Amulon.

"Your voice has returned so conveniently." His gaze traveled from her disheveled appearance to the ensuing panic of the settlement.

Everyone scurried about, knocking on huts, yelling out instructions, and gathering weapons. Maia took a step away from Amulon, but he grabbed her arm and held it firm. He narrowed his eyes as he glared at her, then his face twisted into a smile. "Were you planning on escaping while the Lamanites hack your people to death?" Amulon said, practically growling.

He looked at Paan. "No one is running from the Lamanites today—not me, not my wife, not Maia. We're a community now, and we will stand together, no matter what our fate." His eyes settled on Maia again. "You're coming with me."

Cochiti came out of her hut, holding two knives. Her expression was tight with fear, but she walked with a determined step toward them.

Maia wondered if Cochiti planned on fighting against the Lamanites.

She stopped and handed a knife to Inda, who took it calmly. Cochiti turned her gaze on Maia, who saw the betrayal there. Maia's secret was out.

"Let's go," Amulon said, keeping his hold on Maia as they walked through the center of the settlement. "Gather the women and bring them to the edge of the field!" he shouted as he moved in that direction. Cochiti, Paan, and Inda followed close behind.

Maia stared at the amassing army. They had come down the hill—at least three hundred of them now.

Amulon stopped at the edge of the field and released her arm. She rubbed the skin where he'd gripped it. Next to her, Cochiti came to a halt, keeping her head raised as she stared at the advancing Lamanites.

Amulon moved away, shouting more orders, and Inda joined Maia. The two women linked arms. "What will they do?" Inda whispered.

They watched the advancing warriors. The Lamanites looked ferocious indeed, but Maia knew their hearts were likely softer than many Nephites—like Amulon. "Perhaps they will spare the women at least."

Inda's grip tightened, and she started to tremble. "I'll beg for protection—tell them who I am."

"It may not matter who you are," Maia said, her stomach twisting with fear. The Lamanites were now close enough that she could see their fierce expressions.

Amulon stood in front of his people and threw a clod of dirt in the air, signaling peace. For an instant, Maia admired his show of respect to the Lamanite army. But perhaps it was just part of another crooked plan.

The Lamanite commander stopped in all his finery. He wore a simple loincloth like the others, but across his shoulders was a feathered cape. His head was shaved except for one long braid on the side, woven with a strip of leather. He was taller than most of his warriors and on the thin side, yet his very presence commanded authority. Maia had seen this commander before at the Lamanite king's palace. She doubted he would recognize her, but he'd certainly know Inda.

Before the commander could issue any death orders, Amulon sank to his knees and bowed. "Spare us!" he called. "Grant us our lives! We'll pay tribute to your people and grant any request you might have."

The commander narrowed his eyes at the prostrated man. "You're the leader of these people?"

Amulon raised his head slightly. "Yes. We are but a small community."

"Nephites?" the Lamanite commander asked, his eyes straying to the women. He stopped when he saw Inda. She stepped forward as the Lamanite commander said, "Inda?"

She nodded.

"You're the Nephites who stole our women," the commander hissed, his eyes back on Amulon. He turned to his men and raised his hand. The warriors drew more tightly together and brandished their swords.

Inda took another step forward. "Please spare our husbands, Commander Zorihor."

"Your *husbands?*" The commander whirled to face her, staring in disbelief. "*Who* is your husband?"

Inda pointed to Paan, who lowered his head in respect. Then she looked again at the commander. "I am with child. Many of us women are." She waved her hand, and several other women stepped forward.

"But you're a Lamanite *princess.*" Zorihor gazed soberly at the women, many of whom had dropped to their knees.

"Please, Commander," Cochiti cut in. "Spare our husbands. We know they abducted us. But they are our husbands, and we carry their children."

"Please," Inda echoed. "We want to honor our marriages in the eyes of the gods who witnessed them." Her voice trembled as she continued. "Do not bring us more sorrow. We've made a home here and have found a new life." She looked at Paan. "And love."

The commander looked from Inda to Paan, then to Amulon, who remained kneeling. The moments of tense silence seemed to stretch for hours.

Finally, Zorihor said, "These Nephites abduct our women and marry them—and now they plead to spare the enemies' lives?"

Several more of the Lamanite women took bold steps forward and added their pleas.

After a few minutes, the commander raised his hand to stop the pleadings. "I cannot understand all of the reasons you desire to stay with these Nephite men. But I respect your wishes and will consider them."

Amulon rose to his feet and bowed deeply. "We are men who have been made outcasts by our own people. We no longer call ourselves Nephites. If you'll spare our lives and allow us to preserve our marriages and new families, we'll join you as brothers."

Drawing in a deep breath, Maia watched Zorihor as he arched a brow and studied Amulon. *He wants to become a Lamanite?* She shouldn't have been too surprised, since Amulon had always done whatever King Noah asked of him—as long as it gave him the greatest advantage—even when it meant disowning his daughter and abandoning his home.

But this seemed the greatest treachery of all—joining the enemy.

Maia watched the commander closely as several expressions crossed his face. His surprise turned to curiosity, then consideration. He studied Inda the most, as if debating whether she or the other women had been coerced into speaking for their husbands.

Finally he said, "I'll give the women the opportunity to leave their Nephite husbands and be fully protected by us until we return them to their home." He gestured to the women. "Step forward now." He waited. The warriors surrounding him looked at the women, waiting too.

But no woman crossed to the soldiers.

Take me, Maia wanted to say. Remaining here with Amulon ensured that he'd make her his wife soon. But these Lamanites weren't looking to rescue a Nephite woman. She might be worse off with the Lamanites than she was now.

Amulon bowed again, and the women followed suit. Soon all of the Nephite men and their wives were bowing before the Lamanite commander.

All except Maia. She looked down and twisted her hands together. She'd paid no obeisance to King Laman, so why should she bow to this commander? She was a widowed queen without a home, without a country—yet she couldn't outright defy him either. If he was going to allow the women to stay with their husbands, Maia wanted to be close to Inda to help her with the coming birth of her child.

"You," Zorihor said, and Maia snapped her head up. He was staring right at her.

She didn't know if she was expected to reply, so she simply looked at him. "I know you," he said.

Inda immediately rose to her feet. "She was my servant in Shemlon. My father brought her from the city of Nephi." She looked over at Maia as if to ask her permission to share so much information. "She's a queen, married to the former King Noah of the Nephites."

"Yes," the commander said, his gaze boring into Maia's. "I thought I'd seen you before."

Not like this, Maia thought. Her appearance was quite disheveled compared to the way she'd looked while in Shemlon.

He continued to assess Maia when Amulon said, "The Nephite woman belongs to me."

Zorihor's gaze landed on Amulon. "You do not have a Lamanite wife?"

Amulon straightened. "I have one, but Nephites sometimes have more than one wife."

The commander's eyes narrowed. "You married both women?"

"I'm not married to the Nephite yet," Amulon said.

"If you are to be subject to our rule, then you will not take more than one wife." Zorihor studied the other men, then said, "Come forward if you have more than one wife."

No one moved.

"There are more women here than men," the Lamanite observed. "Who is yet unmarried?"

The collection of younger women stepped forward.

Zorihor folded his arms across his chest. "You are welcome to come with us or remain here."

The women looked at each other, then hurried to stand behind Zorihor.

"And you," the commander said, looking directly at Maia. "You're coming with us."

CHAPTER 18

Forsake her not, and she shall preserve thee:
love her, and she shall keep thee.
(Proverb 4:6)

The smell of charred meat woke Maia, stinging her senses into focus. It took her a moment to realize where she was. Turning her head, all she could see was the black goat-hair panels that made up the small tent in the Lamanite camp. At least she was alone for a few moments. And for that she was grateful. Although Amulon's threats to marry her had died after the Lamanites had taken over, she knew he wouldn't have any qualms about bedding her as a secret concubine. And Maia could think of no other man more vile than he.

She sat up carefully, nursing her sore back. Walking for hours the day before had taken its toll. But it was her head that hurt the worst. The throbbing had returned, and she knew it was from lack of food.

"Get up, woman!" a man's voice shouted from outside the tent.

The accent belonged to one of the Lamanite warriors accompanying their small party. Amulon was leading the commander, helping him find the way back to the city of Nephi. Most of the others had remained behind in the city of Amulon, guarded by a portion of the Lamanites. Biting back a groan, Maia moved to her feet and pushed open the tent flap. Instantly the brightness of the morning sun blinded her, and she blinked several times.

"Over here," a different voice said. The Lamanite commander motioned toward the cooking fire, his black eyes assessing her.

Maia swallowed against the lump in her throat as she stared at Zorihor, fear trickling along her neck. He could so easily have his way with her. As a Nephite, she was his enemy, and she did not know if she could trust him.

The smell of blackened meat was stronger, and Maia's mouth salivated with hunger. Cochiti tended the fire. The two women hadn't spoken since the invasion.

Maia moved to her side and gathered the bowls to serve the soldiers. When Amulon came out of his tent, she'd have to spend the day avoiding him, as usual. She sensed that if it weren't for the Lamanites' upper hand, Amulon wouldn't have hesitated making her his second wife.

Every so often Maia felt Cochiti's gaze upon her, and she wished she could explain her reason for keeping silent and not telling Cochiti right away—if there was ever a moment the men weren't around.

Zorihor turned away to talk to another soldier. Out of hearing distance and because Amulon hadn't made his appearance yet, Maia took the opportunity.

"Cochiti," Maia whispered. "I know you're upset with me for not telling you when my voice returned. But I couldn't risk anyone else finding out. I'd rather do anything than become Amulon's wife—especially since he was part of my husband's court."

Cochiti ignored her and continued turning the meat on the spit.

"I didn't intend to betray you."

"That's not it." Cochiti looked at her with a fiery gaze. "I don't want you to become Amulon's second wife."

Maia's mouth fell open. "But I thought—"

"I know what you thought. When I realized your voice was back, I knew he'd make good on his promise." She took a deep breath, her next words shaky. "I don't want to share my husband." Her expression softened. "In my culture, a woman and a man cleave unto each other—and no one else."

"Y-you don't *want* me to marry Amulon?"

Cochiti shook her head.

Just then Amulon stepped out of his tent. He let out a huge yawn and stretched his arms over his head. He gaze settled on Maia immediately, his expression coy.

Maia glanced at Cochiti and saw with despair that the woman's face had reddened. Now Maia understood.

Amulon stopped to talk to Zorihor, and Maia moved closer to Cochiti, touching her arm briefly. "I'll do everything in my power to not become Amulon's wife."

A faint smile touched the woman's face.

* * *

The wedding ceremony was quiet, even though Helam was known throughout the land. Raquel wanted only their families and closest friends to attend. She looked across the intimate circle at her mother, Itzel, who wore a tired but radiant smile on her face. She and Esther had made all the preparations in just a few short weeks. Once Raquel had made up her mind, no one wanted to delay. Gifts and tributes would continue to pour in during the next few days for the couple, but for now there were only a few guests.

Next to Raquel, Helam kept her hand clasped in his. It felt good not to be alone *and* to be next to Helam. He was watching Alma and Ben with amusement. Ben was describing his latest creation of a sword hilt to Alma and trying to convince the leader that everyone in the city needed to purchase one from him.

At the age of thirteen, Ben was already a persuasive merchant.

Helam caught her looking at him, and he squeezed her hand. Raquel's face warmed. She couldn't believe she was married to him at last, and she couldn't believe she was blushing.

On the other side of Raquel, Abe tugged at her arm. "Can I go play?"

Raquel laughed and pulled him onto her lap. "Not right now. This is a special meal."

Abe nestled against her neck. "I know. Because I have a new papa."

"Yes. You're a fortunate boy," Raquel murmured, kissing the top of his head. She caught Helam's gaze and half smile. Her heart calmed at the absolute tenderness she saw there.

Abe wriggled and turned to Helam. "Can we go fishing tonight?"

Helam laughed and tousled the boy's hair. "Not tonight, but maybe tomorrow." He tightened his hold on Raquel's hand.

She tried to breathe normally, although her heart was now racing. She found herself hoping that the meal would be over soon, and everyone would just disappear for the evening—or even for a few days. Nerves twisted her stomach, making her feel excited and jumpy at the same time.

On the other side of the circle, Alma stood. "A final tribute to the married couple."

Raquel turned and looked at him expectantly. The joy in her heart and the love she had for those at her wedding brought tears to her eyes. She wished that Alma could find a wife to make him as happy as she was with Helam.

"We have all been waiting a long time for this day . . . a very long time," Alma said. "The wait is finally over, and a new family has been created."

Abe scrambled off of Raquel's lap. "I have a new family," he said with self-assurance.

"Yes," Alma said with a laugh. "And we've already seen blessings because of it." He paused significantly. "I no longer have to listen to Helam whine and mope around all day. A great blessing indeed."

Everyone laughed.

Then Helam pulled away from Raquel and stood. "Thank you for your kind words, Alma." He smiled. "I'm grateful too that now I'll have a better excuse *not* to spend time with you."

Laughing, Alma nodded and sat down.

Helam sobered. "This day has required years of patience." He looked at his mother. "One person never gave up, although it wasn't quite what she expected." Esther brought a hand to her chest, her eyes tearing up. Then he looked at Itzel. "I'm blessed to have known and loved my new mother-in-law for quite a while before she officially took on that title."

Itzel nodded and mouthed, "Thank you."

"What about me? You knew me too," Abe piped in.

Helam laughed and looked at Abe. "Especially you." His gaze moved to Raquel. "I don't think it's possible for a man to be happier than I am right now." He reached out a hand toward Raquel.

She took it and let herself be pulled up by him. Then he surprised her. He put his hands on her waist and leaned down. In front of everyone, he kissed her. Really kissed her. Not like the quick peck at the wedding ceremony.

Raquel responded, wrapping her arms around his neck and pulling him closer, forgetting that everyone was watching. When Helam pulled back she put her hands to her hot face.

"I think the meal is over," Alma's voice said from somewhere far off.

Laughter floated around her, but Raquel couldn't take her eyes off Helam. He stared back with an unabashed smile on his face.

Someone came up behind her. "See you in the morning, dear," Itzel said, embracing Raquel.

She tried to focus on her mother, but her mind was still distracted. One by one, the wedding guests bid farewell until Itzel took Abe by the hand and led him away with promises of more honey-baked peanuts.

"Come on," Helam said, taking her hand. "I have someplace I'd like you to see."

"Where?" Raquel asked.

"It's a surprise." Helam tilted his head. "Come on."

She let him lead her along the river, wondering where he could possibly be taking her, but he refused to answer any questions. The sun was close to setting, and the twilight hour made the river look dark and deep. Finally he stopped near the bank. "Close your eyes."

Raquel looked around. There were a few scattered huts this far down the river, but not much else. She closed her eyes.

"Stay with me. It will only be a moment."

She let him lead her away from the river, past a stand of bushes with branches that brushed her clothing.

After a couple of moments, Helam came to a stop and released her hand. "All right. You can look."

Raquel opened her eyes. A large building of vertical timbers and a thatch roof stood in the clearing. The last glow of the sunset illuminated the structure against the backdrop of trees. It was the largest structure she'd seen since leaving the city of Nephi.

"What is this place? A new court building?"

Helam laughed. "It's your house."

She looked at him to see if he was serious. "It's much too big."

Helam put an arm around her. "Not if you think about a growing family."

"You're certainly ambitious."

"Perhaps a little," he said, pulling her closer. "Abe will have his own room. And there are two rooms in the back, should my mother or your mother decide to live with us."

"Or both," Raquel said with a shy smile. Her heart pounded at the thought of them being so far away from everyone. Just the two of them. The kiss Helam had given her came back to her memory vividly. She looked away quickly, trying to prevent the blush from returning.

Helam released her. "Come on, I'll show you."

Raquel took a deep breath and followed him. She didn't want to look at the house; she wanted him to kiss her again. But she followed him through each room and let him explain all of the finishing touches. She was overwhelmed at the work he must have put into this and marveled at the time it must have taken. Over each doorway delicate flowers had been carved into the lintel.

"Alma was really the mastermind," Helam said. "Did you know he was a carpenter before he was made a high priest in King Noah's court?"

"No," she said, following Helam into the cooking room. He'd thought of everything. Clay jugs lined one wall, and waterskins hung from wooden dowels. Over the hearth was a handsomely carved mantel. Several baskets stood in the corner, filled with grain.

"This is amazing." She gazed at the wooden stool by the hearth and imagined sitting there on a cool evening, tending the fire.

"Come see the back courtyard," he said.

She followed him outside then stopped and stared. It was nearly dark, but she could see how Helam had fashioned a low stone wall around a large garden plot. She walked slowly toward the patch of earth. Young plants were already poking through the soil. She stooped to examine the plant varieties—bean sprouts, squash starters. "Curaiao?" She rose and put her hands on her hips, looking at him. "Of course you would."

"Of course I would," Helam echoed.

"I thought you hated it when I put the ointment on your face."

He took a step closer, his gaze intent on her. "I never hated it."

She laughed. "Now you say that. So you want me to grow it? That's quite a change."

"I want you to have everything you'll ever need. Right here."

This time she reached for his hand. "I already do."

And as she'd hoped, he kissed her again.

* * *

Raquel let out a sigh as she stared at the moonlit window from across the room. She was in her new home with her new husband. It was incredible. She'd been so afraid to allow herself to love him, to marry him, and now . . . She turned her head and looked at Helam sleeping next to her. She wanted to wake him and tell him she was sorry for making him wait so long, but instead she reconciled herself to nestling against his chest.

He stirred and murmured something, his arm automatically pulling her closer. Raquel listened to the beat of his heart, its pulse mirroring her own. *Safe at last.* She knew pain and loss and unbearable grief, so she cherished having this sweet moment with her new husband more than she ever could have imagined.

In the morning, she'd return to her usual tasks as a mother, a daughter, and a teacher. But for tonight she was just a wife—Helam's wife. She lifted her face and kissed his jaw line. His eyes fluttered open.

"I suppose we're not sleeping tonight?" he asked, his voice thick with sleep.

"I suppose not." She smiled and turned away.

"Oh, no you don't." He grabbed her shoulder and turned her back toward him. She laughed and struggled as if to get away, but he held her firm until she relaxed in his arms. "That's better."

He kissed her until she thought she might burst into a thousand pieces. When he drew away, he was smiling.

"That *is* better," she said.

Helam laughed and wrapped her tightly in his arms. Then suddenly, he released her and sat up.

"What is it?" she asked.

"Someone's coming."

Raquel turned and looked toward the window. Helam pulled a cloak over his shoulders. "Wait here."

"Are you sure?" She hadn't heard anything, but she didn't want to wait alone. She rose and pulled a robe around her, then padded out of the bedchamber.

She heard the murmur of voices as she entered the cooking room, where the visitor held a torch. "Ben?"

The boy looked over at her, his eyes wide in the flickering light. "Alma says we must assemble immediately. There's not a moment to waste."

"Why? For what?" Raquel asked, looking from Ben to Helam.

"An army has been spotted," Helam said in a quiet voice. "Alma thinks it might be Lamanites."

She drew in a sharp breath. "How many?"

Ben shook his head. "Alma didn't say, he just—"

Helam touched Ben's shoulder. "You should go finish delivering the message. We'll gather our family and be there shortly."

Ben nodded and hurried out.

Helam crossed to Raquel and put his hands on her shoulders. "I'll take you to your mother and Abe."

She stared at him, disbelief ringing in her head. What could Lamanites want with them *here*? The valley of Helam was well north of the borders of Lamanite lands.

"What about you?" she whispered, feeling her throat burn.

"I'll have to report to Alma to find out his plan."

She shook her head. "No."

Helam looked surprised. "We don't have time to argue about this, Raquel. I have no idea how much time we have as it is."

She backed away from him, feeling her body start to tremble. "I lost one husband already."

In one step, Helam was at her side, gathering her into his arms. "You're not going to lose me."

She pulled away, blinking back tears. "You can't promise me that."

"Yes, I can. And I won't lose you," he said, holding her hands.

She felt her knees start to buckle. She had to get to Abe and her mother, but she also couldn't let Helam leave her side.

"Raquel, look at me," Helam said, his voice insistent. "The Lord will preserve us."

She shook her head, tears spilling onto her cheeks. "I—I can't believe that. I've been through this before."

Helam touched her chin and tilted it upward. "I don't know what will happen tonight, but we'll be together afterward. I know it." He took her hand and put it on his heart. "I feel it here."

Raquel nodded slowly. "How can you really know?"

Helam held her gaze, unwavering. Then he placed his hands on either side of her face and kissed her.

She clung to him, desperate to forget Ben's words. Finally, Helam pulled away, and she couldn't ignore reality anymore.

"Let's go," he said, taking her hand. "I want you in the center of the city with everyone else. This home is too isolated."

They took nothing with them as they left the brand-new home. Raquel gripped Helam's hand as they hurried along the river toward her mother's. They spotted several other families moving in the same direction. At the top of the bend, the groups turned toward the city.

Helam and Raquel turned in the opposite direction. Soon they reached Itzel's hut.

"There you are," she said from the entrance. "Are you two all right?"

"Yes," Raquel said. "Where's Abe?"

"He's still sleeping. I was waiting until you came for him."

Raquel pushed past her mother and went inside. She scooped Abe up in her arms, and Helam met her at the door. "Let me carry him."

She handed him over and turned to her mother. "How many Lamanites?"

"I haven't heard."

"You're here!" a voice spoke behind them.

Raquel turned to see Esther. She scurried to them, her expression filled with despair. "We need to hurry. Everyone is almost gone."

"Come on then," Helam said.

Raquel linked arms with Esther and Itzel. "I can't believe we're doing this again." The memory of Lamanites attacking their small settlement and burning their huts returned with full force.

"There are many more of us," Esther said as if to comfort, but her tone of voice was far from comforting.

Raquel's stomach churned. She felt literally sick with worry as she stared at her husband walking in front of her. His strong shoulders and powerful body would be a force against any Lamanite, but she didn't want him to take any risk.

As they neared the center of the city, they were joined by several other families traveling in the same direction. They carried bedrolls and sleepy children into the main market, which teemed with people. For such a large gathering, it was relatively quiet—from fear, anticipation, or both.

Helam made sure that Abe was settled on a bedroll. He leaned down to kiss the top of Abe's head then turned to face Raquel. She wrapped her arms around his waist. "Don't leave me."

He held her for a moment. "I'll be back."

Then he was gone, hurrying off through the crowd toward Alma. The leaders of the city hovered around Alma, and when Helam reached them, they welcomed him.

She strained to hear what was going on, but the low murmur from the crowd prevented her from catching any bits of conversation. Around her people whispered their speculations.

Then a ripple went through the crowd. Several blacksmiths had started handing out weapons. A shiver touched Raquel. There was no turning back now. This was real.

CHAPTER 19

. . . [have] patience and faith in all your persecutions
and tribulations that ye endure.
(2 Thessalonians 1:4)

Alma watched the horizon change from dusty purple to pale gray. He stood with Helam and several other men, trying to estimate the number of warriors in the approaching army. A dozen paces behind him, the men of the city stood in organized rows, armed with swords and spears. Thirty of the Nephite men had remained with the women and children.

There weren't enough men to defend their city against any sort of army. This force looked to comprise about three hundred men. Even though the number of trained soldiers probably equaled the number of men in the city of Helam, the battle would be fierce and too many lives lost.

Next to him, Helam spoke his thoughts aloud. "What will this cost us? Our lives? Our freedom?"

Alma's stomach tightened. He hoped these Lamanites would be more merciful than the Nephites of Noah's court. Then he noticed something odd behind the first line of warriors—two hooded figures much smaller than any of the warriors. "Look behind those soldiers on the left. Are those women?"

"Why would the Lamanites bring women with them?" Helam asked.

Alma frowned as they marched closer. Their leader strode with confidence in the center, wearing an elaborate feathered cape.

Taking a deep breath, Alma took a step forward. "Wait here," he told the surrounding men. "If I approach alone, they'll know that I want only peace." He walked slowly, deliberately, feeling hundreds of Lamanite eyes on him. Their bare torsos glistened with perspiration in the growing light, expressions brutal.

Alma stopped about a dozen paces from the first line. He raised his arms slowly and turned around, showing that he wasn't armed. The Lamanite commander extracted himself from his wall of protection and moved forward, stopping a couple of paces from Alma. The two looked each other up and down.

"Who are you people?" the Lamanite commander asked.

"Nephites. We were driven out of the city of Nephi by our king," Alma said. "This is the land of Helam. We cultivated it and built our own city."

The leader's brow furrowed. "King Limhi did not care for your people, perhaps?"

"King *Limhi?* What happened to King Noah?"

"Noah's people killed him a couple of years ago, burning him by fire."

Alma's mind reeled. It was just as Abinadi had prophesied. One of the Lamanites stepped from the ranks and joined his leader's side. Alma stared at the second man in disbelief. The man had thinned considerably, but his body was still muscular. Even with the shaved beard, Alma recognized his former friend. "Amulon?"

The man smiled. "Well, well. Is this where you've been hiding?"

The commander looked from Alma to Amulon. "You know him?"

"Very well, actually," Amulon said. "We served together under King Noah, but this man became a traitor. It was our king's dying wish to bring him to justice."

Alma narrowed his eyes and stared at the imposter-Lamanite. "You're calling *me* a traitor?"

Amulon laughed. "Fair enough." He looked at Zorihor. "Commander, we don't have anything to fear from this man or his people."

Alma bristled but held his tongue. Amulon was not the man in power here, yet he must have some influence with the commander; they were certainly friendly toward each other.

"Ah, that's fortunate for you, then," Zorihor said to Alma.

"We are a peaceful people," Alma said. "We can provide food and drink for your passing army."

Zorihor's eyes lit with amusement. "I'm sure my men would appreciate that." He looked at Amulon, who nodded, then back to Alma. "In fact, since you're a prior resident of the city of Nephi, we would be grateful if you'd direct us that way."

"Another conquest?" Alma asked.

"Not exactly," Amulon cut in. "The Lamanites have controlled the city of Nephi since Noah was exiled."

"I'm happy to provide you with a map and with whatever supplies you might require," Alma said, "as long as you promise to leave our people unmolested."

Zorihor folded his arms across his chest and scanned the valley. "We'll stay a few days and refresh ourselves."

Alma let out a sigh of relief. "Very well. The northern end is a good place to set up camp. There's a freshwater river and plenty of trees for shade."

Zorihor nodded his agreement.

"I'll bring you a map soon," Alma said. When he turned to face his own small group of soldiers, he could see relief in their expressions. He smiled encouragement as he walked back, although his mind was still troubled. Zorihor had been too accomodating. And he didn't trust Amulon at all. The man still had greed in his eyes.

Alma walked to the center row of his waiting soldiers and motioned for everyone to gather around him. "The Lamanites wish to camp here for a few days, and we'll provide some food and supplies for them before they continue their journey to the city of Nephi. Apparently, it's been under Lamanite occupation for some time." He looked into the eyes of the men who trusted him. "I don't want to worry you unnecessarily, but keep your families close until the Lamanites have departed. Also, keep your weapons at hand." He met Helam's gaze, knowing he'd have to tell him about Amulon.

The men filtered away, rejoicing that there would be no battle today and hopeful that the Lamanites would leave them in peace.

As Alma predicted, Helam stayed behind.

"What's wrong?" he asked as soon as they were alone.

"Amulon is with them."

"The second in command?"

Alma nodded. "I don't trust him. He seems to be close to the Lamanite commander—might even be able to tell him what to do."

Helam let out a low whistle. "My father-in-law is a Lamanite now?"

"Apparently so," Alma said, wondering if Amulon suspected that his wife and daughter were here.

"What will Itzel think?" Helam said. "And Raquel is not going to be happy."

"Do you want me to come with you to speak to them?"

"No," Helam said in a quiet voice. "I'll do it."

"Before you do, call together the council. There is much to be done—this is all too convenient for Amulon not to persecute us in some way." He threw a glance in Amulon's direction, then leaned close to Helam as they walked. "I want secret patrols organized and guards at every possible entrance into the city."

"Yes, sir."

* * *

From within the ranks of Lamanite soldiers, Maia watched Alma walk away and become swallowed up in the fold of his men. She couldn't believe it was him. He was even more handsome and commanding than she'd remembered, yet he still had the quiet strength and conviction of a true believer. A believer who hadn't neglected his faith in any way.

Alma's men crowded around him to listen. Maia wanted to cry out and run to him; tell him that she was here and ask him about her parents. But if she did, Amulon would find a way to punish her.

To see him strong and healthy was comforting—perhaps her parents were thriving. Her throat tightened. To know that her parents were alive and well was more than she could ask for. She thought about her parents being protected under such a great leader. What would they think when they saw her?

Maybe I won't show my face until we're gone from this city, Maia thought as she pulled her mantle closer. But how could she not look for her parents? She must see them. Glancing over at Cochiti, Maia wondered how much she could really trust her.

The Lamanite soldiers had started their retreat. Maia followed them, moving as slowly as possible. If she could only catch a glimpse of her parents . . . but the only people she could see were young men. As the Lamanites moved across the field, the Nephite soldiers dispersed, leaving only Alma and one other man.

"Where are we going?" Cochiti whispered.

Maia tore her gaze away from Alma. "We're camping here for a few days, then we'll continue to the city of Nephi."

"Good. I'm exhausted."

Maia touched the woman's arm absently. She was worn out at the end of each day's marching, so she could only imagine Cochiti's discomfort.

They moved north to the far edge of the field, where the Lamanite leader commanded that the tents be staked. Maia and Cochiti unrolled the tents, although most of the men would sleep in the open. They went through the routine, saying little to each other. Maia thought hard about whether she could escape after dark and make some inquiries after her parents.

When the camp was settled, the men started to complain of hunger. Several Nephites arrived with jugs of wine and bundles of fruits and vegetables on their backs. Amulon greeted the men warmly then relieved them of their burden. He took a drink from one of the jugs immediately before passing it on to some waiting soldiers.

Maia kept her mantle pulled close to her face as she scanned the faces of the Nephites, but she didn't recognize any of them.

Amulon caught her looking, and she moved away, dragging one of the bundles toward the cooking fire. She avoided looking at the Nephites again. After the Nephites had departed, Amulon sidled up to her as she cut open a squash and scooped out the insides.

"Looking for Alma?"

Maia's face heated, but she avoided his gaze. "I'm wondering about my parents, actually."

"Ah, Jachin and Lael. They always were good citizens."

Maia cast him a sharp look, and he bellowed with laughter.

"Don't worry. I'm sure Alma can answer all of your questions tonight."

"Tonight?" she practically whispered.

He reached over and touched the edge of her mantle where it framed her face. "When Alma delivers the map, of course. He's going to show us how to get back to the city of Nephi. But I can assure you that I'm not going anywhere. I rather like this valley." He smiled as she glanced at him, his eyes burning into hers. "It's much too inter-esting here. And it will be my pleasure to reintroduce you to Alma."

For an instant, Maia hoped Amulon was being sincere. She could ask Alma about his wife and children. She wanted to tell him how much he'd taught her in that single visit at her parents' home—and that she was still trying to keep the faith.

But when Amulon moved close and pushed back the mantle from her head, she knew that it wasn't going to be easy to face Alma in her present circumstance—even if he was married and happily settled.

"Maybe we can ask him to marry *us* in secret. The Lamanites wouldn't have to know," Amulon whispered, tugging on a lock of her hair. "After all, he *is* a Nephite high priest. It would be more than appropriate, don't you think?"

Maia drew away, repulsed at the touch and suggestion.

"Now, don't you go silent on me again," Amulon said, his tone smooth and demeaning. "In fact, maybe we'll have you sing for our company tonight."

Maia shook her head and blinked against stinging tears.

"It will be a pleasure . . . for everyone." Amulon moved away slightly, his hand trailing along her arm, then lingering at her waist. She closed her eyes as he leaned close and said, "I'll be looking forward to it all day."

When she opened her eyes, he was gone. But his words remained.

* * *

"We want to come with you," Raquel told Alma.

"It's not safe," he said, looking between Raquel and Iztel. Helam hovered behind them, concern on his face. It was nearly dark, just before the evening meal. "I don't trust Amulon, and I don't know the whole story of how he came to be with the Lamanites or what their true intentions are." He wanted to visit with Zorihor as soon as possible and hand over the map, hoping it would encourage the Lamanites to leave sooner than later.

"You mean you don't think they'll leave us in peace?" Itzel asked.

Alma met Helam's gaze. "I *hope* they'll leave us in peace."

Itzel turned away, twisting her hands in agitation. Raquel moved to her mother's side and put an arm around her shoulders.

"It will be better this way," Helam said, adding his words to Alma's. "We'll tell him that you're both here and see what his reaction is. We don't want to put you in any danger."

"All right," Raquel said, obvious reluctance in her voice. She looked at Helam. "I'm more worried about you than me."

Helam smiled. "One of your faults."

"Be careful," Raquel said, not matching his light tone. She turned to Alma. "You, too."

Alma nodded, and Helam joined him. Three other men waited for them, one of them Jachin. They had collected some gifts to bring along, hoping to encourage the Lamanites to leave. The men started out, and Alma cringed inwardly as the sun set, casting its golden web across the homes of the city of Helam. Anyone could see how well tended and cared for the buildings and fields were. At this time of day, its beauty rivaled that of any Nephite or Lamanite city.

Something to covet and desire.

"Amulon once pledged to hunt you down and kill you, right?" Helam said, his voice quiet.

"Yes," Alma said with a grimace. "And I don't think he's forgotten it."

"With King Noah dead, and Amulon's allegiance somewhere else, maybe he'll be more merciful."

"Perhaps," Alma said, although he was far from convinced. Seeing Amulon brought it all back—life in King Noah's court and the waste of a man that he'd allowed himself to become. The first time he'd heard Abinadi preach, and the years it had taken to change his soul. And of course, Maia. Amulon would know what became of her. Had she remarried after the king's death? Was she still a believer? How did she fare paying tribute to the Lamanites like the rest of Limhi's people?

They neared the river and started to follow it as it wound its way to the Lamanite camp. In the twilight, the churning color of the river seemed to mock Alma. It was the exact color of Maia's gray-green eyes, as if she were watching him, asking him what had become of her parents. Would he let these Lamanite soldiers take over the city and allow her parents to fall under their rule?

Was this their fate then? Run every couple of years from the enemy—whether it be Nephite or Lamanite?

The orange glow of the cooking fire reflected off the surrounding trees as they approached the camp. It looked as if the tents had been hastily constructed. Alma hoped that meant they could be hastily taken down as well.

"There *are* women," Helam said, his voice incredulous.

Alma followed his gaze and saw two shrouded forms on the other side of the fire.

"Why would they bring women on a military operation?" Jachin asked.

"Greetings!" a voice boomed from near one of the tents. The tall Lamanite commander stepped into view.

Alma came to a halt, his men stopping with him. "Commander Zorihor." The two women rose and retreated behind a tent.

Suddenly Amulon was in front of them, his greedy smile as wide as ever. "What a pleasant surprise." But his expression said that he was definitely expecting them.

"You brought the map with you?" Zorihor asked.

"I have it here," Alma said, patting the side of his robe. He intended to have some of his questions answered before handing over the map. He motioned to the men who came with him. "We've brought tokens of peace as well."

"Very well," the commander said. "Come sit by the fire. Our women will serve you our wine—as a matter of fact, it's your *own* wine that was sent over earlier."

Amulon laughed, and Alma graciously smiled.

Once the men were settled around the fire, Alma wasted no time in speaking. "Tell us what happened to the city of Nephi and King Noah."

Amulon let out a yawn and folded his arms over his chest. "Let's have that wine first."

Almost directly the two women reappeared, still wearing head coverings, their faces shadowed. Alma immediately felt uncomfortable.

One was obviously Lamanite; her dark hands protruded from her robe. But the other woman had fair hands. *Leave it to Amulon,* Alma thought. The man seemed to mix with strange company—whoever suited him at the moment. Alma thanked the dark-skinned woman who handed over a cup of the sweet nectar and took a small sip. He didn't want to let his mind grow clouded in any way.

The women disappeared again, and Amulon started his story.

Alma concentrated on every word, from the burning of the elders' settlement to Gideon's attack on the king to Amulon's injuries and then to the approaching Lamanites. He was certain Amulon distorted the truth when he talked about how it was impossible for the king and high priests to return to the city without being killed by the Lamanites.

All the while, Alma was desperate to ask how Maia had fared. Was she safe in the city? Had she fled with the people?

Zorihor filled in the rest of the details of Limhi's rule over the Nephites and their two years of subservience to the Lamanites. "Then came that terrible day when we found twenty-four of our daughters missing. King Laman was crazed with grief—his daughter, Inda, was among the missing." He glanced at Amulon. "Limhi and his people were blamed. But Limhi pled his case and reminded the king about the high priests who had escaped."

Zorihor continued. "King Laman was pacified for a time, but still the daughters were missing. Several days later, a battle ensued. When Limhi and his people escaped in the dead of night, I was sent after them." Zorihor clapped a hand on Amulon's shoulder. "That's when we became lost. On our return to the city of Nephi, we stumbled across the city of Amulon."

"We had the daughters of the Lamanites with us," Amulon said in a quiet voice. "We had made some of them our wives—"

Zorihor leaned forward, clasping his hands. "I've never seen anything so extraordinary. Many of our Lamanite women had learned to love their Nephite husbands and wanted to remain in the city of Amulon."

Alma stared at the two men. It *was* incredible.

Leaning back again, Zorihor studied the Nephites. "You have a healthy settlement here."

"Very *small,* but we are happy with it," Alma said, looking at Amulon, who stared at him with amusement on his face. Alma stood and withdrew the map from his robe, then handed it over to Zorihor. The Lamanite studied it in the firelight, while Amulon looked over his shoulder.

"How many days' travel to the city of Nephi?" Zorihor said.

"With men only, probably six or seven."

Zorihor nodded. "Thank you. We'll likely leave in the morning." He looked up at Alma. "If we can have more supplies."

Alma tried to hide his relief. "Certainly. Anything you need."

"Anything?" Amulon asked, a smirk on his face.

Helam and Jachin's expressions tightened. They were trying their best not to break out into a fight.

Moving casually back to his seat, Alma sat. "We have some of your relatives in our city, Amulon." If Amulon was surprised, he didn't show it. Alma hoped that this revelation would encourage the Lamanite commander to have even more compassion upon their people.

"I have a new family now," Amulon said, his eyes glinting.

"One of the stolen daughters of the Lamanites?" Alma said, feeling disgust well up inside of him. Next to him, Helam clenched his fists.

But Zorihor's eyes had brightened with interest across the crackling fire. "Perhaps your relatives would like to join us on the way back to the city?"

Alma suppressed a smile at the shock on Amulon's face. He, for one, knew Amulon's "relatives" would never do such a thing.

"I don't think it would be wise," Amulon said. "I was betrayed by them a long time ago." His gaze seared into Alma's.

"Don't you care to know how they're doing?"

"No," Amulon said in a tone of finality. "I have a new family now. One that will never betray me."

"You mean—you've remarried?" Helam asked.

Everyone looked at him, surprised that the large man had spoken up. Amulon narrowed his eyes. "Yes, I've remarried. We're expecting a child soon."

"A Lamanite woman?" Helam said.

"Who are you?" Amulon stood.

Before Alma could grab his arm, Helam also stood. "I'm your son-in-law."

Amulon flinched, then recovered quickly, pasting a smooth smile on his face. "That's impossible. For, you see, to be my son-in-law, I'd need a daughter. And I have no daughter."

The two men stared at each other across the fire, equal loathing in both of their stares. After a tense moment, Helam said in a low voice, "And it seems that your daughter has no father."

Then Zorihor stood as well, looking between the men. "Should we have our entertainment?"

Amulon's demeanor changed in an instant to friendly ease, and he clapped his hands together. "Yes! It's the least we can do to thank our generous *friends* here." He ignored Helam and looked directly at Alma. "It will be such a pleasure for everyone."

Alma frowned. What sort of entertainment did they have in mind? He tugged on Helam's arm, forcing him to sit. "As soon as this is over," Alma said, "we'll leave as quickly as possible. There's nothing left for us to do here."

Helam tore his fierce gaze from Amulon, then whispered, "Don't you want to ask them about Maia?"

"I do, but I don't think I'd believe anything that came out of his vile mouth anyway."

"I understand," Helam said, his expression sober.

Zorihor shouted to one of the soldiers to bring the entertainment, and in a few moments, the two veiled women appeared.

A Lamanite started playing a drum, and several more soldiers joined the circle to watch as the women started dancing. Alma and his men observed politely, offering none of the cheers that the Lamanites did, although from time to time they clapped in rhythm with the drum beat. Alma took a few quick glances at the fair woman, wondering how she had come to be with these soldiers. Perhaps she was a slave of some sort—or even one of the Lamanites' wives.

The music stopped, and Amulon clapped loudly. "Now we'll hear a song."

The Lamanite woman stepped back, and the fair woman stayed in place. She was on the outer edge of the circle, where the light from the fire just touched her. One more step back and she'd be in the shadows. Then he noticed something odd. Her hands were trembling. A new thought entered Alma's head—*maybe she's as uncomfortable as we are.* He found himself watching her hands in fascination, then in anger. This woman must not be used to performing, and it was cruel of the Lamanites to force her. He felt sick at the thought of whatever else she may have been forced to do.

The woman started to sing in a low voice, which soon climbed in pitch and increased in speed. Alma stared at the shrouded form, listening to the beautiful melody, but it was not the music that entranced him. He rose to his feet, gripping Helam's shoulder in the process.

Now he understood the woman's trembling hands.

But before he could react, Jachin cried out, "Maia?"

The name sent a jolt of shock through Alma's body. Questions tumbled in his mind as he watched Jachin rush around the fire. The woman stopped singing and drew back into the shadows.

Was it really her?

Alma held his breath as everyone stared at Jachin.

"Maia?" he said in a quieter voice this time.

She moved back slightly, then suddenly she stepped forward and threw her arms around Jachin's neck. "Father!"

"It's you! It's really you!" he said, holding onto her and rocking back and forth.

Everything slowed to a crawl, and Alma saw Amulon's mouth open with laughter, his hands coming together in delight. The Lamanites murmured among themselves, stunned at what was happening. Helam had grabbed Alma's arm to steady him or to hold him back. It didn't matter. He was too dumbstruck to move or speak.

Why is Maia with the Lamanites? With Amulon? He watched as she removed her veil, her dark hair spilling over her shoulders, catching the light of the fire. She looked different, yet very much the same.

"Is it really her?" a voice said next to him.

Alma looked at Helam, still unable to speak. He simply nodded, then turned to watch Maia and her father. They had pulled apart, and Jachin was questioning her. Unable to hear her answers, Alma took a tentative step closer, but he froze in place when Amulon said, "Surprised, Alma?"

He looked at his former friend, abhorrence welling up inside him. "What have you done?"

"I'll let her tell you herself." Amulon's grin widened.

Alma shook his head and looked away, his hands clenching in fists. His eyes locked with Maia's across the circle. She still had one hand on her father's arm, but her eyes were on him.

"Please," she said, breaking her gaze and turning to Zorihor. "Let me go to my parents."

Zorihor cast a glance at Amulon, confusion in his eyes.

"We can pay you a price," Jachin said. "The amount that you would lose for her . . . services."

Amulon laughed. "Services? Is that what you call it?" His gaze traveled to Alma. "She has been little pleasure to me." He waved his hand as if dismissing Maia, but she didn't budge. "She's a deceiver at best. And her cooking and serving skills are minimal."

Alma couldn't help but look at Maia again. Her head was lowered as if she was trying to avoid Amulon's piercing words.

"Yet I'm not quite ready to let her go," Amulon announced. He looked at the Lamanite commander, who nodded his approval. "Tomorrow morning she may come to your city of her own free will. *If* she chooses." Then, almost too quietly to be heard, he added, "And *if* you still want her."

The last words were spoken directly to Alma, making his skin crawl.

Maia raised her head but said nothing. Amulon's gaze remained on Alma.

"Thank you," Jachin said in a loud voice. "Her mother and I will be most pleased and grateful."

"And pleasing is what I love to do," Amulon said, his voice thick with sarcasm.

Alma felt Helam's restraining hand on his arm. "We need to walk away," he whispered. "Before we sacrifice all of our people for this one woman."

Alma knew he was right, but there was little else holding him back from attacking Amulon right here and now.

They made formal gestures of departing to Zorihor. Alma didn't dare look at Maia as they left. He knew she watched from the shadows, and he cringed to think of why Amulon insisted that she stay one more night.

As they trudged along the river, Alma's heart grew heavier. Finally he stopped when they were safely out of sight and sound of the Lamanite camp. "I can't leave her, but I can't endanger our people either," he said, careful to keep his voice steady.

Helam was the first to respond. "We'll put together a guard, keeping within sight of the camp. If Amulon tries anything, we'll be the first to know."

"I want to be a part of that guard," Jachin said.

"And you need to return to the city center so that everyone will know that their leader is safe," Helam continued, looking at Alma.

Alma studied his two good friends. "All right. I'll send six men."

Gratitude showed plain in Jachin's expression. "Let's hurry."

CHAPTER 20

I will bear; even I will carry, and will deliver you.
(Isaiah 46:4)

Maia's hands trembled as she folded her veil and set it near her bedroll. She knew Amulon was coming for her. She'd seen him deliberately drink wine with Zorihor—getting the Lamanite so besotted that he'd fallen asleep by the fire. The commander would know nothing until morning; plus he would never believe her over Amulon—their friendship was too close.

She looked at the surrounding tent walls that had been a sanctuary against his leering eyes. Tonight they would confine her to a terrible fate. A fate she knew had been coming for a long time, yet she had continued to deny.

She didn't know if her father or any of the other men understood why Amulon insisted she wait until morning before reuniting with her parents. But *she* knew. Amulon would give her up once and for all only when he'd had his way with her. She'd be tainted, ruined, after tonight. No man, not even one as forgiving as Alma, would want her. She'd spend the rest of her days living as a single, childless woman— her only hope of a man's love extinguished.

But if she resisted or tried to fight Amulon off—or even somehow escaped—the people living in the city of Helam would pay the price. Her one sacrifice would spare them the temper of Amulon and his corrupting influence on Zorihor.

I just have to make that sacrifice, Maia thought as the tears came. *I can do it. If I can survive King Noah, I can survive Amulon.*

But this was different. Amulon wouldn't even marry her first. He'd do nothing to displease Zorihor, as the Lamanites frowned on multiple wives. No, Amulon would do his worst to ensure that when the sun rose she was no better than a broken woman.

Maia sank to her knees, her breath coming in short gasps. She had to gain control of herself. She had to relax. She didn't want to give Amulon any reason or justification to kill her. Despite her loathing of Amulon and her fear of how she might appear in others' eyes, she still wanted to live. Even through the surprise she'd seen in Alma's face when he realized who she really was, even though she could never amount to anything in his eyes, she still wanted to live.

Perhaps it was her basic instinct of survival. *I can close my mind off,* she decided. *I can bear one torturous night to obtain my freedom.* Maia clasped her hands together and closed her eyes. "O Lord," she whispered, "give me the strength for what I now must endure."

Tears trickled down her cheeks as she tried to choke back the impending sobs. "Protect this great city. Protect my family—my parents . . ."

"There you are," a man's voice said.

Maia's heart nearly stopped at the deep voice.

Amulon entered the tent. "What are you doing?"

She scrambled to her feet, her pulse racing. Her throat felt tight as she took in Amulon's appearance. It appeared that he had washed up. His black hair had been slicked back with oil, and his face was clean-shaven, making him look the part of a Lamanite. But nothing had changed about his eyes—they were filled with greed as usual.

His head nearly touched the ceiling of the tent, and he seemed to fill the entire space. Even if she tried to escape, she'd never make it out—she was no match for a man his size.

"I said, what are you doing?" Amulon asked again.

"I was . . ."

"Praying?" Amulon's tone was filled with spite. "That's what started all this in the first place."

Maia looked at him, confused.

"Or have you forgotten that I was the one who had you thrown into prison?" He took a step toward her, lowering his voice. "For insisting on the power of your god."

Maia stiffened as he reached out and touched her face.

"Such a waste," Amulon said in a gravelly voice. "A beautiful face on a liar never did any man any good."

The tips of his fingers moved along her cheek to her jawbone.

She drew away from his touch, but there was really nowhere to go that he wasn't. "I never lied."

Amulon tilted his head, smiling as if he'd anticipated her response. "You're one of the best. That's why I like you so much. If you consider it, we're two of the same."

Maia opened her mouth to argue, but Amulon grabbed her arms and pulled her roughly to him.

"But I didn't lie tonight, my dearest," he hissed in her ear. "Tomorrow you will go and live with your parents, pine after Alma, or whatever else you want to do. But I'm going to make sure that no man will ever look at you except with pity."

His mouth pressed against hers, and Maia thought she'd collapse from terror. His hands held her arms so tightly that she knew they'd soon be blue from bruising. She wanted to scream at him, scratch him, kick him, anything, but knew she couldn't.

As Amulon's kissing became more demanding she fought the nausea in her stomach and tried to think of something else. *Anything.* But it was impossible. Hot tears burned in her eyes and spilled onto her cheeks.

Then, suddenly, he shoved her down and pinned her to the ground. She closed her eyes and turned her face away as he started to pull at her clothing.

Maybe death would be better than this. At least my death. She bit her lip hard, thinking of her parents and how they meant more to her than anything—even one night of agony.

Silent sobs wracked her body as she tried to convince herself that she could endure this one man. His shifted his weight, nearly crushing her, and she could barely move. Then her chest constricted in panic, and she fought to breathe. Something in her mind snapped and there was no longer any calming reason, any passivity.

"No," she gasped, clawing at him.

Amulon slapped her. Hard. "One more sound, and I'll make your parents pay too," he growled in her ear. "Then Alma will be next."

Maia dug her nails into his shoulders and tried to push him off, but he was too heavy.

A whoosh of air touched her feet, but Maia barely noticed it. Then she felt a presence in the tent. Another whoosh of air, and Amulon collapsed on top of her.

Maia felt as if she'd suffocate; she couldn't even get enough breath to cry out. Suddenly Amulon rolled off of her. She gasped for air and looked up. Staring down at her was Conchiti, a bloody rock in her hand.

Maia grasped at her torn clothing, and Cochiti reached down and pulled her to her feet.

"Take this," the woman said, wrapping a robe around Maia's shoulders. "Flee to the city. Amulon will never know what happened." She glanced at the prostrate figure. "He'll think it was Zorihor or someone who didn't want to see a woman assaulted."

Maia wiped her eyes with a trembling hand, then fell into Cochiti's arms, sobbing.

"There's no time for that," Cochiti said in a firm voice, stroking Maia's hair. "You must leave now. I'll tell him Zorihor let you leave. He won't dare question the commander about your departure."

Maia sniffed and pulled away. "How can I thank you?"

Shaking her head, Cochiti said, "Your safety is my thanks."

Maia opened her mouth to protest, but Cochiti raised her hand. "I do not wish to know all that has transpired between you, but my husband's past must remain there. He and I will build a new future together with a new son." She touched her stomach.

"If you ever see Inda again, please explain to her," Maia said. She leaned toward Cochiti and kissed her cheek. "I'll never forget your kindness and your sacrifice." One more glance at Amulon sent a shudder through her.

Cochiti shooed her out of the tent, and Maia entered the dark night. *I am free!* she wanted to shout. Her entire body shook. She'd come so close to being . . . A chill shot through her limbs. If Cochiti had arrived only a moment or two later . . .

Go.

The words pierced her heart. Maia glanced once more at her tent, with Cochiti still inside, and wondered how long the woman would stand vigil over her unfaithful husband. Or what lies she might have to weave.

Maia started toward the river, where she imagined she would have the least possible chance of running into a Lamanite. She intended to cross the river and travel along the opposite side until she reached the city. Pulling the robe tighter about her shoulders, she was filled with even greater gratitude for Cochiti's courage.

She hurried around the tents, keeping as quiet as possible. The sound of the gurgling river loomed closer, slightly easing the fear in her chest. She quickened her pace to a near run along the bank, looking for a shallow place to cross. The farther she moved from the Lamanite camp, the more she felt tears build. If it weren't for Cochiti . . .

But she came just in time, Maia told herself.

"Thank you, O Lord," she whispered as the tears came hot and fast. She had been saved once again from Amulon. As her breathing grew heavy, she eased her pace and wiped the moisture from her cheeks. She had to try to stay calm until she reached the city of Helam and found her parents. If she thought about her close call too much, she would collapse and not be able to move another step.

Her arms throbbed and her face still stung from where Amulon had hit her. She touched her cool hand to her hot face, hoping the bruising would fade within a few days' time.

The river widened and slowed as it bent around a grove of trees. As Maia passed through the trees, she thought she heard a voice. Spinning around, she saw a figure moving toward the trees.

"Maia?" The voice was a loud whisper.

A wave of dread passed over her. Had someone discovered her absence already?

"Maia?" The voice was louder now—clearer.

"Father," Maia said, joy bursting through her. She ran to meet him and melted in his arms—good, strong, familiar arms. He patted her back and held her close. "They let you leave early?"

She nodded against his chest, fighting back the sheer urge to cry and laugh at the same time. "Amulon doesn't know that I've left, but his wife will protect me."

Her father drew back and studied her bruised and tear-stained face. "What happened?" he asked in a horrified whisper.

"He was going to . . . but his wife stopped him before—" Her voice choked into a sob, and her father pulled her close again.

"We'll get you to your mother as soon as possible," he murmured against her hair. "Are you all right to walk as far as the city?"

"Yes," Maia said, pulling away slightly and looking around. "But we should hurry."

Jachin nodded and put his fingers to his lips, then he let out a low, birdlike whistle. A moment later, five men appeared from various hiding places. One trudged across the river from the other side. Maia recognized him as one of the men who had been with Alma—the man with the scarred face who said he was Amulon's son-in-law. That meant Raquel had married this man after Abinadi's death. She shuddered to realize what Raquel would think if she knew what her father had become.

"Maia?" the scar-faced man said. He frowned as he noticed her welts.

She nodded, still clinging to her father.

"I'm Helam," he said. "And we're here to make sure that no more harm will befall you."

Relief washed over her as she stared at Helam and the four others. These men were here to help *her*. It was amazing.

She gave him a tremulous smile and said, "Thank you." It came out as a whisper though, and Maia felt her strength—and courage— fading fast.

It was well past midnight when the small group reached the city. Maia tried to keep up as best as she could, but her entire body ached. She slowed as they reached the first row of huts. "Where is your home?" she asked her father.

"Toward the marketplace, not much farther now," Jachin said. He supported her with one hand and peered at her with concern.

"I'll bring Raquel to treat those bruises," Helam said. "She'll know just the right poultice to use."

Raquel. Amulon's daughter. A tremor ran through Maia. She didn't want the woman to see her like this; Raquel would discover what her father had done.

"Perhaps I should just rest tonight," Maia said.

Helam shook his head. "I'll meet you at your place, Jachin."

And before Maia could say anything else, he was gone.

* * *

Alma hovered at the doorway of Jachin and Lael's hut, then walked away again, pacing. It was mid-morning and several hours since he'd been notified about Maia—and her condition. Jachin, and then Raquel, had assured him she was doing well, but he wouldn't truly be at peace until he saw her for himself.

As soon as first light broke, Alma had ordered his soldiers to station themselves along the edges of the city to keep watch on the activity in the Lamanite camp. Each hour he received a report, and he'd been relieved to hear that some of the tents had been taken down already. He hoped the Lamanites would move out before the end of the day.

Someone exited the hut, and Alma turned to see Raquel.

"How is she?" he asked, watching her face carefully.

She smiled in a harried way. "Maia's sleeping . . . finally. I thought she'd never stop crying, but other than that, the bruises will be gone in a few days."

Alma let out a breath, trying to not lose his temper in front of Raquel. They both knew what her father had tried to do to Maia, yet they also knew that if they tried to seek retribution, they'd put their entire city at risk.

"Jachin and Lael are exhausted from watching over her, but they refuse to leave her side," Raquel said. "I've left plenty of curaiao for the next treatment of poultices, and I've instructed Lael how to prepare them."

"Thank you," Alma said. "I'm sorry all this has happened so soon after your wedding."

"I'm just grateful that Maia is safe and reunited with her parents," she said sincerely. "She's very fortunate."

"Yes," he said in a quiet voice, understanding the deeper implication of her words. "I wish that the outcome could have been better for you and your mother."

"Me too," Raquel said, her eyes bright with tears. "I'm convinced that my father will never change his ways. With a new wife now, he's made his choices clear."

Alma stepped toward her and put a hand on her shoulder. "How's your mother doing?"

"As well as can be expected. I don't think she ever thought the day would come when she'd be faced with meeting her husband again."

"Let her know I'm praying for you both," Alma said.

Raquel brought a hand to her eyes and brushed away a tear. "Thank you." She sighed. "I needed to hear that. If you need anything else at all, please let me know."

Alma nodded and watched as she walked away. Then he stepped to the doorway of the hut, hesitating for a moment. A low murmur of voices came from inside. Maybe Maia was awake. He pushed open the reed door and peered into the dim room.

"Come in," Lael said. Both parents sat on either side of Maia—who looked to be sleeping.

Jachin stood as Alma entered. There were dark circles under his eyes, but he smiled.

"How is she?" Alma asked in a quiet voice.

Lael released Maia's hand and adjusted the coverlet. "Better." Worry dominated her expression.

"I can sit with her if the two of you could use a rest," Alma said.

Lael's gaze caught her husband's, and he nodded. "All right." She stood and crossed to Alma to kiss him on the cheek. "Thank you for your concern."

"If she needs anything, be sure to wake us," Jachin said.

"Certainly," Alma said. The couple shuffled into the back room, and after a couple of murmured sentences, all was quiet. Alma crossed to Maia's side and sat on the cushion her mother had just vacated.

His stomach tightened as he gazed at her bruises. The left side of her face was swollen; it was clear that she'd been hit hard and likely several times.

Alma reached for her hand, then hesitated. He knew he was here to comfort the sick, but seeing Maia again brought back all of the memories of his feelings for her when they lived in King Noah's court. And though he'd repented of his untoward thoughts, circumstances had changed drastically.

She was a widow now, and he was still unmarried. If he believed Helam's theory, the reason was lying right before him.

Is it possible? Alma wondered. *That I still care for her in such a way, making it impossible for me to give my heart to another woman?* He stared at her—her beauty still undimmed even by bruising. "Do you still have my heart?" he whispered.

Maia stirred slightly and mumbled something. Then she turned her face so that the bruised side was no longer visible. Alma gazed at her—this was the Maia he remembered. Beautiful, ethereal, though fine lines had crept near her eyes and mouth, suggesting further trials in her young life. He wondered again how she had come to be with Amulon and the Lamanites. Had she been his prisoner all along?

According to Helam, Maia had said the Lamanite woman was Amulon's wife, and the way that Maia was dressed led him to believe she was not a second wife or concubine. She had worn no jewelry like the Lamanite woman had. No symbol of ownership.

"What happened to you?" Alma whispered. She'd endured so much, and now this. At least she was here where he could protect her now. He'd gather his friends and build her a home near her parents, so that she'd be taken care of in her widowhood.

Maia stirred again, and her eyes fluttered open. Her gaze widened when she saw him, and her eyes instantly filled with tears.

For an instant Alma panicked, wondering if he should call her parents. But as he stood, she struggled to sit up and reached for his arm. "No. Stay."

Alma sank to the cushion, unable to look away from her bruised face.

"It seems you're always coming to my rescue," she said, her voice trembling with emotion.

"Are you all right?"

"Oh, Alma," she cried and reached for him.

He held her for a few moments until her shoulders stopped shaking. She finally pulled away and wiped away her tears. "I'm sorry. I shouldn't have done that."

"Done what?" Alma asked, trying to read her expression, but she was looking down at her twisting hands.

"Thrown myself at you. It's just that I'm so glad to see you . . . and my parents . . . and to finally be away from *him*." She looked up at him, her eyes rimmed in red. "Can your wife forgive me? A poor hapless woman who brings nothing but trouble on herself and forces you to come to her rescue?"

"Maia," Alma said, putting his hand over her twisting ones. "I have no wife."

Her head snapped up. "But . . ." A look of relief flooded her face. "I thought—assumed—that you had married." She brought a hand to her mouth. "Then you must be betrothed—"

"I'm not," Alma said, his gaze holding hers. He focused on the relief he saw on her face. What did it mean? Was this merely relief that she hadn't offended someone? Or did she still feel the same way about him—even after all this time and who knew what had happened in between? "Are *you* married?"

She shook her head, a smile touching her lips. "No."

"What about Amulon?"

Her face visibly paled. "He threatened to make me his wife many times but never did. The Lamanite commander would have frowned upon it." She averted her gaze. "Then last night—"

"You don't have to explain anything to me," Alma said in a soft voice.

"I want to," she said, her gaze meeting his then moving away again. "I want you to know that he didn't succeed." Her voice broke, and she took a deep breath. "He tried, but his wife came in and knocked him out."

"His *wife* did that?"

"Yes," Maia said in a small voice. "You see, Cochiti is in love with her husband, and she saved me . . . from him and from a horrible fate as a ruined woman."

Alma shook his head and reached for her hand. "Look at me, Maia." When she wouldn't, he gently touched her chin and guided her face upward. "No matter what's happened, you could never be a ruined woman."

Tears brimmed in her eyes again. "But you don't know what's happened."

"I know enough."

"I was a slave to the Lamanites for two years. They treated me kindly, and I became a servant to a princess. When Amulon and the priests captured the Lamanite daughters, I was among them and

Amulon intended to take me as a second wife. Only the hand of God saved me when He took my voice so that Amulon decided to wait." She pulled her hand away from his. "But why didn't God save the other women? I prayed for them as well."

"Maia," Alma said, "if I understand the situation, the other women came to love their husbands and refused to return to their people—this is not your fault."

But she shook her head. "You must look on me with abhorrence. Raquel told me you are the leader of this city and the new church. Everyone looks to you with respect and admiration." She looked down and whispered, "I am the opposite of everything you are."

"Do you still believe?" he asked.

Maia nodded, tears splashing on her hand. "With all my heart. The Lord has answered my prayers too many times to count. I just wish that I could protect everyone else as well, including the Lamanite women I've come to love." She wiped her cheeks. "Everywhere I go, I'm in the way, and I bring more sorrow to those who care about me. It's as if I don't belong or can't do any good."

"You belong here. Trust me," Alma said. "We are building a community here unto the Lord. We are raising a righteous genera-tion, and we need all of the faithful believers we can get." He lowered his voice. "I'd be honored if you'd be part of the city of Helam."

She looked at him for a moment without saying anything.

"Maia, I've never seen your father happier than when he held you in his arms last night."

She bit her lip, acknowledgment in her eyes. "Nor I." Then she tilted her head, her eyes clear and dry. "Why is it that a man such as you isn't married? I thought that surely you'd have a wife and children by now."

Alma looked at her in surprise, his heart thudding. Even with her bruising, she was the most beautiful woman he'd ever seen. But it was more than that—it was the way she'd been through so many trials that would have broken another person's character, yet here she was, awake and alive and asking him the question he'd been asking himself for more months than he cared to count.

It was his turn to twist his hands together. "Interesting that you should ask. Helam likes to revisit that question every few months."

"And what's your answer to him?" she asked.

Alma studied her. Here was a woman who had been a queen, once married to the most powerful man in the land. What would she think if he admitted that the moment he had stepped inside this hut, he had known that there was no turning his heart back a second time.

"I say what I always tell him," Alma said.

Maia's expression was curious.

But Alma couldn't tell her yet. He knew that once she healed and became part of the community, the men would flock to her door. She had the right to make her own choice. "Among other reasons, there's been no time."

Maia looked at him for a long moment, then said, "I understand." She leaned back on the cushions, the light seeming to go out of her eyes. She pulled the coverlet up to her shoulders. "Sometimes I wonder if this is a dream, if I'll wake up in the morning surrounded by Lamanites again."

Alma shook his head. "This is no dream." He hesitated as she closed her eyes, a faint smile on her face. He wanted to take back his comment and tell her the real reason he hadn't married—a reason that had little to do with time.

Her eyes opened again and seemed to sear into his soul. "My parents told me you baptized them at the Waters of Mormon. Will you baptize me?"

"Yes," he said.

"I've been waiting for so long to join the Lord's true fold," she said, her eyelids drooping. "Is tomorrow too soon?"

"No," he said. After a few minutes, her eyes closed. She fell into an easy slumber, and he knew it was time for him to leave. But he would be watching her, protecting her, doing everything in his power to make sure she was safe. No matter what.

CHAPTER 21

I have made a covenant with my chosen.
(Psalm 89:3)

Maia and her parents met Alma at the river the next morning. It was still quite early, so the sun hadn't warmed the flowing water yet. But Maia didn't want to wait one more day, or even an hour. Her father had been able to catch Alma before he headed out for another day of ministering to his people. And now he was here, quietly talking to her father.

Dressed in a simple linen tunic, Maia twisted her hair and pushed a carved stick through the knot. She folded her arms against the slight chill in the air and glanced over at Alma. He'd removed his outer robe and now wore only a plain kilt. She had to take her eyes from him, feeling her face heat up as her pulse drummed.

Again she wondered how it was that Alma hadn't married. It was hard to believe. Any woman could certainly see how attractive he was. But more than that was his quiet strength and conviction. And his never-ending kindness. The way he always put others' needs before his own. His bravery to always take the right path—to never back down, even if it meant risking his life. She wished she could be more faithful and hoped that with her baptism she'd be able to share more of the light that her parents and Alma seemed to enjoy every day.

"Ready?" Alma's voice cut through her thoughts, and she met his gaze. His dark eyes were confident and sincere. She walked toward where he stood on the bank and took his hand, letting him help her across the rocky bottom.

When they reached the middle of the slow-moving water, Alma stopped and turned toward her. "It will take only a minute. Then your mother has a rug to warm you."

The water was certainly cool, but not enough to make Maia's teeth chatter. Yet she shivered, anticipating the chance to finally be baptized. "All right," she said, looking into his eyes. The assurance she saw in them surrounded her with comfort.

He took her arm, then said, "Hold onto my arm with your other hand."

She did so, and he gave her a brief smile, then looked toward the sky. "O Lord," he said in an authoritative voice. "Pour out thy Spirit upon thy servant that she may do this work with holiness of heart."

Then his gaze was on her again. "Maia, I baptize thee, having authority from the Almighty God, as a testimony that ye have entered into a covenant to serve Him until you are dead as to the mortal body."

His voice quieted, and his words seemed to breathe warmth until she couldn't feel the water at all. "And may the Spirit of the Lord be poured out upon you."

At that moment, Maia felt as though her skin were on fire from the inside. Tears sprang to her eyes as Alma continued. "And may God grant unto you eternal life, through the redemption of Christ, whom He has prepared from the foundation of the world."

Then Alma lowered her to the water, and she held her breath as the cold river washed over her. When Alma brought her back out of the water, she felt as if her heart would burst. She was baptized. *At last.* Maia threw her arms around Alma's neck, almost pushing him off balance. But his arms steadied the both of them, and for several seconds he held her.

"Thank you," she whispered over and over. When she finally pulled away, she thought she saw tears in his eyes, but maybe it was just from the river.

"Congratulations," Alma said.

She laughed and turned to make her way back to the bank. Alma's hand steadied her elbow until she reached her mother. Lael wrapped a rug around her daughter and embraced her. Then her father came over, tears in his eyes, and held her.

"At last," he said, "we are all baptized into the true faith."

* * *

Worried over the fact that Amulon and most of the Lamanites were still camped outside the city, Alma gave Maia's parents strict instructions that she was never to go anywhere unaccompanied. It had been several days since her baptism, and Alma hoped the Lamanites would depart soon. Yet they didn't. He had ordered gifts of food and agave wine to be taken to them periodically, waiting patiently for them to leave. But so far, only a few of the soldiers had left, heading back in the direction they'd traveled.

What about the city of Nephi? Alma wondered. When were the Lamanites going there?

He didn't trust Amulon, no matter how well his wife could trick him into thinking that Maia had left with good wishes from everyone. The matter troubled him at night, and he slept little. Finally, he assigned one of his teachers to follow her at a discreet distance when she was out in public.

But time and time again, Alma found himself passing near her parents' house looking for her, trying to assure himself that she was well. In the marketplace, he caught glimpses of her with either Raquel or Lael, always surrounded, and always with a guard following.

Still, he couldn't rest easy.

Jachin noticed the deep shadows beneath his eyes.

"You're overworked with worry," Jachin told Alma one evening as they prepared to leave the courthouse.

Alma shrugged. "Until those Lamanites are gone, I won't rest."

"None of us will," Jachin said, "But we need our leader to be strong and well rested. When was the last time you ate?"

Alma raised a hand and rubbed his forehead. The ache there told him it had been a while. "This morning?"

"That's what I thought," Jachin said. "Come to my home tonight, and we'll get you fed."

"Certainly," Alma said, trying to hide the fact that he was more pleased by the invitation than usual. Maybe being able to talk to Maia and hear how she was really doing would put his mind more at ease.

When Alma reached his own home, he washed with water from a jug and changed to a clean robe. His stomach was positively in knots. He chuckled to himself. *I'm nervous,* he thought. *Actually nervous.*

He hadn't spoken to Maia since her baptism, except in greeting. He left his home and began the walk to Jachin's. Along the way, he said hello to those who passed by, even offered advice to one man about a dispute with a neighbor. But the closer he drew to Jachin's hut, the more nervous he felt.

Alma shook his head, trying to rid his mind of its flustered thoughts. It was just dinner. Maia probably didn't even know he was coming. When he reached the door, Jachin welcomed him inside the main room. They sat together talking about some of the cases in court that day while the women prepared the meal. At least, Alma assumed Maia was with her mother. Once in a while he heard laughter coming from somewhere in the back of the house.

"How is your daughter?" Alma asked, as if he hadn't demanded a report every evening from the guard.

"Excellent," Jachin said, a smile on his face. But there was still a hint of sadness in his eyes. "The baptism was just what she needed. She talks about it all of the time. Now she's making new friends and has even caught the eye of a young man or two."

Alma nodded, pleased she had new friends and expecting the latter.

Then Jachin leaned forward. "But I don't think she's ready for too many changes yet. The men treat her with awe, knowing that she's a former queen. It's intimidating for some, perhaps."

"Understandable," Alma said.

A rustle sounded on the other side of the room, and Lael appeared. "Welcome, Alma." She smiled then looked at her husband. "The meal is ready. You'll be eating in the back courtyard."

The two men rose and followed Lael out of the room and around the hut. Dusk had arrived, and they followed the glow of torches coming from the back courtyard. Jachin and Lael had spent a lot of time cultivating the plants and trees surrounding their home and now had an exquisite garden.

In the center of the courtyard a low table was set with bone utensils and plates of steaming food—dishes of squash, sweet potatoes, and tamalitos. Maia stood at the side of the table, the warmth of the surrounding torches reflecting off her face. Alma could hardly take his eyes from her. She simply glowed. He couldn't help but smile, and she smiled back.

"It looks wonderful," Jachin said. "Our guest will hardly know that I only gave you an hour's notice."

Lael's face reddened, and Alma cut in. "I'd be happy with whatever you chose to prepare. Anything is better than the soaked beans and overripe tomatoes in my house."

"You're probably invited to a different home each night," Maia said.

Alma looked at her with surprise. "You're right. So there's not much reason to have a lot of food on hand."

"It's a wonder you even have barley and tomatoes with no woman to cook for you," Lael said with a laugh.

This time is was Maia's turn to redden. Alma pulled his gaze away from her, afraid that he wouldn't be able to if she stood there long enough.

Jachin put a hand on his shoulder. "Will you offer a blessing on the meal and the home?"

Alma obliged, and when he finished, he insisted the women join them. Lael seemed more than pleased, and soon the four of them were seated and eating. It wasn't long before Lael started to ask questions about Amulon and the Lamanites.

"They've been here for almost a week," she said. "Some say that they've seen soldiers scouting the surrounding hills."

"That's true," Alma said. "Although there haven't been any hostile actions yet." He looked at Jachin. "We can't be too careful though. I've already ordered the blacksmiths and their apprentices to double their efforts."

Lael gasped. "But even if all the women and children were armed, we couldn't match them."

"No," Jachin cut in. "But we can't sit around and be afraid either. Action is better than waiting."

Alma nodded his agreement. "We gave them what they wanted, but still they remain. We're trying to find out why they're stalling."

Lael put a hand on Maia's arm with a knowing nod. "Amulon didn't get *everything* he wanted."

Maia lowered her head, but she didn't respond.

"Alma is doing all he can to protect our daughter, Lael," Jachin said.

"We all know what Amulon is capable of—the worst any of us could imagine," Lael said with a shake of her head. She patted Maia's hand, then passed around a platter of sliced avocado. "Do you think Amulon would breach our borders and take her away from us?"

"We have a guard following her during the day," Jachin said, his voice rising slightly, "and she's with us at night."

"Dear husband, I know that, but she's still an unmarried woman. She was fortunate to escape Amulon when she did. There must be something more we can do."

Hoping to diffuse the tension between husband and wife, Alma cut in, "What do you suggest, Lael?"

"That she gets married right away." She grasped Maia's arm. "Tomorrow is not too soon."

Throwing his head back, Jachin laughed. Then his expression sobered. "If you think I'm going to allow my daughter to marry for convenience again, you're mistaken."

Lael looked at Alma, her gaze pleading. "Reason with my husband, Alma. If Amulon were to receive word of her marriage, he'd have less motive to stay near—to try to get his revenge once and for all. At least the Lamanite commander respects the bond of marriage, and Amulon defers to him."

Nodding, Alma thought about her rationale—she did have a point in a way.

"You aren't agreeing with her, are you?" Jachin said, leaning toward him, his expression intent.

Alma looked at his friend. "She's simply trying to think as Amulon might—and her conclusion might be more reasonable than you think."

Jachin glanced at his daughter, who had said nothing thus far. "You've upset her, Lael," he said. "She doesn't want to be married off to a stranger."

"No, *you've* upset her," Lael countered. "She knows she has to be protected. Any woman would choose a stranger—as you say—over a horrible fate."

Standing, Jachin's face went dark red, but his voice remained controlled. "She's already endured a horrible fate, and I will not ask her to marry in this way—"

"I can't bear to see her treated like a prisoner in our own city," Lael said, her voice trembling. "She has *no* freedoms. She can't even walk to the market alone. She needs the protection that only a husband can give her."

"*I protect her!*" Jachin shouted.

Lael's mouth opened, then closed again, shock on her face.

Out of the corner of his eye, Alma saw Maia stand. Before he could say anything, she left the courtyard.

Jachin's face crumpled with regret, and he sat down with a sigh. "Our daughter is a grown woman," he said, his tone deflated. "She's been married, had a child, and endured unthinkable things. It's time we let her decide for herself."

Lael brought a hand to her face and wiped at the tears spilling onto her cheeks. "You're right," she said in a soft voice. "We'll let Maia decide."

Alma made a motion to leave. "I should go now. I know this is a difficult time for your family. Thank you for the delicious meal."

But Jachin put a hand on his arm. "Thank you for coming, Alma. Please accept our apologies."

He left the couple, worry coursing through him over Maia. If only Amulon and the Lamanites would leave the Nephites alone, all of this could be solved quickly. As Alma rounded the house, he saw Maia sitting under a tree in the front courtyard.

She kept her eyes averted as he crossed to her.

"Would you like to go for a walk by the river?" he asked.

She hesitated, then nodded. She stood and led the way down the path and around a grove of trees.

Alma waited until they were a good distance from the row of huts, then said, "Are you all right?"

"Yes. Although usually my parents discuss the matter when they think I'm asleep." She folded her arms. "I imagine you know how I feel about it."

Actually, Alma didn't know, but he didn't interrupt, grateful she was at least speaking.

She stopped on the path. The heavy moon gently traced her delicate features as she turned to look at him. "What would *you* do?"

"Me? I—"

"Not as a man—but if you were in my place?"

He couldn't read her expression. "I think . . . your mother's idea makes sense on one hand, but on the other, your marriage wouldn't stop Amulon from taking any revenge he has in mind."

"That's what I think too," Maia said, pushing a stray lock of hair behind her ear as a slight breeze picked up. "I don't think Amulon is planning on leaving."

Her words chilled Alma. He didn't know if it was the foreboding he felt at Maia's declaration or the fact that he was alone with her—truly alone—for the first time that he could remember.

She turned away, gazing at the moon. "It wasn't as horrible as everyone thinks," she said in a quiet voice. Alma was about to ask her what she was talking about when she continued. "Yes, Amulon always leered at me, but since the Lamanite commander wouldn't let him marry me, one final act to disgrace me was all he could do."

"Maia—"

"No, I want to tell you—*you* of all people need to know what really happened." She turned to look at him and took a deep breath. "I just wanted the suffering to end. And I wanted him to leave the city of Helam in peace. I thought if I obliged him, he'd finally be over his obsession, his anger—whatever drove him—and I'd be free. And my parents would be safe. At a cost, of course, but no more of a cost than other women have paid for one reason or another."

"You can't have wanted to sacrifice yourself that way," he said.

"I saw it as a necessity," she said, her eyes flashing. "I didn't feel there was any choice."

This time, there was no doubt what her expression meant. She was angry. "Maybe he would have left if he'd had his way, and none of this would be happening," she said, waving her hand. "Your people could be out there preparing to harvest crops instead of making swords."

Alma grabbed her hand. "Don't say that. You don't know that. A man such as Amulon can't be appeased, especially if it means sacrificing you. I'd rather see war between our people than send you back to him." He took her other hand, his heart pounding at being so close to her. "Surely you must know how much I care for you."

"You are too kind to me," Maia said, her eyes bright with unshed tears. "You're too good. Sometimes I feel like I might suffocate from all your generosity." She pulled her hands away. "You can't protect me forever, Alma," she said, her voice trembling. "You have a whole city that depends on you."

He reached out and touched her hair. "What about you? Do you depend on me?"

"You've done enough already," she said. "You don't have to be my protector anymore. I have my parents, and I don't need your sympathy at every corner I turn."

"What do you mean?" He took a deep breath when she didn't answer and said, "I *want* to be there for you. Don't you understand? I love you."

"Of course you do. You love everyone."

"Maia," Alma said, leaning toward her. "I love you as a man loves a wife."

Her eyes widened. "You can't mean that."

"I do." He saw the doubt in her eyes, the distrust. "I cannot deny it. This isn't about fulfilling an obligation. When you told me your feelings so long ago, I never forgot your words." He wiped away a tear from her cheek; she didn't move away this time. "I've *tried* to find a woman to marry. I've tried to talk myself into it time and time again. But when I saw you again in the Lamanite camp, I knew that I could never think of asking another woman to marry me."

She turned away.

"Maia, please." He touched her shoulder and gently turned her toward him. She faced him but looked down, her chin trembling.

"And when I sat by your bedside," he said, "seeing you bruised at the hand of a terrible man, I was angry—yes. I wanted to protect you—yes. But when you came into the river to be baptized . . ." His voice caught. "I—when you held me after, it was like a part of me had been restored. A part that had been missing since my parents' death. A part that I didn't even realize *could* be restored."

He spread out his arms. "It felt as if I were finally holding my future in my hands, and I knew exactly what it looked like."

A tear dripped down Maia's cheek as she stared at him.

"But most of all," Alma whispered, "I knew that if I couldn't have you as my wife, I didn't want to marry at all."

He waited, but she didn't say anything, and his heart pounded in his ears, bringing the dread of rejection. After all this time and all that had happened, would he finally lose her once and for all? Maybe it was too soon, and she was overwhelmed by his foolish declarations.

Then, suddenly, she put her arms about his waist and leaned against him, nestling beneath his chin.

Alma wrapped his arms around her trembling shoulders and held her—waiting for her verdict, hardly daring to hope. Maybe this was her way of saying good-bye.

"Am I dreaming?" Her voice was barely a whisper, and he wondered for an instant if she'd spoken at all.

"I hope not," he said, feeling his pulse increase its pace. "It would mean that I'm dreaming too."

Her hands slipped around his back, and her embrace tightened.

Alma had to restrain himself from crushing her to him, so instead he settled for stroking her hair. "Maia?"

Her murmured "yes" was muffled against his chest.

"Will you be my wife?"

She pulled away and smiled through new tears. "Is tomorrow too soon?"

He stared at her, hardly believing her answer. "Tomorrow?"

"Unless you think the city would be disappointed by not having a huge celebration for their esteemed leader."

Alma lifted her up and swung her around, his heart feeling like it might burst. "I'm not marrying the city," he said when he set her down, laughing. He put both hands on either side of her face, expecting his heart to melt as she met his gaze. "Are you certain? I don't want you to feel pressure from your parents to marry just anyone."

"Oh, Alma," Maia said, moving her own hands to his face. "You aren't just *anyone*. You're the one I gave my heart to so long ago. That has never changed."

CHAPTER 22

For ye suffer, if a man bring you into bondage.
(2 Corinthians 11:20)

Amulon rubbed the back of his head. The lump was still there, even after many days. But he smiled at the commander, who was watching him from across the morning cooking fire. The longer they stayed in the land of Helam, the more he would be able to convince the Lamanites to remain.

Cochiti arrived at last, carrying a skin full of pure water from the river. It was the most delicious water he'd ever tasted, and when mixed with crushed maize, the cakes came out absolutely sweet. Amulon indicated for Cochiti to serve the commander first.

When Zorihor took a sip of water, his eyes brightened. "This water seems to get better each time I taste it."

Amulon merely smiled and motioned for Cochiti to serve Zorihor a hot cake. One bite and the commander's face was mapped with pleasure.

"It wouldn't be too hard, you know," Amulon said in a casual tone.

Zorihor twitched an eyebrow. "Too hard to do what?"

"To rule this place," Amulon said, waving a hand. "Our scouts have found more rivers of pure water and an abundance of wildlife. The work that Alma has done to create a city is only the beginning. We could prosper here quite well."

Zorihor took another swallow from the waterskin then wiped his mouth with the back of his hand. "Tell me more."

Amulon concealed the grin that pushed against his face. He wanted to appear as nonchalant as possible. "It would be a fine experiment. Leave me here to guard the land while you visit King Laman in the city of Nephi. Present to him our plan to rule over this land and people—receiving a hearty tribute in return, of course. You won't even have to bother with governing the land. I'd be happy to rule over this valley and take care of any little uprisings."

Zorihor furrowed his brow. "I'd leave you here alone?"

"Not at all," Amulon said with a chuckle. "We'd bring our men and wives from the city of Amulon, and you could leave as many soldiers as you desire."

Rising to his feet, Zorior said, "How many people did you say are in the city of Helam?"

"I'd say five to six hundred."

"How many soldiers?"

"Not nearly enough to match our strength," Amulon said.

"Not a difficult task," Zorihor mused.

"Not difficult at all." Amulon smiled and crossed to the commander. Putting a hand on his shoulder he said, "Drink deeply. This water is only one of many luxuries your people could own in this valley."

Zorihor looked into Amulon's steady gaze. "Tomorrow I will travel to the city of Nephi with a group of soldiers to make the request of King Laman. Remain here and preserve this place for the Lamanite people. Your loyalty will be greatly rewarded."

Amulon bowed with a flourish. "Your command is my duty."

* * *

"What are you doing in here?" Maia asked, staring at Alma. She wore a bridal dress of lightweight linen to which her mother had added some delicate embroidery. The wedding ceremony would start in less than an hour. He wore a finely woven cape, but he looked as if he'd been running.

"There are some troubling movements in the Lamanite camp," Alma said, his voice coming in a burst of breathing.

Fear struck Maia's heart. "What kind of movements?"

Alma grasped her arms. "Our scouts have been watching them day and night. This morning Commander Zorihor left with a group of men, heading in the direction of the city of Nephi. But Amulon and the rest of the soldiers remained."

"Do you think they're recruiting a bigger army to attack?"

"They have enough of an army to attack now if they truly wanted. This has to be something else altogether."

"What?" Maia asked. She couldn't think of anything worse than war—except being separated from Alma.

"I don't know yet," he said. "That's why I came. I have to leave now and confront Amulon. We must know what to expect . . . what to prepare for."

Maia clutched at his arms. "What about *us?*"

He held her gaze. "We'll have the ceremony tonight instead."

"All right," she said, releasing her grip, knowing that the city's safety came before her. "Go then. I'll be fine."

Suddenly, Alma pulled her into his arms and pressed his mouth against hers. Maia clung to him, stunned but kissing him back. Everything was wrapped into that kiss—the long years of despair and loneliness, the deprivation of true affection and love, and the fear of what would happen when Alma went to see the man she dreaded most.

When he released her, they were both breathless. They stared at each other for a moment, Maia wishing he didn't have to leave.

"Did I tell you that you look beautiful?" he said.

She smiled and touched his cheek.

"I really have to go now," he murmured, pulling her close again.

"I'll be waiting."

Alma drew away and looked as if he were about to say something else, but instead he leaned forward and softly kissed her again. Then he turned and left the hut.

Maia watched him leave, her heart racing with fear. Their first kiss—and it was one of farewell.

Trying to push back hot tears, she carefully folded the veil she'd just unwrapped. Then she changed into her regular tunic, laying the wedding garment across her bed. She'd leave the flowers in her hair and hope they wouldn't wilt too much.

"Maia?" It was her mother's voice.

"I'm in the bedchamber," she said. When her mother entered the room, Maia could see that she already knew.

"Father and Helam went with him," Lael said.

"Do you think it will be enough?" Maia asked.

Lael frowned. "I think they wanted to travel in a small group so they wouldn't appear threatening or hostile." She crossed the room and took her daughter's hands. "I'm sorry the wedding has to be delayed."

Maia bit her lip, fighting back the renewed emotion. "If I've waited this long, what's a few more hours?"

Lael rubbed her back. "Let's go to Raquel's home. She lives on the other side of the city—farther away from the Lamanite camp. I'd feel safer there."

"But I want to know the moment Alma returns. I don't want to delay him finding me."

"He'll know where to find you. He suggested it to me before he left."

He always has a plan, Maia thought. "All right, but when the evening draws nigh, and if he's still not back, I want to return here."

* * *

Alma clenched his hands into fists. The closer they drew to the Lamanite camp, the angrier he became. Why couldn't Amulon and the Lamanites take themselves back to wherever they had come from? What did they want with the city of Helam? Alma was afraid of what his reaction would be when he saw Amulon again. Walking next to him, Helam seemed to sense the unease.

"Do you want me to do the talking?" Helam asked.

Alma glanced over at him, then at Jachin. These two men would be faithful until the end. "No, I'll be composed by the time we reach their camp."

Helam laughed. "I'll believe that when I see it."

Alma grimaced—Helam was probably right. The afternoon was a cool one, but Alma hadn't stopped perspiring since running to Maia's home. And the kiss hadn't made him any cooler either. He smiled as he thought about kissing his almost-wife. He'd felt her love for him through that kiss—a feeling he'd never experienced before. Then the anger returned; his postponed wedding made this visit to Amulon that much harder.

Movement on the fringes of the camp let Alma know they'd been spotted. He was surprised to see several soldiers band together, then Amulon appear in the midst of them. It was as if they'd been waiting.

Amulon ambled forward, and Alma was revolted by his appearance—the dark, hooded eyes, greedy smile, and oily skin.

"Congratulations on your betrothal!" Amulon called out as he closed the distance between them.

Alma raised a brow—news had traveled fast.

"I knew you'd marry her, regardless of her tainted past." Amulon grinned and stopped, kicking up the dirt beneath his feet.

Alma sensed Helam close behind him, ready to take any necessary action. Breathing deeply, Alma tried to remain calm. He dipped his head in response to Amulon's mocking congratulations. "We noticed that Zorihor left."

"Yes, so he has," Amulon said in an annoying tone. He brought his hands together and threaded his fingers. "I expected you much sooner." He glanced in the direction of the afternoon sun. "Much sooner than now—Zorihor left early this morning."

"Where did he go?" Helam cut in, his curiosity too great.

Amulon slid his gaze to Helam. "Nosy, aren't we? Let's just say he's on official business for his people."

"You mean *your* people?" Jachin said, a sneer in his voice.

"Ah, the noble father returns, always the protector." Amulon laughed as Jachin reddened.

"What do you want with us?" Alma said. He ignored the increasingly hostile stares of the soldiers that stood behind Amulon. It was clear that with Zorihor's absence, Amulon was in charge now.

"What do *I* want?" Amulon unlocked his hands, moving them to the hilt of his sword. "Everything." His voice was cold, dead, but his eyes burned with greed and passion.

Heart racing, Alma knew Maia had been right—Amulon wasn't going to be satisfied easily.

Amulon took a step forward and thrust his finger against Alma's chest. "You might have Maia, but I'm taking the city of Helam."

A hand shot out and pushed away Amulon's finger. "Don't touch him!" Helam said.

Amulon didn't flinch. "You need your dog to protect you, Alma?"

"I can protect myself—it's *you* who needs an army to conceal your treachery," Alma said.

"*My* treachery? You should be burned for what you did to your king." Amulon's face twisted into an ugly mass. "There was a time when I would have given anything to bring you to justice—to your deserved death. But I realize now that it will be much more enjoyable to make you suffer—ever so slowly."

Alma narrowed his eyes but didn't back down. "And what exactly did you have in mind?"

"Well, my friend," Amulon said, placing a hand on Alma's shoulder. "Let's just say that Maia was only an appetizer."

At the same instant, Alma and Helam lunged at Amulon, shoving him to the ground. Amulon cried out with surprise. Jachin landed on top of the heap, clawing his way to reach Amulon. One of the Lamanites pulled Jachin off easily and sent him sprawling.

Alma drew his knife and pressed it against Amulon's throat as Helam fended off the other soldiers.

"You've told your last lie, Amulon," Alma hissed. He didn't have a time to see what Helam was doing or who he was fighting, but for a charged instant he stared into Amulon's eyes—a pair of the most vile he'd ever seen. He could end this. Right now. This instant.

Someone plowed against his side, knocking him off of Amulon. Rolling over with a groan, Alma found himself staring into the faces of at least a dozen armed Lamanites. Then something smashed into the side of his face and all went black.

* * *

"How long have we been here?" Alma asked, trying to focus on the light that came through the tent. It appeared to be the middle of the day, but the pressure behind his temples made it impossible for him to discern clearly.

"Three days." Helam sat nearby, his voice scratchy and hoarse. A couple of paces away, Jachin snored softly.

"Maia will kill me," Alma said.

"Well, if she doesn't, I will," Helam replied in a dry tone.

"What did I ever do to *you*?" Alma asked, trying to blink away the haziness of his eyes. He sat up slowly, groaning at the pain that seemed to swallow his entire body.

"We never should have let them enter our valley in peace. We should have fought them from the beginning."

Alma was silent, wondering if that were true. At the time, he hadn't wanted to put his people in any unnecessary danger, but now they *were* in danger, regardless. "What about Maia?"

A breath came from Helam. "You have a point there. Except now that she's going to kill you, maybe it wasn't such a good idea to let her into the valley either."

Alma started to laugh—at least he tried to—but it hurt so much he ended up having a coughing fit instead. "What did they *do* to me?"

"Kicked you unconscious—then cracked a few bones."

"And you? You're sounding well."

"Ha. That's just because I was smart enough not to pull my knife on their precious leader," Helam said.

"But you were right there, fighting," Alma said.

"If it makes you feel any better, you can take a swing at me," Helam said.

Alma slowly, painfully turned his head to examine his friend. One of Helam's eyes was swollen, and he seemed to be missing a tooth. "Nah, I don't have enough strength. Maybe tomorrow."

Helam scoffed and shook his head. "I wish Raquel was here. She'd have us fixed up before the Lamanites could decide what to feed us for supper."

"Food? Is there any?"

Helam shook his head. "Jachin ate your portion—said there's no use wasting it, considering how much you were sleeping."

"Ah, such nice friends I have," Alma said, trying to smile. It even hurt to smile.

"What?" the mumbled word came from Jachin. "Who ate my food?" He sat up with an exaggerated groan and rubbed his head. "Oh, you're awake," he said, looking at Alma. "How are you feeling?"

"Hungry," Alma said, glowering as best he could.

"Oh, that . . ." Jachin said sheepishly, then looked at Helam. "Any news yet?"

"No," Helam said. "Last I peeked out of the tent, Zorihor was still talking with the soldiers—it appears he's arranging them into small groups."

"Zorihor's back?" Alma asked.

"Returned yesterday." A grave look crossed Jachin's face. "He's appointed Amulon as king over the city of Helam."

Alma's jaw dropped. "King? How could he? He has no authority—"

"Zorihor obtained his so-called authority from King Laman." Helam moved closer to Alma. "They've already stationed guards around the city."

Disbelief rocked through Alma. He moved to his knees and tried to stand, but the pain in his lower leg was too fierce. So he crawled to the opening of the tent. He could see the legs of the two guards protecting the entrance. He also caught a glimpse outside—the blue sky, the ground, and the soldiers milling about. Soldiers who were armed.

"We have to stop them somehow," Alma whispered. "Warn the people."

"There's no way to stop them," Helam said in a subdued voice. "The people will find out soon enough about Amulon."

Heat flamed in Alma's face. "I should have used that knife when I had the chance." A shuffling noise sounded behind him, and he felt a hand on his shoulder.

"No," Jachin said. "Or you wouldn't be with us."

Alma sank back and turned to Jachin. "Where did we go wrong? I thought if we extended help—"

"It was only a matter of time," Jachin said, his voice calm. "Right now the important thing is to keep ourselves—and our families— alive." His voice filled with emotion, and he looked away.

"You're right," Alma said, scooting farther into the tent. "So we wait?"

"For now," Helam said. He moved past Alma and peered out the tent opening. "I wish they'd let us return to our homes."

Alma nodded, gazing at his two friends. These men had fought with him, risked their lives with him, and now they were separated from their families. The only consoling thought was that if Amulon was still at the Lamanite camp, then he wasn't near Maia.

CHAPTER 23

When the righteous are in authority, the people rejoice: but
when the wicked beareth rule, the people mourn.
(Proverb 29:2)

Raquel tried to comfort Maia, but it seemed to do little good. She'd gone silent on the second day. It was as if she'd retreated to some place where she didn't have to face the fear. So Raquel turned to Itzel, Lael, and Esther for help. They kept up an easy chatter as they tried to go about their regular household chores of gardening, preparing food, and weaving. They took turns tending Abe and visiting with neighbors. Everyone seemed on edge, even though regular reports were delivered by Ben every few hours.

Pockets of Lamanite guards had been stationed around the city since Zorihor's return. Alma, Jachin, and Helam were still in captivity. Raquel hoped the Lamanite commander would be more sensible than Amulon, yet she had no doubt that Amulon was influencing the Lamanites for the worse. Ironic as that seemed.

But more and more Lamanite soldiers joined the guards daily. The people in the city were too afraid to act until they knew the fate of Alma and his men.

By the third evening, the women started praying every hour. Abe joined them, raising his sweet voice in supplication. Raquel clung to the prayers and the company of the women, grasping at their words of comfort. She couldn't think of what might happen to Helam, or what might be happening to him now. It was unbearable. She'd been married for only a short time, and she couldn't think of losing another husband, let alone to the very man—her own father—who had played a role in the death of Abinadi.

She could not endure it.

As the night of the third day deepened, Raquel lit all of the oil lamps in her new house. She passed by the room Maia and Lael slept in to find Maia already lying under her coverlet. Raquel entered the room quietly, and Maia turned at the sound then looked away.

Raquel hesitated, then decided to approach anyway and sit by her. "How are you feeling?" she asked, not expecting a reply. "We're going to get them out, you know. We must." Her voice trembled. "I won't let my father take away my new husband."

Suddenly, Maia sat up with a sob and threw her arms around Raquel.

Blinking in surprise, Raquel held her as she cried.

"I'm sorry," Maia said. "This must be harder on you than anyone."

Raquel shook her head. "I don't claim to be more afflicted than anyone in the city. We are all in this together."

Maia drew away, wiping her eyes. "I know. I'm just caught up in my own selfishness."

A smile tugged at Raquel's mouth. "I don't think it's selfish to be upset that your wedding was postponed."

"Those men's lives are more important than any ceremony."

Raquel put a hand on Maia's shoulder. "It wasn't just any ceremony . . . you and Alma have been waiting a long time. You should have seen him moping about the past couple of years."

Maia's expression brightened. "Moping?"

"Well, not exactly moping," Raquel conceded. "But he worked too hard and allowed himself little time to just enjoy life. But when you arrived, it was like the flowers finally bloomed."

"Not anymore," Maia said.

"Yes, not anymore," Raquel said. "I know that he's probably thinking of you right now. Whatever has happened to our men, thinking of us will help sustain them."

Fresh tears spilled onto Maia's cheeks. "I think we need to pray again."

* * *

Amulon burst through the tent opening, startling the three men who reclined on their mats.

Helam was on his feet first, followed by the other two.

Surveying their injuries and hollow-eyed expressions, Amulon gave a self-satisfied smile. "Follow me!" He turned around and headed out, but not before hearing a quiet moan from Alma. He was the worst off of the three, and rightly so. Amulon had determined that the man would pay severely for drawing a blade on him.

In fact, he'd be surprised if Alma made it out of the tent without significant assistance.

Once outside, Amulon led the prisoners into a circle of soldiers. If they tried anything, their lives would be cut short, Amulon decided. Looking at their tattered state, he knew they understood perfectly.

"Bow to me," he said with a smirk.

The three men looked at him.

"I am your new king, and until you learn to bow to me, you won't see more than the silhouette of the city of Helam."

Jachin was first, then Helam, and finally Alma.

"Very good," Amulon said. "You could all do with a little practice though."

He strode to the prisoners and circled them. Alma was in poor condition, and Amulon wondered if he'd be able to make the walk back to the city. But any delay would give the Nephites too much time to make plans. And then a battle would follow and some Lamanites might die. Highly inconvenient.

"All right," Amulon said. "You look healthy enough." He ordered some water to be brought, and the three men took turns guzzling it down.

"Now listen to me," Amulon said. "We are marching on the city. Anyone who stands in our way will be slain." His glare met Alma's. "You will all show subservience at all times. You'll encourage those around you to do the same—or their lives will be forfeit. No warnings. No trials."

He turned to the soldiers. "Tie their hands and we'll begin."

* * *

Maia watched as the men drew nearer. At least fifty Lamanite soldiers approached, Amulon and Zorihor in the lead, and with them their three prisoners. Maia glanced around her, looking at the many people who had gathered to watch. Men stood with their families, swords in hand, fear on their faces. Children were sober, their eyes wide, clinging to their mothers.

Maia heard Raquel's sharp intake of breath, and she found herself holding her own breath. It was easy to make out Helam—he was tall and seemed to walk with ease. Next was her father, the smallest in the group. His dark blue cape was immediately recognizable. The mass of soldiers concealed the third man, but she caught a glimpse of him, knowing it was Alma.

"They're alive," Raquel whispered, clinging to Maia's arm.

She nodded, tears of gratitude pricking her eyes, but she couldn't speak over the lump in her throat. Something was wrong with Alma. He walked with a limp and his head was lowered.

Adrenaline pulsed through her as she fought off the urge to run toward him. They were a hundred paces from the city wall. Next to her Raquel seemed to sense her urge to run, and she tightened her hold on Maia's arm.

"Something's wrong with Alma," Maia finally whispered.

Raquel wrapped an arm around her. "He's walking—so his injuries must not be too bad."

Just then Alma lifted his head, and Maia and Raquel both gasped. Dark bruises covered most of his face, and one side was so swollen that his left eye was shut. Maia watched in horror as the men drew closer and more details leapt into focus. At fifty paces she saw the torn clothing, at thirty the caked blood on Alma's hairline and ear, at twenty the pain in his eyes. Every few breaths, he shuddered as if the very act of breathing were torture.

What amazed her was that he walked unassisted. Just imagining what he must have endured made Maia's knees feel like they might give out. She took a tentative step forward.

"Wait," Raquel said. "We don't want the Lamanites drawing their weapons on us."

Maia nodded, tears building in her eyes. She tried to hold them back, not wanting Alma to see her falling apart. He needed her to be strong and supportive—whatever that meant.

Zorihor brought the procession to a halt, and Maia glanced about her nervously. The crowd of Nephites waited in tense silence.

Zorihor stepped forward and raised a spear. "Put down your weapons."

No one moved; all eyes were on Alma.

"Put down your weapons," Alma called out from his position. Maia flinched at the sound of his raspy voice.

Movement rippled through the crowd as men, women, and children dropped their weapons to the dirt.

Zorihor nodded, satisfied. "Today is a new day for the people in the city of Helam. You're under new rule overseen by King Laman himself."

A few gasps echoed around Maia, but she continued to stare at Alma and saw the resignation and affirmation in his expression. *Oh, Alma,* she wanted to say to him. *What will become of us?*

"King Laman," Zorihor continued, "has declared the city of Helam and its surrounding valley Lamanite territory. If you don't want to see bloodshed, you will turn all of your weapons over to us today. Our soldiers will conduct searches of every hut, building, and garden for weapons of any kind." He smiled placidly. "And now it's my pleasure to introduce you to your new king."

Maia's eyes widened. She'd assumed the king would be Zorihor.

The commander cleared his throat. "Amulon, a former compatriot, has been given the commission of king over the land of Helam by the supreme authority of King Laman."

Amulon stepped forward and took an exaggerated bow. Then his eyes briefly met Raquel's. If there had ever been love between father and daughter, Maia saw no evidence of it now in Amulon's eyes. His gaze was hard, calculating.

The breath went out of Raquel, and she took a step back as if to avoid her father's cruel stare. *So she saw it too,* Maia thought. It was then that she noticed how fine his feathered cape was—the cape of a leader, of royalty. She brought a trembling hand to her mouth.

"Furthermore," Zorihor said, "Amulon's brethren have been appointed kings over other Lamanite holdings, including the land of

Amulon, the land of Shemlon, and the land of Shilom." He paused, looking over at Alma and Helam. "King Laman deemed the priests who were shunned by their own people to be in the best position to bring order and retribution to the Nephites, as well as the Lamanites. These former Nephites owe their lives to King Laman, and they will serve with loyalty."

His gaze moved to the gathered crowd of Nephites. "As you can see, the Lamanites have taken over all of these lands, including your former home in the land of Nephi." He nodded to Amulon, who turned to face the people.

"In the morning, Zorihor will continue on to the city of Nephi," Amulon said. "Tonight we will hold the ceremony to induct me as king of your land." He looked at the people, then his gaze settled on something in the distance. "What a beautiful temple—the perfect place for my induction." He smiled and turned to Alma. "I trust the city will provide the appropriate celebration and feast?"

Alma's eyes flashed, but his voice was dull. "The celebration will be in the temple at sunset."

"Very good," Amulon said, his expression pleased. "And now, you may lead me to my home."

Surprisingly, Helam stepped forward. "Follow me." He walked straight toward Maia and Raquel.

Helam stopped in front of Raquel, pain in his eyes. "I'll build you a new home." Then he turned and rejoined Amulon, and they passed through the crowd of people.

Raquel grabbed Maia's arm. "Does he mean to—?"

"I think . . ." Maia said, taking a deep breath. "Amulon is going to live in your house."

"No," Raquel cried out. Her eyes turned wild as she stared after Helam and Amulon. Several dozen Lamanites followed, creating a procession of sorts.

"Hush," Maia said. "We must not draw attention to ourselves."

"I can't allow it. It's *my* home. He's already taken enough!"

Maia held on to Raquel. "I know."

Raquel's mother edged to her other side. "Don't create a stir. We don't want to make things worse."

"Someone needs to do *something*," Raquel said, trying to pull away from Maia and Itzel, but the women held firm.

"Not now," Maia whispered. She looked around at the downcast expressions of those surrounding them. It was as if they'd already given up. Then her eyes widened as she saw Alma walking toward her. She wanted to run into his arms but didn't know what his reaction would be. What had he endured? And how had it changed him?

He stopped right in front of her. She couldn't pull her gaze away from his horrible injuries.

Then, suddenly, he was holding her. She wrapped her arms about his neck. "I'm so glad you're safe," she said.

He pulled back, touching her face. "I'm sorry I didn't return that night."

She shook her head, tears spilling down her cheeks. "I'm sorry they did this to you."

"It's nothing that won't heal," he said, but his words weren't very convincing. "We have a difficult experience ahead of us."

She wiped her eyes and nodded. "What do you want us to do?"

Around her, everyone had fallen silent, listening. "We must make the best of the situation," Alma said. "For now, we're under Lamanite rule. I don't want any harm to come to our people, so we must follow their laws."

"All right," she said in a quiet voice.

He took her hand and squeezed lightly. "We can't know what tomorrow will bring. After Amulon's coronation, let's have our own ceremony."

Her face reddened as he spoke—there were so many people about, listening. But she couldn't help but smile. "In the dark?"

"We'll light some torches." His swollen face stretched into a smile.

Maia tightened her grasp on his hand.

Alma turned, still holding her hand, and scanned the crowd. "Esther?" When the woman stepped forward, he said, "We have a feast to plan."

"Yes," Esther said with a dip of her head. "I'll get it organized right away." She moved away, and several women assembled together, planning out the meal.

Alma looked at Maia. "I need you to stay out of sight. I don't want Amulon to get any more ideas now that he's king."

* * *

What should have been a grand ceremony was sorely lacking, Amulon thought as he crossed his arms over his bare chest. At least the food was decent—he'd give credit to the Nephite women for that. But he knew it would take some harshness to gain the allegiance he deserved. First, he needed to have more work done on this building they called the temple. His gaze swept upward—nothing interesting, no carved idols, just stark, plain rock. Dreary.

Cochiti sat at his side. Mixed emotions played across her face, as if she felt sorry for these people.

"Smile," Amulon commanded her several times. She smiled automatically, but there was no light or excitement behind it. "You are a queen now; act like it."

Cochiti seemed to make more of an effort after that.

Satisfied for the moment, Amulon continued scanning the crowd. On one side of the temple, the Nephites stood, waiting to serve when beckoned. Lamanite soldiers occupied the low tables, eating as if they hadn't had a meal in days. Like animals. Amulon chuckled, feeling power course through him. He could tell them to stop if he wanted. He could order someone punished or put someone to death with just a single command.

Even Zorihor sat in his rightful place among the soldiers. By sitting there, he'd paid deference to Amulon's new position, in front of everyone. Just as it should be. A group of musicians played a series of panpipes, drums, and horns—the melody slow and forlorn-sounding somehow. Amulon lifted his hand. "Faster, play faster—something lively!"

The musicians picked up the pace, and a few of the Lamanites rose to the beat, clapping their hands and cheering. Amulon watched with amusement as a couple of soldiers staggered over to the line of Nephites. They each selected a girl and started to dance with them. The girls' eyes widened with horror.

Amulon laughed aloud. Now this was starting to look like a celebration. He kept the grin on his face as he turned to find Alma and

Helam—the two seemed inseparable—at the other side of the room. They both stood watching everything.

An itch crawled along Amulon's neck. He didn't like those two standing there as if they were judging him. He wondered for a moment if he should have them both imprisoned. At least Amulon didn't need to fear an insurrection. It had taken most of the day to collect all of the weapons in the city, but he was satisfied that the homes had been cleaned out and the people frightened into submission.

Tomorrow he'd begin the task of organizing work forces.

Several more soldiers started dancing, sweeping the Nephite women up with them. Amulon clapped along to the rhythm, thoroughly enjoying how it felt to sit on this makeshift throne of wood. Soon it would be of stone and precious metals. He'd need to plan out his palace with its throne room. *Ah, so much work to do.* He wondered if this was how King Noah had felt when he first inherited his kingdom. *I learned from the master.*

His attention went back to where Alma and Helam stood—but they were no longer there. Amulon motioned for a soldier to come over. "Follow Alma and Helam. Find out where Alma lives and how he spends his time." He lowered his voice. "I want regular reports from now on."

The soldier offered a bow, then hurried out of the room.

Amulon smiled after him. He liked the bowing; he could get used to it very quickly. Of course, he'd heard the rumors of Alma and Maia's betrothal. His first instinct had been to forbid the marriage—find some excuse—not that he would need one as king. But he had ultimately decided that the pain of one of them losing a spouse or perhaps a future child would be far greater than if he took action now.

He glanced at his wife, hoping that their coming child was a healthy son. He'd need to ensure his position of royalty in this land. His children would rule over Alma's children, making them subservient. Amulon looked forward to that day with immense pleasure. First he had a lot of work to do—a lot of changes to make—and he'd enjoy each and every one.

* * *

Moments after Alma left the celebration, he sensed he was being followed. Probably someone sent by Amulon. But there was no way he could outrun anyone—not with his limp.

Helam strode alongside him, noticing as well. "One of Amulon's?"

Alma nodded briefly, realizing they'd have to get used to it. "The sooner Maia and I are married, the better." He'd seen the way that Amulon kept watching him at the banquet. Was nothing ever enough for the man? He was now king over the land, the very title Alma had turned down from his people.

Now they'd be ruled by an unrighteous king—as if they had never truly escaped the city of Nephi. Alma had seen the despair in people's eyes. He knew he must buoy up their faith—counsel them not to give up. They needed to continue praying, worshipping, and doing good works. Loving and serving each other would be the keys in this difficult time. But how was he to teach them to love their enemies when their enemies were now found at every turn?

Alma wished he could go faster, not necessarily to shake off the man who followed, but because he had waited long enough to marry Maia. He glanced at the moon, estimating that it was nearly midnight. At this limping pace, the wedding guests might be asleep before he reached them.

He had little energy and knew he still looked quite pitiful, but he didn't want to put off the wedding even one more night. He hoped she hadn't given up on him. Surely she knew he had to remain at the celebration for a decent amount of time so he wouldn't draw undue attention. The quiet footsteps continued to follow behind as Alma entered the lane that led to Maia's parents' home. *Let Amulon know there is a wedding tonight,* Alma thought defiantly. *Let his spies watch, if they have to.*

Then Alma stopped, seeing that the house was dark. He whispered to Helam, "Do you think they went to bed?"

The footsteps behind them had drawn to a halt as well.

"We should knock anyway," Helam said. "Maybe they're staying somewhere else."

Disappointment surged through Alma, but truthfully all that was important was whether or not Maia was safe.

"Alma?" someone whispered to the side of them.

He turned toward the bordering trees and saw a figure in the darkness. Taking a couple of steps, he responded. "Lael?"

The woman nodded. "Follow me into the house."

Alma cast a quick glance behind him and saw the Lamanite leaning against a tree down the path, partially out of sight. Then he and Helam followed Lael into her home.

Once inside, Lael lit an oil lamp and continued to whisper, "She's waiting for you near the river. They've been watching our house all day, so we've made secret preparations." She looked at Helam. "You should leave by the front door, then cut back to the river. I'll let Alma out the back when the Lamanite follows you. Do you think you can lose him?"

"Of course," Helam said, his eyes bright at the challenge.

After ensuring that the Lamanite had followed Helam, Alma and Lael slipped out the back door. They crossed through the courtyard, then along a path that led to the river. The night had grown chilly, and Alma noticed that Lael held her mantle tightly about her shoulders. After a while, he saw a glow up ahead. "Is that the place?" he whispered.

"Yes. They only brought one torch light with them. It might be too bright as it is."

Alma's heart leapt in anticipation. "I was hoping she'd wait for me."

Lael chuckled softly. "She wouldn't consider doing anything else. She about drove us crazy today with all the finishing touches."

"Finishing touches to what?"

"You'll see," she said. Alma could almost hear the smile in her voice.

Moments later, they reached the river. On the other side, a section of trees glowed. "Come," Lael said. "We can cross the river here."

He followed Lael across a carefully placed bridge of logs and moved toward the glow.

The trees lining the bank opened into a small grove. Alma saw Jachin first, holding the torch. His face broke into a smile, and just at that moment, the figure next to him turned.

Alma drew in his breath. Maia wore a veil, but her beauty seemed to shine through the fine white linen. Fresh flowers had been woven along the hem of the veil, and she held a bouquet of orchids. Her lips were drawn into a smile as she extended her hand. "You came."

Alma took a couple of steps and stood in front of her, taking her hand. "Have you been waiting long?"

She laughed, and Alma thought he'd never heard any sound more beautiful. After all that they'd endured, both past and present, to hear her laugh . . . He looked about the grove—all around them orchids and hibiscus had been woven into long garlands passing in and out of branches. The scent was mesmerizing. *She* was mesmerizing. Her ivory linen tunic was edged with intricate embroidery on the neckline and the hem.

"Is Helam coming?" Jachin asked.

"Yes," a deep voice said. Helam pushed through the trees and arrived inside the small grove. His hair was disheveled, and he was out of breath. "Just the four of you?"

"Yes. We didn't want to attract any more attention," Lael said.

Jachin removed woven shawls from under his arm. He handed one to Alma and one to Helam, who draped the priesthood garments over their shoulders. Helam turned to the betrothed couple. "Ready?"

Both nodded, and Helam began the words and blessings of the marriage ceremony.

Alma watched Maia closely, hardly daring to believe this was really happening. Although they were marrying under the cover of night, he felt as if it were a bright and glorious day. When Alma placed his prayer shawl around Maia, he felt a tremor pass through him. She stood so close.

Helam spoke the final words reverently, "What God hath joined together, let no man put asunder."

Then Jachin held out the marriage scroll, which Alma and Maia both signed. Helam continued speaking, pronouncing blessings upon their heads, but Alma barely heard the words. He reached out and took Maia's hands, feeling their softness and warmth.

Her hands felt feather-light in his, and Helam's words seemed to fade away. Then someone nudged him. Helam had concluded the final blessings. Alma had them memorized since he'd officiated in many weddings. And he knew the next step by heart.

Carefully, he lifted the veil from Maia's face. Everything and everyone seemed to melt away in the background. Her warm gaze met his—steady and unwavering. Then he leaned close and lightly kissed her on the mouth. Her eyes closed. He pulled away, smiling, but keeping her in his arms.

The others offered their congratulations, then Lael said, "We should put the torch out."

Darkness enclosed the bright blooms around the grove, and it took Alma's eyes a few moments to adjust.

Jachin's hushed voice said, "We'll start heading back. See you two later."

Maia broke away from Alma and embraced each of her parents, then Helam. The three left the grove, and soon after their footsteps faded, it was silent.

Alma reached for Maia's hand in the new darkness. "It was all over too quickly," he said, pulling her close. His ribs were still quite tender, but holding her seemed to make the pain flee. In the moonlight, the veil outlining her hair made her look absolutely ethereal.

She nestled against him with a sigh. "It's just the beginning."

He smiled, joy and fear clashing in his heart. What would their lives be like under Amulon's reign? *At least we have tonight,* Alma thought. With no idea of what might come in the morning, he didn't want to waste or forget one moment.

Moving slightly away from Maia, he looked at her—his wife. A wave of emotion swept over him as he saw the tenderness and love in her eyes. "I love you."

A smile touched the corners of her mouth. "I'm glad."

He furrowed his brow. "That's all?"

"And I love you too," she said, her smile widening.

He leaned down and brushed his lips against hers, then started to draw away. But to his surprise, she wrapped her arms around his neck and pulled him back. Her fingers tugged at back of his hair as she kissed him, drawing him even closer.

Alma responded, wanting to hold her this way forever—for this moment and this night to never end. Right now, right here, she was safe. She was his.

CHAPTER 24

*A time to weep, and a time to laugh; a time to
mourn, and a time to dance.*
(Ecclesiastes 3:4)

Maia smiled before she opened her eyes. Alma's arm was stretched over her stomach, but she refused to move it. She'd never felt more safe or more loved than she had last night. And the longer she let the feeling last, the longer she could ignore how difficult it would be living under the kingship of Amulon.

Lifting her head, she scanned the bedchamber. It certainly needed some decorating, she thought. Alma's home bore the mark of a man who had been unmarried far too long. He didn't even seem to own more than a few plates and cups. But his home was clean, if sparse.

She suspected that one of Alma's neighbors kept the place swept and aired out for him since he was constantly serving in the community.

Alma stirred and removed his arm. Maia grabbed it and pulled it back over her, relishing the strength and warmth it brought. Suddenly, she felt his gaze on her. She turned her head and found him staring at her, an amused expression on his face.

"I think you fooled me into thinking you were demure and complacent," he said in a raspy tone. The morning hadn't left his voice.

"I've never been demure," Maia said, feigning surprise. "I've merely been selective as to whom I show my real personality."

"Well," Alma said, his gaze filled with tenderness, "I would have liked knowing sooner."

Maia's heart skipped a beat. She couldn't tell if he was teasing or not. "Would it have made a difference?"

Alma leaned closer to her, his expression growing more serious. "Quite a difference."

Maia's stomach tightened. "How?"

"I wouldn't have waited all of those days before asking you to marry me."

She started to laugh, and Alma leaned over and kissed her, stopping the laughter.

"You're not so demure yourself," she said between kisses.

He paused and narrowed his eyes. "I'm a man."

She shoved against his chest and wriggled away. "So that's it? A man can be bold, but a woman can't act on her emotions?"

Alma let out an exaggerated sigh and rolled over onto his back. "You didn't tell me you were impetuous either."

"What?" Maia practically yelled. She tried to swipe at him, but he caught her arm too fast.

"Don't worry," he said, using his weight to keep her captive. "I'll take you with *all* of your flaws."

Her face heated as she tried to punch him again, but he just laughed. Then he was kissing her. After a breathless moment, he whispered, "I've never been so happy in all my life. You are a blessing in every way."

She tightened her arms around his neck. "Let's stay here all day. Then tomorrow we can see about fixing up this house."

"Anything for you."

A knock sounded from the front of the house.

Alma groaned. "Don't they know it's the day after my wedding?"

Maia reluctantly let him go, knowing that the moment was over. The situation in the city was too perilous to keep her husband all to herself for long. Even it if was just after their marriage.

She rose after he left the room and quietly got ready for the day. A hushed conversation came from outside the hut, and Maia was able to make out the word *Amulon* a few times. A tremor ran through her as she thought of poor Raquel having to turn her beautiful new home over to her corrupt father.

Then suddenly Alma reappeared in the bedchamber. He crossed to her and put his arms around her waist. "I have to leave now," he said, regret in his eyes. "I must go among the people and speak to them about bearing our new burdens. I don't want Amulon to be given any reason to punish or imprison anyone."

"Of course," Maia said, touching his cheek. He lifted her up off her feet and kissed her.

"Don't walk the streets alone," Alma said, concern creeping back into his voice.

"I won't," Maia said as he turned and prepared to leave. "When will you be back?"

He turned his head as he tied his sash around his tunic. "At least for supper, if not sooner. It's going to take a lot of patience and praying to get through this."

Maia nodded, her throat tightening. She wondered if *she* had enough patience. When Alma was ready, he gave her a quick kiss, and then he was gone.

She sat on the bed and smoothed her tunic neatly over her legs. Her new bracelets jangled as her arms moved. Alma had given them to her the night before—a bride's present, he'd said. It wasn't much by city of Nephi's standards, but now it was all the jewelry she owned. She'd even slept in them.

Today was her first day as Alma's wife, and she would spend it without him, with only these bracelets for comfort. Taking a deep breath, she steeled her mind against the pressing self-pity that was building. *I should be happy. Alma has returned safely, we are married, and we'll spend the rest of our lives together. I can make it through this day. Besides, there's so much to do.*

Maia left the bedchamber and did a mental calculation of what supplies would be needed for the rest of the house. She'd start off with just a few of the basic necessities for cooking. She was sure she could purchase the supplies on Alma's credit in the marketplace. With a list in mind, Maia tied a scarf about her head, pulling it slightly forward so she wouldn't be immediately recognizable if she should happen to cross Amulon's path. She wondered how long she would have to be so cautious. Now that she was married, she hoped to have more freedom.

But Alma's words and the thought of prowling Lamanites made up her mind, so she set off for her mother's home.

Maia found her mother cutting and gathering young squash in the small garden plot to the side of her house. Lael greeted her daughter with surprise. "Well, I didn't expect to see you so soon."

Maia's face flushed as her mother studied her. "Care to join me in a trip to the market?"

Lael recovered smoothly. "Of course. Let me finish harvesting these squash."

"I'll help you," Maia said. She found a flat rock and knelt in the dirt next to her mother. The two women worked in silence for a few minutes. Maia knew that her mother was waiting for her to speak first.

"Alma went to meet with his teachers," Maia said. "He wants to send out word to all the people that they are not to do anything that would bring punishment from Amulon upon them."

"Very sensible," Lael said. "I think we all naturally want to rebel against anything the Lamanites tell us to do. It's *our* land and *our* homes, for heaven's sake. It's humiliating, to say the least."

"Yes," Maia said. "But our lives are the most important thing, not our possessions."

Lael let out a deep sigh. "You're sounding quite a bit like your husband already."

Maia laughed and put an arm around her mother. "Thank you for the compliment. I wish I could be more accepting of the situation, like he is. He told me not to go anywhere alone, but I still had to convince myself to come here and invite you to the market with me."

Lael placed the collection of squash into her basket. "I'll just put these inside, out of the heat, then I'll be ready to go." She stood and brushed the dirt off her hands.

"Woman," a male voice spoke behind them.

Maia and her mother turned to see three Lamanite soldiers standing at the edge of the garden. Maia's breath caught, wondering what they could possibly want, since all Nephite weapons had been confiscated the day before.

One of the soldiers stepped forward. "Your head scarves are to be handed over."

"What?" Lael said, reaching up to touch the scarf that protected her from the sun.

"King Amulon doesn't want any women going about in secrecy. Only men in the fields are allowed to wear a turban of any kind."

Lael glanced at Maia, who nodded and began to untie her own scarf. After handing over the innocent swatches of cloth, the Lamanite said, "And your jewelry."

"But these were gifts from our husbands," Maia said, her voice trembling.

The Lamanite put his hand on the hilt of his sword. "King Amulon doesn't want Nephite woman to be more richly attired than the Lamanite women."

"What Lamanite women?" Maia said in a sharp voice, then instantly regretted it.

The soldier brandished his sword with one hand and held his other hand out for the jewelry pieces. Lael removed her earrings and necklace. Maia took off the two bracelets that Alma had so recently given her.

"And bring anything else from within the house."

Lael sighed but turned toward the house. The Lamanite with the drawn sword followed her inside.

While Maia waited, one of the other soldiers eyed her, suspicion in his eyes.

"Where are the Lamanite women coming from?" she asked.

"The city of Amulon," the soldier said, then shut his mouth as the other soldier shushed him.

I might see Inda again, Maia thought. A mixed blessing.

Itzel exited the house with a bracelet, adamantly declaring that she owned no more pieces of jewelry. The Lamanites still looked suspicious, but they took the bracelet and finally left.

When the men were out of earshot, Lael said, "What will be next?"

Maia looked at her mother's bare earlobes. She touched the place where her bracelets had been just moments before. It was as if part of her identity had been stripped away. The scarf that Raquel had made for her and the only jewelry that she'd owned in years was now gone.

"Let's go and see if we can find anything at the market for your home," Lael said, her voice sounding falsely upbeat.

Mother and daughter linked arms. As they walked past their neighbors' huts, they saw the same disheartening scene taking place. Lamanites seemed to be swarming everyone's homes, demanding any luxuries or jewelry. Lael and Maia hurried along. When they reached the market, they both stopped and stared.

The place was deserted. Carts had been overturned and goods scattered about. It seemed that everyone had either gone home or never showed up to sell their handmade items or garden produce today.

"What's going on?" Lael said.

Just then a group of Lamanites appeared at the opposite end of the deserted market. They were singing and laughing at each other. When they caught sight of the two women, they headed in their direction.

"Let's go, Mother," Maia said, tugging on Lael's arm. They turned together and started walking away, hearing the men's laughter increase.

"Don't look back," Maia continued. "Just keep walking."

Lael's arm tightened in Maia's as they turned down a side road leading away from the market. They both let out a sigh of relief when the soldiers didn't follow.

As they took a different route to Maia's home, she noticed that the streets were unusually quiet. There were no children playing and no women out working in their gardens. Every once in a while, they saw a group of soldiers entering or exiting a house, carrying valuables.

"They're robbing us all," Lael whispered.

Maia nodded, swallowing against the dryness in her throat. As they made the final turn toward her home, she caught a glimpse of the maize and bean fields on the outskirts of the city. The area was teeming with men. "What's going on there?" she asked, pointing toward the fields.

Lael put a hand to her forehead to shield the sun's glare. "It looks like they're bringing in the harvest."

"It's a little early for that."

"Wait—they're *clearing* the land."

Maia's mouth fell open. "But what about the crops?"

The two women moved closer for a better view. They rounded a house, then climbed up a rising slope. Maia could now see the far side of the field where a dozen Nephite men hauled a fallen tree. Her gaze traveled over the path they were making and she saw other men stripping branches and bark. "What are they building?"

A Lamanite soldier rushed up to one of the Nephite workers, and by his frenzied actions, it was obvious he was yelling about something. Then the soldier shoved the Nephite to the ground, and a pit formed in Maia's stomach. The Nephite men were being treated no better than slaves.

"I wonder where Jachin and Alma are," Lael said, her voice trembling.

"Let's get home," Maia replied. "The sooner, the better."

They hurried down the slope and back toward the rows of huts. A woman peeked out of her window as they passed. "Just a moment," Maia said, and turned into the woman's courtyard.

"Hello there," Maia called.

The woman stuck her head back out, her eyes wide.

"Do you know what they're doing in the north field?" Maia asked.

The woman hesitated, then said in a quiet tone, "They're clearing land to build a palace for King Amulon."

Maia clenched her hands together. *A palace.* She suddenly felt ill as images of King Noah's court reared up in her mind. Somehow she thanked the woman and walked back to her mother.

"They're building a palace for Amulon."

Lael's eyes mirrored the fear in Maia's. They had both escaped the city of Nephi, but now it had found them.

When they reached Maia and Alma's home, Maia entered first, looking for anything that might be missing. She scanned the front room. The soldiers had definitely been here. One of the stools had been overturned, and a rug left crumpled in the middle of the floor. She walked into the bedchamber—the last place she'd seen Alma this morning. His robes and capes were missing.

Maia sat on the bed and lowered her head into her hands. What would Alma think when he returned? Her jewelry was gone, his nice clothing . . . The place felt empty.

Her mother came into the room. "What's going to happen to us?"

Maia looked up, seeing tears trickling down her mother's cheeks. "I don't know." She stood and put her arms around her mother. "But at least we're together."

Lael nodded and sniffed. "Let's find something to prepare for supper for our men."

A new fear arose in Maia's heart. Where *were* their men? And when would they be home?

"All right," Maia said. "I think there's a little maize we can grind here. And I noticed an avocado tree in the back and some wild tomato plants."

Lael smiled faintly. "You certainly have your work cut out for you."

"Yes," Maia said, "I was hoping the market could give me a better start." Her voice quieted. "Now I just hope that Alma comes home all right. Everything else can wait."

* * *

The two women spent the rest of the day cleaning Alma's house and weeding the wild garden in the back. They made plenty of progress, but they were in no hurry, trying to while away the time until the men were released from whatever work they were doing.

Jachin arrived at Alma's home just before sunset. His tired and dusty face was a welcome sight. Maia dropped what she was doing and rushed to him, with Lael right behind her. Both mother and daughter greeted him with a kiss.

"I hoped I'd find you here," Jachin said to Lael. "When I discovered you were away from home, I started to worry. There have already been reports of people put into prison, of goods taken from homes."

"The soldiers have been everywhere." Lael pointed to her bare earlobes.

"Your jewelry," Jachin said, sorrow on his face.

"They even took Alma's clothing," Maia said.

Jachin's face flushed with anger. "The Lamanites' greed has no end, it seems." He shook his head. "I don't know how Alma does it. He spent the morning felling trees and the last few hours counseling and helping people. I can't believe he's still standing."

"Where is he now?" Maia asked.

"Last I saw him, he was helping Raquel and her mother settle into Esther's old home. It will be a tight fit with all of them there, but Helam will start on their new home tonight—after a full day's work already."

Lael leaned against her husband, exhaustion on her face. "It makes my day seem easy."

Jachin put his arms around her and kissed the top of her head. "And mine."

"Tell us about your day over supper," Lael said. The three of them moved to the newly cleared courtyard, and Maia served the simple supper of maize cakes with sliced avocado.

"You've probably heard about the new palace?" Jachin said.

Both of the women nodded.

"Amulon has ordered that all jewelry and valuables be stored at the temple—in a new treasury."

Maia brought a hand to her mouth. "Just like King Noah."

"Close," Jachin said, his face grave. "Ironically, King Laman happens to be more compassionate than Noah. At least he won't allow harlots in Amulon's court."

Maia lowered her hand, not feeling hungry anymore. Darkness had descended over the valley, so she stood and lit a torch.

When the meal was finished, Lael asked Maia, "Do you want to come to our house? Alma will know to find you there."

Maia looked about the darkened landscape. She didn't want to be alone at night with Lamanites about. "I'd like that." She cleared the meal and went inside to gather a few things to bring with her. Just then, she heard her parents greeting someone.

Poking her head out of the door, Maia saw Alma entering the courtyard. Her heart jumped two beats at the sight of him. His face still showed the bruises from his imprisonment, and he was covered in dirt. He exchanged a few quiet words with Jachin, then he saw Maia in the doorway.

Lael and Jachin slipped away as Alma crossed to his wife.

"You're all right?" Maia asked.

He nodded and took her hand. "But I'm filthy."

Maia smiled. "I'll draw you some water."

"No, I'll soak in the river. I don't want you going to all the trouble."

"All right," Maia said, feeling slightly disappointed. She'd have to wait to hear about his day.

"Come with me," Alma said, still holding her hand. He tugged her toward him, stopping just before she could get dirty from his clothing. "I've missed you."

Maia let out a breath. "I missed you too."

Alma smiled through the dirt on his face and led her through the courtyard, still holding her hand.

"Wait," Maia said. She released him and turned back to the house to fetch a clean robe for him to change into. Then she grabbed a robe for herself against the chill of the night.

"Thank you," Alma said when she returned. As they walked toward the river, Maia told him about the items that had been taken from their home—at least what she was sure of; there might be more.

Alma's shoulders sagged. "Most of those things were gifts."

"I thought so," Maia said, stealing a glance at his profile. Even covered with dirt, he was still a handsome sight. "I was going to fix the place up, but the market was closed."

"I know." Alma let out a deep sigh. "Amulon has moved swiftly. It's as if he's been planning this conquest for some time and hasn't delayed making changes. All products bought or sold will have a new tax imposed. The vendors were turned away because they hadn't paid the tax for their space."

"What will they do?"

"I think they'll start trickling back when they know there's no other option."

"Is there no other option then?" Maia asked in a quiet voice.

Alma stopped and turned. "Not yet. I've counseled everyone to obey the Lamanites. We can't fight back right now—we are sorely outnumbered. Several men were imprisoned today already, and I fear there will be many more until we can all humble ourselves."

Maia gave an exasperated grunt. "We can't be like animals led to the altar."

"We can," Alma said, his voice insistent. "We must. Our lives are more important. I don't care about our things. We have our faith, and we have each other."

Maia looked at her bare wrists and held them up for Alma to see. "I know you're right, but when they demanded the bracelets you gave me, I . . ." She looked down, blinking tears.

"Someday," Alma whispered, taking her wrists, "you'll have all the bracelets you desire." His hands moved to her waist and untied her outer robe. "Come."

She smiled and followed him into the cool water. Alma disappeared beneath the current for a moment, then burst back out of the water. He grabbed her hand and helped her walk into the deepest part. Then he put his arms around her.

"You're all wet," she protested.

"So are you." He pulled her even closer, then kissed her.

When he leaned back his eyes were serious. "Maia, I have to ask you to do something."

She nodded, willing to do whatever he needed, yet a knot formed in her stomach.

"I need you to speak to the women of the city. One by one, or in small groups. You can take your mother or Raquel along. We will need the women to temper their men when they come home from the long days of hard labor." Determination crossed his newly cleaned face. "I need the people to humble themselves and subject themselves to the Lamanites' rule. When we're freed from them, I want to have everyone accounted for. We need to lift up our voices to the Lord and plead for deliverance. We need to be as one in our prayers."

Maia pressed herself against him and tightened her hold. "Anything else?"

"I need you to be safe and well," he said in a fierce voice. "If anything happens to you . . . Please don't go anywhere alone. Promise me."

"I won't, I promise," Maia said, and this time she meant it.

His demeanor relaxed. "Let's go. I'm starving." He scooped her up.

"Put me down," Maia said, "You must be exhausted."

Alma grinned as he carried her out of the river. "Not anymore."

CHAPTER 25

Surely the Lord God will do nothing,
but he revealeth his secret unto his servants the prophets.
(Amos 3:7)

"It's late," Raquel said, watching Helam tie the load of sticks into a bundle to carry on his back. The final streaks of sunset were fading rapidly.

"This is the last one," Helam said with a grunt as he hefted the load onto his back, then winced in pain.

"Are you all right?"

"It's nothing."

Raquel walked by his side, wishing she could do more to help build this home. Gathering sticks during the day didn't seem like enough. But every night for the past several weeks, Helam had been building their new hut not far from her mother's. Even though Amulon was building a palace and would vacate their home in a few months, it would likely go to the Lamanites.

But seeing Helam literally work night and day pained her. Each night, other men came to help—Alma was often among them—but Helam always shooed them away to go and help their own families.

They arrived at their new homestead nestled between two other huts. Property was increasingly sparse as the Nephites living on the outskirts of the city were forced to move inside its borders.

About three-quarters of the hut was completed. It would be simple, to be sure—two rooms and a small courtyard. She told Helam she didn't need anything more. After he'd returned from his imprisonment with the Lamanites, she didn't want him out of her sight.

He bent down, and Raquel helped him lower the bundle. He flinched as he straightened.

"Helam?"

"Mmm?" he said, walking away to examine the recently fitted wall of sticks.

Raquel gasped at the dark stains on the back of his brown tunic. "What happened to your back? Did you fall in mud?"

He stopped mid-motion then slowly turned around. By the expression on his face, Raquel knew it wasn't mud.

"Oh, Helam," she whispered. She crossed to him, making him turn around, and pulled down the shoulder of his tunic. It was criss-crossed with blood. She didn't need to see any more to know what had happened. "They whipped you?"

Helam pulled the sleeve over his shoulder and turned to face her. "Not too bad."

She stared at him, incredulous that he could be so casual about this. "Not *too* bad?"

"I'm just not as fast as some of the younger men." His face twisted into a half smile as he pointed at his face. "And as you know, I'm not the most handsome Nephite in the city."

Hot tears burned Raquel's eyes. "You're being singled out because of your scars?"

He touched her cheek, amusement in his eyes. "Why are you so surprised?"

"Because . . . because . . ." She bit her lip, her throat feeling like it had swollen shut.

"I guess I could always wear that hood again."

"Don't you dare," she spat out. "Don't you hide who you are for anyone." She choked on a sob and put her hands on each side of his face. She lifted up on her toes and kissed each cheek. "You are perfect."

Helam wrapped his arms about her, his embrace fierce. "You're the only one who thinks so."

"Everyone loves you just the way you are," she said. "But this must come to an end. I can't take much more."

"Shh," he said, burying his face in her neck. "It *will* end. We just need to put our trust in the Lord."

Raquel pulled away, ashamed tears on her face. "I *hate* my father. If it weren't for him, we wouldn't be in this situation."

His hand went to her shoulder. "We don't know that. The Lamanites would have found us eventually. We couldn't stay hidden forever—there are just too many of them."

She wiped the moisture from her face, despair draining through her chest. "I want to know how long we'll have to endure this. How many times are they going to steal our things? How many times are they going to whip you?" Her voice faltered.

"I liked it better when you were comforting *me*," he said.

She turned and threw her arms around his neck. "Maybe we can get a small group together and escape. We could flee over the mountains."

He tightened his hold. "It might work, although we wouldn't be able to take any young or older people with us. They'd slow us down too much." He breathed in her hair. "And what would the women of the city do without your poultices? And who would teach the girls to weave? What about your mother? She needs you now more than ever. And my mother has only me, so if I left . . ."

"I suppose you're right." She pulled away with a sigh, studying him in the rising moonlight. "Let's get something on those cuts."

Helam winked. "Now there's my Raquel." He took her hand and brought it to his lips. "I'm sorry that our first month of marriage hasn't been what we thought it would be."

Shaking her head, she said, "Well, if you hadn't waited so long to ask me to marry you, we could have had at least a few good months before all of this hardship."

"Me?" Helam said, astonishment on his face. "I told you how I felt years ago, but you completely ignored me."

She laughed. "Maybe I wanted you to work a little harder first."

"*Work* harder?" He chuckled, amusement in his eyes. "I don't think I've ever worked harder in my life at trying to impress such a stubborn woman."

"Well," she said in a coy voice, "you could still work on some things."

Helam's eyes narrowed. "Like what?"

"Like . . ." She blew out a breath of air against a dangling lock of hair. "You could stop hauling so many sticks and kiss me a little more."

"That's *why* I'm hauling the sticks—so we can have our own place," he said, taking her in his arms. Then he leaned down and kissed her until she couldn't think of anything else for him to work on.

* * *

The time passed slowly as the Lamanites tightened their control over the people in the city of Helam. It had been nearly eight months since Amulon was made king, and it seemed that each week there was another new law that suppressed the Nephites even more. A portion of Alma's days were spent reminding people to remember the Lord and to have faith that they would be delivered. As he labored alongside his people, his heart sorrowed at how they were being treated. Men were beaten or thrown into prison for the slightest infractions. Women were made to labor nearly as long and hard as their husbands. On one hand, Alma rejoiced in his people's return to humble spirituality, but on the other, he sorrowed in their afflictions.

A new edict had been given just weeks earlier—no more praying to their God. Amulon had ordered the guards to put to death anyone who was found praying. But the Nephites had taken the edict in stride and continued to pour out their hearts to the Lord in their thoughts. It was as if the command to stop praying had helped them realize how important praying really was.

Alma stood from his workbench, wiping perspiration from his face and neck with a dirty cloth. It was a rare moment when he was alone in the work tent, but the guards had stepped out for some refreshment. Alma had spent the day carving massive doors that would be used in the new palace. He grimaced as he brushed the wood shavings from the design. It was of the feathered serpent god—something he'd been familiar with in his youth—a design that had been forbidden by his father.

Closing his eyes before starting on the second door, Alma said a prayer in his mind. The guards might be back at any moment, but he had more to pray about than usual. Maia was with child—nearing her seventh month. His heart felt like it would burst just thinking about it.

O Lord, Alma prayed silently, *Protect my people as we labor day and night. Soften the hearts of the Lamanites toward us. Bless us with continued good health. Protect Maia and our unborn child. Shield them from persecution and strengthen them against illness. O Lord, give me the strength to continue with my work and also to help others as needed.*

When he concluded his prayer, Alma felt warmer than usual. A breeze had picked up outside, but it did nothing to cool him. Then, suddenly, a wave of heat passed through him and he sank to his knees, trying to catch his breath. At the same moment, a voice spoke to his mind.

Lift up your heads and be of good comfort, for I know of the covenant which ye have made unto me.

Alma gripped the bottom of the door in front of him as the voice of the Lord penetrated his very soul.

I will covenant with my people and deliver them out of bondage.

They would be delivered! Alma's heart leapt.

And I will also ease the burdens which are put upon your shoulders, that even you cannot feel them upon your backs, even while you are in bondage.

The strength returned to Alma's limbs, and his grip tightened on the door.

This will I do that ye may stand as witnesses for me hereafter, and that ye may know of a surety that I, the Lord God, do visit my people in their afflictions.

Tears came to Alma's eyes as the words touched his heart—the Lord had heard them, and they would be delivered. As the voice faded, Alma didn't move for a long time. It wasn't until he heard the commotion of the guards returning that he wiped his eyes and rose to his feet. With trembling hands, he took hold of the carving tool and commenced his work.

"Ah, there he is!" Amulon's voice rang out, startling Alma.

When he turned, he was struck by the contrast of the experience he'd just had and the appearance of the man before him. Amulon wore all his finery—an elaborate headdress and a coat of jaguar skin—not wanting anyone to mistake who the king of the city of Helam was.

Amulon crossed over and studied Alma's work so far. "My old *friend* has not lost his talent, I see." He laughed in a gritty way.

Alma smiled at Amulon, his heart filled with elation as the Lord's promises echoed in his mind. "Thank you, Your Majesty."

The king narrowed his eyes. "So joyful this afternoon? Do share the good news with me. Is your wife finally with child?"

Face red, Alma nodded. He recovered and said, "And congratulations on the birth of your son."

Amulon arched an eyebrow. "Yes, I finally have a child I'm proud to call my own."

The words were a direct insult to Raquel and Itzel, but Alma brushed off the underlying meaning. "My wife has a gift she is preparing for your son."

The king's expression brightened immediately. "Very nice." He spent another moment examining the door and some idols that Alma had carved. "Very nice," he muttered again under his breath. Then he turned to study Alma again, a sly grin on his face.

"Bring your wife to the palace tonight. I have someone I'd like her to meet."

Dread shot through Alma, but the recent words of the Lord seemed to act as a shield. "I will let her know." He offered a formal bow and was relieved when Amulon finally left.

Alma returned to work, hoping to get the door he was working on finished before dark. Then the guards would have no excuse to make him stay. He knew Maia would be upset about going to the palace, but he couldn't wait to tell her of the Lord's promise of deliverance. Just the thought put more strength into his arms. The carving beneath his nimble hands seemed to appear effortlessly.

When he finally finished and looked up, the sun had set. Rubbing his sore neck, then flexing his aching fingers, he turned and smiled at the guards. "I trust the king will be pleased."

The guards just grunted and looked at him, but they didn't say anything as he prepared to leave.

Alma nearly ran home, his heart pounding with excitement and relief. Warmth continued to pulse through his body as he recalled the

Lord's words. He found Maia in the back garden, carefully watering the plants.

"Maia."

"Almost finished." But before she could turn, he put his arms around her waist, embracing both her and the child she carried, and kissed the top of her hair.

"You're back early," she said, turning in his arms and smiling as she let the waterskin drop to the ground.

He leaned down and kissed her again, this time on the mouth.

"Better day than yesterday?"

He grinned and moved his hands until he was holding hers. "The Lord spoke to me."

Maia's eyes widened, and she squeezed his fingers. "What did He say?"

"That He will deliver us," he said in a quiet voice, although he wanted to shout. "He has heard our prayers and wants us to know He remembers us."

"Oh, Alma," she said, her eyes filling with tears. "Did He say when?"

"No. Only that our burdens will be made light—and the time will come when the Lord will deliver us from the Lamanites."

Maia put her arms around his neck and clung tight. The new child stirred within as if he, too, had heard the good news. She pulled back, startled, and touched her belly.

"What's wrong?" Alma asked immediately.

"Nothing," she said with a smile. "I think he heard his father speaking."

He put his hands on her stomach. "You think it's a son?"

With a slight shrug, she said, "A woman sometimes knows these things." She looked up at Alma, her eyes again brimming with tears. "Do you think he'll be born into freedom?"

He took one of her hands and brought it to his lips. "We can only pray."

Maia let out a breath. "Have you told anyone else?"

"Not yet," he said, then hesitated. "There's something more."

Her expression clouded, but she waited for him to continue.

"Amulon came by to inspect my carvings today. He said there's someone he wants you to meet at the palace tonight."

She drew back, putting her hand on her chest. "At the palace? Who could it be?"

"I don't know," Alma said, truly mystified.

Her expression filled with worry, then fear. "Someone from the city of Nephi, perhaps, someone that I used to know—that Amulon used to know."

He put a hand on her arm. "I'll come with you. Don't fear— remember the Lord's promise."

She nodded, but the worry didn't leave her eyes. "I know. I just hope the Lord meant that all of us would be delivered."

"Whatever happens, we'll be together."

* * *

Maia tried to ignore the worry in her heart as she gripped Alma's arm. She was grateful he didn't complain, but she also wondered if he was as nervous as she was. Taking a quick glance at him, she saw that his expression was a mask of stone.

They were now in full view of the palace and the dozens of torches that had been lit on the outside of it so the workers could continue late into the night. The palace was not finished yet, but Amulon had moved in and already occupied the private chambers.

"I should be working with them," Alma said next to her. "The people will wonder what's going on."

"Everyone will assume that Amulon requested an audience," Maia said. "You work just as hard, if not harder, than most."

As they neared the palace, the guards at the main entrance stood and walked to meet them. One of them said, "Follow me."

Maia and Alma followed the guard through the open entrance then past a series of timbers yet to be raised. Torches were positioned everywhere to light the large hall. Nephites filled the room, bent over to lay finely chiseled tile flooring. A few watched them walk past, then quickly turned back to their work to avoid punishment.

The guard stopped at two large doors and rapped loudly. As the doors swung open from the inside, Maia noticed her husband's handi-work on the carved wood. She had heard that the throne room was the first room completed, even before the private bedchambers; that way the king could hold court and order his punishments right away.

Maia stared as they entered—the décor in the room was astonishing. It was amazing how much Amulon had accomplished in just a few short months. Elaborate rugs lined the walls and floor. Finely embroidered cushions had been arranged in small groups. Amulon's throne was massive—a compilation of stone and gold inlay.

Her heart pounded as she tried to guess what Amulon had in store for her. She glanced about the room, seeing several Lamanite women she recognized from the land of Amulon. They were well dressed, wearing plenty of jewelry—jewelry taken from the Nephite women, no doubt.

Amulon stood on the far side, in animated conversation with one of the Lamanite guards. As they moved farther into the room, the king's gaze fell upon her, and Maia felt her skin crawl.

Next to her Alma tugged at her hand, and together they bowed before the king.

Keeping his head lowered, Alma said, "We are here at your request, Your Majesty."

Maia pursed her lips, her gaze on the ground. She marveled at how respectful Alma could be to such an enemy. She had not been this close to Amulon since the night she fled from the Lamanite camp.

He hadn't changed a bit—unless a person could look even more cruel.

A shudder passed through her, and Alma kept a hold of her hand. She could almost feel him bristle next to her, yet his demeanor was calm.

"Welcome," Amulon said, his eyes slowly taking in Maia's appearance. "And may I offer my congratulations?"

Maia's face flamed. Her stomach twisted with nausea as Amulon continued to stare at her. She wished she could turn away and flee this place.

"We appreciate your congratulations," Alma said, moving slightly in front of Maia.

"Ah, I see you've trained your wife well. She has become meek at last," Amulon said with an eerie chuckle. "Or did she just conveniently go silent again?" He laughed, and those around him joined in the empty echo.

He crossed to his throne and took a seat with a flourish. When all was quiet again, he said, "Inda!"

From the collection of women, one stepped forward and removed the embroidered scarf from her hair.

"Inda?" Maia whispered.

The woman smiled—for she was a woman now. Maia guessed that her child would have been born a couple of months before, and the luster of new motherhood made her glow with beauty.

All eyes on her, Inda crossed the room, holding out her hands. When she reached Maia, she kissed her cheek. "Sister."

Maia embraced the woman, forgetting that Amulon might frown upon it.

"Very nice," Amulon's voice boomed, and the two women drew apart. "Just as I thought." He stood from his throne and crossed to Maia. She moved away from Inda, back to Alma's side.

Amulon stopped right in front of Maia, close enough that she could smell the spices on his breath from supper. "I thought you'd be pleased," he said, then looked at Alma. "Isn't it nice to see your wife pleased?"

Alma's reply was quiet, measured. "Of course."

Maia gripped his hand more tightly, unsure of where this was leading.

"Inda has made a request," Amulon said. "And as I like to grant the requests of all Lamanite women in the city of Helam whenever possible, I must comply." He grinned, then winked at Inda.

Maia looked from Inda to Amulon. The nausea was back. Anything involving the king couldn't be good.

"Inda wants you for her maidservant while she is visiting our city," Amulon announced. "And I have granted her wish. There will be no need for you to return home to collect your things—we'll provide everything you need here. You will attend to Inda and her young child. It will be just like the old days." His smile was triumphant as all around him smiled in agreement.

"But I'm a married woman, expecting a child of my own."

Amulon's eyes flitted over her, suddenly looking bored. "Alma, I thought you taught your wife some manners."

"Oh, Maia," Inda broke in. "I've missed you so much. I—I didn't realize you had married."

Maia took a step backward, staring at the Lamanite girl that she had cared so much for. "Yes, I have my own family now. I am no longer a servant—"

"We can do this the easy way or the hard way," Amulon said with a sneer. As if on cue, several Lamanites moved closer, surrounding the small group.

"You cannot ask a married woman to serve in this manner," Alma said, stepping between Maia and the king.

"Oh, but I already have," Amulon said, shoving Alma's shoulder.

He didn't budge.

"As I said," Amulon repeated. "We can do this the easy way or the hard way."

Alma lunged forward, but the Lamanites pounced and had him restrained before he could so much as breathe on Amulon.

The king laughed. "You still have it, old man. You were taught well . . . by me. Unfortunately, another move like that will cost you your life." He raised his hand. "Guards, throw him out!"

The Lamanite soldiers looked momentarily surprised, then started to drag Alma out of the room. Maia ran after him and threw her arms around his neck. "I'll be fine," she whispered fiercely. "Amulon won't dare do anything while I am with child." Tears burned hot in her eyes, but she didn't let them fall. "I'll remember what you told me earlier this evening." Their gazes locked, and suddenly Alma was torn from her arms.

Maia watched him as the soldiers led him out. She bit her lip, refusing to let Amulon or anyone in this Lamanite court see that her heart had just been shattered. Lifting her head high, she turned to the king.

He wore an amused grin.

Maia looked away and crossed to Inda.

The young mother grabbed her hands. "Come to my quarters."

Maia followed Inda, grateful to be out of the throne room and Amulon's appraising eyes.

"I'm sorry, Maia. I didn't realize you had married, or I wouldn't have made the request," Inda whispered as they walked along the halls, some still open to the sky. "Perhaps your husband can work at the palace as well."

"I married soon after I arrived here," Maia said in a stiff voice. She didn't want to bring more attention to Alma than was necessary, so she decided not to tell Inda too much about her husband.

They reached a row of doors, and Inda opened one. "In here." A couple of oil lamps burned in the spacious room, and a woman stood from a cushion. She was a Nephite and bowed to Inda.

"You can go now," Inda said. "I have a new maidservant."

The Nephite woman glanced at Maia, then her eyes widened in recognition. Maia didn't know her personally, but had seen her several times in the circles of women. She felt her cheeks warm—knowing that it wouldn't be long before everyone in the city of Helam would know that Maia was a servant at the palace.

When the other servant left, Maia crossed to the corner, to a sleeping child.

"This is Paan," Inda whispered. "Named after his father, of course."

Of course, Maia thought. *Like my son will be. But will he be born into captivity?*

"He's beautiful," Maia said, gazing at the dark lashes resting on the cherubic face. The babe's black curls looked slightly damp about his forehead.

"So *you* are with child." Inda smiled. "How wonderful. I worried that Amulon would take you as his second wife when your voice returned—and I knew you wouldn't care for that."

Maia decided she had to be careful—how much could she trust Inda? "Amulon released me when we arrived here. Not long after, I married Alma."

Inda's eyes flickered back to her sleeping son. "Well, now you can live like royalty again here in the palace, not in your husband's hut." She smiled at Maia. "My husband is king over the land of Amulon now—so I am a queen. King Laman seems to love Amulon and has made several of his brethren kings over his other lands. I came here to secure Amulon's special blessing on my son. Perhaps when I leave, you might stay on at this palace." A laugh trickled from her. "But for now, you can be *my* servant, and I'll give you all my old gowns just like before."

Maia tried to smile back, but her heart wasn't in it. How had this girl changed so much? She was a mother and a queen now. But neither motherhood nor queenhood had matured her one bit. Quite the opposite, it seemed. *I don't want to be here,* Maia wanted to say. *I'd rather live in a tiny hut with my beloved husband than here, surrounded by wrongful luxury.*

"He should stay asleep the rest of the night," Inda said, her attention back on her infant. "He's been such a good little boy." She turned her beaming face toward Maia. "Imagine! Everything has worked out so well—me a queen—and you my servant again." She brought her hands together in delight. "Will you comb and plait my hair like you used to before bedtime?"

"Of course," Maia whispered. What she really wanted to do was escape this stifling room and run until she reached home—her true home.

CHAPTER 26

That which thou hast prayed to me . . . I have heard.
(2 Kings 19:20)

Alma waited as long as he could stand it then started the walk back to the palace. Even with the Lord's words of assurance, he couldn't sleep, couldn't rest, couldn't stop worrying about Maia.

When the guards had escorted him home, he had walked into a hut empty of his wife's good nature and spirit. The place was hollow. He wanted to say a proper good-bye to her, not be dragged from the throne room by guards. Although he knew he was taking a great risk in returning to the palace, he knew he'd never sleep tonight or any other night unless he tried.

Nearly all of the torches were out by the time he reached the palace grounds. A new set of guards was at the entrance, their body positions telling him that they were relaxed, probably half asleep. Alma made a wide berth around the palace, wondering how he would find the room that Maia was staying in. All of the high windows were dark, so he settled down on a rock to watch and wait.

"Who's there?" someone called after a moment.

Alma stood and spun around, trying to see who had spoken.

Around the corner of the building, two guards appeared. Alma turned and ran, pushing through the foliage that was just beyond the palace. When the guards' voices faded, he slowed. He waited for hours, until the black sky softened to indigo.

Staying as far away from the palace as possible, he found his way back to the city. He needed help. He had to find Helam.

When Alma reached Helam's newly finished hut, he was surprised to see him already outside, sharpening his tools.

"Greetings," Helam said in warm voice, then his expression grew serious. "What's happened?"

Alma blurted out what had become of Maia.

Helam nodded gravely. "I know several men who work inside the palace. We can get more information that way. In fact, I think Ben is working on the tile floors this week."

Alma let out a breath, his burden feeling lighter after having shared it with Helam. Then he told him the good news—the promise that the Lord had made to ease their burdens.

"Maia's burden will be light in the palace," Helam observed.

Alma sighed. "Mostly I worry that she is under Amulon's command once more—how can *that* be easy?"

"Don't you see?" Helam said. "As horrible as it may be right now to be separated from your wife, she'll be well fed and cared for."

"Of course," Alma said. "But I just don't think I can stay in that hut without her—knowing that she might be in danger."

"You're welcome to sleep in my courtyard anytime," Helam said, a brief smile touching his face. "We'll find out where she is and, when the Lord sees fit to deliver us, we'll bring her home."

"All right," Alma said. "Pray that it will be before our child is born."

"I haven't stopped praying yet," Helam said. "Now go; I'll have to deliver the news to Raquel soon—and she won't be pleased."

When Alma left Helam, it was still early. So he moved through the city, knocking on huts and delivering the message from the Lord. The people were overjoyed, and many invited him in for something to eat. But food would not appease the emptiness in his stomach.

Alma arrived in the work tent before the guards. The doors he'd finished the night before had already been transported to the palace, and new ones stood in their place to carve. Exhausted, he took a drink of the stale water from a goatskin then went to work. Somehow, some way, he'd find a means to contact his wife.

The guards arrived, and Alma continued to work straight through the heat of the day, taking little food, and water only when necessary. Jachin stopped at the tent, and after a brief conversation found out what had become of Maia.

By evening, Alma was completely exhausted, having slept so little the night before. On his way home, he walked slowly, his tired limbs almost giving out. He hoped to hear some news from Helam or Jachin on how Maia was faring.

He was surprised to see Raquel waiting at his door.

"Alma," she said, glancing about furtively. "I have something to tell you."

He motioned for her to go inside his hut.

"Ben came to me this evening—after working at the palace today," Raquel began. "He saw Maia a time or two with the Lamanite woman Inda. Maia seemed to be doing fine." Raquel took a deep breath then rushed on in a low voice. "Ben said the king usually retires soon after midnight . . ."

Alma nodded as he listened, cataloging each detail in his mind as Raquel spoke. He thanked her profusely, then when she left, he grabbed a roll of hardened bread and gulped it down. Then he nearly staggered into the bedchamber and fell onto the bed. He'd need to buoy up his strength. He just hoped he wouldn't sleep past midnight.

* * *

Waking with a start, Alma immediately turned his head toward the window. The night was still dark. He sat up in the bed and rubbed his aching neck. His eyes were still bleary from lack of sleep, but by the position of the moon, Alma knew he didn't have much time to waste.

Pulling a thick cloak across his shoulders, he paused and offered a silent prayer. He prayed that by following Raquel's secondhand instructions, he'd be able to see his wife tonight without interference.

Alma quietly left his hut. Curfew was stringent in the city, and guards regularly patrolled the streets. He kept to the side streets and made a few shortcuts behind homes. At last he reached the edge of the north field—now transformed into the palace grounds. The torchlight burning by the palace entrance revealed the two guards who stayed there throughout the night. Neither looked his direction.

Another silent prayer, then Alma was off again, making a wide berth of the palace walls, staying low to the ground. He reached the back of the massive building, out of breath but safe. As the moonlight reflected off the walls, he began to count windows. The eighth one belonged to Inda and her family. The small one off to the side was the room that Ben had told Raquel was the servant's room—close enough to the family quarters so that she could be summoned day or night.

Alma crept to the windows, counting as he moved below them. Finally reaching the ninth one, he waited a few minutes before peering inside. It was high, but with his height it wasn't hard to see inside. The room was quite dark, but he could make out the furniture—a bed, a low table, and two stools. His gaze went back to the bed. It was empty.

Just as he was about to whisper his wife's name, something crashed into the side of his face. He pulled his head back, holding the side of his jaw.

"Alma?" came a whisper.

He looked up, his eyes stinging in response to the blow. "What were you trying to do? Kill me?"

Maia's face broke into a wide smile. "What were *you* trying to do?"

He smiled back and leaned through the window again, taking her face in his hands and kissing her. "That's much better." He flexed his jaw as he released her. "What did you hit me with?"

She lifted a goblet. "You're lucky this is all I had."

Alma chuckled softly, then grew serious. "How are you?"

"It appears that I'm better than you." She looked down at her hands. "I'm fine. Although I'd rather be home with you." She met his gaze. "But I don't want you to do anything foolish to make things worse. You shouldn't even be here."

"I know," Alma said. "But I can't sleep without you."

Her cheeks flushed.

"Move back a little," he said, then hoisted himself up on the window ledge. It was a tight fit, but within a few seconds he was inside Maia's room without making too much noise.

"Alma, someone will hear," she said, but stepped into his embrace anyway.

"I just couldn't stay away," he whispered. "How is the baby?"

"Fine," she said against his chest. "But you can't stay."

"I know."

"You should leave."

"I know." But he only held her tighter.

Finally, reluctantly, Alma pulled away. "Soon," he whispered. "Soon the Lord will deliver us."

"I hope so," she whispered back.

Alma kissed her gently on each cheek. "Be ready. I don't know what the Lord's plans are, or when the time will come, but I'm not leaving without you."

* * *

Amulon spread his hands wide, stretching his fingers. On four of his fingers, he wore jeweled rings—rings fit for the king he was. The day was still early, and there was little to do but wait for his morning meal. He preferred to eat in his chambers alone as he thought over his plans for the day. He smiled to himself, pleased with how things were progressing in Helam; there was only one item that bothered him. The Nephites seemed too happy. They did everything they were asked to with annoying cheerfulness. He'd even overheard the palace workers singing as they worked. When he commanded them to stop, they did so without any hesitation, but they still seemed cheerful.

Perhaps they were finally becoming the obedient servants they should be, he thought. But he expected their postures to be slumped, their expressions dour, their souls beaten—especially with the edict he'd given about no praying to or worshipping their god. Even Alma, with his beloved wife at the palace, still put in a full day's quality work *and* greeted Amulon with pleasantries each day.

Amulon didn't trust Alma, but nothing in his actions or words had pointed to any form of treachery. So Amulon had doubled the guards to watch his every move, night and day. That's how he discovered Alma's nightly visits to his wife.

But instead of immediately imprisoning Alma and putting him to death, Amulon let him carry on. He would wait until the absolutely right moment to rid the city of Helam of its precious Alma once and for all. But first, he needed to be assured of absolute control.

That will be my revenge, Amulon decided. He'd establish his authority once and for all—and the people would forget their prophet and their so-called god. *I will be their god,* Amulon thought. The more he dwelt on the idea, the more he liked it. *The idols will be carved after my image, and the people will worship me.* Of course he'd still pay homage to the nature gods, but *he* deserved more from the people.

Someone tapped lightly at his door. "Enter," he said.

The rustle of footsteps preceded the smell of the morning meal. Amulon turned, pleased to see that it was Maia who carried the platter. She might be Inda's personal maid, but from time to time he requested her services as well. Maia kept her gaze lowered, but Amulon had no intention of letting her leave too soon.

"How is your health?" he asked when Maia set the tray down.

"Fine, sir," she mumbled.

"Look at me," he said, a thrill running through him as she lifted her gaze. "How do you like living in the palace?"

"It's . . . very comfortable."

He smiled. "It can be more comfortable if you should choose." He watched the changing expression on her face—from fear to curiosity. "Ah, so I have your interest. I may be a married man, but I can offer you so much more than any other man in the land."

Her face darkened. "I *am* married."

"Right now you're married, but don't forget you lost your first husband tragically."

Maia opened her mouth in surprise.

"Who's to say that you won't lose your second husband in a similar way?"

She clamped her mouth shut, eyes blazing.

"Just know that I'm watching your every movement—and I know *everything.*" He stood and took her arm. She flinched, but he held fast. "What makes you so special? Why do you marry only the leaders of the land? First Noah, then Alma. Are you really so much a woman that no man can resist?"

Maia's eyes brimmed with tears, but Amulon merely laughed. "You got away once from me, but not again." He pulled her close until he could feel the warmth of her skin next to him.

With a gasp, she pushed away from him. "What do you want from me? You have a wife, a son, all the women of the court if you choose, all the power in the land . . . why me?"

Grabbing her by both arms, Amulon leaned down and whispered fiercely in her ear, "I only want to finish what I started all those months ago." Then he shoved her away, hard.

She fell against a table, then staggered to her feet. She wiped at the tears on her face. "You're despicable to the core—you have a beautiful daughter, a grandson, and a wife who all cared for you."

Amulon stared at her in disbelief. How dare she speak about his former family? "They abandoned me!" he roared. "They're alive today because of *my* mercy. Their desertion could be punishable by death."

She started trembling but still held his gaze. "No matter your power, no matter how many Nephites or Lamanites you put to death, you are still nothing. You are still not worthy of any woman or child's love."

"Get out!" Amulon yelled. "*You* will not see the light of day again. Your dear Alma will not live to see his child born. This I assure you!"

Maia stumbled toward the door, which was flung open by a guard. Several more guards appeared, and immediately they seized her and dragged her to the underground prison.

His room empty once again, Amulon strode to the table and with one sweep of his arm, sent everything crashing to the floor.

* * *

"O Lord, please spare my husband's life. Protect him from Amulon's hand. Please deliver me from this place," Maia whispered to herself. She'd only been in the prison for a few hours, but already despair had set in. How long would it be before Alma found out? What would he do? What about Inda? She certainly knew by now; maybe Inda would be able to persuade Amulon to release her.

It was ironic, Maia thought, as she gazed at the rocky prison walls and the earthen floor, that Amulon had built this prison right next to his palace. The guards had led Maia through the palace, for all of the Nephite workers to see, then along the north side of the building. Here, several prison cells had been dug out of the earth, then lined with rocks, and the only way in was to be lowered by rope.

When she first arrived, she heard a few of the other prisoners—men—call out to the guards for food. Her stomach now grumbled, and she wondered if she'd be fed.

She gazed around the dim interior and saw no sign of rats—which meant that food and water were strangers in this cell. Then she looked up toward the light coming from the top and prayed silently again, remembering the assurance she'd seen in Alma's eyes when he'd told her about the Lord's promise of deliverance.

She was ready for it.

As the day progressed, she prayed constantly—for Alma, for herself, for her unborn child, for the Nephites, even for Inda. She eventually dozed off, feeling weak with hunger. When she opened her eyes, the light was more orange, and she felt strangely warm and relaxed.

I don't feel hungry anymore, she realized, surprised not to feel nauseated either. Rising to her feet, she stretched her stiff joints. She paced the small area for a while, then sat down again to wait—for what she didn't know.

Dark came and still no food. No sign or sound of the guards or any of the nearby prisoners, either. Maia said another prayer, then spread her cloak beneath her and tried to sleep.

As she slept, she dreamed that Inda had come to rescue her, but Maia couldn't reach the rope dangling above her head. Suddenly, she opened her eyes, realizing that someone was calling her name.

She peered through the darkness. "Inda?"

"Maia, are you down there?" the voice came again.

"Yes!" Relief flooded through her. Maybe her dream would become reality after all.

"I'm sorry," Inda said, her voice echoing against the stones that surrounded Maia. "I shouldn't have insisted that you come to the palace in the first place."

"Can you get me out?" Maia called up.

There was a period of silence, then Inda said, "The king said I can take you with me to the city of Amulon. We leave in two days."

Cold seeped into Maia. "What about my husband?"

"He has to stay here," Inda said. "But you'll be free of this place if you come with me. If not, you'll die in this prison."

Maia's shoulders slumped. She would never leave Alma, even if it meant wasting away in this prison. Her hands went to her stomach. But could she live with a decision that would harm her baby?

"I brought a round of bread and some water," Inda said, and something landed near Maia's feet.

She stooped to retrieve the waterskin and wrapped bread. "Thank you."

"I'll try to come tomorrow night."

Maia didn't answer but nodded to herself, tears forming in her eyes. She sat on her cloak and drank from the waterskin then bit into the bread. The taste melted on her tongue and she ate slowly, relishing every bite.

When she finished with the bread, she grabbed the waterskin and drank deeply, but saved some for the morning. "Alma," she whispered. "Please come and find me." Yet in her heart, she didn't want him to risk his life. She closed her eyes, trying to picture him in her mind, his loving gaze and whispered words from only the night before. Then her body went cold again. Amulon would surely be waiting for Alma tonight if he chose to appear.

"Alma, don't come—don't come at all. O Lord, please protect my beloved," she whispered, tears budding at her eyes. She wrapped her arms around herself and lay down, knowing that sleep would not come easily this night.

CHAPTER 27

. . . for the Lord preserveth the faithful.
(Psalm 31:23)

Alma paced the length of his home. His wife was in prison—Ben had just confirmed it upon his return from working at the palace that morning. Alma's first reaction was to gather a group of men and deliver an unpleasant surprise to the king's guards. He knew this would set in motion a chain of events that could ultimately be devastating, but he felt literally ill when he thought of his wife, in her condition, on a cold prison floor. Yet something had whispered to his mind that he needed to wait.

So he'd waited, going through the painful motions of the day's labor. Yet all day he'd felt as if something were about to change. All day he'd prayed in his heart that his people's deliverance would come soon. As the hut darkened with the night, he continued to pace, thinking about the magnitude of moving such a large group of people, and worrying about the safety of his wife.

For the umpteenth time, he sank to his knees and bowed his head. But this time, instead of repeating the words that seemed to be constantly on his lips, a whisper came to him—the whisper of the Lord.

Be of good comfort, for on the morrow I will deliver you out of bondage.

Alma's shoulders relaxed, and joy pulsed through him. He clasped his hands tighter, listening intently to each word.

Go before this people, and I will go with thee and deliver this people out of bondage.

When the Lord's words had faded away, Alma opened his eyes and stood. It was time. Tomorrow they would be delivered. But first, they needed to gather the flocks and pack up grain and other supplies to take with them. No one would sleep tonight.

* * *

"The flocks have been gathered," Helam said.

Alma turned and rubbed his hands together. They ached from carrying goatskins filled with grain to the market center. He glanced at the sky—still dark, but dawn was fast approaching.

"Do we need to find weapons, too?" Helam asked.

"No," Alma said. "The Lord will not deliver us with violence." He didn't know how exactly the Lord would deliver them, but he knew it wouldn't happen through fighting. "When everything is ready, I need to rescue Maia."

"I can see to the last details," Helam said in a quiet voice. "Or do you want me to come with you?"

Alma let out a breath. He should be dropping from exhaustion, but somehow he still had strength as if he'd slept a full night and hadn't been working all night with the people to gather flocks and supplies. "You stay here; I won't be long." He gazed across the open market where families had gathered. Many of the children slept while the adults made preparations. It was a miracle they hadn't been discovered by the Lamanite guards—a miracle that only the Lord could have brought to pass.

With a final glance of reassurance to Helam, Alma left the market and hurried to the palace. Since learning of Maia's imprisonment, he hadn't stopped praying. At least he knew she was away from Amulon, but he also feared for the unborn child's health. Somehow he would find a way to rescue her—the time for the Lord's deliverance had arrived.

When he came within view of the palace, the torches still burned at the entrance, but he was surprised to see no guards. He crept closer, wondering if they were patrolling and would appear around the corner at any moment. Then he saw two shapes on the ground.

Slowly, he moved toward them, looking about for anyone who

might be watching him. When he reached the side of the first Lamanite, he reached out and touched his chest. The man was breathing, but seemed to be sleeping. Alma looked at the second guard—he appeared to be sleeping too.

A gentle warmth rushed over him. Could this be the Lord's doing?

Alma rose and walked along the palace walls, toward the far side where the prison cells had been constructed. He slowed as he neared the area, keeping alert for any guards.

At the entrance, two guards lay on the ground, sleeping. Alma watched them for a couple of minutes to be sure, then crept toward the first cell. He lowered the rope as he called out, "Hello down there."

It only took a moment for a man to respond.

"Grab onto the rope," Alma instructed. When he felt the tug, he pulled the man up.

The Nephite emerged from the hole and blinked at Alma in surprise. "What's happening?"

"We're leaving," Alma said. "The Lord has caused the Lamanites to fall into a deep sleep. We've spent the whole night gathering our flocks and grain for the journey."

The man embraced Alma. "Let me help you free the others."

The two men worked side by side until they had lifted five more bleary-eyed men above ground.

"The woman must be in this one," one of the men said.

Alma looked down into the hole, his heart leaping as he thought of his wife. "Maia?" he called out. He waited a moment, holding his breath, but no answer came. He called out again, but still no answer.

"I'm going down." With a couple of men holding the rope, he lowered himself into the cell. Once he hit the ground, he scanned the darkness. Then he saw her, curled up against the wall. He crossed to her and knelt by her side. Touching her shoulder, he was relieved to find her warm and breathing. "Maia?"

She moved and lifted her head.

"It's me."

"Alma?" Her voice was hoarse.

"I'm here," he said, scooping her into his arms. "Are you all right?"

Her arms wrapped around his neck. "You're here?" She clung to him, inhaling deeply. "You're safe. That's all that matters now."

"Can you stand? We must get out of here quickly."

Maia nodded against his chest, and he helped her locate the rope. He secured the rope beneath her arms to give her added support. When she was safely outside, the rope came tumbling down for him, and he hoisted himself up.

The sky was starting to lighten as Alma climbed out of the cell. A quick glance told him that the prison guards were still sleeping soundly. He smiled as he saw Maia, and she embraced him again. "I thought I was dreaming when you called my name."

Alma held her tightly for a moment before releasing her. "I'm relieved to see you're all right."

He turned to the others. "More of our people are inside the palace. We need to collect them quickly and return to the market-place where everyone is waiting."

"What about the palace guards and the king?" one of the Nephites asked.

"The Lord has caused a deep slumber to come over all of the Lamanites—we should be able to wake the Nephites to help them leave." He turned to Maia. "Can you walk?"

She nodded and grasped his hand.

The small group of Nephites hurried to the palace and walked unimpeded through the front entrance. They split up, taking torches to light the way, and moved through each room, waking the Nephite servants.

Maia stopped Alma as they walked along a corridor. "Inda and her family sleep here," she said in quiet voice. She slowly pushed the door open and peered inside. Then she drew back into the hallway. "Inda wanted to take me back with her to the city of Amulon, where her husband is king."

"When?"

"The day after tomorrow."

Alma drew her into his arms. "The Lord's deliverance came just in time then." He kissed the top of her head, shuddering at the thought of Maia being carted away—again. "Do you have anything you need to retrieve from your room?"

"No." Maia looked at him. "Everything I need is right here."

Alma grabbed her hand. "Then let's get out of here." They moved toward the entrance of the palace, joining the freed Nephites. There were several dozen of them gathered at the entrance, their faces filled with awe.

Leading the group and still holding Maia's hand, Alma left the palace and walked back to the marketplace, where the crowd had almost doubled in size. Helam came forward, Raquel right behind him.

"Are you all right?" Helam asked Maia.

She nodded as Raquel crossed to her and took her arm. "Let me get you some food and water," Raquel said and led her away.

Alma watched them go, then turned to Helam. "How close are we to leaving?"

"Everyone is accounted for," Helam said. "How did you get the people out of the palace?"

"The Lord has caused a great sleep to overcome the Lamanites," Alma said.

Helam nodded. "Several reports have come in that the guards at the outpost are also sleeping. It seems to affect only Lamanites."

"Of course," Alma said with a smile.

Helam returned the smile, although his expression remained weary. "The sun will rise in a couple of hours; how long do you think the sleep will last?"

"Until we are delivered," Alma said in a quiet voice. He put a hand on Helam's shoulder. "The wait is over. This moment we'll begin our journey to freedom once again."

Helam turned to the crowd and sent word among them that it was time to leave. The instructions passed like wildfire, and small groups formed, organizing themselves into long rows. Children were awakened and morsels of food passed around. The men lifted heavy sacks of grain on their backs, and the women carried clothing and rugs rolled into bundles.

Raquel and Maia appeared, and Alma took his wife's hand. "Ready?"

"Yes," she said with a smile. He could see the exhaustion in her eyes but hoped that she would have the necessary stamina.

Alma started to walk, passing along the familiar streets muted in waning moonlight—the streets that he and his faithful people had built with their hands. They passed their homes, their courtyards, their carefully tended gardens. They reached the fields west of the city, out of sight of the palace, where several dozen men and boys stood guard with the flocks.

The Nephites joined together, Alma leading the way. As the terrain changed and grew steeper, Alma noticed Maia's labored breathing. "Do you need me to carry you?"

She tightened her hold on his hand. "No—I don't feel as tired as I look."

"I think everyone has been blessed with greater strength today."

As they crested the first hill, the early signs of dawn touched the land. Alma turned and looked down upon his people as they climbed the hill. Some of the children ran ahead of their parents, then stopped and waited for them to catch up. The elderly leaned on arms of the young. Men carried small children on their shoulders, adding to the weight of the grain bags they bore. And lastly, the flocks were driven, livening the air with animal bleating.

And still the city of Helam slept.

"I'll miss it," Maia said, standing next to Alma.

"I will too," Alma said, his throat thick as he looked down on the city that the believers had built with their own hands, perspiration, and love for their God. A life on the run was not what he'd have ever guessed for himself while living in King Noah's court. But if fleeing meant living free of persecution and being able to pray aloud to the Lord, the sacrifice was worth it.

"I'll never forget the river," Maia said, nestling against Alma's side. "The place where you baptized me. The place where we were married."

Alma wrapped his arm around his wife's shoulders. "We will soon have new memories." He looked down at her growing stomach. "Ones that we can share with our little family."

* * *

Alma scanned the green valley. The climate was cooler than the city of

Helam, but he could see plenty of water—a small lake with several streams running into it.

Next to him, Helam stopped, his gaze following Alma's. "This is it?"

"Yes," Alma said, taking a deep breath as tender warmth spread through him. This place felt *right*. For how long, he didn't know, but his people needed a rest. They had been traveling all day, and now evening approached. He looked over at Maia, who stood with a group of women, Raquel included.

Maia caught his glance and smiled. "It's beautiful," she called out. It was as if she'd read his mind.

"Yes—almost as beautiful as you."

She shook her head, laughing, then patted her stomach. "Even though I'm as large as an alpaca?"

"Never," he said.

"Come on, you two," Helam interrupted. "You're making Raquel blush."

Raquel opened her mouth in protest, then pursed her lips, glowering at Helam.

"Careful, Helam," Alma said, "or you won't have a tent to sleep in tonight."

Helam laughed. "I guess I don't have anything to lose then. While we're speaking our minds, I have a suggestion." He leaned close to Alma. "We're not calling this place *Helam* or any such name—I propose that we call it the valley of Alma."

"Very nice," Maia exclaimed, her eyes twinkling. Several others around them murmured their assent.

Alma rubbed the back of his neck. "What about the valley of Abe? Or Raquel?"

"Nice try," Helam said with a firm shake of his head. "I've done everything you asked. It's time you listen to me for a change."

"Oh?" Alma said with a smirk. "Is that how you feel?"

"That's how we all feel," Helam said, crossing his arms. He turned from Alma and called out, "Who's in favor of naming this valley after Alma?"

Dozens of "yeses" chorused around them. Helam turned back to Alma, a triumphant smile on his face. "There you have it."

"All right," Alma said, trying to appear nonchalant. But inside, he was overwhelmed by Helam's suggestion and the people's support of it. "Let's get to work then. Sunset is only an hour away."

The Nephites streamed into the valley, excited chatter bubbling from everyone. Finally, they would be laboring for their own benefit, and not for a greedy and selfish king. When most of the people had passed by him, Alma turned to Maia. She gazed ahead, a strange look on her face.

"What's wrong? Do you think we should change the name of the valley?"

Maia's eyes widened as she turned to look at him.

"Maia?" He stared at her, taking in her ashen face. "What's wrong?"

"I—" She gripped her stomach. "I think . . ." Her eyes rolled back in her head, and Alma reached her just in time to stop her from hitting the ground. Gritting his teeth, he lifted her in his arms.

"Raquel!" He didn't know how far ahead she'd gone, but if Maia's pain was what he feared, she needed a woman's attention.

Those who were closest to him turned as he continued to call for Raquel. He tried to quell the panic in his voice, but desperation flooded through him.

Finally Raquel returned his call. She came running up to him, concern on her face. "What's happened?" She touched Maia's forehead, then moved her hand over her face and neck.

"I don't know," he said. "She was holding her stomach and fainted."

A flicker of fear passed over Raquel's face, then it returned to calm. "I think the child might be coming."

"It's too early," he said, recalling Maia's first babe, also born early, who had not lasted long in the world.

"Babies have survived this early before," she said in a quiet voice. "Fresh water will be important. You need to carry her to the nearest river. We'll set up a birthing tent."

Alma nodded, feeling numb. It was good to have someone else tell him what to do. Maia stirred in his arms, and hope rushed through him. "She's waking up."

Raquel walked by his side, holding Maia's hand. "We need to get her out of the heat as soon as possible. The journey has probably been more difficult for her than we guessed."

Itzel, Lael, and Esther were soon by his side. Helam rushed ahead and started constructing a tent using the panels that several Nephites offered. By the time Alma reached the river, carrying Maia, the birthing tent was up. He stooped to go through the flap and set Maia on the rugs that had been spread out.

Raquel and Lael followed him inside. They immediately set to work cooling Maia's skin with wet cloths. "Tell Esther to find willow bark and tobacco leaves. Abe can help her," Raquel told Lael, who bowed out of the tent.

"Let me help you," Alma said, taking the cloth that Itzel had left.

"We need to take off some of her layers of clothing," Raquel said.

Alma helped Raquel, careful not to disturb Maia too much. She moaned a few times but remained unconscious. Then he noticed that her lower skirt was soaking wet.

Raquel saw it at the same time. "It looks like she will be having her child soon—hopefully before morning."

"Is something wrong?" Alma asked.

"Not necessarily. But once the waters break, the child must be born soon or . . ." She didn't finish, and he was grateful for it.

Raquel pulled out a satchel tied to her waistband and took out a pinch of dried herbs. She glanced at Alma. "You may want to leave now. This should wake her up, and she may be in some pain."

Alma shook his head. "I'll stay as long as she'll let me."

Raquel held the herbs in front of Maia's nose, and her eyes startled open.

She looked wildly about, and Alma grasped her hand. "It's all right. You fainted." Her gaze focused on him, then her face contorted with pain.

Raquel put a hand on Maia's stomach. "The labor pains are stronger now," she said just as Maia cried out.

"Is she all right?" Alma said, perspiration heating up his face and neck.

But Raquel ignored him. She leaned over Maia, looking into her eyes. "You need to stay awake, no matter how much it hurts."

Maia cried out again and tugged her hand away from Alma.

He tried to take her hand again, hoping to give some comfort, but she batted it away. Her breathing came fast, and she closed her eyes again. "What can I do?" he asked.

"You can bring a good supply of water to the tent and find some more rugs," Raquel said.

He tore his gaze away from Maia, who seemed to stare past him.

Raquel put a hand on his arm. "You should let the women handle it from here. We have plenty of experience in these matters."

He nodded, but inside he ached for his wife. What would the outcome be for her? For their child?

When he stepped out of the tent, he was assaulted by questions from Esther, Itzel, and Lael. But he couldn't answer any of them. "Raquel needs your help."

Lael squeezed his arm, concern in her eyes. "We'll keep you apprised of any news."

Alma nodded and watched the three women enter the tent. Rubbing the back of his neck, he turned and walked the several dozen paces to the men gathered near the river—Helam, Jachin, and Ben, who held onto Abe's hand. Crossing to them, Alma lifted his hands.

"They took over, did they?" Helam said, his tone light but his expression worried.

"Sent me right out." He shuffled his feet.

Just then, another cry came from the tent.

Abe's eyes rounded. "What's wrong with her?"

Helam crouched by Abe. "Maia's not feeling well. She'll be better tomorrow. What do you say we try this river out and see if there are any fish in it?"

Abe smiled and grabbed his hand. Helam turned to Alma and asked, "Want to join us?"

"No," Alma said, "I need to fetch the water. Besides, I want to stay here in case there's any . . . news." He watched Helam, Ben, and Abe walk off. Then he turned to Jachin as another cry reached their ears. "How am I going to endure this?"

Jachin folded his arms. "One moment at a time, just like she is." He looked past Alma. "When Maia was born, she gave her mother a difficult time. That's why we couldn't have any more children."

"Was she this early?"

"No, a little late if I remember right."

"You're not making me feel any better," Alma said, attempting a smile.

"Not much can, except praying." He sighed. "Here, I'll help you with the water."

The two men grabbed some goatskins and waded into the river together to fill them one by one. Then they placed the goatskins by the tent. Alma heard the murmuring of voices coming from inside, but no more cries for now.

"Do you want to walk down the river a ways after the others? I can come fetch you if there's anything to report," Jachin said.

"No," Alma said, looking around. "I'll wait here. You can let people know where to find me if anything is needed." He walked back toward the river and perched on a rock. The minutes passed slowly as he watched the water ripple around the protruding rocks. The trees above provided ample shade, but the heat seemed to filter through even the thickest leaves. Alma wiped perspiration from his forehead and loosened the sash on his tunic.

He was mostly left alone, except for a few people who came to offer him words of comfort. The sun's rays were just starting to wane when someone called his name.

Alma turned to see Raquel walking toward him.

He stood, watching her face. Was she happy? Distressed? He hurried to meet her. "How is she?"

Raquel let out a low breath of air. "Not well. The baby has made no progress, and Maia is feverish. She is too weak to even cry."

Dread pulsed through him. "Take me to her."

"Alma, this is women's business. All that I ask is that you pray for your wife."

"No," he said. "I have been praying, and the Lord knows my heart. My wife needs me now." He pushed past Raquel, who seemed too tired to try to stop him.

When he entered the tent, the women inside looked surprised. His eyes immediately sought out Maia. She looked worse than before. Her skin was pallid, her eyes open, staring into nothing.

"Maia?" he said, hoping that she'd respond to his voice. He moved to her side and knelt, touching her forehead. She was hot.

There was movement behind him, and Alma sensed that one or two of the women had left. When he turned, only Raquel and Lael remained inside the tent.

"Can anything be done?"

Raquel held out a damp cloth, and he took it from her. He swabbed it over Maia's face. She blinked but otherwise didn't respond.

"Here," Raquel said, taking Alma's hand and guiding it to the top of Maia's stomach. It felt as hard as a rock. "It's a birthing pain—it should be very painful, but she doesn't respond."

"What does that mean?"

"I'm afraid she might be bleeding inside, that her body has given up."

"Given up?" Alma said, his throat dry. He turned to Maia. "We can't let her. Maia, can you hear me?" He stared at his wife, willing her to focus on him. But her mouth was slack, her breathing shallow.

Alma placed his hands upon her head and started to pray over her. "O Lord, thou hast delivered us from the hands of our enemies, King Amulon and the Lamanites. If it is Thy will, please deliver Maia from this difficulty. Spare her life, and the child's life. Give her the strength to bring it into the world." He continued to pray until his voice was hoarse. When he finally exhausted his pleadings, he lay down beside Maia and cradled her head in his arms.

"I won't leave you," he whispered. "I told you I'd never leave you." He heard one woman sniffle, but he closed his eyes and whispered in Maia's ear—alternating between words of encouragement and his personal pleadings to the Lord. He was dimly aware of the gentle movements of Raquel and Lael as they continued to keep Maia's skin cool with moist cloths.

Unexpectedly, Maia's body jolted. Alma's eyes flew open, and he pushed himself up on one elbow.

Maia's eyes were wide. "The baby's coming."

"Did you hear that?" Alma said. "She said the baby's coming."

Raquel nodded and looked over at Lael. "We need to help her stand." Her gaze landed on Alma. "You can choose to stay or—"

"I'm staying."

"All right. You support her from the back," Raquel said in a flat voice. "She'll have very little strength."

New worries plagued Alma at Raquel's tone. Had *she* given up hope?

He stood in the low tent and held onto Maia as Raquel and Lael took their positions in front of her. It was as if Maia had suddenly come to life. She gripped Alma's arms and cried out with each push, but at least she was feeling something. Alma hoped that was a good sign.

What seemed like an hour later, Maia finally heaved one last push, then collapsed. Alma carefully laid her back onto the rug. He kept his eyes on his wife's exhausted face, afraid to look at the baby. Raquel and Lael spoke in hushed tones.

When Alma looked over, all he could see was a bundled shape and dark hair poking out of the opening of the blanket. There was no sound.

Raquel met his gaze. "He's very small, but seems to be all right."

He realized he'd been holding his breath. In a rush he said, "The baby's all right?"

A gentle smile crossed Raquel's face. "It may be too early to know for sure, although—"

"It's a boy?" Maia's voice caused everyone to look in her direction. The warmth was back in her complexion, her eyes brightening. "Let me see him."

Raquel handed the bundle to Alma, who felt as if he were holding a fragile egg. Carefully, he transported the babe into Maia's waiting arms.

She slowly unwrapped the bundle, and Alma drew in a breath. It was possibly the smallest human he'd ever seen. The babe was red and wrinkled, but beautiful all the same. Maia leaned over him and touched the downy hair on his head, then kissed the infant's cheek.

Just then, the child wailed in a loud, clear voice.

Alma looked at Raquel with alarm.

"That means he's going to be a fine, strong boy," she said with a chuckle.

Alma reached out a hand and touched the child's tiny fist. He'd never felt anything so soft. At his touch, the babe quieted.

"He already knows his father," Maia said, looking into Alma's eyes for the first time since the birthing pains had begun.

He leaned over and kissed her forehead. "I was so worried."

She nodded, her smile weak. "Thank you for staying with me."

Alma cradled the child as Raquel and Lael continued to care for Maia. After a while, the women seemed satisfied.

"We'll give you two a few minutes with the new baby, then you'll need to let Maia rest," Lael said, looking at Alma.

He flashed her a grateful smile. As Raquel and Lael slipped out of the tent, Alma scooted near his wife. Then, pushing a damp lock of hair from her cheek, he moved closer and wrapped his arm about her shoulders.

"What should we name him?" Alma asked in a quiet voice.

Maia nestled her head against the inside of his shoulder. "Are you going to let me decide?"

"You did all the work."

"All right then. I think we should call him Alma—after his father *and* after the valley he was born in."

Alma stroked the infant's cheek. "How will the people keep us straight?"

"You'll be Alma the Elder, and he'll be Alma the Younger."

Chuckling, Alma tightened his arm about her shoulders. "That makes me feel old already."

"Well, you *are* a father now," Maia said, turning her face and kissing his cheek.

"I am." Alma gazed at the babe in his wife's arms. *I am a father,* he realized, wondering if this was how his father felt when he was born. It was a combination of joy and angst, combined into one sense of elation. Studying each feature of his new son, Alma wanted nothing more than to see this child grow strong, to know where he came from, and to feel the love of the Lord.

"Our son was born free," Maia said in a quiet voice. "Imagine that—he'll grow up surrounded by the teachings of the true gospel, with intimate knowledge of the Lord's ways."

Alma nodded, his eyes growing moist. "He'll know firsthand the faith of his parents and the legacy that he was born into. He'll grow up without persecution, and instead he'll enjoy all the privileges the Lord sees fit." His finger traced the sleeping infant's face and neck, stopping at his gently rising chest. "Our son will truly be blessed."

Voices came from outside the tent. "I think that's the signal that I need to let the women back in." Alma kissed his wife again, then leaned over the babe and kissed the downy cheek. Reluctantly, he left his new little family and stepped outside.

The women smiled and bustled past him, carrying rugs and baskets of herbs.

He paused for a moment, listening to the exclamations from inside the tent, then looked up at the violet sky. The Lord had certainly delivered them. Alma's heart was full, almost ready to burst. He wanted to run to the camp on the other side of the river and shout the good news. Instead, he walked slowly, savoring every step, every blessing, and pondering every guidance from the Lord.

There were not enough words to express his full gratitude, but tonight, he'd be on his knees before an altar of thanksgiving—an altar he would build to thank God for his people's deliverance, his wife's health.

And for his new son, Alma the Younger.

Chapter Notes

CHAPTER 1

Scriptures referenced: Mosiah 18:4, 8–10

According to Hugh Nibley, Alma was a direct descendant of Nephi. This meant he had the priesthood and was entitled to serve in King Noah's court. When Alma took Abinadi's side, King Noah had to get rid of him. Here was a young man who had royal blood, who was taking a stance against the king. Noah had little choice but to wipe out Alma (*Teachings of the Book of Mormon—Part Two*, 77). Later, when Alma performed baptisms, he did so under the power of the priesthood, which he already held (90).

Games were played throughout Mesoamerica in ancient times, dating as far back as 1300 BC. There's not enough evidence to know whether the commoners and the elite society played the same games, but games were prevalent and an important part of life. John L. Sorenson notes that "the best known game was a contest with a rubber ball; the game was called by the Aztecs *tlachtli*." This game was played on a rectangular court, by striking the ball using only hips and elbows. Gambling on the winner was also part of the game. Other ancient games included *patolli*—similar to the board game Parcheesi (*Images of Ancient America*, 99).

CHAPTER 2

Swords and cimeters were common weapons in Mesoamerica—and were used by the Nephites and Lamanites (see Alma 43:17–18).

Matthew Ropers points out that that the main difference between a sword and a cimeter is that a cimeter has a curved blade, similar to that of a modern machete tool (*Journal of Book of Mormon Studies:* "Swords and Cimeters in the Book of Mormon," 8:1, 1999, 41). Various swords and knives were used by the Mesoamericans, including wood-bladed swords, swords of steel, and the macuahuitl sword (38). The macuahuitl, made of wood and obsidian, was the most formidable of all. It was reported by Bernal Diaz that "their swords, which were as long as broadswords, were made of flint [obsidian] which cut worse than a knife, and the blades were so set that one could neither break them nor pull them out" (36).

CHAPTER 4

Scripture referenced: Mosiah 18:7

CHAPTER 5

Scriptures referenced: Mosiah 18:8–14, 16, 34; 23:1

In Mosiah 18:11, we are told that the people clap their hands for joy when Alma tells them that they will be baptized. Joseph L. Allen makes an interesting observation on this point. When he and his wife were traveling through Guatemala, a native Quiche-Mayan woman took them on a tour through a church and museum. When she became excited, she would laugh and clap her hands (*Sacred Sites,* 38).

Two hundred and four people were baptized by Alma, as recorded in Mosiah 18:16. More would follow as believers continued to arrive at the Waters of Mormon. When Alma baptized Helam (and himself) in Mosiah 18:13, we notice that the words of the baptismal prayer are different than the prayer we use today. We must remember the baptisms that Alma performed took place before Christ lived on the earth and before His Atonement. Nibley points out that the baptisms were not for the remission of sins, but as "a witness and covenant only" (*Teachings,* 89). Nibley says that Alma was "following strictly the order before the time of Christ" (90). Thus, the wording of the prayer is different. The people are baptized as a "testimony," and to enter "into a covenant." Ultimately to become as one—one heart, one church.

In this chapter, I'm not too specific about the types of flocks owned and maintained by the Nephites. Sorenson believes that the flocks and herds of the Nephites were probably limited to goats and fowls, such as turkeys (*Images*, 46). Sheep are mentioned for the Lamanites, but it seems logical that if the Lamanites had sheep, the Nephites did as well. Other domesticated flocks and herds may have included quail, duck, dogs, and the tapir (47–49).

CHAPTER 6

Scriptures referenced: Mosiah 18:17–21, 23–25, 27–28

CHAPTER 8

Scriptures referenced: Mosiah 13; 23:3, 7, 17–18, 20

Scholars differ in opinion as to where the location of the land of Helam might be. In truth, no one quite agrees. Joseph Allen points out that the village of Almolonga fits the criteria, near the city of Quetzaltenango, Guatemala (*Sacred Sites*, 28). We know that Alma's people traveled eight days from the Waters of Mormon to Helam. In this book, I've placed Helam northeast of the traditional theorized location of the Waters of Mormon. One bit of research that inspired this idea was information on the Los Cimentos region of Guatemala. The land there is rich and productive, boasting five rivers of pure water. It's also a hotspot of controversy since the indigenous people have been driven out time and time again.

Sorenson notes that multi-story structures in Mesoamerica were very rare. More likely, the homes would be added to horizontally. Upper-class citizens would have extra rooms for visiting guests (*Images*, 61). Sometimes if a home became large enough, it would become a community building when the family moved on. Homes of the wealthy consisted of a home with a courtyard and elaborate gardens, whereas homes of the lower class would possibly have only one or two rooms. Gardens and fruit trees were kept right next to the home in the less populated areas (60).

Since ancient times, men and women have eaten separately. Sorenson says that meals "were eaten seated or squatting on a mat on the floor." They probably ate outside as well since the people of Mesoamerica spent most of their time outside (ibid.).

Chapter 9

Scriptures referenced: Mosiah 19:4–7; Alma 3:4

Throughout Mesoamerica, three levels of authority existed. Sorenson notes that there were high priests, supervisory priests, and regular priests, who fell under the "dominance of the ruler." The priests worked in areas such as keeping records, astronomy, engineering, overseeing offerings, praying, fasting, schooling, and making sure "the elaborate calendar of ceremonies was carried out." If a community had adequate priests, a shaman working in the area would be a specialist in "healing, divination, witchcraft." If not enough priestly authority existed, the shaman would take on additional roles (*Images*, 148).

Midwives were a common part of Mesoamerican society. They assisted and presided at childbirth. In return they would receive a gift or even a fee. They had to have knowledge of obstetrics, and, of course, herbal remedies. They also offered ritual blessings and instruction as they talked the birthing mother through the process (*Images*, 70).

When Noah climbed the tower to escape from Gideon, he saw an army of approaching Lamanites. Sorensen notes that a tower, or similar type of structure, "may have been the most essential feature" and proved that a community was prominent (*An Ancient American Setting for the Book of Mormon*, 172). Towers also held religious significance in that "they were thought of as artificial mountains on whose tops deity could dwell, or come down to visit men, in sacred privacy" (ibid.). Noah's towers likely had both political and religious meaning.

CHAPTER 10

Scriptures referenced: Mosiah 19:9, 12

Burial practices in Mesoamerica included burial in a grave or a tomb. Sorenson notes that in some cultures the dead were cremated, possibly accounting for the reason that archaeologists have failed "to find nearly enough human remains to account for much of a proportion of the ancient dead." Yet, Sorenson believes that the lack of remains is a result of the dead being buried away from their communities (*Images,* 154). Regardless, the dead were revered, especially those who were of a high rank (ibid.). In the Book of Mormon, "mourning for the dead was characterized by extreme weeping, wailing, prayer, fasting, and possibly self-sacrifice of blood" (156).

CHAPTER 11

Scriptures referenced: Mosiah 18:18–29; 19:13–20

In Mesoamerica, preparing the land for planting was a man's job. Sorenson says that clearing the fields included "hand-cutting trees and bushes and then burning the debris when it had dried out" (*Images,* 32). The ash served as fertilizer. Seeds were dropped into small holes made by a sharp stick (ibid.).

Maize was the staple of all Mesoamerican diets, although other grains were grown and consumed, e.g., wheat, barley, neas, and sheum (Mosiah 9:9). Allen points out that all of the crops mentioned in Mosiah 9:9 are indigenous to Guatemala. Interestingly enough, the corn was planted first, then the beans—and the cornstalks served as beanpoles (*Sacred Sites,* 33–34). In addition to tortillas, fish "were consumed where it was convenient to obtain them." Allen also notes that a variety of insects and fungi were eaten (ibid). But the fundamental staples were corn, beans, and squash (*Images,* 36).

Sorenson notes that "obsidian was crucial in Mesoamerican technology." The hard volcanic glass was used in weapons, cutting tools, knives, and woodworking tools. Wood was used for making boat paddles or planting sticks. Bone was another useful material and was turned into needles, scrapers, and utensils (*Images,* 51).

CHAPTER 12

Scriptures referenced: Mosiah 12:3; 19:22–23, 26, 28

CHAPTER 13

Scriptures referenced: Mosiah 23:15, 19–20

CHAPTER 15

Scriptures referenced: Mosiah 20:1–5

Although in the story the Lamanite daughters are very surprised to be abducted and forced to marry the Nephite priests, this type of incident dates back to ancient customs. According to Hugh Nibley, German anthropologists have explained how *frauraub,* "the robbing of brides" worked. It was required that the men steal their brides outside of the tribe. The Hopi Indians still practice this custom to a degree—they don't marry within their own clans (*Teachings of the Book of Mormon—Part Two,* 97). In fact, in the Bible (Judges 21), the Israelites "instructed the Benjaminites to kidnap the daughters of the Israelites who lived at Shiloh while the young women danced in the vineyards." (*Rediscovering the Book of Mormon:* "The Stealing of the Daughters of the Lamanites," by Alan Goff, ed. John L. Sorenson, Melvin J. Thorne, 68). The kidnapped virgins then became the abductors' wives. For a discussion of the legal dimensions of this act of kidnapping, see S. Kent Brown, "Marriage and Treaty in the Book of Mormon: The Case of the Abducted Lamanite Daughters," *From Jerusalem to Zarahemla: Literary and Historical Studies of the Book of Mormon* (Provo: BYU Religious Studies Center, 1998), 99–112.

Music and dance were ancient traditions in Mesoamerica. Public events and ceremonies almost always included music and dancing. The most common musical instruments included the rhythmic drums, rattles, and scrapers; and the melodic panpipes, horns, whistles, flutes, and shell trumpets. The Bonampak murals (ninth century AD Mayan murals) show "long wooden trumpets blown as part of a procession of nobles." Sorenson notes that "no remnants of actual music have been preserved for us to hear today" (*Images,* 178–179).

In Mesoamerica the moon goddess was called Chak Chel or Ix Chel, or "Lady Rainbow." The Mayas believed she helped to ensure fertility and refused to be a victim of oppression. Historian Michael D. Coe says that she was the goddess of "weaving, medicine, and childbirth . . . the snakes in her hair and the claws with which her feet and hands are tipped prove her equivalent of Coatlicue, the Aztec mother of gods and men" (*The Maya,* 216).

CHAPTER 16

Scriptures referenced: Mosiah 23:19–23

Casting lots has been a traditional practice since ancient times. One method used in Mesoamerica was casting maize kernels or beans into a tub of water. If the kernels dropped in the water and then floated on top in groups of 2, 3, 5, or 13, a decision or prediction could be made. Determining the cause for an illness, choosing the day to marry or to plant, or selecting the name for a newborn were all decided by casting lots (David C. Grove, *Social Patterns in Pre-classic Mesoamerica,* 80).

CHAPTER 18

There is not a standard time period in which a widow remarries. History shows that some have married quite soon after widowhood. For example, when Abigail's husband, Nabal, was struck dead, David offered to marry her (1 Samuel 25:3, 42). Bathsheba also married David soon after her husband, Uriah, died (2 Samuel 11:3; 12:24).

CHAPTER 21

Scriptures referenced: Mosiah 18:12–14

CHAPTER 22

Scriptures referenced: Mosiah 23:27–29; 24:1–2

The story and influence of Amulon is not to be taken lightly in the Book of Mormon. We know him as a distasteful figure, but Nibley points out that he was one of the worst characters. Amulon's ambitions lead him to survive the assassination of King Noah, have a settlement named after him, get away with kidnapping twenty-four Lamanite women, and rise to power over his former people—Alma included. To top it off, he was made a king over the land of Helam by the Lamanite king (*Teachings,* 123). During his kingship, Amulon took all he could get and "started persecuting in grand style" (124).

CHAPTER 23

Scriptures referenced: Mosiah 24:1–4, 8

CHAPTER 25

Scriptures referenced: Mosiah 23:27; 24:10–14

Michael D. Coe notes that the Maya god—the Feathered Serpent—is the "early form of the later Aztec god Quetzalcoatl" (*The Maya,* 89). Relief figures made out of stucco date to the early classic period, which includes "a puma, an anthropomorphic bat, birds of prey, a squirrel, a warrior with goggled eyes . . . [and] the Feathered Serpent" (109).

CHAPTER 27

Scriptures referenced: Mosiah 24:16–22

I have stayed relatively close to the timeline laid out by S. Kent Brown in *Voices from the Dust.* Brown suggests that Abinadi died in 128 BC and that King Noah was killed between 128 BC and 125 BC. Some scholars believe that the people of Alma lived in the land of Helam for a couple dozen years, but following Brown's timeline, I've kept them there for about three years (218).

Selected Bibliography

Allen, Joseph L. *Sacred Sites: Searching for Book of Mormon Lands.* American Fork, Utah: Covenant Communications, 2003.

Brown, S. Kent. *Voices from the Dust.* American Fork, Utah: Covenant Communications, 2004.

Coe, Michael D. *The Maya—Seventh Edition.* New York: Thames & Hudson, 2005.

Nibley, Hugh. *Teachings of the Book of Mormon—Part Two.* Provo, Utah: FARMS, 2004.

Sorenson, John L. *An Ancient American Setting for the Book of Mormon.* Salt Lake City: Deseret Book, and Provo, Utah: FARMS, 1985.

Sorenson, John L. *Images of Ancient America: Visualizing the Book of Mormon.* Provo, Utah: FARMS, 1998.

About the Author

H.B. Moore is the award-winning author of the Out of Jerusalem series: *Of Goodly Parents, A Light in the Wilderness, Towards the Promised Land,* and *Land of Inheritance.* The fourth volume in the series, *Land of Inheritance,* won the 2007 Whitney Award for best historical fiction. Heather is also the author of critically acclaimed novel *Abinadi* (2008), which won the 2008 Whitney Award for best historical fiction and the 2009 Best of State Award in Literary Arts for historical fiction.

Moore graduated from Brigham Young University with a degree in fashion merchandising and a minor in business management—which have nothing to do with writing novels. But at least she can color-coordinate her kids' school clothes and balance a mean checkbook.

Moore is also a member of the League of Utah Writers and the LDStorymakers. She appreciates hearing from her readers, who can contact her through her Web site, www.hbmoore.com.